Bridge Over the Atlantic
By
Lisa J. Hobman

This is a fictional work. The names, characters, incidents, places, and locations are solely the concepts and products of the author's imagination or are used to create a fictitious story and should not be construed as real.

5 PRINCE PUBLISHING AND BOOKS, LLC
PO Box 16507
Denver, CO 80216
www.5PrinceBooks.com

ISBN 13: 978-1-939217-43-1 ISBN 10:1939217431
Bridge Over the Atlantic
Lisa J. Hobman
Copyright Lisa J. Hobman 2013
Published by 5 Prince Publishing

Front Cover Viola Estrella
Author Photo: Craig of Craig Photography Studio copyright 2013

First Edition/First Printing March 2013 Printed U.S.A.

5 PRINCE PUBLISHING AND BOOKS, LLC.

For Rich, my soul mate; my inspiration; my muse

ACKNOWLEDGEMENTS

I would like to thank my husband, Rich, for believing in me and giving me the opportunity to pursue my dream. Thank you to my beautiful daughter, for being very proud of me and making sure I know it. I love you both with all my heart.

To my Mum and Dad thank you for raising me to believe that I can achieve whatever I put my mind to. Although the distance between us is now greater I love you more than ever.

Thank you to my BFF, Claire H for being there for me even though I moved so far away. It's been seventeen years and you still put up with me. What would I do without you? I love you, Chick.

Ali, you kicked me up the bum when I needed it and were there when I needed you. You're a star and I love you to bits.

To Ali, Liz and Claire M, thank you for being my beta readers; for laughing and crying in all the right places and for wanting me to write more. Also for supporting me throughout this journey. I appreciate your help and encouragement more than I can express.

Throughout this journey I have met some wonderfully talented authors who have provided advice and spurred me on. Heartfelt thanks to Allan Bott, Jan Romes, Melodie Ramone and Jon Rance to mention but a few. And thanks to Viola for interpreting my cover art request so perfectly.

Last but by no means least, I would like to thank my editor Bernadette Soehner, who became a lovely friend in a very short space of time; for her guidance and for putting up with my incessant questioning. And to all the wonderful staff at 5 Prince Publishing for believing in my debut novel and giving me the opportunity to be published. Thank you all so very much.

Dear Reader,

Firstly I would like to thank you for taking the first step on the journey with Mallory and me. I hope you come to love Mallory as much I do.

The year 2012 was a bit of a rollercoaster journey for me. Not only did I move hundreds of miles north of home (*Yorkshire, England*) to my favourite place in the world, *Scotland*, but I also embarked upon a whole new career. Whilst leaving behind my friends and family was one of the hardest things I have ever done, I don't think I would have been able to begin writing if we had stayed.

Writing this book has been a bit of a dream come true and I have loved every single minute. I have learned so much and met some wonderful people both in my new home town and through social media.

So…I'm a *Yorkshire* lass, living in *Scotland* with an American publisher…as you can imagine things have been very interesting! There were discussions around the language and whether I should Americanise it or stick with Anglicised versions. I am hoping we came up with a happy compromise.

I hope you enjoy the story and tell your friends about it too. Book number two is waiting in the wings and is a stand-alone story with its own twists and turns. Watch this space!

Lisa J Hobman

www.lisajhobman.co.uk
https://www.facebook.com/LisaJHobmanAuthor

Bridge Over the Atlantic

Chapter One

January 2011

"You can *NOT* be serious?" Mallory Westerman recoiled. It wasn't a habit of hers, to inadvertently quote 1980's sports stars. But even *she* was surprised when she heard John McEnroe's words fall from her lips.

Thankfully, her fiancé, whilst obviously bemused at her reaction and frustrated by her lack of enthusiasm, didn't really notice the similarities between her and the wiry haired tennis supremo. He was much too busy stroking the print-out in front of him, on the table, as if ironing out the creases would make his suggestion a more viable proposition.

"Honey, imagine the life we could have there right now," he pleaded. "The open spaces, the fresh air-…"

"The midge bites, the lack of internet connection, no other civilisation for miles." She rudely interrupted. She immediately felt guilty when Sam's eyes took on the appearance of a scolded puppy dog. She slid her arms around his neck caressing the sides of his beautiful face. "I'm sorry, sweetheart. I just don't see me…either of us, really, taking to a permanent life out in the middle of goodness knows where at *this* point in our lives, surrounded by sheep and wearing wellies and Tweeds!"

"Now you are being terribly stereotypical and insulting to all things countryside, Mallory," Sam chastised in his Canadian drawl. "And besides, I think you'd look very fetching in wellies…just wellies that is, nothing else." He grabbed her playfully and squeezed her. His green eyes flashed with a mischievousness Mallory had come to adore.

She giggled and gazed up at him, lovingly recalling the first time she had found herself utterly mesmerised by him.

~~~~~

December 2009

Mallory had lived in *Yorkshire* all the twenty-eight years of her life. Since dropping out of her PR course at Uni, through sheer laziness, she had endured a run of soulless jobs. Nothing ever really pushed her buttons. That was until an inheritance from her dear Aunt Sylvia had given her the opportunity to do the *one thing* she truly wanted to do.

Her little gift emporium, *Le Petit Cadeau*.

It had been the brain child of her Aunt many years before, when Mallory had taken to making her own Christmas gifts one year when, as was the case on more than one dreadful occasion, unemployment occurred on the brink of the festive season.

She had sobbed and sobbed when the solicitor informed her that her Aunt had left her the large sum of money under strict conditions that she was to, 'get off her backside and do something fulfilling for once!' She remembered almost laughing aloud at the point when the solicitor had uttered the quote directly as her Aunt had written it. Even in death, feisty Sylvia knew how to draw a chuckle from her beloved niece.

It was a fairly quiet early December Wednesday in *Leeds*, well perhaps *quiet* was not the right way to put it. The city centre was the usual bustling metropolis, but the Victoria Quarter was, ostensibly, being given a somewhat brief reprieve from the usual barrage of festive shoppers. Mallory huffed as she watched a swooning couple canoodling whilst browsing in the window of the lingerie boutique.

"Sod this for a game of soldiers. I think I need a break," she informed one of the cute, jointed, Steiff teddy bears sitting, looking pensive on the shelf next to where she perched. "I reckon there is a tall, caramel macchiato with my name on it somewhere!"

Grabbing her oversized bag she chalked *Back in 20 mins* on her very own, handmade door sign. Once she had dropped the latch she headed out into the sea of suited business people and Christmas shoppers. She smirked at the vast number of pre-school children who were sporting cheap red Santa hats lovingly procured for them, she guessed, by harassed parents as bribery for good behaviour.

The paved precinct area was buzzing. Mallory loved *Leeds City Centre* with its designer boutiques and quirky shops. At this time of year, however, there was something transcendent about the atmosphere. Maybe it was the twinkling lights strung from building to building or the way that each and every shop was decked in sparkling silvers and gregarious gold. The myriad Christmas songs, being played in numerous outlets all out of synch with one another, were an assault on the senses. The stalls all laid out, down the centre of the precinct, were vying for the attention of passers-by with their brightly coloured gifts and trinkets. A delicious aroma of roast chestnuts wafted through the chilled air and into Mallory's nostrils making her tummy grumble.

She rounded the corner heading for her favourite coffee shop when suddenly she involuntarily lurched forward. Her stiletto heel had become lodged in between two paving slabs, sending her and her belongings, hurtling into the arms of a passing stranger.

"Whoaaaa there!" The startled man grabbed for Mallory, in a bid to stop her inevitable collision with the pavement. "We haven't been formally introduced and yet here you are throwing yourself at me!" He laughed. His accent was noticeably of the North American variety.

Rather dazed, heart pounding and feeling more than a little bit embarrassed, Mallory slowly lifted her gaze to look at the Knight in shining armour, whose strong, muscular arms had come to her rescue. She was met with vivid green, laughing eyes and a very, *very* handsome countenance. Suddenly the weight of what had just happened hit her like a stack of tumbling gift boxes and she realised she was holding on for dear life and staring, just staring at this poor bewildered guy. She quickly came to her senses.

"I-I am so sorry, how clumsy of me. My...my shoe...erm...oh no, it's still bloody stuck!" She stammered almost falling for the tall stranger a second time, as she fought with the shoe, which was determined to stay bloody-well put, thank you very much. Perfect!

"Here let me help you." The man aided Mallory into an upright position. He crouched in front of her. "Hold onto my shoulder and take your foot out of your shoe."

Mallory silently obeyed her strikingly handsome saviour. She felt the flushing of her face, which was surely glowing like a Belisha beacon. Passers-by smirked in her direction, further increasing the heat in her cheeks. He twisted at the shoe until the heel finally allowed itself to be freed from the crevice, *rather like the sword Excalibur*, Mallory pondered. *Hmmm, that would make him the dashing King Arthur...yum.* She giggled at the errant thought.

He looked up and offered her the return of her shoe, whilst still on bended knee. She sighed as she reached out for it. *Oh if only I knew you and this was a diamond ring and I was in the midst of the most romantic proposal ever...*she shook her head to dislodge the ridiculous, mental intrusion and snatched the shoe. *Good grief, I have been single far too long!*

"Thank you so much for helping me, I feel like such a muppet."

"Don't mention it. It happens to us all. But only usually on a weekend for me." Then, with a fake and over-exaggerated glance around for ear-wiggers, he leaned in close to whisper. "My high heels are seriously frowned upon at work, and let's not even *mention* the stockings." The man chuckled, obviously pleased with his joke, his emerald eyes sparkling.

Smiling and *really* hoping that his last sentence was in no way a true reflection on his life, Mallory tilted her head at the stranger in an enquiring manner,

"You're not from here," she mumbled. Yup, she had just stated the blooming obvious, she realised as she was caught in his gaze and unable to look away. A wide grin spread across his gorgeous face. He wagged his finger, "Do you know…I knew there must be a reason why people keep on looking at me funny when I speak." He paused and held out his hand, "I'm Sam, by the way. Samuel Buchanan, in case you wanted to know my full name. You know, for when you report my dashing act of valour to the *Yorkshire Evening Post*." His emphasis on the pronouncement of 'shire' made her chuckle.

"Nice to meet you, Sam. I'm Mallory Westerman." She shook his hand. "And we locals pronounce it York*sher*, as opposed to York*shyre*." She felt smug at getting him back for his sarcasm.

"Well thank you very much for the insider info." He laughed "So Miss Mallory York*sherrr*," he joked rolling his 'R' "Mallory is quite an unusual name, huh?" His tone was questioning.

"Hmmm, that's what you get for having quirky parents I suppose." She rolled her eyes once she realised this comment needed further explanation. "My Dad was an avid rock climber in his youth and his hero was the climber George

Leigh Mallory." Sam look nonplussed and she continued, "He was apparently a famous climber who was killed attempting to climb Everest in the 1920's." Sam's expression indicated that he still had no clue what on earth she was rambling on about. It didn't much matter really, she surmised. His nose crinkled, probably through bored confusion she figured.

"So, where were you off to before throwing yourself into the arms of a complete Canadian stranger?" Sam teased.

"Ah, Canadian, eh? I just thought you were from America."

Samuel winced and shook his head in mock disgust. "Youch! Hold your tongue there, Miss Yorksher, a proud Canadian could get highly insulted, you know, next you will be saying we all sound alike."

"Sorry." She held her hands up in apology. *Well, actually you do, to me.* Her subconscious blew a raspberry in his general direction. "I was on my way for coffee, just up there." She pointed up the paved precinct, toward her favourite coffee shop. "I'm taking a break whilst things are quiet in my shop."

"Oddly enough, I was going to go for coffee too." He paused, looking thoughtful, almost hesitant as if he wondered whether he should say what he was thinking, but really hoping she made the suggestion first. "Soooo, how about you buy me one, by way of a thank you for saving your ass?" He winked and immediately cringed regretting the cheesy facial expression.

Her jaw dropped in mock surprise at his forward manner although secretly, she quite liked it.

Smiling and rolling her eyes she held out her arm as if to gesture 'after you'. He took this to be an answer in the affirmative and began walking in the direction of her extended hand.

Sam and Mallory sat in the coffee shop for a lot longer than her door sign had denoted. They found lots to talk about in their hour and a half long conversation. Mallory discovered that Sam was thirty-one and was over in England following his brother's request for him to take the reins at the UK arm of his asset management business.

"I'm renting an apartment in what I believe is some kind of converted warehouse." he told her with a bemused, questioning look, "Seems to be the *in thing* in *Leeds*."

"Yes, there are a lot of run down old industrial buildings around here. I think someone saw a bit of a niche in the property market."

"Yeah, I think so...the rooms are very spacious." He smiled cheekily, "and I have a *great* view from my bedroom." Mallory blushed and fiddled with her coffee cup. Sam cringed again. *Idiot*, he chastised himself.

Mallory cleared her throat, "So, where in *Canada* are you from?"

"A town called Kingston, in Ontario. I grew up on the outskirts of the town. My Dad was in construction and he built the family home. His father was a builder too, so I think he just fell into the industry. He was good at it."

"*Was* good at it? Is he retired now?" Mallory sipped her coffee.

"Ahhh, no, sadly he passed away two years ago of a heart attack." Sam looked understandably sad.

"Oh… gosh I'm so sorry…I-I didn't mean to pry."

"No, no, please, it's fine. My Mom is amazing. She won't allow us to be sad. She says we should always remember the good stuff and so we do." He looked pensive, "I think she tries to protect us both. Even though we're adults."

"Hmm, that's what Mum's do I suppose. So is your brother still in *Canada*?"

"Yeah, he just got married and his wife wasn't ready to move all the way out here…so…here I am."

"Mmmm, here you are…" Mallory said with a little gravel to her voice, making her blush again.

He had a strange effect on her. She tucked her hair behind her ear and looked at him from under her eyelashes. He smiled, knowingly, as he sipped his coffee.

Mallory surveyed his well-groomed, clean-cut, suited appearance which was in total contrast with his unruly, windswept mop of shaggy, brown hair. *A hazard of the Yorkshire winter weather*, she mused. She could tell that he was quite toned and muscular, simply by the hang of his suit. She already knew from earlier that he had strong arms and as he talked she imagined those arms encircling her. She fought to hide the shiver that travelled through her as she began to picture him naked.

"So, tell me about you." He leaned back in his chair, folding his hands in his lap.

"What do you want to know?" She asked shyly, pushing her glasses up her nose.

"Everything…where you grew up…where you live…your friends…the whole nine yards."

Mallory took a deep breath, "Well…I'm twenty eight, I live a short drive away from *Leeds* in a little railway cottage. I have a little Patterdale terrier called Ruby…she usually comes to work with me, but Josie, that's my best friend, has taken her today. She 'borrows' her sometimes." She smiled at how silly that must have sounded, "I've always lived here in *Yorkshire*. I've never lived abroad or been to *Canada*. I've been to Spain a few times…" she trailed off realising she was waffling a little.

"So what about your shop? What do you sell?" Sam enquired.

"Local crafts mainly. Gifts and cards, things like that. I make little hanging signs and sell those in the shop. My Aunt Sylvia insisted I open it. She left me the money to set up when she died, bless her."

"Sounds like an amazing woman." Sam offered.

"Hmm, she was. Very opinionated and sometimes irritating as hell but lovely all the same." She continued to tell him enthusiastically about her shop and the different crafts people she had met.

Sam smiled and listened intently. He found her quite beautiful. Her long wavy hair fell in chocolate tendrils around her shoulders, where it had escaped the grasp of the claw pinning the rest of it in a loose pile atop her head.

He discretely ran his eyes over her body. Her curves were accentuated by the fitted skirt and top she wore, giving her a timeless Marilyn Monroe-esque appearance. Every so often she would push her spectacles up her nose, even when there was no need to do so. He thought that was really cute. Her bright blue eyes sparkled and he couldn't help but smile at the way she waved her arms around as she spoke; so expressive. She was clearly a nervous talker. He felt the urge to stop her mouth with his. Not because she was boring; no she was *anything* but boring. He just wanted to kiss her. It took all the will he had not to just do it.

At the end of their conversation they stood outside the window of the coffee shop in the chilled December afternoon. Mallory felt sure she had bamboozled him with her non-stop jabbering and her life history. *Good job, he's way out of my league really*, she thought to herself. *At least I won't see him again to remind him what a clumsy, fat, chatterbox I am.* Hmmm, there was that low self-esteem rearing its ugly head again. She had always felt herself unattractive and had pretty much given up on the yo-yo dieting. After all, she was single and busy with *Le Petit Cadeau,* so it didn't really matter that she had crept up three dress sizes since her youth.

Expecting this to be the start *and* end of a beautiful friendship, she held out her hand. "It was very nice to meet you, Sam with the *Canadian* accent." She smiled. "Thank you for rescuing my face from a date with a concrete pavement."

"You are very welcome." He let out a long breath, but didn't move. He wasn't making a run for it. "It would have been such a shame to spoil such a pretty face with a bashed up nose and cracked teeth."

Mallory chuckled as she saw him outwardly cringe as the words escaped his shapely lips. "Well, thank you…I think." She glanced upward as if trying to decipher the compliment.

"You sound as if I'll never see you again." He looked sad, "Is that it? Is this the end? How could you? After all I've done for you?" He held his knuckles to his teeth and bit down in mock, melodramatic actor mode. The back of his other hand pressed to his forehead.

This guy was funny. She found herself allowing a small hope to shine through, that this was not the end. Perhaps he *did* want to see her again.

~~~~~

Later that night she sat, snuggled up on the sofa with Ruby, watching a re-run of *Friends.* It was the one where Brad Pitt's formerly fat character, Will, is invited for Thanksgiving. He has an aversion to carbs because of his past and is scared to go back there. He fights himself when the yams pass him by and initially succeeds. It was one of her favourite episodes. *Humph, if only I had that amount of willpower!* She thought to herself.

She was just munching through another carb laden mouthful of cereal when the phone rang. Her heart leapt.

Surely he wouldn't be ringing so soon? She and the rather yummy Sam Buchanan had exchanged phone numbers at the end of their lunchtime chat and she had almost skipped back to the shop, avoiding all the cracks in the pavement this time around.

"H-hello?" she stammered hopefully, into the receiver.

"Hi ya, Chick! Are you okay? You sound a bit odd." Perceptive as ever, Josie, who had been her best friend since school, was not known for beating around the bush. They had been friends through thick and thin. The *thick* boyfriends, who Mallory regrettably discovered were either too self-absorbed or more interested with cars and staring at other women's tits. The *thin,* on the ground patches where loneliness and reluctant celibacy seemed to be the way of life thrust upon her. Josie was her touch stone, her voice of reason. She was glad to have the opportunity to spill the beans on the potential new guy in her life.

"Oooh Mally, he sounds dreamy." Josie had swooned after Mallory had imparted every last detail she could remember; and there were many.

Josie loved listening to details about Mallory's love life, since she had been with Brad since high school. They had been childhood sweethearts and had no intentions of ever being with anyone else. Still, Josie loved to live vicariously through her best friend any time a new man came on the scene. "Did you kiss him? Does he smell good? Is he well off?" Josie barraged her friend with questions.

"Good grief, Josie! Talk about the *Spanish Inquisition.*" There was a pause and the whirring of their brains was almost audible.

Suddenly the girls cried out in unison in their best *Monty Python* voices the oh-so famous line from the oh-so famous Python sketch.

"Anyway," Mallory continued after they had stopped laughing hysterically, "I did notice he smelled rather gorgeous when I fell on him. Kind of fresh and Calvin Kleiny? And *no* I didn't kiss him. What do you take me for, woman?"

"I take you for a gorgeous girl who has not had a good orgasm in almost a year! That's what! You deserve something good, Mally!"

"Thank you, Josie, but you know I don't just go about jumping into bed with random men who save me from smashing my two front teeth in." She giggled.

"No, you just wait and wait to find that the bloke you have been waiting for is more interested in his bloody vintage *Mark II Ford Escort.*" Josie reminded Mallory of her last disastrous relationship. Mallory groaned.

"Don't go there, Josie. I honestly thought Craig's obsession with that canary yellow passionless wagon was endearing at first."

"Yes. Until you found out that he used to tuck it in every night." The two friends howled with laughter. "So, *is* he well off?"

"Josie! Really, I don't ask such questions. Anyway, I'm guessing he's comfortable. His job sounds quite high flying. Honestly though, Josie, I don't care about that stuff. I just want someone who looks at me as though he could ravish me on the spot; someone who wants to make a life with me; someone who won't mind that I'm not super-model thin." Mallory sighed at that last thought.

"Hey! What have I told you about that? Men prefer curves." Josie attempted to stomp on the negativity.

"Yeah? Shame that none of them are prepared to admit that in public. Eh?"

"So do you think he *will* call you?" Ah there we go, Josie had asked the dreaded, million-dollar question.

"Oh I *really* hope so, Josie. I had a really good feeling about him."

"In your knickers I bet." Josie gave a coarse cackle, making her sound like a fish wife. Mallory tutted and shaking her head, decided she was tired out.

Giving a yawn she mumbled, "And on that note, Josie Gardiner, I am hanging up. Night night."

"Night night you spoil sport. Love you squillions, babe."

"Love you too, you cackling banshee!" The conversation came to its usual banter-filled end and Mallory was once again alone, save for the little black Patterdale terrier with staring brown eyes pawing at her for attention.

~~~~~

Mallory's shop was crammed the next day. She was rushed off her feet and even had to call in Josie for assistance. Together they smiled, chatted, served customers and had the old fashioned cash register make that fabulous *kerching!* noise over and over again. When five o'clock finally came around, Mallory locked the door heaving a huge sigh of relief.

"Phew! Thank goodness it's time for home." She slid down the door, landing with a bump on her ample bottom.

Josie smiled down at her friend holding out her hand to pull her back up. "Come on you. Let's get back to yours and have a bite to eat and then we'll wander down to the Railwayman's for a couple of pops." Josie wiggled her eyebrows suggestively. It sounded like a bloody good plan.

Mallory put the day's takings in the money bag and fastened Ruby's lead onto her bright rainbow coloured collar. "You've loved today haven't you, Rubes? All that attention." Ruby wagged her tail and pawed at Mallory's skirt in agreement. Just then her cell phone began to vibrate in her bag. She opened her bag and rummaged around in its cavernous depths frantically searching for the phone. Finally putting her hand on it she swiped it up to her ear, "Hello?" She gasped feeling flustered.

"Well, hello there, Miss Yorksher." A familiar voice kissed at her ear, making her shiver with excitement.

"Oh, hi! Sam, right?"

"Oh great, you've almost forgotten me already, huh?" He sounded perturbed.

"No-no! Not at all. I was just checking. You'd be surprised at how many Canadian men have been ringing me lately." She chuckled.

"Ah well, I'm afraid I'm going to push to the front of the line. I wondered if you'd like to meet for a drink or a bite to eat later...I know it's short notice."

"Ah, I was actually going out with my friend, Josie, tonight I'm afraid."

Josie heard her declining the offer of a date and began to make throat slitting gestures and wave frantically in her face. Mallory screwed her face up in confusion, mouthing "what?"

"Just go on the bloody date, Mal, you moron. You can see me any time." Josie whispered loudly. Chuckling became audible from the other end of the phone.

"Ummmm, I think you should take your friends advice, Mallory. She sounds like a very sensible girl."

"Oh, if only you knew the truth, Sam, if only." She sniggered as she saw Josie's expression turn from horror to relief. "Okay, well, there is a little pub near my home. It's not flashy but they make a fab steak and kidney pie."

"It's a date!" Sam trilled and Mallory's face almost split in two, thanks to the cavernous grin on her face. They made their arrangements and Mallory floated from the shop with a smile as a new permanent fixture.

When she arrived home, Mallory frantically searched through her wardrobe. *I really need to go shopping,* she sighed to herself. She grabbed something which she felt was passable out of her limited wardrobe and showered. Just as she climbed out of the shower the doorbell chimed.

"Oh, bollocks!" Why did the doorbell always ring when you had either just stepped in, or out of the shower? She wrapped a bath sheet around her voluptuous figure as she hurried down the stairs. She tied a towel-turban on top of her head and opened the front door.

"Ta-daaaaaaa." Josie waved jazz hands around. Josie was petite, blonde and very pretty, until she opened her mouth. Subtlety was not a trait she was famous for. She stood there in jeans and a hoody, *UGG* boots and a woolly hat with flaps that covered her ears.

"Your timing, as always, is impeccable, Miss Gardiner." Mallory grumbled dryly.

"I thought there may be a chance you might need these." She handed a green and white paper bag to her best friend.

"Oh, Josie, what have you done?" Mallory had a feeling she knew what the contents of the bag were. She reached inside and pulled out the small blue box which, sure enough, had the word *Condoms* emblazoned on the side.

"They're ribbed ones too," Josie wiggled her eyebrows giving her a double thumbs up.

Mallory tried to look indignant. Shaking her head and huffing out a sharp breath she stared at her friend, "Seriously, Josie? Do you *honestly* think I am likely to *need these*? I've only just met the guy."

"Well, I bloody well hope so. You daft bat!" Josie was now the one to appear indignant. "Anyone would think you were hunch-backed and covered in warts and boils. He sounds bloody gorgeous and you obviously fancy the pants off him. This is post war Britain and the rules have changed, Mallory. In fact there are no rules. So, stop worrying about your body and go get you some nice, juicy ass, girlfriend."

Mallory laughed at Josie's appalling attempt at an American accent and "gangsta rappa" stance. She sighed, rolled her eyes and shaking her head, slammed the door in Josie's face.

~~~~~

Sam and Mallory sat at a small table beside the fireplace in the Railwayman's Arms; Mallory with her glass of red wine and Sam with a pint of 'Sleeper Ale' the pubs homemade brew. They chatted easily.

"So, tell me about your last boyfriend. I was shocked when you told me you were single. I expected you'd have been snapped up by some lucky son of a gun long ago" Sam blurted suddenly, totally changing the subject and catching her off guard. He, genuinely, *did* seem surprised at her marital status which both pleased and embarrassed her.

"Crikey, get right to the point, eh, Sam?" Mallory could feel her face flush as heat rose to her cheeks. After a pause to see that Sam was, *actually*, interested she began.

"Hmmm, how long have you got? Tell you what, I will give you the abridged version…Craig Spencer was a mechanic, a year older than me, divorced from a marriage that began when he was only twenty-two. He was obsessed with his car. In fact, he loved *IT* more than he did me. I *thought* it was love, but he just wanted a fling, even though we went out for a year. Then one day I realised that if there was *ever* to be some kind of an ultimatum the car would win hands down. So I ended it." The words rushed out all in one breath. She gasped air back into her lungs.

"Wow!" Sam looked stunned. He gazed at her and took her hand. "I cannot believe that dumb son-of-a-bitch loved a hunk of metal more than a beautiful, funny, sexy-as-hell girl like you." He looked down at their hands and freed hers, "S-sorry, I didn't mean to be so…forward. I mean I don't know the guy…I am sure he—"

"Hey, it's fine, honestly." Mallory missed the now absent contact and wanted to reach for his hand in return, but refrained. "You've pretty much got him pegged." She smiled.

They sat in silence for a few moments when something dawned on Mallory. "Wait a minute. You think I'm sexy?" Her eyes widened at the realisation. His lips turned up into a scrumptious half smile that made her toes curl.

"Hell yeah!" He nodded and there was a mischievous glint visible in his verdant eyes.

Mallory sat up a little straighter, feeling quite boosted by this unexpected compliment. "So tell me about your last girlfriend? It's only fair."

"Touché," Sam said. He thought for a moment and then began, "Where do I start? Syd was…uhh—"

Mallory gasped, "Wait. Sid? Like the actor Sidney Poitier? As in a…*man*?" She feared that she had just opened up a whole new can of worms and discovered that her new, potential true love was bi-sexual. She wasn't sure she was *that* open minded.

Sam slapped his knee as he threw his head back and guffawed at her shock. "Sydney *was* and still *is* as far as I am aware, a girl!"

"Thank goodness for that." Mallory burst out laughing with him, "I was just wondering what on earth to say next."

"Sydney Lowery was a secretary in my brother's firm. I met her when I worked in the office in Ottawa to do my internship. She was lovely at first."

"What did she look like?" Mallory interrupted

"Hey, no fair. I didn't ask you what that douchebag, Craig looked like. A little irrelevant don't you think?" He briefly raised his eyebrows but continued to smile.

"He was tall, skinny and hairy with big ears. Nuff said. Humour me, Sam. I'm just curious."

Sam chuckled after she gave him a vision of her ex.

"He sounds as ugly as he was stupid." He gave her a wink. "Okay, she was about five-eight, long curly auburn hair, with green eyes." He rubbed his forehead as if trying to remember.

"Was she thin…chubby…?" Mallory trailed off, looking down at her hands and as she fiddled with her nails. Sam reached over and gently squeezed her forearm as if trying to reassure her.

"Mallory, she is who she is. I didn't ask her out because of her size. Anyway it's a moot point. We split. She was seeing several people behind my back. The one she really wanted broke her heart. She came back to me, but I wasn't interested."

"Hmmm, well she sounds like a *douchebag* too then." Mallory defended him

"It would appear so." He smiled, tilting his head to one side, "Good for us that our former partners were so crappy, huh? Or we may never have met." He kept his eyes locked on hers and she melted inside.

~~~~~

Mallory took out her keys as they arrived at her cottage. Wondering what the *hell* she was doing bringing Sam back to her place. What if they ended up kissing? Or worse still, what if they ended up in bed? He would see her *naked*! *Oh-my-God! Oh-my-God! Oh-my-God!* She panicked as her breathing increased. She fumbled, trying to get the keys into the lock.

"Hey, are you okay? You look a little shaky?" *Damn!* He had noticed.

"Y-yeah, yeah I'm fine, no problems…just can't get the key in with my gloves on, silly me. What a dufus," she rambled. He took her shoulders and turned her to him. Gently he cupped her face in his warm leather clad hands and gazed into her eyes.

"Hey, it's coffee, that's all. Don't be nervous." He smiled, planting a light kiss on her forehead. "I am not expecting to jump into bed with you, Mallory. I am *so* not that kind of guy."

"Well," she let out a sigh, "that's good to know." She clambered for some poise. "And I wouldn't expect you to want to…erm…anyway." She tried to turn her attention to the door.

"Wait, what? You wouldn't *expect me to want to?*" He frowned, "What's that supposed to mean?"

"Nothing, forget I said anything. Really. I was thinking out loud." She hadn't meant that last part to be audible at all! *Dammiiiiiit!*

Still grasping her shoulder with one hand, he tilted her chin back to look at him with the other.

"Hey, Mallory, believe me when I say this, as I don't say things I don't mean. *Oh I want to, really I do.* All I've been able to think about since we met the other day is how much I wanted to see you again. How much I would just die to kiss those luscious lips of yours and how good it would feel to run my hands over your sensuous curves. You're so sexy, so feminine. You're the way a woman *should be.* Don't *ever* think that you are not exactly what men want; what *I* want. Popsicle sticks do nothing for me. Curves are what turn me on. And *man* do yours turn me on. I just don't want to scare you off by groping at you on our first, official, date. I really think we have something here. Don't you feel it too?"

Mallory gazed into his emerald eyes, unable to move; almost unable to breathe. She felt a little like a rabbit in headlights; stunned by his honesty and floored by his almost palpable desire for her. All she could muster was a little nod of her head.

With that he leaned down, pausing to seek her consent. She closed her eyes in anticipation. His breath felt warm against her chilled skin and then, finally, after what felt, to Mallory, like forever, he took her mouth with his own. His firm lips moulded to hers and his tongue dipped inside just a little. He tasted delicious and his cologne filled her nose as she breathed him in. Her hands reached up and found his hair as she drew him nearer. His kiss was soft but oozed passion and longing and gave a glimpse of what could be. Her legs became weak. And she clenched way down *there*.

When the kiss ended she felt a little light headed; almost drunk from the oh-so-brief exchange. She had *never* been kissed like *that* before. She raised her fingers and touched her lips where his had been only moments before. They tingled. She tingled. She turned her gaze once again to the door and this time unlocked it with ease.

Sam followed her inside, holding her hand in his. She watched as he made an assessing glance around at his new surroundings. The fireplace wall was adorned in a sumptuous wallpaper of red and gold whilst the rest of the walls remained a rich, neutral cream. She loved art work; unusual art work at that and had displayed as many of her pieces as she could without cluttering up the small room. Sam stood in front of the mantle appraising one of her most prized paintings. The scene showed a couple walking along a moonlit beach. The painting was almost black and white but for a bright red umbrella that the couple carried together.

"Very romantic." He said as he turned and smiled at her. A little sigh escaped her throat, "Nice little place you have here." He said nodding in approval.

"Thanks. It's small, but I love it. My parents bought it for me before they died."

"Wow, that's a thoughtful gift."

Mallory shrugged, "They wanted me to have a safe place to live when I moved out of home. They didn't have much money but they bought this place and rented it out until I was old enough to move in." She looked around her lounge, "It's big enough for the two of us. Well, more like one and a half." She said as a little black dog ran into the room making a beeline for the visitor in her home, "This is Ruby."

Sam crouched down to greet the fluffy canine.

"Hey there, cutie-pie, aren't you just the sweetest wittle fing I have ever seen? Yes you are. Yes you are." Sam cooed at the dog, which clearly approved of him.

"So…coffee?" She asked and Sam tore himself away from the black wiry bundle of fur skipping around his feet.

"That'd be great, thank you." He answered brightly.

He followed her into the kitchen still glancing around. She had painted the uneven walls in duck egg blue to compliment the handmade pine storage units. There was just enough space for a dining table, against one wall. The rest of the available spaces on each wall were filled with old, metal advertising signs and little plaques displaying phrases such as 'I kiss better than I cook' and 'Never trust a skinny chef!' Mallory heard Sam chuckle as he read the words.

When they re-entered the lounge, Mallory set the tray of cups, cafetiére, cream jug and sugar bowl on the little coffee table which was made from an old piece of tree stump with a highly polished top. They sat beside each other on the couch.

"Wow cool table. And come to think of it cool tray." Sam ran his hand along the nobbled sides and smooth top of the furniture.

Mallory switched on her stereo and flicked to Snow Patrol's 'Eyes Open' album— her favourite— and hit play.

"Oh, great choice. I love this album. So what's the story with the table? And the tray?" Sam asked.

"The coffee table is a creation made by Brad, my best friend Josie's boyfriend. He studied carpentry. He's also responsible for the kitchen." She gestured in the direction of the other room. "And the tray is me. It's just a plain old seed tray that I tarted up a bit."

"Tarted up?" Sam mimicked her accent, grinning cheekily.

"Oy!" She playfully hit him with a throw cushion. "Yes I make stuff. Or I buy bits and pieces and make them look pretty," she said proudly, pleased at his earlier compliment.

"Well, you are one talented lady, Miss Yorksherrrr."

"Why thank you, Mr. Canada." Mallory proceeded to pour the delicious smelling coffee and hand a mug of it to Sam.

"Can I ask you a very personal question?" Sam twisted to face her. He rested his elbow on the sofa and leaned his temple on his fist.

"Oooh, you can ask but can I decline to answer if I see fit? It always sounds ominous when people challenge you like that."

"Have you always been self-conscious about how you look?"

Blimey, that was blunt and to the point. She sighed, paused and wondered how the heck to answer without making herself sound, well, utterly pathetic.

"I suppose I have since my folks died. They were such wonderful parents; so supportive and loving. When I lost them I think a little bit of me died too." *Uh-oh…too deep!* She chastised herself as tears began to sting the backs of her eyes.

Sam placed his cup down on the tray, "Hey, I am so sorry; I didn't mean to make you cry. I'm such a tactless idiot." He moved in closer to her.

"No, no, it's fine. Don't worry. I get a bit melancholy sometimes when I think about them, that's all." She lifted her glasses briefly and dabbed the tears that were threatening to emerge.

"Of course you do, that's totally understandable." He touched her cheek lightly, catching an escaped tear. *'Chasing Cars'* began to play in the background; Mallory's favourite song.

"I love this song." He let out a deep breath and closed his eyes for few moments. When he opened them Mallory was staring into space with a serene smile playing on her lips. He watched her for a moment. "You really are beautiful, Mallory. I wish you believed me."

She covered his hand with hers. "Me too," She smiled. "But for now I'll settle for the fact that you think so."

Sam took Mallory's cup and placed it beside his on the tray. He moved in closer still and tucked a stray strand of hair behind her ear. "I hope that one day I get to *show* you how beautiful I think you are."

Mallory gasped.

Great, he'd done it again with his 'speak first, think later' mentality. *Idiot*, he reprimanded himself. It was true though. He couldn't deny it and why should he? And furthermore why shouldn't she know this? He wanted her. He wanted her *now*. He had to stop himself from ripping at her clothing right there and then like some crazed animal.

No, he breathed, trying to calm his thoughts. He was willing to wait. He didn't want her to think of this as a pity fuck. He truly desired this woman. She was everything he had ever wanted. She was beautiful…no…stunning, but beguilingly unaware of the fact. She was intelligent, hilariously funny, kind, and passionate. The idiot with the car must have been crazy.

Mallory saw a mix of emotions flash across Sam's beautiful face. *I would NEVER sleep with a man on our first date!* She reminded herself thinking back to the gift she had received from Josie. *Although, technically, this could be counted as our second…and if I was to be really picky, we have changed location so this could be counted as our third!*

Before she could stop herself, she launched herself forward and flung her arms around his neck. She grabbed at his shirt with one hand and his hair with the other, pulling him toward her. She pushed her tongue between his full, luscious lips and deepened the kiss, desperate to taste him again. It was a hot, lust fuelled, needy kiss, and, in that split second, she hoped it conveyed that she wanted him desperately and NOW!

He didn't make a move and so she started to pull away thinking she had made the most stupid mistake of her life. *Oh God he thinks I am a tart! Even worse, a tart that he had no intention of sleeping with tonight! Aaargh!* Her breathing was ragged.

She dared to glance into his face. And he was staring open mouthed, his breathing, too, was erratic.

"I'm sorry. I'm sorry. I don't know came over me." She stood quickly, feeling a little head rush as she did so.

Suddenly Sam rose to his feet too. She expected he was going to make his excuses and leave. She wouldn't blame him. She had just molested him on her sofa! *Hussy!* Her Aunt Sylvia's over used word sprang immediately to mind.

Sam just stood there looking at her, panting; clearly searching for words which seemed to evade him. This was getting worse! She covered her eyes with her hands. He had said he desired her. He had talked about her curves; *he* had kissed *her* first, for goodness sake! He said he wanted her, in a roundabout way! What the hell was going on then?

"I'm not usually like this," she began backtracking. "I don't launch myself at men, well, of course not unless…unless my heel is stuck in a pavement…and…and I don't have any choice in the matter, but even then I don't stick my tongue down their throat and expect them to be happy about it. Obviously, not that I have ever actually found myself in *that exact* scenario until I met you. Oh God, I can't believe I just did what I just did! What a moron. And I can't believe I'm still talking," she rambled. It was truly ridiculous.

Sam walked over to her and looked down, peering into her eyes. He placed a hand on either side of her face.

"Would you please, just shut the fuck up for one second." Despite his harsh words, his expression was warm and he was smiling.

Oh, gosh! She wasn't one for foul language, but his accent made it kind of sexy.

Without further words he slid his hands into her hair and lowered his mouth to hers. This time the kiss was searching, passionate, deep and lusciously wet. This time *his* tongue entered *her* mouth and she welcomed it with her own.

He caressed her back, tangled his fingers in her hair and brushed his fingers over her face. His movements were prurient, yet somehow loving. Every so often he would break free of her mouth to gaze into her eyes; almost as if he disbelieved that this was real.

She took his hand and bravely led him toward the open stair case. He followed her, willingly, up the stairs. She opened the door to her bedroom. And holding both of Sam's hands, never taking her eyes from his, she backed slowly inside. He gazed down at her with hooded eyes, full of lust. Although shy and self-conscious, she was about to trust this gorgeous man with her body.

Mallory had never felt so desirable and it had filled her with a new confidence. Sam stroked her hair as she began to unbutton the light blue cotton shirt that he had looked so very handsome in. She removed the shirt and threw it aside.

Next, she tugged at the hem of his white T-shirt, he lifted his arms and in one smooth movement, she swiped it off over his head. She gasped as she laid fresh eyes on the beautiful, muscular, naked torso in front of her. Okay, he wasn't male model material, but gosh, to her he couldn't be more perfect.

Sam's heart pounded in his chest, so much so that he feared she could see it about to burst forth from his skin. He swept her hair away from her shoulders and removed her glasses.

"Oh, Mallory, you have the prettiest eyes." He breathed out long and slow, mesmerised by their sparkle.

He unfastened the top three buttons of her fitted black shirt to reveal a hint of ambrosial cleavage. His breath caught in his throat. Gently, he continued down until her lace covered breasts were exposed to his hungry gaze. He discarded the shirt.

"So beautiful," he whispered.

Mallory's cheeks filled with color. He lent forward to plant a gentle kiss on her collar bone.

It was so soon, but he knew that this was more than just sex to him. He wanted to communicate this to her somehow. He slid his arms around her waist and pulled her to him, in a warm sensual embrace. He ran his fingers up and down her spine. Her smooth, creamy skin heated under his touch. He rested his chin atop her head. She was just the right height. She reciprocated and smoothed her hands down his sculpted back. He pulled away gazing at her once again.

Sam tilted her chin up towards him. "Are you okay, Mallory? We don't have to do this. I'm happy to wait. We have time."

"I don't want to wait, Sam. I don't know why, but this feels right. I want this…I want you."

On hearing these words his desire was fuelled. He slowly crouched down before her, turned her around and slid down the zip on the back of her black fitted skirt. He shimmied the skirt down her rounded hips onto the floor.

He kissed her lower back just above the top of her black lace panties. She shivered under his touch.

He turned her around and stood before her. He took a step back to appraise the gift he had just unwrapped. Suddenly, he sensed her discomfort at his gaze.

"Mallory, please don't feel embarrassed," he reassured. "I can honestly say that I have never desired any woman more than I desire you right now."

She seemed frozen to the spot. He unfastened the fly on his jeans and slid them down his legs until he was standing in front of her wearing just his fitted boxers. Only then was his arousal, completely and unavoidably visible.

Mallory's core clenched with desire. She wanted to see all of him; feel all of him. With a deep breath she slid the straps of her lace bra down over her shoulders and bent her arms back to unfasten the clasp. She held the bra in her hands feeling exposed and vulnerable as her full, rounded breasts heaved with a mixture of fear and desire. Sam took the bra from her hands and threw it onto the little arm chair in the corner of the room. A wry smile appeared on his face.

"Wanna do this last part together?" he whispered. Mallory nodded, "Okay, on three...one...two...three." They both removed their remaining undergarments and stood there, naked before one another. *Oh my God this is really happening* the scrambled thought rushed through her mind.

He was a spectacular specimen of sexual male, she thought. His erection was strong and powerful. She felt her desire increase and her sex felt damp.

"C'mere." Sam held out his hands to Mallory, who gladly stepped into his arms. He kissed her again; their tongues dancing around each other's mouths; breaths shallow and wanting; hands wandering and exploring. Sam cupped her right breast, worshipping it with, first his palms and then his fingers. He toyed, gently, with the little pink protrusion which had hardened under his touch.

Mallory's hands grasped at his hair as she moaned at the myriad sensations that, like shooting stars darted throughout her body. She ran her hands down his back, hesitating a little just above his buttocks. She summoned up a little more of that new found courage and ran her hands further down, squeezing and kneading, pulling him closer to her body. She delighted in the moan that escaped Sam's throat as his erection pressed into the softness of her belly. She felt her own desire throbbing between her thighs.

Still wrapped around each other they tumbled onto the bed, kissing and caressing. Sam kissed her neck, sending little electric shocks right through her over-sensitised body. She stroked his smooth taut skin, bringing little sexy growls of pleasure from Sam's throat yet again. He slowly slid his hand down to her stomach. She flinched and tried to push his hand away. He grabbed her hand in his and brought it up to his lips, kissing each finger gently. Then to her horror he slid down the bed and trailed his tongue down her abdomen as he did so.

When he reached her smooth rounded belly he looked up into her eyes briefly and then lowered his mouth to kiss it reverently.

"I love that you are so, so soft…and so…feminine," he mumbled in between the kisses he feathered over her least favourite body part. She had just relaxed into that sensation when he began to move his kisses further down towards her sex. *Oh my God, Oh my God!!!* She inhaled sharply. *He is not going to kiss me there is he? No no no no no…mmmmm…or maybe yes…* She tensed again as he nuzzled the soft hair at the apex of her thighs. And then it happened.

Sam moved her leg ever so slightly and kissed her womanhood gently at first. Those delicious electric shocks ravaged her body again and she couldn't help but writhe and arch at the pleasure. He continued, his kisses becoming firmer; more insistent; more urgent; exploring with his tongue; tasting and revelling in the very essence of her. She felt the pressure began to build, deep down between her thighs. Her breathing became more and more ragged. She felt like she was soaring at high altitude, climbing higher and higher; she was light headed and a little dazed.

As if feeling her pleasure rising, Sam's pressure increased, he swirled his tongue faster and faster until finally her delicious orgasm took hold and she cried out, grasping at Sam's hair, her hips moving to their own rhythm. It was glorious.

He climbed back up the bed toward her pausing to caress first her stomach and then her ample breasts. His erection pressed into her hip as he stroked her hair back from her face and kissed her deeply. Slowly he moved until he was almost on top of her, still worshipping her with his mouth.

"I-I'm so sorry, Mallory, but I don't have any protection with me. I didn't want to seem presumptuous. I don't want to let you down, but I also don't want us to do anything silly," he breathed feeling very disappointed. She looked shy and pensive for a moment. "Is everything okay?" he questioned, fearing he had disappointed her.

"Josie, my friend called over with a little gift earlier. It's in the top drawer of the bedside table."

He opened the drawer and a grin formed on his lips. "Ah, I see your friend likes to look after you?"

"Likes to interfere with my sex-life more like."

"Well, I don't know about you, but on this occasion I am *so* glad she did."

"Hmmm, when you put it like that, I suppose I should thank her." Mallory smiled up at him.

Sam ripped open the box and took out a foil packet. He opened it and took out the condom. After sliding it down the length of his erection, he knelt between her thighs. He crouched down to kiss her passionately.

"Are you sure you want to do this?" He breathed, caressing her cheek.

"I'm very sure, Sam. I want to feel you inside me…Please make love to me."

He slowly slid into her and she gasped as she welcomed him in. It felt so good; so right. He kissed first her forehead, then her nose, her cheek, her neck. He continued down to her breast, cupping it gently before devouring her nipple with his warm mouth, making her gasp again as her climb began once more.

This had never happened *twice in one night* to her before. But then again, no man had ever taken the time to bring her pleasure so selflessly. She grabbed his hair with one hand and reached for his left buttock with her other hand, pushing him deeper inside. His breathing became shallow and she knew he was joining her in the ascent.

They couldn't seem to get close enough to each other. He broke away from their kiss and gazed down at her. Tiny beads of sweat covered his chest. She leaned up to taste him there, finding her way with her mouth across to his right nipple which she caressed with her tongue. He threw his head back, pushing deeper and deeper; his breathing rougher and his movements more determined. He grabbed onto her hip, lifting her onto him. He thrust faster into her and once again she was lost at the top of her Everest. Seeing him in such ecstasy pushed her over the edge and she began to climax, whimpering as she tightened around him, until a split second later he cried out and joined her in free-fall.

When they had floated back down to earth, Sam collapsed back onto the bed, pulling Mallory into his side. Quite exhausted, she wrapped her arm around him and nuzzled into his neck. They breathed heavily, still speechless from the passion they had just shared. Sam turned his body to face her.

They stared into each other's eyes, caressing each other's fingers and exchanging gentle kisses, whilst their breathing calmed and their heart beats settled back to their resting rates.

"Wow," was all Mallory could manage to say after the long silence as she gazed deep into the eyes of her lover.

"You're telling me!" Sam inhaled deeply and rolled onto his back, raising an arm above his head. She lay beside him not knowing what else to do. He turned to face her again and softly said, "Hey, penny for 'em?"

"I'm just thinking that was probably the best sex I've ever had, but don't go getting all big headed and arrogant now." She poked his bare flesh playfully. He scooped her up and pulled her into him once again.

"If I told you that I felt exactly the same way would that help?" he asked, stroking her hair.

"If it were true then yes, I suppose I'd feel pretty good." She said in a small voice.

"All I can say, Mallory, is that I hope we do *a lot* more of that and on a regular basis too. In between the odd conversation and meal of course," he teased. "A man's gotta eat." She nuzzled into his neck again, smiling and relishing his words.

~~~~~

Sam had returned to *Canada* for Christmas a couple of weeks later. Mallory missed him terribly. He had left her a little gift under her tree and given the strict instructions that it was not to be opened until Christmas morning.

Josie and Brad had arrived to stay on Christmas Eve and they had all drank champagne and prepared the veg for their festive feast. They had eventually gone to bed at around midnight, after playing a very long game of scrabble, which Brad had won and boasted about for the rest of the wine fuelled evening.

Mallory awoke at nine Christmas morning and made her way downstairs, eager to open her gift from Sam. Brad and Josie were still sleeping and so she switched on the tree lights and admired her beautifully decorated, *real*, tree. She inhaled the fragrance of the garland over the fireplace. She loved Christmas so much. She held the rectangular box wrapped in Santa paper and read the tag,

To my beautiful Yorkshire Rose lots of love from Santa Sam. she grinned widely and ripped the paper off eagerly. Inside was a red velvet box. She opened it slowly and gasped at the contents. A stunning white gold bracelet of linked hearts, each with a diamond at its centre. Wedged into the lid of the box was a note. She unfolded it and read, *Mallory, I give you my heart, forever*. She wanted to cry and wished so much that he was here with her. She missed him desperately.

Lunch was amazing but they all ate far too much. At two o'clock the phone rang and Mallory almost vaulted over the sofa to answer it.

"Hello? Sam?"

"Hey, baby, it's me. Merry Christmas."

"Oh Sam! Merry Christmas to you too. I miss you so much."

"I miss you too. Been telling my Mom and Ry all about you," he told her. "They want to meet you. How would you fancy a little holiday out here sometime?"

"Sam, that'd be amazing. We'll have to arrange it. I opened my gift by the way."

"Yeah? What did you think?" He sounded hopeful.

"It's just beautiful, Sam. I love it."

"I'm so glad. I just wanted you to have it when I saw it."

Hearing his voice made her heart melt and made her miss him even more. Being apart at Christmas was difficult even though, relatively speaking, they had only just met. They chatted for a while until Sam had to go.

"I'll see you soon. Can't wait." She sighed into the receiver.

"See you soon…I love you."

Her heart skipped a beat when she heard his words.

"S-sorry?"

"Whoops…I should maybe have said that to you in person, huh? Well, it's out there now so I'm going to say it again. Mallory, I love you."

Tears began to cascade down her face. "Oh Sam, I love you too."

~~~~~

January 2011

"Just at least say you'll think about it, Mally?" Sam pleaded as Mallory rested her head on his shoulder in a warm embrace. "I mean, we could go up there for holidays a few more times first before we relocate completely?" He implored. "And Josie is more than capable of running *Le Petit Cadeau* for you now. She's there more than you are. The cottage has a workshop and you could concentrate on making stuff for the business again, which you know you would love." He desperately tried to convince her of the prospect of such an idyllic lifestyle.

Mallory turned and picked up the print out of the pretty white washed, stone built cottage and began to read the description. Three good sized bedrooms, one en-suite, one family bathroom, lounge, dining room, farmhouse style kitchen, utility room and best of all a workshop. She and Sam had spent several happy holidays over the past couple of years in Argyle and had visited the Isle of Seil with its pretty, stone, hump-backed bridge. They had admittedly talked of living there eventually. *Eventually!* Not right now! Not when they were so happy here and things were going so well.

Sam had been doing his usual 'just looking' on the Scottish property websites and had discovered the cottage near the water's edge in one of their favourite places and had simply fallen head over heels for the place. He had decided that he had spent too much time in his brother's shadow and wanted to buy a place of their own, do something different, maybe write a book. They could afford it now, with the shop doing so well and Sam's inheritance—a combination of money left by his beloved Father and from Uncle Jacob, his father's eccentric and wealthy brother. Why wait until they were too old to really enjoy it?

"It does look very pretty," she mumbled, not realising she had done so out loud.

"Does this mean you'll think about it?" The look on Sam's face was reminiscent of an excited schoolboy. How could she possibly resist?

"I will *think* about it. But I mean *think*." Almost before the words had left her lips he swept her up in his arms and swung her around, kissing her passionately, before leading her up the stairs to their bedroom.

Chapter Two

January 2011

Mallory awoke to a bright, January Saturday morning. She blinked a few times to acclimatise her eyes to the sun streaming through the ridiculously thin curtains. Sam was wrapped around her, his naked limbs tangled in the cotton sheets and one buttock peeking out. She suppressed a giggle *and* the urge to spank him quickly to rouse him from his slumber.

Stretching her arms above her head she thought back to last night's delicious love-making. Sam had been even more attentive than usual, which was saying something. He was a *very* attentive lover under normal circumstances, but last night she had felt as though he was on some kind of mission. Or was he thanking her for agreeing to 'think' about the move to *Scotland*, to their dream cottage. Maybe he was trying to convince her. Who was she kidding? She needed no convincing. She knew for a fact that they would be moving, lock, stock and barrel if they could only secure the deal before some other lucky so and so beat them to it.

Realising she needed to go to the bathroom, she slid out of bed, as carefully as was possible considering she was pretty much wearing a six foot two male about her person. She grabbed her fluffy robe and shrugged it on, tiptoeing to the bathroom.

When she returned to the bedroom, Sam was gone, but there was the distinct sound of out-of-tune wailing and whistling coming from elsewhere in the little cottage. Rolling her eyes and smirking to herself, she drifted down the stairs to find her gorgeous man clattering around the kitchen with serious intent.

Caterwauling, as only Sam could, along with the sounds of Radio 2, he was oblivious to Mallory's presence in the room. She stood silently watching him as he danced around with a couple of mugs and sang into the coffee scoop along with Bon Jovi's *Livin' on a Prayer*. He really was a delight to behold. His grey checked 'lounge' pants—he wouldn't be seen dead in pyjamas, he had once told her—hanging low around his hips; the light spattering of hair on his chest, begging to be nuzzled; his unruly bed-hair sticking out at all angles. She sighed and suddenly felt the need to hold him.

Wandering over silently and standing behind him as he waited for the kettle to alert its readiness, Mallory slid her arms around his smooth skin, kissing his back as she did so.

"Well, good morning, Miss Mallory Yorksher." The pet name had stuck from their very first encounter, even though they had been engaged for over a year and she was soon to be Mrs. Sam Buchanan. "Did ya sleep well?"

"How could I not sleep well?" She replied.

"Oh I just wondered if you had maybe been lying awake, you know, thinking about little Highland cottages, or maybe mentally setting out your new workshop." He turned to embrace her and gently kissed the top of her head.

"I said I would think about it Sam, but that's all." She reminded him sternly.

"I know, I know." He sighed, turning around as the kettle clicked off.

She felt a pang of guilt at his obvious sadness. What could it hurt, really? It was what they had dreamed about for a long time. Admittedly she never expected they would be able to fulfil the dream until later in life, but hey, why wait? It would mean a totally different lifestyle and a fresh start. She knew that initially they would be overrun with guests, maybe for the first year, until the novelty wore off for family and friends travelling such a distance. But it would be their very own little piece of paradise. Maybe it wasn't everyone's idea of paradise. *Scotland* wasn't renowned for its tropical weather but that really didn't matter a jot. It was their dream location—theirs.

Sam had dreamed of writing a book since before he met Mallory; he had a head full of amazing ideas, but never had the time to get them down. Plus, it wasn't as if they couldn't afford to take the leap. But it was scary. It was a huge change. But the more she thought, the more the butterflies in her tummy danced the hot shoe shuffle. She was excited. She wanted to do it.

They sat at the little kitchen table munching on toasted bagels and cream cheese, drinking freshly brewed coffee, as was their weekend ritual. Sam was chatting away keen to plan the day ahead. Mallory, on the other hand, was finding it hard to concentrate on Sam's suggestions to jump in the car and take a trip to the seaside for some fresh air and good old Scarborough fish 'n' chips. She was consumed with to-ing and fro-ing over the minutiae of the possible move in her mind.

"Penny for 'em?" Sam finally gave up on his one way conversation when he realised that Mallory's eyes had glazed over and she sat in an almost trance like stupor.

Suddenly Mallory jumped up, "We should go for it!" She blurted out the thoughts in her head.

"Are you saying what I think you're saying, Mally?" Sam's eyes danced like fiery green amber. His excitement expressed throughout his whole body.

"Yes!" She gasped and lurched over to him. She flung her arms around his neck knowing that he had only ever wanted the best for her. "A million times, yes! Get the phone quick, ring the agent."

Sam grasped Mallory in a strong embrace and covered her face with kisses. She laughed uncontrollably, almost hysterically, at the realisation of what they had just decided. It was immense.

"Have I told you how much I love you, Miss Mallory Yorksher?" He whispered breathlessly into her hair.

"Yes but tell me again." She stared into his loving gaze, eager to hear his words.

"I love you, no, I adore you, no—I worship you." He continued to pepper her with kisses "My beautiful, beautiful Mallory. I can't wait for you to be my wife and I can't wait to spend our nights holed up in that little cottage, making love in front of a roaring fire and the wind blowing outside. I don't care how cliché that sounds. I want the cliché. I want to spend my life with you in our little piece of paradise." He uttered the very words she had been thinking earlier. It was as if they were one person with a single mind-set. She loved that. She loved him.

"I'll call the agent first thing Monday morning and make arrangements for us to go visit." He breathed into her long matted birds nest of morning hair.

"Hmmm, well, if we have to wait until Monday, what are we going to do to occupy ourselves until then?" She fluttered her long lashes provocatively at her fiancé. He didn't need any more hints. Whisking her up into his arms he carried her over to the squishy old couch that had seen better days and laid her down, hunger gleaming in his eyes.

~~~~~

It took forever for Monday to come around. Thankfully it was Josie's day in the shop and so Mallory didn't have to make the journey into *Leeds*. She would probably have been as much use as an inflatable dartboard. Sam had taken a day's leave too, which rarely happened. Despite the opportunity for a blissful lie in with her hunky man, she could fight the excitement no longer and tugged at Sam's ear lobe in a bid to wake him from dream land. If that hadn't worked, plan B was to send Ruby in to jump on him in her giddy canine fashion. How could he be asleep when there were things to be done? She stressed. Sam begrudgingly opened his eyes.

"What time is it my little *Yorkshire* puddin'?" He yawned.

"Half seven. I couldn't sleep, Sam, I'm so excited."

"Ya don't say." He mumbled rubbing his weary eyes.

"Shall I go and make coffee?" She urged, leaning in for a kiss.

"That'd be grrrrand," Sam replied, rolling his 'r' in his best attempts at a *Yorkshire* accent.

Bashing him playfully with a cushion she told him, "that accent still needs work, Mister."

Mallory clambered out of bed, scrambled into a pair of yoga pants and a T-shirt and headed down to the kitchen.

When Sam had finally crawled out of bed and spoken to the agent later that morning, it was suggested that it would be best for them to go up and view the interior of the property as soon as possible and that there had been a lot of interest from other parties. This was unwelcome news and it filled Mallory with dread. But Sam didn't falter. He simply proceeded to book a Bed and Breakfast a short drive from the cottage for them to take a few days break in the area the following week. They would have to wait, hoping and praying that no one would pip them to the post.

~~~~~

After a ridiculously early start, they arrived at noon at the B and B they had found located at Easdale, just along the road from the cottage. The owner greeted them with homemade Scottish shortbread and fresh coffee. Their appointment wasn't until one o'clock and so they had an hour to relax in their room. The problem was that Mallory's nerves were on end and she found it hard to sit still, never mind relax. Her palms were sweating and her heart rate could rival that of someone running a trolley dash. She kept glancing at her watch.

Sam smiled and shook his head, "Mally, you are driving me crazy. Would you please just calm down. We're here. It's not long now." He pulled her into an embrace on the squashy bed and kissed her. The kiss was enough to temporarily fog her brain into a calm trance-like state as his delicious lips moved over hers. She sighed against his mouth and felt him smile. Suddenly Mallory's phone began to beep.

"Ooh, it's time!" She leapt from his arms. "Come on slow coach!" She tried her best to pull him from the bed. He allowed her to pull him upright shaking his head again, a grin firmly fixed on his face.

"Yup, crazy." He muttered to himself.

The drive along the road to the cottage took all of ten minutes. There were jagged rocks rising skyward to Mallory's left side with a few houses dotted just in front. Mallory looked out of the window next to Sam as he drove, killing two birds with one stone. On the one hand she was able to look at Sam's handsome unshaven face and on the other she could look over the water. The winter sun glistened like scattered diamonds on the sea and the rocks way out in the distance looked like a stationary ship that had dropped anchor just off the stunning coastline. She couldn't help but allow the small smile that had been curling up the corners of her mouth to spread into a full on grin. *Why on earth it took me so long to agree to this I'll never know.*

They past a pub on their left hand side. That's handy, Mallory thought as she appraised the old white building with its wooden outdoor benches. Across from the pub was a small parking area and what looked like a little tourist information hut. The bridge stretched out over to their right. A large beautiful stone structure where she and Sam had stood before and admired the spectacular vista.

The road curved around to the right and traversed over the bridge, but they pulled off to the left onto a little track that ran parallel with the water as it swept along under the bridge and out to sea.

The double fronted, whitewashed cottage stood looking out over the water. The little path that led up to the front door was dusted with frost where the sun hadn't yet reached. They were greeted by the estate agent. He was quite young and not what Mallory had expected.

"Ah, Mr and Mrs Buchanan I presume?" The suited man held out his hand, "Jim Warriner of McTavish and Co."

"I wish," Sam smiled shaking the man's hand. "She has agreed to marry me but we haven't done the deed just yet."

"Mallory Westerman. Pleased to meet you."

"Well, the door is open, feel free to have a good roam around. I'll wait in my car so you have some privacy. Oh and there are still a few bits in there belonging to the owner. He hasn't quite cleared the place out yet. It should all be done by the end of this week."

"Great, thanks. We'll see you soon."

The estate agent returned to his vehicle and the couple made their way into the house.

They stepped into the tiny entrance and were greeted by two doors, one to the right and one to the left. Straight ahead was a set of stairs. Mallory reached for the door on the right. She gasped as the door opened onto the lounge. Some of the owner's effects were still dotted around the place but Mallory could see through it and virtually place all of their furniture. A brick inglenook fireplace sat under a large, gnarled and pitted oak beam mantle on the wall opposite the door. The log burning stove stood in the middle of the slate hearth with a thin layer of dust atop it.

"Oh Sam, it's a Christmas house." She exclaimed as her eyes travelled around the white walls that were in need of a freshen up.

"Sorry, a what now?" Sam's brow furrowed. And she knew it wasn't the first time he didn't know what she was talking about.

She turned to Sam with an excited grin, her hands splayed out in the air. "Okay, imagine this…" She walked over to the fireplace. "The log burner is crackling away with a fresh pine log…there is an evergreen and berry garland stretched across the mantle..." She gestured wildly to where the adornment would sit, and then moved to the corner of the room. "Over in this corner is a real Christmas tree, not one of those plastic artificial things…" Her nose scrunched at the thought. "No, a real tree trimmed with baubles and beads, filling the air with its fresh scent." Glancing over to where Sam stood in the centre of the room she crouched, "under the tree are little brightly coloured packages, tied up with ribbons, waiting to be opened…" She rose again and moved back over to the fire place and waved her hands at the empty floor space, "there's a rug in front of the fire and Ruby is curled up fast asleep…" crouching again she reached out her hand, "eventually there will be a mini Sam or Mallory sitting, wide eyed waiting for Santa to come…although, explaining how he'll get through a stove may be tricky." She laughed as she imagined that scenario. Standing again, she moved over toward the door that led through to the kitchen and closed her eyes. "There's a delicious aroma floating through the house of spiced fruit cake…" her fingers flickered around in the air, "and in the background Bing Crosby is singing about snow…" She brought her arms around her body and sighed. Breaking herself from her vision she turned to Sam. "Hey, are you okay honey?"

His eyes had misted over. Sam strode across the room and wrapped her in his arms. Taking a deep breath he kissed her forehead. "Babe, I can honestly say that I can see every little thing you just described and it's perfect. I can't wait for it all. I can't wait to share it all with you. What you described…it kinda took me back to my Christmases at home. My family will love this place. My Dad would have loved it."

She tiptoed to brush his lips with her own and smiled lovingly. "You big softy. It will be perfect because we get to have this adventure together. And I can't wait for your family to see it. We have to get this house, Sam."

He laughed, "we haven't even seen the rest of it yet."

"Don't have to. I just know when something's right. I just know." She pulled away and took his hand. They walked through the lounge toward the back of the house to find the kitchen. The walls were fitted with rustic pine units and granite worktops, very similar to those at Railway cottages. It needed freshening like the lounge but it wouldn't take much. There was enough room for a small table where you could sit and look out over the pretty garden—once it had been tidied up; it was rather overgrown in its current state.

They exchanged smiles and walked from the kitchen almost in a circle back around to another room at the front of the house. This was the dining room they had longed for. There was an open fire in this room too and plenty of space for a large table, right in the middle, which would look wonderful surrounded by friends and family at Christmas time. It would certainly beat dinner on a tray which is what their friends were subjected to when they visited their current home.

Back to the hallway and up the stairs. There were two bedrooms to the front which felt spacious despite the lower than average ceiling heights. The master bedroom had a small en-suite shower room in one corner and a window that overlooked the little front garden. The view out to the water was so beautiful.

"Wow, Sam. Imagine waking up to that every morning." Mallory slid her arms around her fiancé's waist as he soaked in the view.

"It really is a beautiful place, Mally. We've always loved it here. Since we visited on our first holiday as a couple we always said we wanted to live here eventually. And now we've seen this place I can't think of anywhere I would rather be."

"Come on, let's go look at the bathroom." She grabbed his hand eagerly once again and pulled him to the door which led onto the landing and led to another bedroom to the front, two smaller bedrooms to the rear and finally the bathroom.

They both stood open mouthed at the large roll top bath with its antique brass taps and telephone style shower head. The stone walls had been left exposed giving the room an old world, rustic feel. It was Sam's turn to slide his arms around Mallory.

"Mmmmm, I think that tub is big enough for two, babe." He nuzzled her neck sending shivers tingling down her spine. She turned in his arms and kissed him languorously.

"I think we need to make that the first thing we try out." She wiggled her eyebrows suggestively, making him laugh.

The two bedrooms at the back were plenty large enough for double beds and so guests would be very comfortable. The walls in one room were striped in blue and white and the other was a pale yellow. The other front bedroom was the same size as the master and it too looked out over the water. There was so much potential and the details really didn't do it justice at all. It felt so much more spacious inside, rather like *Doctor Who's Tardis.*

The back garden was totally overgrown, but at the end of a long path was another building. Mallory almost ran toward it and Sam dashed after her. She shoved the stiff door open and looked inside. A wave of disappointment washed over her.

"What is it?" Sam asked, with a hint of concern in his voice.

"Hmm. It's going to take a lot of work to get this place in a fit state." She grumbled

Placing an arm around her shoulder he leaned close to her ear. "Ah, but with your vision, like you had back in the lounge, surely you can see it for what it could be?"

He was right, she surmised. She had vision and determination. With the pair of them going at it together they could do it. They could make it the perfect place to run *Le Petit Cadeau* from. Positivity reigned supreme.

The couple reluctantly tore themselves away and handed the keys over to Mr. Warriner, the agent. Once they were alone again they went for a stroll. They stood on the midpoint of the stone bridge and looked out over the Atlantic Ocean.

Sam slipped his arms around Mallory's waist and pulled her into him. He looked deep into her eyes. They sparkled today like he had never seen them before. He was mesmerised. He kissed the tip of her nose,

"So whaddya say Miss Yorksherr? Are we going for it? We would have our favourite bridge right on the doorstep. We could walk up here every day and look over that massive expanse of sea and it would be just like it was our own."

Stroking a finger down his cheek and no further thought needed she gave her reply, "I say let's do it."

After viewing the cottage they took a long drive to Glenfinnan to sit by the Loch and take in the view. The air was chilled, but they huddled together and sat on the old tree trunk that had been there for years. As the sun began to descend they made their way back to the B and B where they were booked in for dinner seeing as the owner had given them the option on check in. It meant they could share a bottle of wine and relax whilst they discussed the house.

Sam watched Mallory as he tucked into his steak. "Penny for 'em?" he asked, as his fiancée drifted off somewhere and her eyes glazed over.

"Oh sorry. I think I was back in the cottage for a moment." She shook her head as if to bring herself back to the present.

"And?"

"Well, all I can say is I never expected it to be so…so…"

"Perfect?"

"Perfect."

~~~~~

On the Monday morning following their mini-break the all-important call had been made to put their offer forward. They had both adored the cottage. They just needed to secure it, but unfortunately it was in the hands of fate…well, the estate agents to be exact.

After three hours of pacing the floor, negotiating and nail biting, the final call came through from *Scotland*. Sam answered his cell phone and Mallory clung onto the hem of his shirt anxiously waiting for Sam's facial expression to reveal the news.

"Ahuh…yes…okay…oh, yeah?…hmmmm…okay, well thanks for all your help Mr. Warriner, it's much appreciated." Sam hung up; his face stoic. He closed his eyes, ran his hands through his hair and let out a long breath. Mallory's heart sank. Her eyes welled up. The dream was gone.

"Well, that's it I guess." Sam finally spoke in a low resigned tone.

Mallory stifled the sob that was desperate to lurch from her throat, "I guess so." She slumped onto the sofa. Although she had been filled with trepidation about the whole thing, initially, to know that it wasn't happening broke her heart a little. There were a few moments of silence as she tried to come to terms with the news.

"Yup…I am soooo not looking forward to all the packing." He huffed, shaking his head.

Mallory hesitated, pondering that last sentence. She looked up slowly into the face of her beloved only to see the huge grin that had transplanted itself onto his flawless face.

"You rotten sod! You absolute mean GIT!" She screamed as the realisation of the truth dawned on her. She flung herself into the arms of the fibber and burst into floods of warm, ecstatic tears.

April 2011

Sam had been worrying about Mallory as the stress of the move was taking its toll on her appetite and she had lost weight. Even *she* admitted it wasn't like her, but she put it down to excitement mostly. During one of their packing days he slid his arms around her and noticed the change.

He nuzzled her neck and said, "Hey, don't you be turning all twiggy on me now! I love your curves. They are what make you so delicious." He moved away to build yet another box.

"Believe me, it's not intentional. I think it's just the stress of moving so far away. You know, leaving Josie and Brad…the business…"

"I know, babe. But it will be so worth it when we get there, eh?"

"I know. I *am* looking forward to it. I think I'll just be happier when we actually get there and we can relax." She looked around at the boxes that surrounded them both. "And how on *earth* did we accumulate so much stuff?"

"Beats me, babe. I think most of it's yours anyway." He teased. She threw a cushion at him playfully but he caught it, "Want me to pack this?" She stuck her tongue out at him as he laughed.

"There is one positive thing about me losing weight."

He came over and kissed her neck again, "Really? I can't think of a single one."

"Hmm, I would need to buy a whole new wardrobe." She grinned.

Sam slid his arms around her, "Nah, if I have my way when we get to bonny *Scotland* you'll be spending most of the time naked." He wiggled his eyes suggestively making her giggle.

Sam pulled the loft ladder down and climbed up. "Oh.My.Gosh. Mallory, you thought down there was bad...you ain't seen nothing yet, baby. Not by a long way."

Mallory cringed, "Oh no. I haven't been up there since I moved in. Not properly. I slide the Christmas decorations just inside the hatch every year but avoid going up there at all costs."

He lowered his head through the hole in the ceiling, "Well, as they say, there is no time like the present! C'mon. Time for a clearout."

Mallory groaned at the thought. Grabbing some black refuse sacks she climbed the ladder and pulled herself up beside Sam.

He handed her a box, "What's in here I wonder…okay, *Mallory's school stuff* is what it says. Should be interesting." He pulled out a report card and laughed heartily.

"What? Oh no what have you found?" She snatched the card from his grasp and read aloud, "…*Mallory has the potential to be a very bright girl, if she would only stop daydreaming long enough to apply herself.*" She read in her poshest voice, mimicking Mrs. Gloria Sanders, her prim and proper high school English teacher.

"Hah! No change there, huh?" Sam poked her in the ribs, making her scream in shock and punch him on the arm in playful retaliation. "We have to keep these to show our children how *not* to behave." He sniggered.

"Cheeky." Mallory retorted dryly. "Ooh, what's in this one? Aww, keepsakes." She opened the lid and stared inside, "Oh wow, these are my mum's things." Mallory lifted her hand to her mouth. She placed the box between them so that Sam could see.

"Hey, I found a little photo of you as a toddler. So sweet. Look at your curls!"

"Oh, yes. My mum used to spend hours trying to tame my birds nest. Here's one of me with my mum."

"Hm, now I see why you ended up so darn gorgeous. She was a beautiful lady, Mally"

"She was…I miss her so much, Sam. I wish you could've met her."

Sam pulled her to his side and kissed her hair before resting his head on hers, "I know baby, me too."

"She would have loved you."

"That's 'cause I'm so loveable." He smiled, "I'm sure she and I would have been great friends."

Mallory's eyes began to sting, "The thought that she won't be here to see her grandchildren, Sam…"

"Hey, hey, baby don't cry." He cupped her face in his hands and kissed her, his own eyes becoming glassy, "We'll make sure that our babies know all about all of their grandparents and how much they loved them even though they never met."

Mallory sniffed and wiped her eyes, "Yes, we will."

Eleanor, Mallory's Mother had passed away when Mallory was fifteen after a long battle with illness. Her heartbroken Father, James, joined her a year later after never having recovered from losing his soul mate. Her Aunt Sylvia had taken over the role of parent, which usually consisted of frank conversations and blunt advice. But Mallory had loved her all the more for it.

They sorted through several more boxes when Mallory came across some of Sam's boxes. "Hey, how did these get up here? I thought we had dealt with all your stuff?"

"Ahem…I kinda sneaked a few things through the hatch that I brought back from *Canada*. I didn't want you thinking I was taking over your life *completely* when we got back from my mom's."

"Hmm, very sneaky, Mr. Canada. But seeing as I adore you I will let it go. And as a matter of fact, I don't mind you taking over my life completely."

"Thanks Miss Yorksherrr." He rolled his 'r' in that way she loved.

"That certainly was a memorable trip." Mallory paused, staring into space.

"Which one?"

"*Canada*…seeing your mom of course."

Placing his hand at the back of her head he pulled her face to his and kiss her deeply, "That's because you agreed to marry me on that trip and made me the happiest man alive."

"You made me the happiest woman alive by surprising me like that."

They snuggled together in the loft and reminisced about July 2010 and their life changing trip.

July 2010

They were met at the airport by Renee, Sam's mom. She was an elegant lady. Tall and slender with grey hair in a stylish bob, which she wore tucked behind her ears. She wore grey pants, a cream round necked sweater, pale grey cardigan and a set of pearls around her neck with matching earrings. Her embrace had been warm and Mallory had liked her instantly. She had said how lovely it was to finally meet the wonderful woman who had *deserved* to capture her son's heart.

Sam's family home was beautiful. Compared to the houses in the UK it was more of a mansion. The double fronted façade was so incredibly pretty with its carved portico and shutters. There was a huge apple tree at the front which, Mallory learned, Sam used to climb up if he was sneaking home after his curfew.

The back 'yard' as they called it was also tree lined and larger than any garden Mallory had been in other than at hotels or stately homes. The furniture in the garden was a mix of white painted wrought iron in the tree lined seating area and huge modern looking outdoor wicker sofas on the huge BBQ and patio area.

The inside of the home was very traditional, but extremely classy with its cream walls and antique dark oak furniture. It felt very homey indeed and Mallory was completely at ease.

They had spent a wonderful two week break at the Buchanan family home and Sam had shown her the delights of *Kingston*. It was a huge town with a mix of architectural style from modern grey concrete buildings to beautiful old stone churches, complete with pretty carvings and fenestrations. The streets were much wider than Mallory was used to and everything seemed to be on a grander scale.

They had met with Sam's brother Ryan and his lovely, pregnant wife Cara who Mallory had hit it off with straight away. Ryan was a typical big brother; teasing Sam playfully at every given opportunity.

They spent a day at *Fort Henry*, where Sam had spent many of his school trips; they had braved the chilly waters of the beach at *MacLachlan Woodworking Museum* with its pretty old log house, before taking a romantic stroll to see the wildlife. It was wonderful. Mallory had felt like she was on her honeymoon.

On the morning of their last full day in *Canada*, Sam and Mallory lay snuggled together in his old room, surrounded by blue and white striped wallpaper and posters of his childhood sports star heroes, in his mahogany sleigh bed.

"I've booked a table for us all to dine at *Aqua Terra* tonight, baby; it's a seafood restaurant with fantastic views. I hope that's ok. Ryan and Cara are coming over too. I thought it'd be a nice way to spend our last night here."

"Ooh that sounds good; I remember walking past signs for that place when we were out in *Kingston* on Tuesday. It sounds lovely." Mallory squeezed her man lovingly.

"We are booked to dine at 8pm so we have all day to do as we please." Sam wiggled his eyebrows suggestively as Mallory grinned up at him.

"Hmmm, what *will* we find to do, I wonder?" She asked, kissing his chin lightly.

Sam growled his sexy growl and pulled the covers over their heads. Mallory let out a squeal of delight.

They spent the morning in bed, making love at their leisure. It was divine. In the afternoon they had gone shopping and Mallory had bought a sexy midnight blue dress that clung to her curves in that sensuous way that Sam just adored. When they had returned home they had shared a luxurious shower, devouring each other's bodies once again. Then it was time to get ready for dinner.

Sam sat perched on the edge of the bed in his smart black pants, pristine white shirt and black jacket. He waited patiently for Mallory to come out of the bathroom and reveal herself. She first poked her head around the door.

"Ooooh, Sam, I'm so *not* sure about this dress." She stressed. He rolled his eyes and shook his head.

"C'mon, baby, you looked gorgeous in the store, why would now be different?" He encouraged her.

She stepped, nervously, out of the en-suite bathroom, opened her arms and did a 360 degree turn.

Sam gasped. His pupils dilated. "See – you take my breath away." He looked genuinely taken aback by her elegance. Her hair had been styled perfectly, thanks to the help of Renee who had created a beautiful cascade of chocolate curls falling down from the diamante clasp holding her hair loosely at the top of her head. She had applied smoky grey shadow to her eyelids and a glossy pink shade to her lips. The midnight blue dress was off the shoulder and fitted to her knees; very Marilyn Monroe. Her silver clutch and matching high heeled sandals finished off the look with perfection.

Mallory was truly a vision to him. He wanted to scoop her up in his arms and take pleasure in removing that dress, slowly caressing every inch of her sexy, curvaceous shape. But that would have to wait. Tonight was going to be special.

They arrived at the restaurant and met Ryan, Cara and Renee in the foyer. They exchanged hugs and kisses. Once they had said their hellos they were shown to their table overlooking the waterfront, by the owner, who happened to be a good friend of Renee. Mallory looked out over the glistening water as the sun began to set and the twinkling lights of the boat masts danced like fire flies in the July breeze.

They chatted comfortably, ate escargots, crab and lobster and drank several bottles of Sauvignon Blanc. The house band played romantic tunes in the background. The dulcet tones of the handsome, young male vocalist lilted through the air and many of the restaurant clientele hummed along to familiar tunes like *The way you look tonight* and *I've got you under my skin.*

As they chatted, the music stopped and the band shuffled their sheet music. They began to play again. The music seemed to take on a different tone. This tune had a more modern feel to it. *Dum dur dum dur dum dur…*the intro sounded familiar and out of step with the earlier lounge music. The guitarist plucked the opening notes and a shiver travelled down Mallory's spine. She looked around the room to see if anyone else had noticed. She *did* recognise those opening bars; it was the beginning of Snow Patrol's *'Chasing Cars'*. She turned to acknowledge this fact to Sam, but he wasn't in his seat. Suddenly there was a hush across the whole restaurant. She realised that all eyes were on the stage.

Slowly she turned and saw Sam standing there, looking scared to death. *What the heck is going on? Oh no, he's not going to sing, is he? Please no!* She cringed. Sam was not renowned for his vocal talents. In fact she had once joked that his voice could curdle milk. Thankfully, the band's singer began the words that meant so much to the couple whilst Sam stood gazing at Mallory, his hand held out to her, needing her full and undivided attention.

Her eyes welled up with tears at the words she had held dear since their first night together. She rose to her feet and looked down at Renee whose eyes were filled with tears now too. Her hands were clasped in front of her face as if praying and a smile played on her lips. Ryan had a huge grin on his face as he looked up at Mallory and gestured that she should go to Sam; he was in on whatever was happening. The lovely but extremely hormonal Cara just sobbed.

She looked back to Sam who still beckoned her to him, the song continued and the magical words floated through the air like feathers on the wind; she began to walk towards him but her legs had suddenly turned to jelly. The singers beautiful voice went on coaxing her towards Sam whose gaze never broke from hers. She reached Sam as he stepped down from the stage and took her in his arms.

"Will you dance with me if I promise not to sing?" He whispered.

"Did you ask for them to play this?" She asked stroking his cheek. He nodded and planted a kiss on her nose. She giggled and slid her arms around his shoulders as they swayed to and fro in time with *their* song. The moment felt so perfect, even though they were now the centre of attention. All eyes were focused on the besotted couple as they danced. They gazed into each other's eyes as the song carried on in the background. Suddenly Sam stopped dancing and silently mouthed the words that followed.

New tears sprang from her eyes as the song began to draw to a close. The musicians quieted down until their music was a faint whisper and the singers voice rang clearly out across the room, Sam continued to mouth the words along with the voice that was much better equipped than he to express them musically.

During the last bars of the song Sam dropped to one knee and with tears tracing the line of his handsome, smiling face he looked up into the eyes of his beloved, holding aloft a little velvet box containing the most beautiful ring Mallory had ever seen.

He took a gulp of air before he spoke, "Mallory Westerman, will you waste time *'chasing cars'* with me for the

rest of our lives? Will you please marry me?" Wrought with
emotion he struggled to get the words out.

Mallory stared down at the only man she had ever *truly*
loved and the answer was easy.

"Yes" The restaurant erupted into thunderous applause as
the couple sealed their engagement with a kiss.

April 2011

After spending far too much time in the loft talking about
their romantic engagement, they went back to clearing out.
They cleared out as much 'tat and rubbish' as they could
possibly muster up the heart for and packed everything else
over the following week. Mallory then set about cleaning
around their essential items in order that the little cottage
looked pristine for the new owners. Leaving the house was
going to be very hard for her. But she was excited about the
prospect of a total change of pace and a new adventure with
the love of her life.

At eight-thirty, on the morning of moving day, there was
a timely knock at the door. The bleary eyed removal team had
arrived to take her whole life hundreds of miles northwards.
She directed them here and there as to which items had been
inherited by the new occupants of No.3 Railway Terrace.
Where the heck was Sam? He had only nipped out to get
some cash for their journey. Trust him to miss this bloody
bit. She grumbled to herself and winced as she got a paper cut
from a sheet of labels. Suddenly her cell phone rang.

"Where the bloody hell are you?" She scolded as she
answered Sam's call.

"Hey honey, I am soooo sorry but I got a call from Ryan,
while I was on my way home from the ATM. There's been a
major crash on one of the client databases over here and he is
stressing like a crazy person. He really needs me to go in

there to help out, just for a couple hours. They've been on it all night but Ry didn't want to bother me unless it was absolutely necessary. He does understand how important today is, babe, he just really needs my help."

He sounded apologetic but Mallory was unimpressed that this job, which he was supposedly leaving behind, was getting in the way of the most important day of their lives so far.

"Well that's just bloody great, Sam. What am I supposed to do? Go without you?"

"Honey, I am so sorry. Please don't be mad. You know I would do anything I could to change this but I can't. No one else knows the system like me and Ry and it's just not feasible for him to get on a plane right now when I know I'll be able to fix it. I'll get this thing dealt with and I will get on the road as soon as humanly possible. I love you so much, you know that, right?"

"Well, I am mightily pissed off with you right now. And you can tell, Ryan to stick his problem where the sun don't shine! This is so unfair, Sam, of all the days your brother needs you he chooses today? Really? It's just not fair."

She realised how immature she must have sounded when one of the removal men, barely out of his teens, grinned at her sulky retort. There was a long pause on the other end of the phone then Sam suddenly burst out laughing.

"You are one crazy Yorkshire terrier, do you know that? Hey, baby, I will get there ASAP. I promise." His tone changed to a husky whisper, "and I can't wait to get you on the rug in front of the fireplace and kiss every inch of that sexy body of yours. In fact, make sure the champagne is chilled, baby. I intend to get you good and drunk and take advantage of you tonight." He growled that deep sexy way that made her legs turn to jelly and her lower regions quiver with anticipation.

"Well make sure you do get up there ASAP. You have a lot of making up to do for this, Mister." She gathered herself, glancing around to ensure no one could see the heat rising from her chest to her face.

"I love ya, Miss Yorksher," he whispered.

"I love you too, Mr. Canada." She smiled. It was impossible to stay mad at him.

Her anger totally abated, Mallory joined the three men out at the truck to give them directions. When she got back to the house after waving off the truck filled with all of her worldly possessions, she stood in the lounge looking at the bare walls and floor. Tears stung the back of her eyes and she remembered back to the day she moved in…

October 2001

"Good grief, Mal! How much bloody stuff have you got?" Brad exclaimed as he humped another box from the self-hire van into the little house. Josie and Brad had been together forever, it seemed. He was tall, very muscular and had that dirty blonde 'surfer dude' floppy hair going on. He was ruggedly handsome and had a scar above his left eye where his brother had hit him with a Tonka truck when he was five. Mallory looked at him as the older brother she never had. Being an only child it was great to have someone tough looking out for her.

"Ooooh, only another three hundred boxes, Brad don't worry." Josie laughed as she and Mallory had set to the unpacking.

"I don't get how you two are just allowed to sit there doing the easy bit. I am *one man* you know!" Brad moaned.

"Ahhh, but what a man you are." Josie jumped up and ran over to her man, reaching up and slinking her arms around his neck. She kissed him deeply.

Mallory threw a cushion at the loved-up pair. "Aaargh, get a bloody room you guys."

"Hey, Westerman, I think a snog is the least I deserve for helping out," Brad complained pulling a face at her.

"Oh don't worry, by the look of it you'll be getting payment in kind from lusty lips there tonight." Mallory laughed and Brad's eyebrows wiggled suggestively at what she implied.

They had finished unloading and unpacking by ten o'clock that night and were all completely and utterly enervated. Pizza was ordered, but when it arrived they were pretty much past the point of being hungry. Brad had commented that they should just save it until morning. After all, there was nothing, what so ever, wrong with pizza for breakfast. The girls had laughed hysterically whilst Brad tried to justify not wasting good pizza.

Josie had produced a warm bottle of fake champagne and they had drunk it from mugs raising a toast to Mallory's new home.

"May you have many happy years here, sweetie pie." Josie had hugged her friend hard. "Enjoy tonight because Sylvia will be here tomorrow to tell you that your taste in IKEA furniture is deplorable." She laughed uncontrollably and Mallory knew that she was absolutely, unequivocally correct. She loved her Aunt so very much, but boy could she be cantankerous and opinionated. It was going to be an interesting visit.

Aunt Sylvia had arrived the next morning sharply at nine. She was dressed in a lilac twin-set and her hair had a matching hue. Mallory stifled a giggle.

"Daaaaahling!" Aunt Sylvia yelled in her usual pseudo-posh accent hugging Mallory hard as if years had passed since their last meeting; in actual fact, it had been the previous day when Mallory had finally moved out from the 'Manor House'.

Sylvia was her Dad's older sister by around eight years. She had married a very wealthy man who had owned a string of butcher shops throughout *Yorkshire*. She had gradually become the stereotypical *Lady of the Manor* but she had a heart of gold. "Come on then, lovey; show your old Aunt Sylvia around your new crib."

Mallory burst out laughing at the attempt Sylvia had made to be *down with the kids*. "My what?" she spluttered, holding her stomach for fear of her sides splitting.

"You know…they do it on the *MTV* programmes on Sky, haven't you seen them? Oh, you really should watch it, Mallory, dear. You need to stay abreast. Anyway, they all go around and look inside the grand homes of the rich and famous and see where the magic happens, darling. You really should keep up with what's *en-trend*, you know, young girl of your age."

Sylvia didn't crack a smile. She was unabashedly self-righteous in her explanation and subsequent dressing down of her niece.

"Okay, Aunt Sylvia, I will try harder." Mallory smirked, "Come in, come in." They stepped inside the lounge which was still full of boxes.

"Oh, it's…um…compact…erm…delightful, darling, delightful." Sylvia scanned the room almost with disdain. "It will be nice when you get it all sorted and have been with your friends to that Swedish furniture place you youngsters can't seem to avoid. Honestly it must be like walking into the same house over and over when you all visit one another." She looked to Mallory and her expression softened. "Sweet heart, you know you always have a home with me. Come back any time if you decide you don't wish to be alone…here."

Mallory saw a mixture of emotions behind her Aunts grey eyes. Perhaps it was *she* who was concerned about loneliness;

after all Uncle Harold had died three years previously and that manor house was so big. She hugged her Aunt.

"Come through, Aunty, and I'll make tea. I have little china mugs that I got from that antique place in Marsden. You'll love them!"

At the end of the visit, after she had waved off her Aunt, Mallory found an envelope on the mantle. She opened it and inside was a card.

Wishing my dear Mallory a wonderful new life of independence, love Sylvia, P.S. don't you dare eschew the enclosed gift. It is meant for you to invest as you see fit in order to make your new adventure a little more facile, much love.

Mallory rolled her eyes at her Aunts formal tone. Sure enough inside the card was a cheque for £500.

April 2011

Finally, and with more than a little trepidation, Mallory said goodbye to her happy little house of memories, locking the solid wooden door behind her. After a brief detour via the solicitors, to leave her keys, she and her little dog Ruby set off up the motorway on the first leg of their great adventure, surrounded by the essentials they would need on arrival at their Scottish destination.

The little yellow car was stacked to the hilt and the engine was somewhat protesting at the extra weight. Ruby sat on the passenger seat staring out the window whilst Mallory listened and sang along, emphatically, to the compilation CD of life affirming tracks and love songs that Sam had presented her with the day before. Tears streamed down her face as she sang along to their song '*Chasing Cars*' by Snow Patrol. She missed him already even though she knew she was going to see him in a few hours' time.

Mallory gazed out of the window as she passed the large hotel at Scotch corner. She smiled fondly as she remembered the time she had been to *Scotland* with her parents when she was nine and she had got very excited because they had reached this place and she'd presumed that they had arrived. She was very disappointed when she discovered the truth. Scotch corner was nowhere near Scotland! *What a silly place*, she had thought sulkily.

Mallory made a brief stop at Annandale water services for Ruby to do what dogs do and to stretch her legs. She grabbed some chocolate and a bottle of water, from the shop and then they travelled on.

Glasgow was bustling by the time they were approaching the Erskine Bridge. The cosmopolitan city was bursting with life. People shopping; people dashing around in business suits, carrying briefcases in one hand take-out coffee in the other; obvious tourists with their bags of souvenirs, silly tartan hats and 'bum bags'. *What is it about tourists and bum bags?* Mallory mused. She chuckled to herself as she spotted an elderly couple gesturing wildly and fighting with a large, crinkled map that had, apparently, acquired a mind of its own and was flapping, kite-like as they tried to tame it.

Further down the road they had another brief sojourn at the well-known *Green Welly Stop*. It was always part of their journey whenever she and Sam came to *Scotland*. She felt like she was truly on holiday when they pulled into the car park and she glanced up at the cartoon green Wellington boot with its smiley face.

Twenty minutes or so further on and they were past the Bridge of Orchy with its stunning hotel and out into Rannoch Moor. What Mallory could see of Rannoch moor's fifty square miles of boggy moorland and rocky outcrops was eerily bleak with its muted colour pallet. It was utterly breath-taking in its vastness and natural beauty; framed by the Black

Mount in its severe, snow-capped splendour, reaching towards Glen Coe in the distance. Mallory's heart leapt.

Almost eight hours after leaving her old life behind she had collected the keys from the solicitors and had finally pulled up outside the white painted cottage. It felt good to be here but she really wished that Sam and she had made the journey in tandem as originally planned.

The heavily laden removals van was going to be another hour or more and so she decided to open the front door into their new haven. The door was stuck and so she had to push it hard, with her shoulder. Once inside she found that the cottage was just how she had remembered it from their visit a few months earlier. It was clean and dry with mainly white-washed walls. *A blank canvas.* Mallory thought to herself. She let Ruby out into the back garden and watched for a few minutes as the little dog explored, picking up new smell after new smell; her little stubby tail wagging frantically.

Mallory busied herself unpacking the few essential items she had prepared for their arrival. She plugged in the kettle and took out the mismatched china mugs in readiness. She made herself a quick cup of tea and went to stand in the front garden to admire the view. Just up the road was the beautiful little stone bridge she had fond feelings for. She remembered her first visit here, when Sam had regaled her with his knowledge of the locale.

"This is the bridge over the Atlantic." Sam had informed her as they stood huddled together at the mid-point of the pretty little arched stone structure, admiring the view and watching the sun dance upon the water.

"What? It can't be!" Mallory had been totally befuddled by the fact.

"It's true. The water down there is the Atlantic Ocean. Over there is mainland and over there is the Isle of Seil. The bridge was built in 1792 by an engineer called Robert Mylne."

She had been very impressed with how much research he had done prior to their holiday and she smiled as she remembered his enthusiasm and eagerness to share with her what he had learned.

As she sat there, cup in hand she mused about how strange things had turned out. A couple of years ago they stood atop the bridge admiring their surroundings and soon, hopefully *very* soon, when their furniture and Sam arrived, they would be living a literal stone's throw from that very spot.

Later, Mallory decided to go for a wander and so she clipped Ruby's lead onto her collar and strolled away from the cottage to the main road. She paused for a moment on the bridge to reminisce once again about their conversation and walked a little further. She came to the pub on her right. It was a white washed building with a welcoming orange glow emanating from the windows. She took a breath and decided to go in to say hello. The warmth of the roaring fire was a welcome change from the early evening temperature outside, where it had gotten cooler as the sun had begun to descend.

With Ruby tucked firmly under her arm she strolled over to the bar. A couple sitting in the corner were chatting quietly and eating a rather delicious looking meal. Mallory began to salivate as her senses were bombarded with both savoury and sweet aromas. *No, I'll wait for Sam*, she chastised herself. An elderly gent sat at the bar drinking a pint of beer and reading a newspaper. Mallory smiled kindly and he returned her smile with a nod.

Eventually the bar tender came through from a back room, drying a glass with a tea towel and holding it up to the light to inspect it before sliding it back onto a shelf above his head. He was a tall man; broad and muscular with fairly long, shaggy hair which was almost black except for a slight smattering of grey. He had a goatee beard which also showed signs of age but this was contradicted by his youthful face. He was ruggedly handsome and tanned. Mallory felt quite taken aback by how appealing this man was to look at. *I'm only looking*, she smiled to herself but then shook her head to rid her mind of such thoughts as the man looked up, hesitated and then came over. He leaned on the bar in front of her and stared right through her with dark brown eyes that almost matched the colour of his hair in the dim lighting of the pub.

"What can I get you?" He almost growled in a strong, Scottish accent. She felt a little as though perhaps her being here was an inconvenience to him, somehow.

"Erm…Can I just have a diet cola please?" She whispered feeling like the request was almost definitely unreasonable judging by this man's surly demeanour. Who was *she* to order a beverage in a public house for heaven's sake? He didn't answer. Turning away from her he walked over and picked up a glass. She noticed his sculpted forearms as he placed the glass under the tap and drew down the dark brown, fizzing liquid, keeping the glass slightly tilted.

He was wearing a fitted grey V-neck T-shirt and black jeans. Around his neck was a tight black cord necklace with a stone pendant which sat close to his throat. The pendant appeared to have some kind of image carved into it but she couldn't quite make it out. Peeking out from under his sleeve was the jagged edge of a tattoo which looked rather like barbed wire.

He brought the drink back over to her and plonked it on the mat in front of her, spilling some of the contents as he did so. What was his problem?

"One eighty." He stated. She handed over an English five pound note which seemed to disgruntle him further. He handed her the change and went back to polishing glasses. She sat there perched at the bar whilst Ruby lay patiently at her feet dozing off.

"I-erm-that is *we*...are new here," she offered. "We've bought one of the cottages just by the water." The bar tender glanced over at her and shrugged as if to say "So? And your point is?..."

She fidgeted with the glass and against her own better judgement she continued; she always talked too much, especially when she was nervous,

"Yeah, me and my fiancé have moved up here from Yorkshire. We might become regulars in here, living so close." She forced a small laugh.

"Lucky us." The man snorted and turned his back to her. She felt tears sting her eyes. There was no need for him to be so dismissive and cruel. After all, she was just trying to be polite and make small talk. She hoped that this wasn't the shape of things to come. She emptied her glass and rose to leave. The elderly man from the other end of the bar rose to leave too and walked over to her.

"Don't mind, Gregory, he's a grumpy old fart some of the time but he's a heart o' gold, honestly." The man gave her a friendly, reassuring smile and continued "Aye, he's had a rough few years, poor man. Doesn't excuse his rudeness but it does go some way to explain it."

Mallory was grateful to the man for trying to put her at ease. "And I always thought that bar tenders were supposed to have people skills." She sniggered.

"Aye, well, I think he was at the back o' the queue when they were given out." The old man whispered with a chuckle. "I'm Ron, by the way. I live up in the opposite direction from you."

"I'm Mallory and my fiancé is Sam. He's on his way and should be here soon. It was nice to meet you Ron." She shook his hand.

Ron bent to fuss Ruby and she welcomed the attention. "Well, Mallory, I hope you and Sam will be very happy here.

And don't you worry, we're not all like him," he said behind his hand, gesturing toward the bar tender.

"Thank goodness." Mallory smiled and made her way outside and back down to the cottage.

By nine o'clock the furniture had been unloaded, the contents of several boxes had found their way to their new rightful places and Mallory had discovered that mobile signal was dependent on network provider. Much to her chagrin she had also discovered that her particular network was rubbish. Sam was still AWOL and her failed attempts to contact him via this method had left her with no choice but to go back over to see Mr McHappy at the pub to beseech him for the use of his land-line. *It'd be just bloody typical that Sam will have broken down in a "no signal" area and will be sitting at the side of the road waiting for the RAC to rescue him.* Mallory chuntered to herself, immediately feeling bad when she realised that if he was sitting waiting he could very well be soaked, as the rain was now bouncing down outside.

Ruby was snuggled up asleep on the rug in in front of the fire that Mallory had built about an hour before and was clearly not prepared to go anywhere. Mallory grabbed her water proof coat, pulled on her very fetching Wellington boots and opened the front door. The rain was coming down in torrents. She pulled up her hood and scrunched it around her face holding it tightly closed under her chin and she trudged to the pub in the dark.

When she got to the pub door she rubbed her hands down her face to rid her features of the excess water she had managed to amass on the short walk. The pub was alive with chatter and she could see the man from earlier, Gregory, standing behind the bar with a towel slung over his shoulder. She made her way over to him and he turned to her. His face broke into a wide, mocking grin as he tried not to laugh at her. That was it; the final straw. She snapped.

"Oy! I don't know what your problem is, Matey, but I tried to be friendly earlier only to receive the least warm reception I have ever had the displeasure to encounter from a 'bar keep' and now I walk over here in the pouring rain for you to laugh at me?! Well, I would very much like to borrow your public telephone and then you can get stuffed and I won't be bothering you again!" The pub had fallen silent making her voice sound very loud and Gregory looked dumbstruck; his smile had disappeared and Mallory thought she noticed his cheeks colour infinitesimally. He frowned and without making further eye contact he made steps toward her.

"Public 'phone isn't working. You'll have to come through to the back and use the private one." He lifted the hinged area of bar up to allow her through. She followed him reluctantly. "There. And you might want to look in a mirror before you come back through." He turned sharply and went back through to the bar.

Mallory first tried Sam's mobile number but had to leave a message when it went straight to voicemail.

"Sam where on earth *are* you? It's gone nine o'clock and you should've been here ages ago. I'm so worried. Please just ring me and let me know where you are. I love you."

She tried his work number; then Ryan's number; then his mom in case they had heard from him. She could get no answer at any of them. *Where the heck is he?* She was getting very worried now. She hung up and left a couple of pounds by the 'phone out of courtesy. As she passed the hallway mirror she glanced at herself.

"Oh great." The reason for her nemesis having a joke at her expense became clear. She looked like some kind of Kiss tribute band reject, as the streaks of eyeliner and mascara had left tram lines down her pale, wet face. She made her way down the hall to the door with the letters w.c. and closed the door behind her. She proceeded to remove the remnants of Gene Simmons from her face.

When she came out, Gregory was leaning up against the wall waiting. He smiled when he saw that she had cleaned her face.

"So, you're a *Yorkshire* lass, eh?" He had very smiley brown eyes when he wasn't being a grumpy-arse.

"That's what I said." She wasn't having any of his attempts to be friendly now. That ship had well and truly sailed.

"I have friends in York," he offered. She found herself smiling at his rolled "r" when he said that. He smiled too.

"Look, I'm sorry for being an arsehole earlier." He pushed off the wall and stood in front of her. "I've been having a shitty time of it lately but I had no place being like that."

"Don't worry about it. We're not friends. You don't have to explain yourself." Her words were clipped.

He raised his eyebrows and opened his mouth to speak but thought better of it and closed it again. She glared at him expectantly with her arms folded across her damp coat.

"Oh, okay. I get it…that's fine then. I'll be getting back to the bar."

He looked a little hurt at her sharpness. *Serves him right,* Mallory justified as she tried to shake the feeling of guilt. She stormed through the bar and back out into the rain.

She opened the door to the cottage, shivered the excess water from her garments and locked the door behind her. Ruby opened her eyes and her tail gave a little greeting wag but she dozed straight back off again. Mallory paced the floor for the next half an hour. She made more tea but didn't drink it. It was just something to do.

At five past eleven she awoke with a start and found herself curled up on the rug with Ruby. She had only lain down to cuddle the dog for a minute but must have nodded off. The reason for her rude awakening became clear as she heard tapping on the front door. She jumped to her feet, suddenly feeling very excited. She struggled with the keys but eventually fumbled them into the lock. *Finally! He's here, he's here, oh yeah,* and she did a little happy dance in her mind.

She opened the door ready to fling her arms around his neck and cover him in kisses, she'd tell him off later. As she pulled the stiff door free of its sticking frame, she gasped.

"Mallory Westerman?" The police officer asked quietly. Another officer stood silently behind him. Mallory nodded as the colour drained from her face. He reached out to touch her elbow. "May we come in please? I'm afraid we have some bad news."

Chapter Three

Mallory sat stoic whilst people dressed in black fussed all around her. She loved that people cared, but she just wanted them to all just sod off and leave her alone. She hadn't cried yet. She had just felt completely numb. The ache inside her had been replaced with a strange feeling of…nothingness. People talked about her whilst she sat; as if she had suddenly become invisible. *Does she want a cup of tea? Should she have a lie down? Has she cried yet? Do you think she will move back to Yorkshire?* It irritated her, but she hadn't the energy to fight.

Mallory kept replaying the Police Officers words repeatedly in her mind. "We're so sorry Miss Westerman, they couldn't revive him, they tried but the injuries from the crash were just too severe. Is there anyone you'd like us to call?"

As soon as they had found out, Renee and Ryan had flown straight over to be with Mallory. Cara had to stay home with their new baby boy, Dylan. They had all been amazing, but due to the absence of Sam's family in the UK, initially, Mallory had been the one asked to identify his body. The image just wouldn't leave her, it was etched on her cerebral cortex like a horrific tattoo; irreversible; a permanent fixture for her memory amongst all the happiness she'd had up to then. The experience had left her feeling almost anaesthetised.

There had been a discussion about funeral arrangements. Mallory had felt she had no right to even join in the conversation, after all she was *only* his fiancée; they were his *family*. Much to her surprise they had decided that Sam should be cremated and the service held near their new home. Renee and Ryan felt that Sam would have wanted that if he'd had the chance to decide for himself. Plus, they added, Mallory needed Sam to be near her. She should choose what to do with the ashes. After all, Mallory would not be returning to *Yorkshire*. There was nothing to go back for. Aside, that is, from her business and two best friends.

Mallory couldn't express her overwhelming gratitude for the kindness of the Buchanan's. She couldn't really express anything. But she did thank them with a silent hug. Both Ryan and his Mom had cried. Mallory had not. Ryan had felt responsible and had apologised over and over, *If only I hadn't asked for his help…if only he had followed Mallory as planned…if only.* Mallory had assured him as best she could that she didn't blame him. What was the point?

The cremation service had been lovely; if that's even a possibility for cremations. People had come from far and wide to pay their respects. She had sat and listened as people eulogised about her fiancé. Their words had been so kind. She had been asked if she wanted to say anything at the funeral, but she couldn't even attempt to muster up the words to express her feelings of anger, loss, emptiness and most of all sadness.

She thought about what Ryan had said and about his apologies. She wanted to go back; to make him not go into work on that day. Maybe Ryan was right? Maybe then he would still be alive. If he had followed her instead, maybe that lorry driver would not have lost control on the narrow, rain covered road by Loch Lomond. When she had, for a couple of moments yesterday, been granted a little bit of mobile signal, a voicemail had come through, so very cruelly. She had played the message over and over again…

'*It's me my little sexpot! I've just left work…it's about…aaahhh…noon…you must be driving or something…anyways, I'll be on my way in the next hour…I am sooo excited, baby! You, me and Rubes will have the best time, you'll see! The BEST!! I love you more than life, I hope you know that and I am so sorry about today. I promise I'll make it up to you. Don't go 'chasing cars' 'til I get there, ok babe? See you soon! Love you.'*

Each time she played it she could pretend he was still alive. She could pretend he was just at the other end of the line. It comforted her to hear his voice; the voice of the funny, loving, kind, sexy man who had come into her life and given her so much—loved her so much. How could that be over? It just didn't seem real. Maybe that's why she couldn't cry. When they had attended his Uncle's funeral over in *Canada* six months ago, Sam had hated how sombre the whole affair was. They stood in the church whilst the choir sang *Abide with Me* and Sam had fidgeted uncomfortably.

"When anything happens to me I want you to promise me you'll make sure that people wear bright colours, get drunk and laugh about the good times!" He'd whispered.

"Shhh! I am not going to talk about you dying!" She had hissed back at him, feeling rather cross.

"I'm just saying, I think it's sad when people die and all, but you have to try to remember the happy times." He had squeezed her hand and understanding what he meant she had squeezed his back.

Back in her new reality, the scent of flowers filled the white washed lounge of her cottage. *Her* cottage. Funny how in such a short space of time the plural had become singular.

Ryan had gone straight to the airport after the service. He had to get back to Cara and the baby. Mallory completely understood. She had insisted he go when he faltered at the door of the taxi that had come to collect him.

"I am only a phone call away, Mallory. I consider you my sister and I want you to feel able to pick up the phone if you need anything, okay?" Mallory had nodded and hugged him hard. She felt so guilty for not crying. As if he had read her mind he touched her cheek and said "You'll cry when you're ready, don't feel bad." *Sweet, just like his brother*, Mallory had thought.

Renee squeezed her shoulder. "Mallory, honey, you should rest" Mallory looked up into sad, bloodshot eyes. "You must be exhausted. You haven't slept for such a long time and you need to keep your strength up."

Keep it up for what? Mallory had wanted to ask it out loud but didn't. *It's not as if I have anything to look forward to.*

As if she had read her mind Renee continued, "Mallory, come on now, it may not feel like it right now, but you will get through this. We will all help you; you can't get through this alone. When I lost my husband it felt like my world had come to an end, but it does get easier, honey. But you do need strength to get through this. Please go to bed and sleep."

The mother of her precious Sam, who should be concentrating on her own grief, was selflessly helping Mallory through hers instead. She couldn't be bothered to argue or to even speak for that matter so she let Renee lead her upstairs and she laid on the bed she had shared with Sam and drifted off into an uneasy, fitful sleep.

She awoke with a start to an empty bedroom, breathing heavily and sweating. She must have cried out because she heard footsteps bolting up the stairs.

Josie burst through the door. "Mallory?" She lurched toward her distressed friend and embraced her "Oh, Mallory, sweetheart." She stroked her soothingly "You cried out his name, shhhhhh, it's alright, shhhhh." They embraced for what felt like an hour. But then again, time meant nothing anymore. After a while Josie broke away and said, "Do you want to come and eat something? Renee and Brad have made some food. You should've seen them, Mally, they were working together like a well-oiled machine those two." She smiled and held Mallory's face in her hands. "Come on, lovely, come downstairs and eat, eh?"

Josie, Brad and Renee sat at the dining table with Mallory. Brad and Renee had made sandwiches and had arranged a few other items on plates to try and tempt Mallory's appetite to return. She hadn't eaten properly for such a long time now and her weight was falling too rapidly. She tried to eat a little, but really couldn't be bothered. She hadn't really spoken to anyone. She simply couldn't find her voice.

While Josie and Brad tidied up Renee went to lay down in her room. Mallory found herself sitting alone. Looking around her, she suddenly felt claustrophobic, as if the walls of her new home were closing in on her and she needed to get outside; to escape. She wanted to feel the cold air on her skin and to be out there, where she and Sam had made memories. Without another thought she opened the front door, tugging it past its sticking point and walked outside.

The air was cold on her bare arms but she didn't care. It felt good to feel goose bumps prick her arms. In fact, it felt good to *feel*. She gulped the cold into her lungs and began walking. It was quite dusky out. She walked up onto the bridge and paused at the mid-point. She could hear Sam's voice here. The wind was getting up and made the air even chillier. She looked out to the Atlantic. Sam had crossed that sea first to come to the UK and then a few more times with her by his side. He would never make that journey again.

She couldn't bear to look at the view any longer and began walking again. As she walked her feet felt sore. She looked down and realised she hadn't put shoes on. Her feet had been stocking clad but now the stockings had torn through. It didn't stop her. She picked up her pace and began to jog; her jog became a run. She had no clue where she was going, but she kept on regardless. Eventually, she came to a stop and looked around her.

It had dropped quite dark by now. She wandered across some rocks and down to the water's edge. She looked out into the distance past the spit and could see a boat with its light swaying in the wind. Suddenly, a wave of emotion took hold of her body and she let out a loud, angry scream. She screamed and screamed. A blood curdling noise filled with anguish and pain erupted from her body. She dropped to her knees and the tears finally came. The scream turned to a heart rending sob that shook her whole body to the core.

She hadn't noticed the figure running across toward her from the water. Suddenly she was scooped up and wrapped in a large blanket, or was it a coat? She didn't know and didn't care. She had no clue who had picked her up, but it didn't matter.

She must have passed out as she seemed to rouse back into consciousness as she felt herself being placed into a vehicle of some kind. The engine started and the heaters were turned up full. The welcome warmth began to melt her ice cold skin and she opened her eyes. She couldn't see much. It was night time. The figure that had climbed into the driver's seat flicked on the map-reading light.

"Here, take this," the deep, Scottish accented male voice resonated through her. She looked up slightly to see a flask lid filled with steaming liquid "C'mon *Yorkshire* lassie, drink it. You need to get warm. You could've caught your death out there."

"I don't care." She finally spoke without looking at his face. Her voice was frail and wavering.

"Aye that's as maybe but there are plenty that do care. Now drink." Mallory took the cup and warily took a sip. It was coffee but it had a kick that burned her throat and made her cough.

"You're not a whiskey drinker I take it?" The voice spoke again. He sounded familiar but she hadn't even looked up. *He could be some axe wielding murderer,* she thought. Then she reasoned, *okay maybe there aren't that many axe wielding murderers who rescue their victims from freezing beaches and then give them whiskey before they chop them into little bits.* She looked up to see who the Good Samaritan was and gasped.

"You?" Was all she could muster.

"Well, I was me last time I checked, but then again I have been known to have a grumpy-arsed side too." He smiled. They sat in silence for a few moments. "I didn't catch your name *Yorkshire* Lassie but I'm Gregory. My friends call me Greg."

"So you mostly get called Gregory then on account of having no friends?" She replied snidely, immediately regretting her comment.

He held his chest as if he had just been shot, "Ouch, I think I deserved that, eh?" His eyes were warm. "So are you goin' to tell me your name, Miss Yorkshire Lassie?" He asked.

"Please don't call me that." Tears stung her eyes and one escaped down her cheek.

"Okay, so tell me your name then?" His voice had softened.

"Mallory," she informed him, wiping away the single tear with the back of her hand.

"After the mountaineer, eh?" She nodded; surprised that he didn't need the explanation that most people did. There was a long pause. "Did he call you that?" He rubbed his nose, "The name Miss Yorkshire Lassie I mean. Is that what he called you?"

"A version of it, I suppose…Miss Yorkshire…that's what he called me." She smiled as she heard his voice in her head.

"Ah, I see. Sorry. If I had-a-known I would've called you something else."

"What would you have called me? You didn't know my name anyway."

"Probably *'Wee Crabbit Lassie'*" His mouth curled up at one side so she knew he was jesting.

"And what does that mean?" Her eyes squinted at him suspiciously as she was fully aware that it was probably an insult.

"Ohhh…it means pretty and quiet."

"It *does* not! I know you're being mean. Tell me the truth," she chastised.

"You sure? Okay, you asked for it. *Wee* as in little and *crabbit* as in bad tempered." He visibly winced, as if he expected her to thump his arm.

"Huh, you can talk!"

"Aye, that's true."

Greg knew she was right. He hadn't exactly made the best first impression to the village newcomer. He deserved all he got. He watched as she stared into the cup of steaming liquid and his heart ached. He understood her grief more than she could possibly know. He wanted to reach out and comfort her; tell her things would get easier. But what was the point? She clearly didn't like him, so what would his words mean?

After a few moments he dared to speak again. "You alright now?" he asked his guest passenger.

She didn't speak. She just shook her head slowly as the tears came again. She covered her face with one hand as her shoulders shuddered.

Greg removed the cup from her hand and he moved toward her sliding an arm around her shoulders. "Hey, c'mon, shhhhhh, you'll be fine. Shhhh. It gets easier, I promise you that."

He stroked her hair as she let more of the raw emotion spill out onto his denim jacket. He sat there comforting her for what felt like hours, just letting her cry, holding her tightly and fighting back his own tears of grief that had bubbled to the surface.

Finally, she raised her head as her tears subsided. He looked into her red, puffy eyes and saw the raw pain she was feeling. He reached up and almost touched her face to express his empathy, but he thought better of it and placed his hand on the steering wheel.

"C'mon, we'd better get ye home. They'll all be wondering where you've got to."

Greg put the vehicle into gear and released the handbrake. It was a gutsy vehicle. She noticed the *Land Rover* badge on the steering wheel. *That figures* she thought. Looking at his left hand she noticed the indentation where a wedding ring had once been. She wanted to ask him about his family and his wife, but decided to save those questions. She wasn't sure she could digest any more information at the moment.

They pulled up outside the cottage and the front door opened immediately. Brad, Renee and Josie came running out. They shouted out in unison, some unable to hold their feelings.

"Mallory, thank fucking goodness!" Josie clapped her hands over her mouth when she received a disapproving glance from Renee.

"Oh thank, God, Mallory!" Renee exclaimed "We've been worried sick!" She pulled her cardigan around her shoulders to guard against the chill wind.

Greg appeared at the passenger side and opened the door. Mallory tried to get out of the vehicle.

"Whoa there lassie, you've nothin' on your feet." He scooped her up with ease and began to walk toward the door. Brad did not appear happy about this gallant action and quickly followed him inside.

"Who are you, pal?" He asked in a rather threatening manner, his broad *Yorkshire* accent becoming more evident in anger. "Why does she look like she's been dragged through an 'edge?" Brad clenched his fists at his sides.

Greg's jaw clenched at the insinuations as he placed Mallory on the sofa.

"I found her on the beach sobbing her heart out, if you must know. She's nothing on her feet and no coat. Have you any idea how cold it gets out there, *pal?*" Greg fronted up to Brad.

Mallory panicked at the sudden confrontation. "Whoa, hey! Knock it off, please!" She implored. "Brad…Greg came to my rescue when I went a bit crazy tonight, and Greg…Brad wasn't responsible for my lack of appropriate clothing. I went out like this of my own accord. So can you please just back up and shake hands?"

It was the most she had spoken in a while. They all stared at her, open mouthed, as if a miracle had just occurred.

Greg nodded to the two ladies and held out his hand to Brad. "I'll be going, now that I know you're okay."

Brad grasped his hand and shook it. "Look mate, why don't you stay for a coffee or summat? Warm you up a bit? And thanks for helping Mal. She's like my little sister and I would never forgive myself if she got hurt."

Greg looked to Mallory for her consent. Mallory shrugged.

Greg sat beside Mallory on the sofa. The others busied themselves sorting coffee and Renee went to call Ryan to let him know Mallory had returned.

Greg nudged Mallory's shoulder with his own, "See, you *have* people who care. Don't go scaring 'em like that again, okay?"

"When we were in your car, you said it gets easier…how do you know that? How can anyone say that?" She pleaded.

"Well, only those who've experienced loss and grief and have come out the other side can really know, I suppose." He frowned, staring into the flames of the fire.

"You've been through this?" She asked gingerly.

"Aye," he continued staring. His voice was clipped.

"Your wife?" she asked, remembering the indentation of the wedding band.

"Na. My…" He inhaled deeply. He rubbed his brow as if it hurt to think about it. She wanted to ask more; to find out whom he had lost. For her own sake admittedly, which was selfish, but she wanted to know how he had got through it, so she could at least start to try. But she didn't. "Look, it's late, I'd better go, I've got an early start the morrow. Got to pick Rhiannon up and I can't be late. Tell your family I'm grateful for the offer of a drink, but I really should be off." His voice cracked as he briskly walked to the door, pulled it open with ease and left.

Mallory stared at the door, a little bemused as to why he had gone in such a hurry. She had no clue who Rhiannon was, but she was clearly very demanding. Josie and Brad returned to the lounge with a tray and glanced around the room.

"Where's Cutie McHunky gone?" Josie tried to lighten the mood. Brad elbowed her. "Ow!"

"I think I upset him," Mallory admitted. "He said he'd been through this situation and so I asked about it," Mallory's bottom lip began to quiver, "then he left and I feel so awful." The tears sprang from her eyes as guilt washed over her.

"Hey, hey, it's okay, don't worry about him, you don't even know him from Adam," Josie soothed, "it's you that you need to be concentrating on now."

Mallory nodded, but deep down she knew there was more to what had just happened. He had been so caring; it was as if things were still raw for him. She regretted questioning him. She would have to apologise.

May 2011

In the few days that followed the cremation and her mini breakdown, new neighbours made themselves known to her. Her tragic circumstances had spread around the village like a wild fire. She was touched by their condolences, offers of kind, reassuring words and help.

Colin and Christine, the proprietors at the village shop, stopped by with homemade carrot cake; Colin's specialty they had told her. Ron from the pub came by to walk Ruby several times and the lady from a couple of doors down, who had lost her husband a year ago, called by with flowers, a card and an understanding hug. Mallory had shed tears at how wonderful these, to all intents and purposes, strangers were being. She felt sad that her welcome had been under such sad and painful circumstances. But they had welcomed her nonetheless.

Friday evening came around and Josie and Brad felt that Mallory really should get out of the cottage. They decided that a nice walk in the fresh air and then a couple of drinks at the pub was in order. Mallory took some convincing, but eventually she conceded and readied herself. Renee had agreed that Ruby should stay home and she was happy to doggy-sit.

Mallory pulled on a baggy sweater, jeans and a fleece. She scraped her hair into a low pony tail and slid her spectacles up her nose. When she examined her appearance in the bathroom mirror she was shocked at just how pale and drawn she had become. She lifted her glasses and dabbed on some under eye concealer to rid herself of the dark circles and rubbed a tinted lip balm onto her lips.

The walk was short, but helped clear some of the fuzz that had taken up residence in her head. They stopped at the midpoint of the bridge on their journey toward the pub.

Mallory inhaled the cool sea air into her lungs and fought the tears that once again stung her eyes. Would she forever be plagued by this sinking feeling whenever she stood here, she wondered. Josie and Brad, who flanked her, enveloped her in a group hug. It felt good.

"C'mon guys," she squeezed her friends' shoulders. "To coin a well-known Josie Gardiner phrase…'*let's go get rat arsed!*'" this brought giggles and overly enthusiastic grins to her friends' faces. They made their way toward the lights of the pub and its warm welcome.

Mallory stopped when she saw Greg leaning on the bar at one end; pint in hand. He wasn't in his usual spot, grumpily serving the locals and visitors. He looked fidgety and rather nervous. He was wearing a dark blue shirt which had little pale blue flowers on it. It suited him, Mallory mused. He looked smart. *Probably on a date*, she deduced.

The three friends sat by the fireplace with their drinks and chatted. Josie and Brad doing their best to keep the conversation light hearted. Mallory began to enjoy a relaxed feeling brought on by the alcohol she imbibed.

They had just begun their third round of drinks when someone began to speak over a PA system. They turned to the direction of the voice. Much to their mutual surprise, Greg sat on a stool in front of a mic stand, clutching an acoustic guitar.

"Ahem…evening all," he coughed. "Good to see you. Ahh…for those of you who haven't had the pleasure of being served intoxicating liquor by my good self…I'd better introduce myself, eh?" He fidgeted nervously again. "My name is Greg McBradden and I'm the local handyman, bartender and all round grumpy arse." He looked directly at Mallory who cringed and felt rather guilty considering he'd come to her rescue on the beach so readily. He laughed to himself at her obvious recoiling. "Anyways, I'm going to do my best to add '*entertainer*' to my list of talents. Thanks to Stella, the owner here, she seems to have a disliking for all you locals as she's agreed to let me sing to you." The pub customers roared with laughter; some heckled and some booed.

Lifting his guitar aloft he went on, "Anyways…I'd like to introduce you to Rhiannon…my guitar…named after a Fleetwood Mac song that got me into playing in the first place…so you can blame them if you don't like ma playing." A rumble of laughter travelled the room. "She has just been repaired at the guitar hospital…also known as a music shop for you heathens…so she sounds grand…If any of you's get up and leave, don't forget I know where most of you live." Greg chuckled.

"Right, well, seeing as this is my first night I'm not going to scare you away with my own compositions. This first one, you should all know, but don't bloody sing along. I hate that," he laughed. "It's a little number that I like to call '*Trouble*'…because…erm, that's its name." Another rumble of laughter. "It's by a guy called Ray LaMontagne and I'd like anyone who knows him or follows him on Twitter to tell him I'm sorry." The customers laughed again.

Greg began to strum the opening chords and closed his eyes as he did so. Mallory, Brad and Josie exchanged looks which pretty much meant *Crikey! I should cocoa!* They laughed together at their mutual shock. An amazed silence blanketed the room as everyone listened, mesmerised by the voice of this erstwhile loner who had appeared to have come out of his shell right before their very eyes. *He named his guitar? Bit odd…*It did, however, explain who Rhiannon actually was. Mallory pondered, letting the bizarre nugget of information sink in.

Song after song had everyone swaying and, contrary to Greg's insistence, singing along. It was wonderful to hear someone with such a soulful voice doing justice to some of the best songs from last decade.

Mallory and her friends drank and drank. But Mallory, feeling relaxed, was surprisingly sober. She sang along and felt as if all her sorrows had melted away for that brief period of time. Without giving his next song any introduction, Greg took a quick gulp of his beer and began to play a series of singular notes. Shock gripped Mallory and she felt frozen to the spot. Her heart began to pound and she felt the minimal colour she currently had drain from her face as Greg began to sing. Mallory's eyes widened as her friends exchanged worried looks.

"Oh shit, Brad, it's bloody '*Chasing Cars*'!" Josie growled at her boyfriend whose mouth had just fallen open in realisation.

Before she could stop herself, and before Greg pierced her heart with the chorus, Mallory rose and dodging the people at the tables nearest to her, bolted for the exit, closely followed by Josie and Brad.

Mallory burst into the evening air and gulped as if she had just come to the surface of a very deep lake. She was struggling to breathe. Her heart was making its most earnest attempts to escape its bony cage as Mallory ran. She collapsed to her knees in the middle of the bridge where she began to sob uncontrollably. When Josie and Brad reached her, Josie dropped to her side and encircled her in her arms.

"He's gone, Josie!" Mallory sobbed, "he's gone and I can't bear it. I don't know what to do. I'll never hold him again." Her body convulsed as emotion wracked her, "he's gone." Brad too crouched to join the girls and stroked Mallory's hair. The same sorry words fell, over and over, from her lips, as if she was determined to make them sink in. "He's gone...he's gone and he's never coming back."

Carefully Brad lifted Mallory into his arms and the friends made their way back to the cottage. Eventually, Mallory's sobs subsided and Brad carried her upstairs to her bedroom under the concerned gaze of Renee who stood, hands clasped over her mouth and tears caressing her cheeks. Josie helped her friend undress and tucked her into bed. She cried herself to sleep, this time with gentle, pain filled silent tears.

~~~~~

Mallory awoke and glanced over at her clock; ten forty-five. She sat and felt the most horrendous pounding in her head, which forced her to lie back down. Sunlight streamed in through the curtains. The same silly, tissue thin, curtains that she and Sam had endured at the cottage in *Yorkshire*. They never got around to buying new ones. It had been on their 'to do' list. She heard a knock at the front door and managed to scramble over to peek out of her room to see who it was. She had no intention of answering it herself. Josie had opened the door, "Oh, hi. What are you doing here?"

On hearing Josie's somewhat hostile greeting Mallory cranked her neck so that she could see who it was without being seen herself. Greg stood there looking like a rabbit in headlights.

"I came to check up on Mallory." He fiddled with his car keys as he spoke, "I saw her run out last night and was worried she was sick or something." He ran his hand through his hair.

"Oh, yes, of course. Thanks." Josie took a deep breath and shifted from one foot to the other. "You played *'Chasing Cars'*. That was the song that was played at her engagement. It meant a lot to her and Sam…It was their song."

Greg's eyes widened and he inhaled sharply. He looked horrified. "Oh my God. No fuckin' wonder she ran out." He covered his face with one hand and blew out a huge breath, as if letting all the air from his lungs escape. "Please…fuck, oh I'm sorry to swear, but fuck. Please tell her I'm so, so sorry. Fuck. What a fucking idiot!"

"Hey, Greg, you weren't to know. Honestly don't beat yourself up, eh?" Josie was trying to reassure the broad, six foot plus man who had almost visibly shrunk away to nothing in front of her.

"Fuck. Fuck. Fuck. Oh, God sorry, my language." Upstairs Mallory had to stifle a giggle at his reaction. She couldn't help it. *Bless him.*

"Don't worry, mate, Josie has said much worse." Mallory heard Brad shout from somewhere toward the kitchen. *Hmm, he has a point.*

"Every time I see that girl I seem to put ma fuckin' size ten in my mouth." Greg shook his head. "I'm going to go before I do any more damage to the poor wee girl. As if she hasn't been through enough, eh?" He turned to go, a look of despair played over his features. "Seriously, please tell her I'm so sorry. I'll be keepin' out her way I reckon." Mallory's heart sank a little at his words. Poor Greg. It wasn't his fault.

"That won't be necessary, Greg, honestly. You weren't to know. You're not to blame." Mallory was glad that Josie did her best to try and relieve his anguish but he turned and walked away, muttering expletives at himself as he went.

Sunday brought the sad reality of goodbyes. Renee had to fly back to *Canada* to be with her family. She was missing her new little grandson. They stood at the taxi which had pulled up and been loaded with her bags. Renee hugged Mallory as if she never wanted to let go.

"Now you listen, young lady," Renee choked back tears, "you had something so special with my son. He adored you and that makes you family. You must get on a plane and come to stay soon, okay?" Mallory nodded, wiping away her own tears.

Renee placed her hands on Mallory's shoulders. "Please don't sit home feeling sad though, honey, you are young and you must not let this terrible grief become who you are. Sam would hate for you to sit around looking so sad. He always said what a beautiful smile you have and he was right, darling. You and I know that Sam would have wanted you to make the most of this new adventure here in *Scotland*. He was so excited about being here." She kissed Mallory and cupped her cheek.

Renee slid into the back seat of the car and closed the door. She dabbed at her face with a lace handkerchief and rolled down the window. "Promise you will visit soon?"

"I promise, Renee." The car pulled away and Mallory raised her hand to wave. Josie slid her arm around her shoulder and hugged her as they turned to walk back inside.

During the week that followed, Brad and Josie helped Mallory to finish unpacking and they even managed to convince Mallory to put her photographs out on display. That particular task had been difficult. But they had all laughed at the one showing the four of them at a 1970's fancy dress bash last New Year. Sam had sported an afro wig, long moustache and fake chest hair. His flares were a little too snug and he had spent the whole evening re-adjusting himself as the others made fun. Brad had been a hippy dude with long hair and round glasses. He'd had to defend his choice of outfit, insisting it was a *kaftan* and not a dress. It felt good to laugh.

After they had given all the framed pictures a new home Josie had made coffee whilst Brad went out to buy beer for that evening.

Josie sat next to her and nudged her shoulder gently. "So, honey bun. What do you think you will do now?" She inquired.

"About what?"

"Well, will you sell up and come home to Yorkshire? Will you stay here?"

"Oh, Josie I honestly don't know," Mallory sighed. "It's a bit too soon to be thinking about that. Sam wanted to be here and so I feel I should stay. But I do worry that I'll be lonely. Back in Yorkshire I have you, Brad, the shop…" She hoped Josie realised the weight of such a decision and that it was not a decision she could attempt to influence.

As if reading Mallory's mind Josie said, "you have to do what's right for you, babe. Never mind us. You know you'll still see us. You can't get shut of us that easily you know." Josie laughed. "Brad and I are going to get home tomorrow. Maybe you need some time to adjust. You can't really do that until we are out of your way."

"I don't know. Maybe you're right. I wish you didn't have to go."

"Me too, Mally, but the shop won't re-open itself. We all need to get back into a normal routine. Brad has had a few calls asking when he is free to do a kitchen for that family in Adel that he worked for before and he really should take the work."

The shop in *Leeds* had been displaying a 'Closed until further notice due to bereavement' sign for over three weeks and Brad had dropped everything to be with his girlfriend and her best friend. He was quite a guy, Mallory thought. But they were right. The time had come for Mallory to move onward. It was going to be the most difficult time of her life, apart from the death of Sam, but she needed to move on.

Two weeks into May, Brad and Josie packed up their belongings into Brad's van. It was time for another goodbye. Mallory had said far too many of them recently. They weren't getting any easier. She tried hard not to give in to her emotions but failed miserably, quite literally.

"Oh don't cry, babe." Josie clung onto her friend. "We'll come up in a few weeks for your birthday! It's the big three-oh! We'll take you out if you like. Or we could stay in, whatever you want. Let's see how you feel, eh?" Josie kissed Mallory and climbed into the passenger seat before she too erupted. Brad hugged Mallory.

"Take care of you, Mal, right?" He kissed the top of her head.

"Thank you both for everything. I really don't know what I would have done without you. I'll miss you."

"That's what friends are for, Mally," Josie said through her open van window. Brad climbed into the van and they drove away. Josie hung out of the car waving frantically until they were out of sight.

Mallory walked back into the eerie silence of the house. She looked around the room at her old brown leather sofa that had seen better days, her burgundy rug complete with curled up dog, the solid oak sideboard displaying photo memories, the widescreen TV that Sam had insisted they needed, the beautiful artwork on the walls, some that Mallory had before Sam and some that they had bought on visits to *Scotland* together. And there above the beautiful inglenook fireplace, on the mantle sat the urn.

"Oh Sam, what do I do now?" She touched the cold surface of the container. "I feel a little lost. I miss you so much. I can't imagine the rest of my life without you. Why did this have to happen to you?" She wiped away a tear as Ruby jumped up, stretching her little fuzzy body along Mallory's thigh.

"Come on Ruby-doo, let's go get some fresh air eh? Want to go for a walk?" She picked up the little dog and nuzzled her spikey fur. Ruby wagged her little stumpy tail in excitement at her second favourite word; the first favourite being dinner.

Mallory clipped on Ruby's lead, grabbed her fleece and set off out into the afternoon sunshine. It felt surprisingly warm compared to the chill of recent weeks. The pair strolled along stopping at the same place she always did when crossing the bridge. She loved the view and the memories that the place evoked, no matter how painful. As they continued on a *Land Rover* pulled up alongside them and stopped.

"Hey, Mallory," Greg shouted through the lowered window. "How are you doing?"

"Oh hi, Greg. I'm okay, I think. Having my moments." She smiled.

Greg climbed out of the vehicle and came round to where she stood. "Look, I wanted to apologise for that night in the pub." He ran his hand through his hair. "If I'd have known…"

"Look, don't worry, you had no clue. How could you have? I'd had quite a bit to drink too which I don't think helped. Really, please don't worry." She smiled trying her best to reassure him.

"I just felt so bad. I came round the day after."

"Yes, Josie said so. You don't need to worry."

"Aye, but I just feel that every time I speak to you I put my foot in it."

Mallory smiled kindly. "Well, if it's any consolation, up to that point in the evening I thought you were really good," she enthused.

Greg blushed; he actually blushed! Mallory found it quite amusing that this surly, sky scraper of a man could be a little shy about his talent.

"Really? Thanks. I'm hoping to do it again soon. You should come along. Are there any other songs I should avoid?" he asked cautiously.

"No, just that one."

"Okay, noted. Keep a look out for the blackboard at the pub…well that is when I've made one. Right, well, I'd better go. I'm off to fix a leaky tap at Colin's. He tried to do it, but I think it's something a bit more serious than he thought." He made back to the car and climbed in. "I'm glad you're okay…well, as okay as you can be, eh?"

He fastened his seatbelt and looked back to where Mallory still stood. "Anyway, you should come up to the pub for some food sometime. Stella makes the best steak pie and you've lost too much weight since you moved here, you're looking like you could use a good meal." He clamped a hand over his mouth as soon as the words had fallen out. "Fuck. I really should just not talk to you, eh?" He shook his head as if he was annoyed with himself and drove away quickly without another word.

Mallory frowned and looked down at her disappearing frame. Maybe he was right? She shook her head in disbelief, she and Ruby continued on their stroll.

Chapter Four

The next day, Mallory decided to get stuck into organising her workshop. Hearing Greg talk about making a blackboard had given her the desire to get stuck into making things. *It'll be a good way to take my mind off things.*

She went upstairs into her room to hunt out her scruffy old denim dungarees. They were torn in places and covered in an array of coloured paint splats, but they were what she always wore when she was creating and they were so comfy. She pulled them on and to her horror they were enormous. She walked over to the full length mirror in the corner and looked at her figure. She remembered how Sam used to look at her and caress her curves. They were disappearing fast. Her vivid blue eyes looked larger. She vowed to take Greg's suggestion seriously and would endeavour to try Stella's steak pie someday soon. She scraped her long, wavy, chocolate brown hair into a high pony tail and doubled the band over so that it sat in a knot atop her head.

Armed with a CD player, a bunch of discs, a bucket of soapy water and wearing an old scarf threaded through the belt loops of her scruffy old denim dungarees to stop them from falling off, she walked up the uneven path to the little stone building at the top of the garden.

She pushed open the rickety old wooden door and flicked on the light. There was a film of dust over all of the work surfaces and enough cobwebs and creepy crawlies to make Tim Burton salivate. It really was like the set of a horror movie; she half expected *Frankenstein* or some other such monster to come crawling out of the woodwork. It was clear that the place hadn't been used in earnest for years and Mallory decided that was about to change. She set to, cleaning and sweeping. It felt cathartic to be doing something physical. *Maybe tonight I'll sleep.*

She placed the CD player near the nearest socket and selected '*Jagged Little Pill*' by Alanis Morissette. *Nothing like a bit of Alanis to belt out to whilst I'm cleaning*, she mused. The old sink in the corner had a rusty old tap which wouldn't even turn. So after emptying the filthy, dank water from her bucket she went back into the house to refill it. Ruby followed her everywhere like a little four legged shadow.

After a good three hours hard graft the workshop was coming together nicely. The work surfaces all along both lengths of the building were clean. The floor was swept and to her delight Mallory had discovered that under all the dirt there was a terracotta tiled floor. The pot sink was back to its original off white and the whitewashed walls were free from cobwebs and spiders. It needed a lick of paint and maybe a noticeboard and some bright pictures to give her something pretty to look at whilst she worked.

She unpacked her various table top saws, sanders and routers from their boxes and place them along one length of the work surfaces. Fortunately, she had discovered that the place appeared to have been rewired for a similar purpose and so there were enough power points for all her gadgets.

Mallory decided that she would venture over to the pub later and ask Greg about what could be done to mend the tap so that she could begin work straight away. She had an idea of a trade-off that would mean they both got a good deal out of the situation.

Once she had finished setting things up she made a quick inventory of her supplies and wrote a shopping list of things she would need in order to get working. She decided she would go shopping the next day.

She showered away the grime and rough dried her hair until it fell shaggily around her shoulders then she set about hunting for the old suitcase she kept with her 'slim' clothes in. It was in one of the spare rooms under a pile of things ready for the loft. Today she was thankful that she had kept a few items away from eBay and charity shops as she was rapidly running out of clothes that fit. She found a pair of grey trousers and a red v neck sweater that would do. The trousers had been too small when she bought them and now they fit perfectly. Checking that they didn't smell damp from being packed away she ironed the outfit.

Once dressed, Mallory applied concealer to the ever present, dark under-eye circles and a rose coloured gloss to her lips. On assessing her appearance in the mirror, she hardly recognised herself, which was quite a disconcerting feeling. *Sam would have been so disappointed* she mused. She pulled on her black boots and black waxed jacket and set off to the pub.

It was eight o'clock and the pub was lively with couples and families enjoying the home cooked food. The aromas emanating from the kitchen made her stomach grumble in need of satiation. She wandered over to the bar and perched on a stool. Greg was serving a very well-spoken middle aged gentleman who was enquiring about the local guest beers. Greg was imparting his knowledge and chatting pleasantly. *I bet he doesn't tell him he's too bloody thin*, Mallory growled in her mind. Then she chastised herself. After all, she had spent the past goodness knows how many years feeling self-conscious about her figure and here she was, almost two sizes smaller through no work of her own and she was offended because some bloke she hardly knew had commented that she had lost weight! *Stupid bloody cow.* She scolded herself.

Greg finished serving the middle class gent and came over to her. Tonight he was back to his normal self; a black T-shirt with a strange emblem and the words 'A Perfect Circle' on the front, black jeans and his usual chord necklace.

She could still only see the very edges of the tattoo on his arm. He nodded in greeting but didn't smile. *Hmm, back to the status quo then, eh?* She said to herself.

"You came out then," he said, stating the obvious.

Ya think? "I guess so, or else I'm very realistic hologram." She too spoke without smiling.

"Aye. Well, what you drinking? It's on me." He flung the towel he was holding over his shoulder like some bartender in a western.

"I'll push the boat out then and have a Jack and Cola." She smiled. She hadn't had one of those for months.

"Ugh! Have you no taste at all? First you ask for Jack when you're in a Scottish pub selling the best single malts you'll ever taste…then you kill it with Cola?" He closed his eyes and shook his head as if slowly realising he had just about done it again. Mallory just stared at him. He gulped, "Coming up." He wandered over to the glasses and measured out a double Jack, topping up the glass with Cola. When he had placed the drink in front of her he passed her a menu. "Steak pie is my recommendation, but see what you fancy." He walked away to serve someone else.

"Nice chatting to you." She said sarcastically, but he was out of earshot. She perused the menu and settled for the steak pie after all. Once he was done serving he came back over and stood leaning on the bar in front of her.

"What are you eating then?" he asked sharply.

"Well, you recommend the pie so I'll go for that please." She tried to be pleasant, but he wasn't making it easy with his brusque manner.

"Mashed tatties or chips?" he asked.

"Mash please." She smiled acerbically.

"Chips it is then." He grinned.

"Oy! I said…" he had already walked away through to the back. *Git.* She thought.

Mallory moved over to sit at a table near the roaring fire. She felt a little like a Billy-no-mates sitting there all by herself. Glancing around at all the tables occupied by couples, families and groups she felt uncomfortable. Greg placed a steaming plate of delectable looking food in front of her and then walked away without a word. Shaking her head at his rudeness once again she began to tuck in. She hated to admit it, but Greg was right, it was absolutely delicious. The chunks of steak were melt-in-the-mouth good and the pastry was short and buttery. She even had to admit that the home made chips hit the spot nicely.

After a few minutes Greg appeared again, pulled up a chair and sat right opposite her at the table. He didn't even have the courtesy to ask if it was okay. God he could be arrogant.

"Nice, eh?" He nodded at her plate of food. She nodded in agreement, chewing on a tender piece of succulent beef. He smiled as if proud to be proved right, "Told you it was good."

"You did," she mumbled, still with a mouth full. He was a real master at stating the bloody obvious. She was now trying to decide which was worse, sitting alone to dine or having her mercurial audience of one. It was a toss-up.

"Anyway, have you got that workshop sorted yet?" he enquired.

"How did you know about that?" she asked, trying to remember if she had ever mentioned that the house had a workshop.

"The guy who lived there before, James McLaughlan. I did a bit of work for him a few years back. A bit of rewiring and stuff. He moved up north to be wi' his family. Nice guy. He used to make wooden toys for the hospital and the hospice in Oban," he informed her.

"Oh right, that's nice." She thought that James must have been quite a guy to do such thoughtful, selfless things.

"Aye, he was a top man. Anyways, what are you going to do with the space?"

He was incredibly nosey, she decided.

"I make things. It'll be my workshop, if I stay." She put another forkful of the delectable pie into her mouth.

"Oh right, what do you make then?"

Good grief did he ever give up?

"I make little signs with phrases, picture frames, chalkboards and a few other bits and pieces." She decided there was no time like the present to put forward her proposal. "Funny you should mention the workshop actually." She swallowed the food and took a gulp of her Jack and cola.

"Aye? Why's that?" Greg asked inquisitively. His eyes narrowed suspiciously.

"Well you mentioned earlier that you were fixing Colin's tap and I wondered if you could come and have a look at the sink in the workshop?" She hesitated, "if you have the time, obviously, no pressure."

"Oh right. Aye, I could come and have a wee look. What seems to be wrong with it?"

"I think it may need a new tap altogether. It won't budge." Greg looked thoughtful, scrunching his eyes up as if trying to do a mental calculation.

She placed her cutlery down. "If you can, I thought maybe I could make you that chalkboard you mentioned when I saw you earlier. You know by way of payment and to save you a job." Greg smiled and held out his hand toward her. Mallory looked puzzled at the gesture.

"Got yourself a deal, Mallory." *Ah, right.* She thought. They shook on it. "I'll come around tomorrow and have a wee look if you like?"

"Great." That was easier than she had expected. She smiled, relieved.

"I'll bring you a dessert menu," he said whisking away her plate before she'd really had time to decide if she'd finished or not. Mallory was too full to even consider a dessert and so she decided to make a quick exit before he could return. She felt a little guilty, but figured he would get over it.

She stood outside briefly to gaze up at the stars. It was a very clear night and there was little up light so she could make out millions of tiny white dots of light and a few constellations that she learned about from her dad.

It took her back to one of the times her dad had taken her out onto the Yorkshire moors when she was around eight years old. They had packed a flask of hot chocolate and Mum had given them a Tupperware box of home-made flapjack. They packed her dad's telescope and set out at ten o'clock on a chilly October night. They had pulled up in the middle of a picnic area car park near Sutton Bank and gazed up at the stars from the boot of the old car. She had snuggled up to her dad with a little mug of the sweet chocolaty drink as he had pointed out Orion and The Plough; Mars and Venus. They had looked at the clear image of the face on the moon and had named him Boris, just because it was funny and suited his expression. He was such a kind and gentle man; and a wonderful father.

Smiling at the memory she walked toward the cottage. The fire was so welcoming when she opened the front door. She put up the guard and slumped onto the sofa. It was almost ten and she felt exhausted after her busy day. She couldn't be bothered to watch TV or read. She let Ruby into the back garden and on her return into the house gave her a little cuddle.

"Come on Rubes. Time for bed." The two companions went up into Mallory's room where she undressed, brushed her teeth in the little en-suite and pulled on her snuggly pyjamas. She climbed into bed and switched off her lamp. Ruby made her way to her favourite place; under the covers beside Mallory's feet. Mallory smiled when she thought back to the first time Sam had stayed over…

January 2010

"Well, I don't know about you my little love muffin, but I'm bushed." Sam stretched once the film they had been watching had finished. The movie '*The Hangover*' had been both hilarious and cringe-worthy.

"Yup, me too." Mallory got up from the beat up old sofa and took the empty popcorn package and wine glasses into the kitchen. "You go on up, I'm just going to wash these few dishes whilst you do your teeth."

Sam followed her into the kitchen, slid his arms around her waist and nuzzled her neck. "Mmmmm, are you sure you are okay with me staying over? It's not too soon is it?" They had been seeing each other for a few weeks but, apart from Christmas, they had been virtually inseparable since that first passionate night.

"Of course I don't mind. It's been three weeks and every night you've gone home I have missed you like crazy." She arched her neck and he nibbled her earlobe, sending shivers down her spine.

"Okay, well I'm glad you feel the same, Miss Yorksherrr," he purred. "Now don't be long, we have some serious heavy petting to do when you come up." He squeezed her bottom and made his way upstairs. Mallory nibbled at her lips, but couldn't stop them pulling upwards into a grin that almost made her face hurt.

She finished up the dishes and went upstairs, Ruby following closely behind. Sam had finished in the bathroom and was lying in bed, in all his scrumptious, naked glory. Mallory brushed her teeth, washed her face and climbed in beside him in her own birthday suit. He groaned with pleasure when he felt her naked skin against his own.

Suddenly he jumped out of bed. "WHAT THE FU-!!" He switched the light on.

Mallory sat up abruptly. "What on earth is it?" She panicked.

Sam flung the covers back from the bottom of the bed to discover a bleary eyed Ruby staring up at him from her usual spot beside Mallory's feet.

After things had sunk in they both collapsed in fits of hysterical laughter.

"I thought…I thought…" Sam gasped, trying to get his words out between loud guffaws, "that you must either be the *hairiest* woman I've ever met, or worse still that you had a huge hairy pet tarantula that you'd forgotten to tell me about!" He held his stomach.

Tears of laughter streamed down Mallory's cheeks as she visualised herself braiding her leg hair whilst holding the leash attached to her giant pet spider. When their laughter had subsided they were both drained. They cuddled up together, feet either side of the little black dog who seemed unfazed by the whole episode. Every so often one of them would give a little chuckle until eventually they dozed off.

May 2011

Mallory awoke and felt a little strange. She looked around to discover that she was standing at the mid-point of the Atlantic bridge. Had she been sleep walking? Confusion clouded her mind.

"Hey, Miss Yorksher" a familiar voice came from behind where she stood. She spun to the direction of the voice; heart pounding. A familiar handsome face smiled warmly at her.

Her mouth fell open. "Wh-what's happening? You…you're…" she gasped for breath, shaking her head; not quite understanding the surreal situation she found herself in.

Sam stroked warm fingers down her cheek, "Don't worry, baby, you're dreaming."

"No, you're real…you…you *seem* real." Mallory felt her eyes well up with tears. It couldn't be a dream. She didn't *want* it to be a dream.

"Let's not dwell on that, I'm here now. Let's make the most of it, huh?" He enveloped her in his arms and for the first time in weeks she felt calm and serene. She melted against him. The familiar feelings washed over her as she nuzzled his neck and he sighed. "I wanted to ask you about something you said today."

"Mmm, anything." She didn't want to let go. But she gazed up into the emerald eyes that locked lovingly with hers.

"You said that the workshop would be where you would run your business *if* you stay." *How could he know this?* Thoughts buzzed around in her mind like bees around a hive, but then reality hit and she realised that this was most likely an interaction with her subconscious.

"I feel lonely without you, Sam. I don't know if I want to stay here. Maybe I should go home."

"You *are* home, Mallory. This is where you and I wanted to be. Your *heart* is here. Look at where you end up on every walk you take and now even in your dreams." Mallory looked around her and took in the beautiful scenery from the bridge. The sun was beginning to rise over the sea and the sky was an array of glowing orange shades; causing a glistening sheen on the sea as if it were on fire. He was right.

"But how do I cope without you?" She sobbed, nuzzling into him once again.

"You remember the wonderful times we had, just like my mom said. You make friends. You start to do what you love in that workshop and it'll all work out right." He paused, squeezing her into him, almost as if to buffer her from the blow he was about to deliver. "At some point, Mallory, you will have to scatter the ashes."

She shook her head frantically looking up at him in desperation. "No! I can't do that. It'd be like losing you all over again!" Her heart ached at the thought.

"No, Mallory, it's something you *need* to do. I'm not in that urn, baby. I'm in here and in here." He touched first over her heart and then her head. "You need to set the ashes free into all the places we've visited and loved up here. When you're ready, you'll know." He let go of her and turned to walk away. "Remember how much I loved you Miss Yorksher…with all of my heart."

She felt physical pain and grabbed for him but he was out of reach. She tried to run but couldn't move. Her feet seemed glued to the bridge.

"Sam! Saaam! SAM!!"

She lurched to a sitting position; covered in sweat, or tears, or a mixture of the two; heart pounding; breathing ragged. How cruel to dream such a realistic vision of her beloved and then have it snatched away so quickly. Ruby appeared at the side of her, nuzzling her hand where it lay clutched into the bed clothes.

When her breathing and heart rate finally resembled normal, she looked at her clock: six forty five. She lay back and tried to recapture the dream but it was no good. A whirlwind of emotions swept through her mind, scattering her thoughts like torn pieces of newspaper on the breeze. She tried to replay the dream in her memory; thinking and rethinking the conversation, but decided her attempts were futile and so she went downstairs. Ruby followed.

Mallory ate breakfast on the patio, in her checked pyjamas with un-brushed bed hair. The sun warmed her skin as she drank her freshly brewed coffee and looked over the jungle that, at some point, she was sure, used to resemble a cottage garden. It certainly needed work.

She had found an area of ground near the workshop, yesterday, that had been formerly used as a vegetable patch. There were a few pegs with seed packets attached still remaining, pointing out where potatoes and other veggies had been grown. That was a project she quite fancied attempting, she decided.

She heard a thudding which she eventually realised was coming from the front door. She checked the kitchen clock which read eight o'clock. *Who would be calling around this early?* She huffed making her way through the house to find out.

"Morning! Am I too early? Just thought I'd call in as I was out and about so…shall I have a look at that tap?" Greg stood there in a sleeveless T-shirt and combat pants. *It is too early and it's not that bloody warm*, she mentally rolled her eyes at his attire and his persistence to turn up in front of her uninvited. She guessed he was trying to be friendly but he apparently had no social skills whatsoever.

"I'm not exactly…er…" she gestured at her pyjamas, hoping he would get the hint.

He trailed his eyes down to her attire and back up to her face. Smiling he said, "Oh, no bother, they're very fetching. Get the kettle on, eh?" *Good grief, this man takes no hints*; she pursed her lips at the smiling buffoon in front of her. Reluctantly she let him in with his large metal tool box. "Shall I just go away up there? I know my way," he said walking past her.

"Why not, you probably will anyway," she chuntered under her breath.

Greg paused and turned to her. "Sorry? I didn't catch that."

She mustered up as much cheeriness as she could manage. "Yes, sure go on up, it's open. I'll get the kettle on."

When the coffee was made she trudged up the garden, with minimal enthusiasm to the workshop. When she had made the suggestion to Greg, she had expected a little notification of his intention to call round, or for the visit to at least be at a more sociable time of day. She felt guilty for being so negative; he was doing her a huge favour after all. She pushed the door open with her bottom and found Greg lying on the floor under the sink. She placed the coffee down and leaned against the work surface.

"How bad is it?" she enquired, hoping the answer would be a positive one.

"Hard to say at the moment, the nuts are all seized…and there's nothing worse than seized nuts!" He laughed heartily at his own joke. Mallory chuckled. It was quite funny after all.

She switched on the portable CD player and stuck in a *Foo Fighters* disc. Greg began to sing along as he worked. She stood and drank her coffee in silence as he faffed around with spanners, hammers and bolts under her sink. She realised she had a very clear view of his tattoo now. Something she had been curious about since her first encounter with Greg. She had always had a fascination with ink, but had never dared go under the needle herself. Greg's tattoo was puzzling. The image showed the alphanumeric 'K2' wrapped in barbed wire.

"That's an interesting tattoo on your arm, Greg, what does it mean?"

Greg stopped working and sat up. He pretended to examine the mangled bit of metal in his hand.

"Ah, it's just something I had done last year," he said glancing up at her. His expression told her he wasn't going to elaborate.

"Oh right. Why K2? What's the significance?" she pushed, figuring he had been personal so why couldn't she?

"Maybe it's a story for another time, eh?" He rose to his feet, scraping his hair back off his face. He came to where she stood, took a gulp of his coffee and went back to work. *That's the end of that conversation then*, she surmised. She decided to take the empty cups back into the house and jump in the shower.

"I'll be in the house if you need anything, okay?" She didn't wait for an answer.

She felt refreshed after she had showered, towel dried her hair and applied moisturiser. When she was dressed she went up to the workshop again where Greg was just finishing up. He stood wiping his hands.

"You finished already?" Mallory enquired, hopeful.

"Na. You'll need a new tap. I'll pick one up and come back to fit it tomorrow if that's okay?"

"Sure, if you don't mind. I don't want to keep you from anything."

"It's fine. I'll squeeze it in. It's not a massive job. I've got to go now 'cause I'm working on my boat this afternoon and I need to get lunch before I go." He tucked the dirty cloth into his back pocket and closed his tool box.

"Oh I could've made you some sandwiches or something to take, it's the least I could do."

"I'm quite capable of making my own sandwiches, thank you," he snapped.

Seriously, what is his problem?! She opened her mouth to snap back, but thought better of it.

"Fine. See you later then." She wasn't sure what she was supposed to have done wrong.

"I'll see myself out. See you." He walked away. As he did so his mobile rang. "Aye, what is it? No I'm just finishing a job…where did they find it?" He froze. "Aye, okay. Thanks for letting me know." He shook his head as he hung up the call. He turned to look at Mallory, "See you tomorrow." There was a hint of sadness to his gaze. Before she could ask if he was okay, he was gone. Mallory wondered what the call must have been about. It sounded serious judging by his reaction.

After lunch, Mallory decided she would go for a walk with Ruby. This had become somewhat of a daily routine now and she enjoyed the fact the weather was improved of late. This time she decided to take a slightly different route, avoiding the bridge for once. As she walked past the houses one of the neighbours waved to her. She seemed to remember her name was Aileen. She had called around with a pot of Irish stew which Brad had devoured in one sitting. It was a good job Mallory had no appetite at the time as she didn't get a look in.

"Good afternoon! Good to see you out and about, hen." The neighbour called. Mallory waved back and smiled. It brought tears to her eyes when people she hardly knew showed such kindness.

The walk took her past the pub which was closed. She wondered how Greg was. He had been impolite on leaving this morning, but he seemed to be upset by the call he had received. Perhaps it had been bad news. She'd have to try and cut the guy a little slack, after all she knew there was something painful in his recent past and she could understand what that was like.

She called into the little shop to get a bottle of water. The shop owner, Colin, greeted her with a huge friendly smile.

He came around the counter to give her a hug. "Oh Mallory, it's so good to see you out." He stepped back holding her at arm's length. "I know we don't know you all that well, but if you need anything, anything at all…" he didn't need to finish the sentence.

She smiled and nodded, biting her cheek to halt the tears that threatened. He was such a kind, thoughtful man.

"I was wondering, Colin, I'd like to get some fresh air and see some nice views. Where's the best place to do that without having to go by car?"

Colin tapped his chin as he thought. "You know what? You need a boat trip." He proceeded to give her directions down to the marina where there was a daily outing run by one of the locals. He said that she would get to skim the coast and see some stunning views and maybe even some seals. It sounded perfect.

She set off with a renewed enthusiasm, following the directions in her mind and hoping that she hadn't 'missed the boat' already.

When she arrived at the little marina she stood for a few minutes to take in the view. There was a scruffy old chalkboard displaying the words,

BOAT TRIPS ON LITTLE BLUE,

£10 PER PERSON,

DOGS FREE

She looked around for the captain. She spotted someone with their back to her. He was wearing a woolly hat which was odd considering it was now May and it wasn't cold. He turned and spotted her and a grin spread across his face. Greg.

"Hey, you're out again. It's becoming a habit."

Why did everyone greet her as if she had been in prison? *And why is he so mercurial?* She wondered. She strolled toward the boat.

"This is you then, eh?" she asked gesturing at the boat. She wondered how many jobs this guy actually had. "I hadn't twigged that you did excursions when you said you were working on your boat this afternoon."

"Aye, it's my day job." He smiled. "You up for a trip out?" he asked.

She thought he almost looked hopeful.

"Why not? I could do with a bit of fresh air. How many of us will there be?" She wondered where the other passengers for the trip were.

"You're it." He carried on making the boat ready. "Bit of a slow day. I was just about to give up and go out by myself."

"Are you sure you want me to tag along?" She suddenly felt a little uncomfortable, remembering his attitude toward her earlier.

"Aye, why not? I get sick o' my own company. Get enough of it, day in day out." He held out his hand to help her on board. She blushed as she took his hand, stepping on the 'Little Blue'. She held out a ten pound, but he waved it away.

"Cute name." She gestured to the sign, "the boat, I mean," she clarified. "It has a cute name." She watched as he tightened ropes and did a lot of other things that she didn't really have a clue about.

"Aye, named it after my old dog; had him as a boy; he was a black lab; when he was a pup he almost looked like there was a blue tinge to his fur; hence the name." Greg gestured to Mallory to take a seat which she did immediately.

"Aww, that's sweet." Mallory saw yet another new side to this man she hardly knew. She looked out into the distance as Greg started the engine and steered the boat away from its mooring.

"Do you want the running commentary that I give to all my passengers?" Greg enquired of the sole occupant of the boat trip.

She gave him a puzzled glance.

"You know," he gestured out to sea, "…and on my left we have a seal and on my right, oh look there's another seal." He chuckled.

She smiled and rolled her eyes at him. "No, it's okay. I just wanted to get some fresh air, to be honest. Colin in the shop recommended a boat trip. Feel free to pretend I'm not here." Mallory sighed and closed her eyes as she faced into the sea breeze. Ruby's front paws were propped on the side of the boat as she looked out too; her little tail wagging.

When they got far enough away from the coast Greg switched off the engine and took out a flask. He sat opposite Mallory and offered her an empty tin mug.

"Thought we could sit and chill for a bit here, is that okay? It's usually a good place for seal spotting." He poured coffee into her cup.

She wasn't sure how she felt really. But she *was* enjoying being out in the fresh air.

"Yes I suppose. Am I not keeping you from anything? Another job perhaps?" She smiled

He shook his head and took a slurp of his coffee. "Na, Pub at night, boat trips three days a week and odd jobs two days a week…oh and entertainer at the pub on my nights off now, that's me." He sounded so matter of fact about the number of different things he had going on.

"Crikey! I'm not sure I could keep up with all that. I think I'll just stick to making stuff, plain and simple." The thought of juggling several jobs bewildered her.

"Aye, you should do that. It's good to have something to focus on at times like this." he said, knowingly. Her inquisitive streak was surfacing again. She wanted to pry about his situation but wasn't sure if she should.

There was an awkward silence. She could feel Greg watching her. She suddenly felt sad again; lost even.

He leaned forward resting his elbows on his knees. "It sounds like a cliché, but it does get easier with time." He looked down at his coffee. "You just need to keep busy."

"Is that what you are doing with your gazillion different jobs?" she asked.

He looked up and they made eye contact. For a brief moment there was a sympathetic look in his dark gaze. But suddenly something changed in his demeanour, yet again.

"Na. I like the variety. Don't get bored that way." He straightened up in his seat and took another sip of his steaming drink. Why he kept reassuring her in one breath and putting up the shutters in the next one, she could only wonder. "Have you started eating properly yet?" he enquired, once again the question a little on the personal side.

"Why do you seem so interested in my eating habits?" She was frustrated by his insistence on being so direct and interfering.

"Sorry, I just see you wasting away, that's all." He looked out to sea. "You look different than when you first moved here."

"Well, no offence, but that's nothing to do with you." She retorted harshly.

He held his hands up in surrender. "Okay, okay. Sorry I spoke. It's just that if my little sister was refusing to eat I would have something to say about it."

"Well, thanks for your concern, Greg but I am not your *little sister*. I am a twenty nine year old woman with her own life and I am fine. Don't be so bloody patronising." It was her turn to avoid eye contact and look out to sea now. They sat in silence for quite a while.

"So, you made any other friends in the village yet?" Greg asked.

Mallory let out a surprised snort at his insinuation that *they* were friends and then immediately felt cruel.

"Sorry. That was mean. I was just surprised to hear you class yourself as my friend." She explained. "We haven't exactly got along very well since we met, wouldn't you agree?" Greg looked hurt and she felt terrible. "Great, now it's my turn to put my foot in it, eh?" He didn't answer. She had clearly hurt his feelings. They sat in silence again.

Suddenly he leaned forward again. "Look, I know I can be an arse, alright? I've never had a female friend, I suppose. I've two brothers who never dare let me meet their girlfriends for fear I'll speak to them how I speak to you. I spend a lot of time on my own, by choice I hasten to add, and I feel sorry for you."

Anger rose inside Mallory's gut at his words. "You feel sorry for me?" she spat, "I don't want you to go out of your way to be *your version of nice* simply because you pity me." She was horrified and it showed as her voice rose.

"No you misunderstand me." His voice rose too now, "That's not what I meant. See? This is why I don't do…this." He waved his hand back and forth between them.

"What are you on about? You don't do what?"

He placed his cup down and rubbed his hands over his face. He was clearly exasperated, but Mallory wasn't sure with whom; her or himself.

"Look, that night on the beach, I really felt your pain." He paused as if calculating each sentence. "I felt so terrible for what you were going through. I understood…I understand." He looked skyward as if the words he was searching for may be written up there. "It's not pity, it's…it's…argh...what's the fuckin' word?..*empathy*!" He raised his hands up in a swift 'Eureka' type of gesture.

Mallory's eyes began to sting as tears threatened. He was relentless. Couldn't he just shut up? Clearly he couldn't.

He took a deep breath, leaning forward toward her again his voice had calmed. "I know how hard it is. You're in a strange place where you hardly know anyone and you've lost the *one person* in your life that would've made that whole situation okay." He took off his hat and ran his hands through his flattened hair. "I get that. I get what you're going through. I felt I wanted to help; no that I *needed* to help, but it turns out I keep making it worse." He looked into Mallory's eyes again. "Oh fuck and now I've fuckin' made you cry again."

Mallory sniffed and wiped at her eyes. "It's fine. I'm not your responsibility!" she exclaimed, "I get that you understand, but every time I try to ask you anything, you go all mean and moody on me. I have no clue how to take you. If you want to be friends you have to change how you act around me. I can't do with trying to second guess your mood and wonder if I have overstepped the mark."

He slid over to sit next to her. "Right, this is stupid. Can we please just fuckin' start over, eh?" He clamped his hand over his mouth. "Fuck, I'm sorry I keep swearing," he apologised.

Mallory smirked, "It's fucking fine! Just don't fucking do it again, okay? It's fucking rude!" she shouted. They stared at each other and then burst out laughing.

Once they had calmed down a little Greg nudged Mallory's shoulder with his own. "So I'm guessing you'll want to know my story, then, eh?"

She felt a little guilty for pushing him again. "Only if you want to tell me. We still don't know each other from Adam."

"Aye, well, I know your stuff so I guess it's only fair." He inhaled deeply. "What are your burning questions?"

She thought about it for a moment, "Look, it's up to you how much you do or don't say. I know that you lost someone. Maybe you can just leave it there if you prefer?"

"She was my girlfriend."

Mallory glanced as he subconsciously rubbed his wedding ring indentation. "She was the love of my life if the truth be known." He went on, "I'd been separated a few years and I met Mairi up near The Buckle by Glen Etiv whilst I was travelling around, camping. She was absolutely *mad* about climbing." He smiled and closed his eyes. "She'd started as a wee bairn with her dad travelling all over the place just to climb. That's what she was doing in that area when I met her. She called it Munroe bagging...Oh, err, that means that she—"

Mallory interrupted him, "Greg, my name is *Mallory*, I was named after a climber. My dad was a climber. I know what Munroe bagging is." She nudged him.

"Oh, of course. I forgot." He rolled his eyes and carried on. "Anyway to cut a long story short; she'd done all the big climbs in the UK and most of the European ones. She was one of the youngest female climbers ever to achieve Scottish Grade 3 and she'd been dreaming of something even bigger. Anyway, she'd been saving up to go to Pakistan since she was a teenager; it was all she could go on about. Her face just lit up when she talked about it." He paused as if finding it difficult to continue.

"She was so beautiful. But when she talked about climbing..." he shook his head as he trailed off. "I've always been quite outdoorsy myself. She managed to convince me to go with her a couple of times, but I just didn't *get it* like she did. In fact, if I'm honest it scared the willies out of me being so high up." He laughed. "Last year she met up with a team of professional climbers who she met through one of the big climbing websites she was always going on. They'd arranged a trip out to Pakistan and invited her along. She had the money and asked me if I minded. How could I mind? I wasn't going to stand between her and her dreams, was I? Anyway, they set off in June to climb K2. She was in touch until they started the main ascent and then…nothing."

Mallory didn't quite understand. "What do you mean nothing?"

Greg huffed the air out of his lungs. "The news stations over there reported a freak storm." His eyes welled up with tears. The memories clearly still very vivid and equally as painful. He cleared his throat. "None of the team made it down. The bodies were never recovered. I never saw her again. I never got to say goodbye and my sweet, sweet girl was gone." His voice trailed off. A shiver travelled down Mallory's spine. "I went out to Pakistan to see what else I could find out, but they gave up searching pretty damn quickly. She was declared dead on August twentieth along with the rest of her team." He spoke through clenched teeth as he pinched the corners of his eyes with his finger and thumb. His anger was evident. "This morning at your house, I had a call to say they had found what they thought was part of her kit. Turns out it wasn't hers."

"The tattoo…is that for Mairi?" Mallory asked carefully, not really knowing if she should.

"Aye. K2; the wretched place. The barbed wire represents the pain that place caused me. It's there as a reminder that you have to be careful what you wish for."

She understood; completely.

"I'm so sorry, Greg. I'm sorry for being so hard on you. I do understand." She smiled at her unlikely kindred spirit. There was a long pause before she went on, "I dreamt about Sam last night. It was so real. He spoke to me about my fears around staying here. I told him I wanted to go back to Yorkshire, but in my dream he said I should stay." Her own eyes began to blur with tears again as she recalled how lifelike the vision of Sam had been.

Greg's eyes widened. "Really? Wow. I bet it was hard to wake up from that dream, eh?"

"So, so hard. I keep expecting to see him standing on the bridge; or for him to come through the door and apologise for being late."

"Aye, I know what you mean. Every time I see a girl with long red hair I want to rush up and grab her to see if its Mairi...then I realise it can't be." He thought for a moment, "So you've been thinking about leaving, eh?" He seemed surprised.

"To be honest I just don't know what to do. I have friends back in Yorkshire. I have my shop...but this is where Sam wanted us to be. This is where we wanted to be together. I think I feel closer to him here than I would in Yorkshire; even though I met him there."

"I get that. Every so often I take off up to The Buckle, where I met Mairi. There's a turn off the main road that leads to Glen Etiv. I usually park in the little lay-bay just past the bridge. A bit further up there's this little rock where I like to sit. There's an amazing view of the Buckle from there. I like to wait for the sunrise. I just sit there looking at the changing colours of the dawn. I usually take my sleeping bag and sleep under the bridge for a couple of nights. I feel her there, you know?"

Mallory nodded.

Greg fiddled with his hat looking lost in his thoughts. "You don't need to feel lonely here you know." Greg informed her after a few minutes of a more comfortable silence. "People around here are great. They're warm, friendly people. From what I've heard, people have nice things to say about you. It's funny you know, some people can move here and be here for years and never fit in. Not you, though. People love you already." He sat upright snapping to look at her. There was a glint in his eyes that she hadn't witnessed before, "Hey, you know what you should do?"

Mallory was sceptical about what was coming next. "Hmmm, you seem rather excited and that worries me." She squinted at him suspiciously.

"A way to meet people. Stella is looking for an extra bartender for the evening. I could put a word in for you." He suggested.

Mallory thought about it for a moment. Actually it'd give her something to focus on; evenings *were* going to be difficult.

"But I have no clue how to pull a pint and I can't add up in my head." Panic started to take over when she realised she was actually considering this.

"Aye, well I can train you to pull pints and we have an electronic cash register you know. We don't live in the dark ages up here."

"Okay, well, have a word with her then. I could come in for a trial to see if I like it and if Stella likes me."

"Aye, well Stella employs *me* don't forget, so being likeable can't be one of the requirements." Greg laughed and Mallory joined in, thinking his self-deprecation was kind of sweet.

Chapter Five

They sailed back to shore both feeling as if the air had been cleared between them. They had come to a mutual understanding. Mallory really felt for Greg. His emotions were still raw which wasn't surprising considering it was less than a year since Mairi had been declared dead. Although it had been a horrible experience, Mallory had the chance to cremate Sam; there had been some sense of closure for her. Greg hadn't had anything like that. Nine months had passed for this poor man since he had lost his love and there were still unanswered questions. He had no peace. She admired the immense strength of his character and silently forgave him for his attitude on their first encounter and those that had occurred since.

As they climbed off the boat and back onto terra firma Mallory broke the ponderous silence that had fallen between them once again. "What are you up to this afternoon then? More leaking sinks to repair?" She smiled warmly at him, feeling more at ease.

"Nah…I'm away to pick up Angus and I think we might go for a long walk."

Mallory scrunched her nose feeling puzzled. "Angus?"

"Aye, I don't bring him on the boat too often. He can get sea sick and sometimes he bothers the customers." Greg informed her.

Angus hadn't been mentioned before. "Is Angus your son?" she asked hoping she wasn't prying.

Greg threw his head back and guffawed loudly.

"What's funny?" Mallory smiled but wasn't sure why.

Greg shook his head, his laughter still erupting. "My son…actually, he *is* rather spoiled so I suppose in a way he is." He glanced up at her. "He's my dog. Stella looks after him sometimes when I'm out on the boat."

Heat rose in her cheeks. "Ah right." She couldn't help but laugh now at her earlier thought. "What type of dog is he?" Mallory had always loved dogs.

"He is a Lab-satian."

"A what?" *That's a new one on me.*

"Labrador Alsatian cross breed. He's bloody huge, greedy and daft as a brush." He smiled fondly.

"Oh lovely. I'd love to meet him sometime. I can't believe you have a sea-sick dog." The thought made her giggle.

"Aye, I wasn't too impressed the first time I took him out I can tell you." They walked toward his Landy. Greg agreed to speak to Stella that evening and let her know about the job "See you tomorrow." He waved and drove away.

"Bye for now!" she shouted after him. She and Ruby turned to head for home. It was almost time for dinner. Mallory felt genuinely hungry for the first time in weeks. As they walked she replayed their conversations in her mind. Greg had opened up so much more and she appreciated his honesty.

She knew that there was also a tale to be heard about why his marriage had ended, but that would wait. She felt she had found a kindred spirit in Greg; someone who understood and felt her pain. Maybe they could help each other to come through their grief. Maybe, just *maybe* they could be friends…

She walked through her front door and glanced around. *I do like this place, maybe I should give it a try?* The ashes still sat in their plain container on the mantle in the lounge. She knew that a decision would have to be made soon as she couldn't be one of those people who hung onto to something like that. Worse still she didn't want to become one of those people who *talked* to the urn and its contents. Now that's the type of thing Sam would have taken the mickey out of for sure.

Mallory made herself a chicken stir fry and noodles and poured herself a glass of wine. After she had eaten she watched the first part of a movie on TV, but kept dozing off and so she decided to go to bed. It was only ten o'clock, but she felt exhausted. It had been quite a day.

She was awakened by someone pounding on the front door. She sat bolt upright and looked at the clock. Wow, she must have been tired–it was nearly half past ten in the morning. She dashed out of bed and down to the front door; she rubbed her bleary eyes and opened it.

"I was beginning to think you'd done a moonlight flit." Greg stood there, worried expression on his face, tool kit in hand, excitable dog by his side.

"Sorry, I must have slept really deeply. I've only just woken up." She yawned. *Good grief, once again I look a sight when Greg calls round. He must think I live in my jim jams.*

Greg looked her up and down and smirked but didn't say anything. He was wearing a T-shirt with an image of some kind of rabid wolf and the words 'Faith No More' emblazoned over the top of the image. She wasn't a fan. He had an interesting array of T-shirts, she mused. She stepped aside and gestured for him to come in.

"I brought Angus, is that okay? You said you'd like to meet him." Mallory nodded as Ruby came up to greet the new canine visitor. The two dogs sniffed each other inquisitively, their noses stuck up each-others rear end. Greg pointed at the two dogs. "I hope you don't expect me to greet you like that."

Mallory burst out laughing. "No, a simple hello will suffice." She bent to say hello to Angus who slobbered all over her face.

Greg laughed. "I'll not do that either, I promise."

Mallory wiped her face on the back of her sleeve. "Thank goodness!" she retorted.

Greg headed straight through to the kitchen. "Sit yoursel' down, I'll make us a coffee." Mallory couldn't be bothered to argue, so she sat. "I got that new tap sorted. I just need to fit it and then you're away." He called over the increasing noise of the kettle.

"Great." She yawned and stretched. She felt like she had run a marathon.

Greg came through to the lounge with two steaming mugs. *Just what the doctor ordered*, she thought.

"So, I spoke to Stella last night." Greg grinned; she guessed this meant she had a new job. "She says you're very welcome to come and give it a go. See what you think. What do you reckon, eh?"

She pursed her lips. "Oh…great, yes, thanks."

Greg waved an arm at her. "No, no, calm down with your mad enthusiasm you'll do yourself an injury." *Sarcastic sod.*

Feeling a stab of guilt Mallory shook her head, "Sorry. I just…I've had second thoughts…I'm not sure I'm ready…it's only been a few weeks, Greg."

"Hey, no one knows better than I do about this shit. And I say, grab the bull by the horns and get out and meet people."

She knew he was right. Life would go on; she didn't know how, but go on it must.

"Anyways, I said you'd be there tonight at about six so I can show you the ropes, eh?"

"Okay." She cringed. "I'll be there."

They finished their coffee, making small talk about the weather, things on the news and the fact that her friends were going to come up for a visit in June for her birthday. Greg latched onto the last bit with enthusiasm.

"So, am I right in thinking you'll be the big three-oh this time, eh?" He grinned.

Mallory gaped open mouthed. "How do you know?" *Are there no secrets around here?*

"Remember the other night when you told me off for worrying about your eating habits?"

She nodded sheepishly.

"You said then, and I quote 'I am a twenty nine year old woman' I don't forget stuff. I have a mind full of useless information." He laughed.

"Don't remind me. I feel old." She rubbed her face and her shoulders hunched.

"Ah, rubbish. You're a wee bairn." He shrugged off her comment. "Wait 'til you're my age then you'll feel old."

"What age is that then?" She had wondered this since she met him. She reckoned he was one of the people who hid their age well…but just how well?

"Guess." He challenged her with a glint in his eye.

"I may offend you," she warned.

"Na. I don't offend that easily. Age is just a number."

"Okay…you asked for it…" She pretended to ponder for a moment. "…erm…fifty five?" she teased.

A look of horror spread across his face and he sat open mouthed.

"Ahhh you said you wouldn't get offended! Age is just a number you said!" She punched him playfully on the arm.

"You cheeky wee mare." He laughed. "Go on, seriously, how old would you say I am?"

"Seriously? About thirty four…maybe thirty five?" It was genuinely what she thought.

His chest puffed out. "Na. I'm thirty eight next birthday." He seemed proud of the fact. "I just look bloody good for my age." He laughed again.

So that explains why he talked about me as his 'little sister' the other night.

"Yes, it's your modesty I admire the most." She mocked sarcastically. He really didn't look thirty seven though.

He made a face at her. "Right, I'm off to get this tap sorted. I need that chalkboard making and if it's the sink holding you back, I will make sure it doesn't stand in your way."

Greg put his empty cup in the sink and headed straight for the workshop. Just like last time, she ran upstairs, showered, dressed in leggings that she had found in her 'slim' clothes and a long sleeved blue tee. With the stress of the move and then losing Sam she figured she had lost just over fourteen pounds. Not good.

She strolled up to the workshop with more coffee and got out the bits and pieces she needed to start on Greg's board. She decided she was going to paint a top section in the same blue as the pub door and then write 'Greg McBradden Playing Live Here:' The bottom part would be chalkboard so he could write the dates on. She found a piece of wood in amongst her off cuts that would be the perfect size. She set to undercoating the board. They both worked in silence apart from the CD player, this time belting out a little Pearl Jam. Greg sang along.

Once the tap was finished it was around lunch time. He showed her that the tap was working and she was over the moon.

"Right, I'll be off then. Think I'll give the boat another try today. There seemed to be a few tourists around and I think the rental cottage just up from the shop has a large family staying, so fingers crossed." She waved him off at the front door and got back to work on the board.

At five that night she showered again, to rid herself of the paint splats. She was very pleased with the job she had done on the board and was happy that the weather had been warm enough to enable it to dry and be completed all in the day. It was ready to take with her when she went over to the pub.

She rummaged through her 'slim' clothes again looking for something suitable for her first night working in the pub. She found a pair of black trousers and a fitted, v-necked, black and grey top with a paisley pattern. She straightened her long tresses and applied make-up. When she looked at herself in her full length mirror she actually liked what she saw for the first time in ages. She didn't look quite so pale and her skin seemed to be settling into to its new shape so she didn't look quite as drawn as she had been.

She opted for contacts, pulled on her black jacket, picked up the brown paper wrapped board and set out for the pub leaving Ruby curled up in her favourite spot in front of the fireplace.

Her nerves were shredded by the time she had walked the few hundred yards to the pub. Stella greeted her warmly. She was such a lovely bubbly woman. She put Mallory at ease straight away.

"I'll leave you in the capable hands of Greg then. It's my night off and I really feel like putting my feet up." Stella lifted up the bar to allow Mallory through. She hung her coat in the back and took the package back through to Greg who was chatting to Ron at the bar.

A huge grin spread across Greg's face. "Is that what I think it is?" he asked.

"Hmmm, depends what you think it is." She toyed with him.

"I think it's my chalkboard," he said hopefully.

"Then in that case you would be correct." She handed him the package and he ripped off the paper like a kid on Christmas morning. She laughed at his enthusiasm.

He held the board at arms-length. He didn't speak. His grin was gone. *Oh great, he thinks it's rubbish.* Mallory worried to herself.

Greg shook his head as a huge grin returned to his face. "Mallory, Mallory, Mallory…it's bloody brilliant!" *Phew!* Mallory silently breathed a sigh of relief. "Bloody brilliant!" He repeated, "I love it!" He turned it to show Ron.

"Aye she's a talented lassie, our Mallory." He nodded, smiling. *Our Mallory.* Her heart warmed at Ron's choice of words. Greg put the board down leaning it up against the bar. He turned to Mallory and for a moment looked rather awkward. Eventually he grabbed her and hugged her hard. She felt winded. Her cheeks heated at his show of gratitude. When he freed her she just smiled, not really knowing what to say.

Greg's cheeks coloured. He fidgeted and ran his hands through his hair. He didn't seem to do public displays of affection comfortably. He muttered something under his breath about keeping it out of the way so it didn't get damaged and walked out toward the back of the pub. Mallory looked at Ron and they both chuckled.

When he returned he had pulled himself together and began to show Mallory the ropes. He showed her how to operate the till, take food orders, where the glasses were kept, how to measure out shorts, and everything else he could think to teach her.

Then came the moment she had been dreading. She knew how folks, especially men, could be rather persnickety about the way their beer was served. She was aware that too much froth— "It's called a head," Greg had corrected her–was a bad thing but not enough froth—"Head, Mallory!"—was just as bad.

She gulped as Greg showed her how to tilt the glass at just the right angle. Not too far. The beer slid down the side of the glass and he slowly brought it to an upright position as the glass filled. *Impressive, he makes that look easy.* Mallory felt cocky.

It was her turn. The first pint was all froth—*sorry, head.* Greg and Ron howled with laughter. Mallory felt her cheeks heat again. The second, all beer, no head. The men laughed again. Mallory was annoyed and stamped her foot like a petulant child. The third was better and had potential, according to Greg and Ron.

Greg decided it was time to let Mallory loose on the customers and so he stood back and gestured for her to serve the couple who came to the bar. Once she was done and had managed to get their order correct *and* give them the right change, she felt quite proud of herself. Greg and Ron gave her a mini round of applause.

"Aye, you're a natural lassie." Ron beamed, "and you'll certainly brighten this place up, if you know what I mean." He gestured toward Greg and winked at her, making her giggle.

"See, I told you you'd be fine." Greg thankfully didn't see Ron's gesture. "Now you'll need to decide what hours you'd like to do, but really I could do with some help on the night's I'm playing here. You know when the crowds hear about my gig and they come swarming in droves." He chuckled. Mallory rolled her eyes.

June 2011

Mallory was really enjoying working at the pub. She had made several new friends and had mastered the art of pint pulling in the two weeks since she had begun perfecting the skill. Greg had been great and they had laughed a lot during their shifts together. The chalkboard had made an appearance when Greg had played his second gig.

It was a week until her birthday, but she hadn't heard anything from Josie about when they were coming up. She felt a little disappointed. As her birthday fell on a Saturday this year, Greg had made suggestions that they should have a barbie on the beach and Stella had given them the go ahead for a night off. Mallory wasn't bothered. She just wanted to see Josie and Brad.

She stood behind the bar. It was Greg's third gig tonight and he was, as always, dressed for the occasion. Tonight, he wore a white linen shirt and he had married it with khaki combats. Very smart, Mallory smiled. Although, why he felt he had to look different on the other side of the bar befuddled her.

"You look terrified," she commented as he stood drinking a glass of cola. "What's up?"

"Ah, nothing. I always get like this before I go on. Goodness knows why. I'm a grown man."

"Age has nothing to do with it. We all get nervous, Greg. You'll be fine."

He checked the clock and so did she. Eight, time to go on. The bar had filled up nicely. People enjoyed coming and hearing him sing and Mallory enjoyed it too. He took his position at the mic and lifted his guitar onto his lap.

"Evening all, anyone would think something was going on with all of you's turning up tonight," he joked. "As always, I'll steer clear of my own stuff but be warned, one of these days I'm going to sneak one in when you're not looking." A low mumble of laughter ran around the pub. "Don't forget, no singing along, it puts me off and you's lot can't sing anyway." The usual jovial boos and light hearted heckles came.

"Right, this first song is a wee bit obscure, but I love it so tough." He smiled. "It's by a band called Nirvana who take me back to my younger days. I'd like to dedicate this to someone who I think I can now class as a good mate. This is '*About a Girl*'."

He began to strum his guitar and his eyes closed as they always did when he first started to play. Mallory felt quite touched by the gesture and smiled her approval over at him as she bobbed around to the music. He nodded and winked at her with a cheeky grin. The song felt quite appropriate too given their long chats about their lost loves.

Greg's set was very well received and he even had a swarm of young women around him by the end of the night. They had been in last time, but hadn't dared approach him. This time they had obviously acquired a little Dutch courage. They giggled and played with their hair while they chatted to him. He seemed a little embarrassed but also appeared to be enjoying the attention. Mallory chuckled at how the girls flirted and batted their eyes.

"Get you with your groupies," she joked when he came over to the bar, finally rid of the mini Harem.

"Aye, they cannae resist." He blushed. "What did you think tonight, Matey?" he asked. She smiled at the new term of endearment she seemed to have been allocated.

She scrunched her face up. "I thought it was a bit rubbish really." She carried on emptying the dish washer under the bar. He looked hurt. "God, for someone who doesn't get offended easily, you get offended…easily!" She threw a bar towel at him. "You were fab as always, you numpty."

Greg frowned. "Great choice of words. Remind me to get you to critique my first album, eh?" He threw the towel back at her.

"I especially liked the Nirvana track you opened with."

"Aye well, that'll be before your time, eh? You being such a kid," he teased.

"Oy! I remember Nirvana very well thank you." Mallory went through to the back to get her coat.

"Are you finished up here? I'll walk you over home if you like?"

"Why? Scared some of your groupies are jealous that you dedicated a song to me and will be waiting outside?" Her turn to tease him now.

"Funny." He made a face at her. "Actually, I could murder a coffee and I've none left at home." He grinned.

"Cheeky sod." She laughed.

They walked back to Mallory's and were greeted by a very giddy little black dog. Mallory went to put the kettle on.

"Your answering machine light is flashing," Greg hollered into the kitchen

"Oh right, thanks." She made the coffee and carried it through to the lounge placing it on the tree stump table. She hit 'play' on the answering machine.

"Oh hi, Mally. It's Josie…look I'm really sorry, but we can't make it up for your birthday. Brad has a lot on with his latest job and we just won't get the time to come up. I'm sure you'll understand, babe. I'll ring you later. Love you! Bye, bye."

Mallory slumped onto the sofa. She was devastated. Josie and Brad hadn't been up since the funeral and she missed them like mad. How could they miss her birthday? They promised they'd be here. Greg sat beside her and rested an arm loosely around her shoulder.

"Don't worry. We'll still have a laugh. I'll keep you entertained."

But she was so disappointed.

He nudged her. "Look, we'll have drink at the pub and then take a bucket barbie onto the beach and I'll cook a steak, eh?" He was being very kind, but it just wasn't going to be the same.

She forced a smile. "Yes, thanks, Greg, I appreciate it."

"My pleasure, you're only thirty once, eh? I will expect the same, mind you, for my fortieth."

Saturday, June eleventh came around very quickly. Mallory had a lazy day. Stella had insisted she took the day off and not work on her birthday. She had received cards through the post from friends in Yorkshire, from her 'family' in *Canada* and from some of her local friends. She had felt a little depressed and had got the photo album out of her last birthday when Sam had taken her to Edinburgh as a surprise.

They had stayed in the four poster suite in the stunning *Dunstane House Hotel* just minutes away from the shops at Princes Street. They'd had the most wonderful time. They visited the Dungeon and had a silly photo taken of Mallory pretending to chop off Sam's head. The museums were fascinating and the architecture superb. They'd shopped in Jenner's department store and Sam had bought her the most beautiful dress to wear for dinner on her birthday. It was a deep purple fabric with a chiffon overlay. The bodice fitted her perfectly and made the most of her curves. Sam had been desperate to get her out of it after their dinner out at an exclusive restaurant. He had been undressing her with his eyes for the whole evening. She loved it. She sighed as she remembered...

June 2010

"My God, you are just so sexy in that dress, Miss Yorkshire." Sam kissed her hand as they sat side by side in the cab on the way back to the hotel.

"Why thank you, Mr. Canada." She giggled. She loved the way he looked at her.

He leaned toward her. "I've been imagining you naked all night," he whispered.

Mallory checked to make sure the driver couldn't hear their conversation. "I've been imagining you getting me naked all night too," she whispered back.

They arrived back at the hotel and almost ran up the stairs to their suite. Once inside the door, Sam grabbed Mallory by the waist and removed the clip which pulled some of her hair back from her face. He devoured her mouth with his own and explored with his tongue. He set her body on fire with his passionate kisses. She grabbed at his hair pressing her tongue into his mouth.

He stopped kissing her and turned her around. He slid the zipper down to where it finished just above her bottom. She had dressed in the bathroom and so he had no idea what lay beneath the jewel colored fabric. He slid the dress down over her hips and gasped when he saw the basque and stockings. He turned her round, dropped to his knees and gazed up at her, his eyes filled with lust. Without warning he nuzzled her through the lace of her panties. She moaned as pleasure washed over her. He slid her panties down her stocking covered legs and rose in front of her still fully clothed. He gently caressed the flesh at the top of her breasts where the basque had pushed them up into creamy white mounds. Then he kissed where he had just touched.

She loosened his tie and unfastened his shirt, sliding it off at the same time as his jacket. They stared longingly at each other, unable to wait any longer. Sam unfastened his trousers and slid them off quickly. She loved the heat in his eyes. They tumbled on to the four poster bed and within seconds he was making love to her.

June 2011

Mallory was snapped back to the present by a knock on the door. She answered to a rather giddy looking Greg who stood holding a bunch of helium balloons with 'Thirty Today!' emblazoned on them. She giggled when he began to sing *'Happy Birthday'* purposefully out of tune and far too loudly.

She grabbed the front of his jacket and yanked him into the house. "Come in you nutter."

She felt she ought to save the poor neighbours ears.

He had a little gift bag in his hand which he handed over when she had shut the door. She opened the bag to find a wrapped parcel inside. "Oh, I get it, it gets smaller the more layers I take off it, eh?" she teased.

"Na. That's it. Last layer," he assured her.

She ripped off the paper and took out the box. It was a set of new craft pens. "Oh, Greg, that's lovely. Thanks ever so much."

His cheeks flushed. "There's something else in there too." He pointed at the bag so she delved back inside.

She took out a little black velvet box. "Oh," her voice was almost a whisper as she held on to the box. Her eyes darted nervously between it and Greg who had a small smile curving at the corners of his mouth.

She opened it and gasped. Inside was a silver chain with a silver Celtic looking pendant hanging from it.

"It's a Celtic knot," Greg informed her. "It's the symbol for friendship." He smiled.

Her eyes welled up with tears. "Oh, Greg, it's beautiful." She threw her arms around him and hugged him. A sudden unwelcomed heat surged through her body at the contact and she gulped pulling away and stepping back immediately. Greg ran his hand through his hair, his eyes looking anywhere but hers.

"Here put it on me."

He pulled her hair around to one side and placed the chain around her neck. He fastened the clasp and then let her hair fall back over her shoulders. She turned to face him.

"Gorgeous." He smiled.

She walked over to the little porthole mirror near the front door. "I love it, Greg. Thank you so much."

"Well, I figured you're the closest thing I have to a best friend around here, so…"

"Well, I'm honoured to be your friend. It's such a thoughtful gift. They both are."

Greg cleared his throat and ran his hand through his hair again. "Anyway, it's all arranged, I'll pick you up at half seven. We'll go over for a couple of drinks and then we'll go down to the beach for that steak, okay?"

"Wow, you have it all organised." She appreciated how kind he was being and how much of an effort he was making to ensure her thirtieth birthday went with a bang and not a fizzle.

"Aye, I have. Make sure you wear something very smart; the beach is an exclusive place to dine, you know." He put on his best 'posh' accent and winked. "And it's quite warm out," he added. He opened the front door and turned to her. "I know it's not the same as you'd wanted, but I hope you still enjoy your birthday celebrations, Mallory." He smiled.

"Oh, I'm sure I will. So far so good." She gestured to her necklace. He was gone.

She ran herself a bath and added some relaxing essential oils, poured a glass of her favourite red wine, and climbed in. The warm water was soothing and she began to relax whilst the heady aroma of jasmine filled her senses. She couldn't help still feeling a little disappointed with her so called friends. This was a milestone birthday. Plus it was her first birthday since Sam was gone. She wasn't sure how she would cope. He always made such a fuss of her. Tears stung the back of her eyes. She fought them back. *No, you are not going to do this Mallory Westerman!* She chastised herself. *This is your birthday and you will bloody well smile and enjoy yourself.*

Once the water had gone cold, and she resembled a shrivelled up prune, she climbed out of the bath and wrapped herself in a huge, soft bath sheet. She surveyed her miniscule wardrobe of 'slim' clothes that had now been promoted from the suitcase under the bed.

She found a long floaty skirt in shades of turquoise and black and slipped it on feeling unsure as to whether she would end up freezing at the beach. *Oh sod it; I'll take a blanket just in case.* She decided. She accompanied the skirt with a pale turquoise fitted T shirt which showed off her, now smaller, bosom with just a hint of cleavage. She slid on her favourite flat, jewelled flip flops and her short denim jacket. She felt summery.

Greg called as promised right on time at half seven. She opened the door and did a twirl.

"Will I do for the posh dining experience?" she asked with a smirk.

"You look…great." Greg seemed a little taken aback, but Mallory presumed she had misread his response. "Come on; let's go get a birthday drink." He held out his elbow to her and she linked her arm around his.

They wandered over to the pub. As they got to the door Greg opened it and gestured for her to go inside before him.

"Why thank you, such a gentleman," she kidded as she walked through the door.

"SURPRISE!" The pub full of people all shouted in unison.

Mallory stood there frozen, open mouthed as she was bombarded by party poppers, camera flashes and cheers all at once. She turned to Greg who was leaning against the door with his arms folded. A smile playing on his lips, he looked quite pleased with himself for his part in the deception.

She gasped and pointed to him, narrowing her eyes. "You knew?"

He held up his thumb and finger. "Little bit." He chuckled as he gestured.

All at once Mallory was surrounded by people hugging her. She burst into tears when she spotted Josie and Brad. Brad lifted her and spun her around. Josie was crying too.

"But…but you rang! You weren't coming!" Mallory sobbed.

"You daft cow. Do you think I'd miss this?" Josie hugged her friend tightly. "Not a chance. We were always going to be here, but we were the first people Greg rang when he decided to plan this thing."

Mallory froze. "Greg did all this?" She covered her mouth with her hand in total shock.

"He sure did. Look who else is here." Josie stepped aside and Mallory was swept into a group hug by Renee, Ryan and Cara. Cara was holding a cute little blonde baby boy.

"Dylan?" She cried, "he's gorgeous Cara." She dabbed her eyes with a hanky someone had handed her. "It's so good to see you all." Mallory was hugged from all sides by neighbours and friends.

Colin and Christine from the shop, Ron, Aileen, Stella, and a group of friends she had made since working in the pub—they were all there. This was so special. The only one missing was Sam.

A while later Mallory heard Greg's familiar voice over the pubs PA system. *Oh brilliant!* Mallory was overjoyed.

"Evening party people!" he shouted as if he was some famous radio DJ hosting 'Party in The Park' or something similar. It made Mallory giggle. "Well, we're all here tonight

to celebrate the fact that Mallory is and I quote 'Getting old'."
Everyone laughed and looked at her.

She felt her cheeks heat. She would have to get him for
that. "I reckon the first number tonight requires a bit of
audience participation. Which as you may know is not
something I usually encourage. You all know the words and
this time you can sing along!" The crowd cheered.

They all broke into a loud rendition of '*Happy Birthday to
You*,' and then the pub erupted into cheers, applause and
whistles. Mallory's face could have split in two with the grin.

When the ruckus had died down, Greg smiled over at her.
She mouthed the words "Thank you" at him. And he
mouthed back "You're welcome."

"Right, that's enough of you lot singing! It's my turn now
and you know what I always say?"

"DON'T BLOODY SING ALONG!" Everyone shouted
in unison. Mallory threw her head back with laughter.

"Aye, that's right and don't you forget it." He put his
plectrum in his mouth whilst he adjusted the guitar on his lap.
He took hold of the plectrum and spoke again, "Okay, now
as we know, Mallory is the big three oh today." Someone
whooped. "Aye and so this night is dedicated to her. I'll play
loads of her favourite songs, that's if her friends have told me
the right ones and I'm not going to get into trouble later." A
rumble of laughter rolled around the pub. This first one is a
song I dedicated to my good friend once before. He played
the opening bars of '*About a Girl*'.

He sang the song so well and with such feeling.
Throughout the night the audience was delighted with some
fantastic music. He had clearly been speaking to Josie as she
had pretty much given him a soundtrack to their history.

"This next one is by a band who you may have heard of.
Foo Fighters." The audience cheered. "You've never heard of

them?" He joked, "oh well this is a little song they did a few years back, it's called *'Learn To Fly'*."

"Apparently, I'm told this next one will take Mallory back to her shoe gazing days, *'Wonderwall'* by Oasis…"

"A little insight into Mallory's teenage years next. I'm told this next one reminds her of her first love. A long haired lout from the next village along. It's called *'Runaway Train'* and it was done by a bunch of long haired louts called Soul Asylum."

"Now everyone will probably remember this next one being done by a band called the Commodores, but I have to say my favourite version was by an alternative rock band called Faith No More, it's called *'Easy'*."

The audience totally disobeyed Greg at this point and all joined in on the choruses, singing loudly and mostly out of tune. Greg could hardly sing for laughing.

"This next one is a beautiful song that I'm going to throw in just because I love it. So there. And you can't stop me coz I have a mic and you don't! It's by a local fella called Dougie McLean." A loud applause ensued. "It's called *'Caledonia'*."

"Now there can't be a single person in this place who has never heard of Neil Diamond?" Again, there were loud applause and cheers. "Aye, everybody loves Neil Diamond. I'm told it was Mallory's folks' favourite song so this is for them, God bless them. It's one his best loved songs, *'I am, I said'*. No bloody singing along!" Once again his demands were ignored and the audience erupted into song.

"Now I'm personally going to dedicate this song to the birthday girl. It's by one of her favourite bands but the message is loud and clear, do you hear me, Mallory? Fleetwood Mac *'Don't Stop Thinking About Tomorrow'*."

Mallory gasped at the touching gesture. She smiled and Greg's smile beamed back in return.

He sang with such conviction and Mallory loved the sentiment behind the words. Renee gave her shoulders an affirming squeeze and a little wink as they swayed to the music.

The party had been wonderful. Greg had played so many of her favourite songs and had even danced with her to the jukebox when he had taken a break, twirling her around rather like a ragdoll and making her howl with laughter. The night was drawing to a close and Mallory had enjoyed every single minute. She had been presented with flowers and cards. Colin had made her birthday cake; it was his wonderful specialty carrot cake complete with candles, but thankfully not thirty of them.

Greg began to speak again, "Well, I'm hoping the birthday girl has had as wonderful night as the rest of us, eh? It's been great to have you all here. But I have to say, when it comes to singing, don't go giving up your day jobs. Leave it to the professionals. Know what I'm saying?" The audience booed and heckled in fun. He shrugged at them as if to say, "What? You know I'm right!"

"I'll finish tonight with another of Mally's favourites and I have to say that it's grown on me this week whilst I have been practising it. It's by a bloke with an interesting name, if nothing else. He is a mighty talented guitarist, not unlike myself." A groan rumbled around the room, "Okay, okay. He's a young guy called Newton Faulkener and this is a beautiful song for a beautiful...ah...friend and it goes like this." He used the guitar as a multitude of instruments, just like the songs composer. Mallory's eyes glistened and after the musical intro, Greg began to sing *'Dream Catch Me'*.

His eyes were closed whilst he sang, but suddenly he opened them and made direct eye contact with Mallory at a very poignant line in the song. Was he telling her in no uncertain terms that he was falling in love with her? *Oh my word!* Mallory's breath caught in her throat, looking behind her to check if he was looking at someone else, but he wasn't. Greg's gaze remained fixed on Mallory's for the rest of the song, a sweet smile playing on his lips. Mallory shivered.

She loved that song so much, but she felt strange when he sang the words, especially when they were directed at her. It didn't seem right. Josie hugged her friend, singing along and a little tipsy.

"Oh, Mally, this takes me back. And I think maybe Greg is a tiny bit taken with you, don't you?" Hearing Josie say the words made her cringe. They were friends. They both knew it.

At the end of the evening, gradually, everyone filtered out of the pub. Renee and her family had rented a cottage and would be around for a week. Josie and Brad had stayed at the pub the night before, but were hoping to crash with Mallory and travel home Monday.

Greg came over to say goodnight as she had said the last farewell to Ron who hugged and kissed her cheek. He waited patiently for Ron to leave.

"Och shit, Mallory, you're looking old now you know," he teased. She hit him on the arm and he pretended to fall over. "Have you had a good time?" he asked.

"The best. Thanks so much for doing this for me, Greg. It was so sweet of you."

"No bother. That's what friends do. And like I said, it's my fortieth in a wee while." He wiggled his eyebrows.

"Well, I'm guessing you won't let me forget that." She rolled her eyes.

"Am I allowed to hug you?" he asked opening his arms, "I think I made a total balls up of the last time I hugged you. You know? The incident I now like to call 'Chalkboard-gate'. I cringe whenever I think about it. What a complete spanner." He laughed shaking his head. She walked into his open arms for a hug. He embraced her briefly but strongly.

"Thanks again, Greg. You are a really good friend," she told him, looking directly in his eyes as she said it. Hoping he'd get the message.

"Aye, you're not so bad yourself, Matey."

She reached up and kissed his cheek. His cologne filled her nostrils. He smelled of sandalwood. Her heart did a strange skip and she shivered again. *What the heck is wrong with me?* She was immediately angry with herself for even noticing his cologne, let alone allowing it to have any kind of effect on her.

She pulled away and said goodnight. She grabbed Josie and they made their way home.

Mallory walked so fast that Josie's little legs could only just keep up. Brad managed quite easily, but did ask what the rush was about. Mallory didn't answer.

When they got inside, Josie whispered something to Brad who went out to the van, which he had moved to Mallory's house at some point during the evening. He collected their bags and took them straight up to the guest room, that they had claimed as theirs last time they were there.

"Right, missy, spill the beans will you." Josie stood arms folded as Mallory removed her denim jacket and hung it up on the coat pegs by the door.

"What are you on about?" Mallory knew exactly what she was getting at, but didn't want to talk about it.

"You know very well what I mean. Something's up with you and I want to know what it is." Josie tapped her foot like she did when she was annoyed.

"Josie, if you have something to say, just say it." Mallory didn't want to be the first.

"You've been a bit distant ever since Greg sang that last song." She pointed out accusingly.

"Yeah? So? It was weird; he was looking at me as he sang that line."

"What line?"

Tears began to sting Mallory's eyes. "You know what line!" She raised her voice.

"Why don't you remind me?" Josie demanded.

Mallory sighed, running her shaking hands through her hair. "The line that talks about falling in love. That bloody line! Alright?" Tears escaped her eyes and slid, unwelcomed, down her face.

"I knew it. I bloody knew it." Josie threw her hands up in exasperation. "And now you are worrying you've led him on, or what people will think if they notice he has feelings for you, and what Sam's family will think if they notice? Am I right?"

Mallory nodded and a sob escaped her lips as she slumped onto the sofa.

"Mallory, you are not," she tilted Mallory's chin so that she looked at her, "…hey, listen to me, you are not responsible for other people falling for you. Well you are because you're so lovely…but that's not what I mean…what I mean is people can't help who they fall in love with or when it happens. It's not your fault. It doesn't mean you have to reciprocate. It doesn't mean you are betraying Sam in any way. Do you understand?"

"I do understand, but I really like Greg and I don't want to hurt him. I may be totally missing the mark here anyway. Maybe it was just a coincidence that he looked at me? Maybe I'm wrong. He does keep saying I'm his best friend and he keeps calling me 'Matey' so I could be imagining it?"

Josie sat beside her friend and put her arm around her shoulders. Mallory had always been guilty of putting others feelings before her own.

"Mally, honey bun, Brad and I saw him looking at you on more than one occasion tonight. He threw the party for you; he arranged everyone to come. He somehow managed to get people here from Canada for goodness sake; he arranged the food; he learned all your favourite songs. He bought that beautiful necklace. I'm sorry to be the one to pass on the news babe but he is smitten."

The undesired words hit Mallory like a ton of bricks and she burst into tears again. She was sure that this was the end of their friendship. After all she didn't feel the same. She couldn't.

Chapter Six

Sunday morning was dull and rainy. It matched the mood that had cast over Mallory since the night before, after the party. She sat in bed thinking about Greg and what she could do or say to make things different. He hadn't said anything at all to her about any such feelings. Perhaps what was left unsaid was best left exactly that.

When she eventually went downstairs, Josie and Brad had busied themselves making a cooked breakfast. Brad had been up and out at stupid o'clock for a run and had called in to Colin's to pick up the Sunday papers and all the necessary ingredients for a heart-attack inducing fry up. It was half ten. The smell of the breakfast was wafting its way through the house and made Mallory's, and Ruby's, mouth water.

"Sleep okay?" Josie enquired as Mallory sat herself down at the kitchen table, clad in pale blue fleece pyjamas.

"Shouldn't I be asking you that? You're the guest." Mallory yawned her answer.

"Well, I'm guessing you had lots to think about," Josie stated.

"I've decided to do nothing and say nothing. Greg hasn't said anything directly to me, so I've no intention of bringing it up in case I ruin the best friendship I have up here."

"That's up to you. But just be careful, Mally. Don't get yourself into situations that will cause you more upset."

Mallory's anger toward Josie began to surface. She hadn't wanted to confront the idea that Greg may have feelings for her, but Josie blurting it out last night had meant she had to do just that. It wasn't fair. She didn't want to have to think about that crap every time she saw him. Why couldn't she have just kept her mouth shut? Ignorance is, as they say, bliss, after all.

Frowning at her friend she rose from the table. "I'm off to get a shower and then I'm taking Ruby out...alone." Mallory declined the cooked breakfast and sulkily retreated to the bathroom.

Brad and Josie were still sitting in the kitchen chatting when Mallory descended the creaky staircase. She didn't interrupt them. She clipped on Ruby's lead, slipped on her jacket and left the cottage.

The air was cool and the sky was heavy as if it would rain soon. She walked up to the midpoint of the bridge. She thought about all the things that had happened since she moved here. It had been a period of almost three months, but such a lot had occurred. She hadn't had the best start at friendship with Greg, but when they had ironed out their differences he had become a good friend. He was there for her. She needed that. She didn't need Josie making something out to be there that wasn't. She vowed that she would carry on as if Greg had not made eye contact with her at that crucial part of a love song. Things *would* be fine.

As she stood there she heard a deep, excited bark coming from the direction of the pub. She turned around and saw Angus barrelling toward her, tail wagging frantically. He jumped up to greet her and managed to lick her face. She laughed and wiped the dog yuck away with the back of her hand.

Greg came jogging up the road after him. "Angus you bloody mad hound! Come back here!" He stopped and shook his head, throwing his hands up. Mallory laughed at his lack of control over the friendly canine. He looked frustrated as he made his way to the bridge. He waved and began to jog again but wasn't even out of breath when he reached her. "I obviously didn't do my job right last night, eh?" He observed clipping Angus's lead back on.

"Meaning what, exactly?" She raised her eyebrows.

"Well you don't look in the least bit bloody hung over! What were you drinking at your birthday bash? Earl Grey?" He grinned.

"Do you know, when I come to think of it there was so much going on I didn't actually have much time to drink." She giggled when she realised the truth.

"Aye, well maybe you're one of those weird types. You know, the ones who don't need alcohol to have a good time." He teased.

Mallory rolled her eyes at his remark. "Where are you off to, then?" she enquired scratching the top of Angus's golden head.

"Just for a wee walk. Want to join us?" he asked sounding hopeful, "It'd be nice to have some company."

Mallory thought for a moment. *Oh for goodness sake, he is your friend and it's a dog walk. Get over yourself*, she mentally chastised.

"Ruby and I would love that," she chimed and they headed up the road in the direction of the beach.

On arrival at their destination both friends unclipped their dog's leads and let them run. They watched in amusement whilst the two, little and large, ran around chasing each other as if playing a game of catch. *Even the dogs have become friends*, Mallory mused.

"So...it was a good party last night, eh?" Greg didn't look at her, but kept his eyes on the view.

"It was wonderful, Greg. I can't believe you did all that for me." She too didn't attempt eye contact, for fear of what unspoken words may pass between them.

"Well, I figured that's the kind of thing Josie would do if you were down Yorkshire way."

Mallory snorted a laugh. "Maybe not with so much gusto though," she admitted. "Josie would have done the pub and the friends, but they would have been their own entertainment."

"Well, I'm just glad I did you proud." He briefly put an arm around her roughly as if she was 'one of the boys'. Relief washed over her. They stood in a more comfortable silence watching their dogs play together, when a few spots of rain began to fall.

Pulling her hood on Mallory announced, "I think I might head over to the holiday cottage and see Renee and the family."

"Okay, I'll walk with you." Greg smiled, "I have a free day today and I intend to do bugger all but relax and maybe read a book." He gasped and put a hand over his mouth dramatically.

Mallory giggled.

They clipped their dogs back onto their leads and headed briskly in the direction of the cottages as the rain gained intensity and the drops became larger and more determined to soak them through.

Greg looked pensive as if there was something he needed to say. Suddenly he stopped and gently took her arm. She turned to look at him. The rain was now pouring down and his lack of hood or hat meant that his wet, dark hair looked black. He swept it back out of his face. Raindrops dripped off the end of his nose.

He took a deep breath and after a pause said, "I have to say something. Please just let me speak and don't say anything, okay?"

Narrowing her eyes Mallory said a hesitant, "Oooh kay." She frowned at his urgency. Not knowing exactly what to expect, she worried in case he was about to declare his undying love or something ridiculous.

"Mallory, you and I didn't get off the best start, we both know that. I feel that now, though, we're friends, good friends?" He nodded at her, clearly needing affirmation. She nodded in acknowledgement. "Seeing you look so happy last night made me feel amazing. Knowing I had a part in it. You know? But I think I may have given you the wrong impression. I know for a fact you felt uncomfortable at one point when I caught your eye…in the last song?"

Mallory knew exactly what he was getting at, but couldn't speak for fear of saying the wrong thing.

After another pause Greg continued, "Now, I want you to know that I put your friendship above anything…I would never want to jeopardise that. If I made you feel uncomfortable by the way I looked at you then I am so, so sorry. I just…you know…I sometimes get caught up in the meaning of a song…it didn't mean anything."

He ran his hand through his wet hair again, but his actions were futile as the weight of the water was simply dragging it straight back over his face. "Like I said before, I'm crap at this friends business. And if I'm completely honest, and I think I should be, I do find you attractive. But there are *so many* reasons why I can't and won't even bother to dwell on that fact. So please don't worry. Do you understand what I'm waffling on about?"

Mallory chewed her lip and scrunched her brow. Confusion invaded her mind. She was wondering how the hell he had just dived into her head and read her thoughts without her feeling a thing. The rain hammered down.

Greg was soaked but didn't seem to care. "Basically, what I'm trying to say is that, if we'd met under different circumstances, if we were closer in age, if we weren't both so broken, if I was braver, if you even remotely found me attractive, then maybe things would be different. But I know that things are how they are. We're friends and that's enough. Please promise me that you won't start to withdraw and avoid me for fear of hurting me or doing...saying the wrong thing. I'm a big boy. I can handle it. I'm happy to be just friends."

Suddenly Mallory felt washed with emotion. She felt the desperate urge to hug him. He had just given her the biggest gift; the gift of real friendship. She needed him so much to be a part of her life but could offer him no more. He had looked into her soul and known that and had relieved her of her burden. He found her attractive, but if she was honest, she thought him attractive too. But there was a difference between seeing the beauty in someone and wanting to do something about it. Evidently they were on the same page.

She threw caution to the wind and embraced the soaked man in front of her; knowing that he would not read into the gesture after all. He returned her embrace, this time without awkwardness.

Deep inside Greg surged an unwelcomed emotion, which felt a little bit like sadness....

"Mallory, sweetheart. How lovely to see you." Renee helped her off with her wet coat and embraced her warmly.

Cara came to join in the hug as Ryan bounced baby Dylan around on his hip, smiling.

"It's great to see you all too. I had no idea you were coming. It was such a wonderful surprise."

"Well, we knew it was your thirtieth birthday and wanted to come over to celebrate with you, but didn't want to intrude. Anyway, when we received Greg's call we accepted his invitation without giving it a moment's thought."

So it was true, Greg had done all the inviting. *So sweet.* Mallory smiled to herself.

"He is quite the character isn't he?" Renee stated rather than questioned, smiling at Mallory.

"Yes he is a good friend. He has been so helpful since I moved here." Mallory wanted Renee to understand that friendship is all it was.

"Yes, he seems to care a lot about you which is so reassuring, especially knowing that everyone else you care about is so far away. It must be good to know he is there for you." Renee hugged her again.

Ryan stood. "I'm going to go and put Dylan down for his nap and then we can all catch up properly." He walked through the large one story building toward the bedrooms.

"Tea, Mallory? And perhaps a slice of this delicious carrot cake that the owners of the cottage left for our arrival?"

Mallory smiled. She hadn't realised that Colin and Christine owned the cottage, but the signature carrot cake made the fact apparent.

"Oh yum. Yes please," Mallory accepted enthusiastically. Renee disappeared into the kitchen.

Fiddling with the hem of her top Cara touched Mallory's arm. "Mallory, can I speak to you in confidence?"

Mallory placed her hand over Cara's. "Yes Cara, course you can. What's up?"

"Renee and I have been chatting about you lately. We are both a little worried."

"Worried? Why?" Mallory didn't quite understand.

"Well, Renee is concerned that you feel you will never be able to move on. You know, meet someone new?"

Mallory suddenly wanted to make a quick exit and looked to the door. She couldn't have this conversation. Not with Sam's family. Not now. Cara didn't stop there.

"Renee wants you to feel able to fall in love again someday. She's terrified that you'll feel you're betraying Sam or the family if you do fall in love. But that's not the case."

They heard Dylan crying and Renee came into the room with a tray full of tea and cake. The two young women looked as if they had been caught with their fingers in the cookie jar.

"Giiirls? What are you talking about? Come on now. Don't stop just because the old lady walks in." Renee looked saddened.

Cara cringed a little. "Mom, I was just telling Mallory what we had been saying about her recently."

"Ah, I see." Renee blushed under her beautifully done, natural, photo-shoot quality make-up. "I didn't want to interfere, Mallory, dear, but I think you should know that when the time comes, as long as you're happy and the man who wins your heart treats you well, you'll have the whole families blessing, darling."

Why was everyone so intent on matching her up and making her move on? She felt annoyed, but did her best to soften her tone as she spoke, "Renee, how can I think of moving on when I'm still in love with your son? It's only been two months or so since he...since...it's too soon to even be thinking like that." Mallory looked pleadingly at the Mother figure that she held in such high regard.

"That may be, honey, but we still wanted you to know how we felt, sooner rather than later. We'd hate to think of you falling in love and dreading telling us. You're so young. Too young to spend your life in mourning for what you lost. You owe it to Sam to go and be happy. That's all he ever wanted for you." Renee was right and it was good to know, but it was knowledge that she would fasten away in a little box in the depths of her mind with a sign on it saying 'In emergency break glass.'

Mallory had tea and cake with the Buchanan family and then left with Ruby. The rain had eased and Mallory was glad to be going home. She needed to apologise to Josie for her stern nature and to tell her that everything was okay with her and Greg.

When she arrived home she gave Josie a blow by blow account of her conversation with Greg. Josie listened avidly. But she still had a look of concern on her face.

Josie scrunched her face. "Why is he so hung up on the age thing?" she asked. "It's seven or eight years. You're both adults. Age is *not* an issue."

Mallory felt frustrated at this response. "That's *all* you got from everything I just said?"

Josie blushed. "Well, I'm just saying. Age doesn't matter."

"No, Josie, age doesn't matter but *love* does! I don't *LOVE* Greg! I *LOVE* Sam! And I'm sick of people telling me that it's okay to move on when it isn't! Even if I loved Greg it would be too soon. When will you lot get that through your thick skulls?" Mallory's risen voice and her outburst expressed her frustration at the whole situation. She stormed up to her room and slammed the door.

For the first time ever, she actually wanted to be alone. She wanted everyone to go and just leave her be. She sobbed into her pillow for a while.

She awoke to gentle knocking on her bedroom door. She must have cried herself to sleep. She sat upright and croakily called, "Come in."

Josie sheepishly walked into the room. She hesitated and then shook her head. Walking toward her she sat on the edge of the bed.

She rubbed Mallory's arm. "Hey, you." She smiled. "Are you okay?" Her expression was filled with concern. Mallory's heart twinged.

"I'm as well as can be expected given the circumstances."

Josie nodded. "Well, Brad and I have packed our things; we'll head home after dinner. Brad has made us a curry. It smells yum." She encouraged Mallory to smile.

Mallory sighed. "Josie you don't have to go tonight, that's silly. You were supposed to go tomorrow. I'm sorry for being so grumpy."

Josie squeezed Mallory's hand. "No, no, it's fine. I shouldn't have interfered. I'm just worried about you getting hurt. You're my best friend in the world and we've been through so much. I just don't feel like I can help you with all this and it gets to me."

"I know you only mean well. I just feel like everyone is forgetting about Sam and *that* gets to *me*." Mallory explained.

"Lovey, no one is forgetting Sam, not at all. We all know how special he was and how happy he made you. But we just don't want you to give up on loving someone in the future."

"Well, that has to be in my own time. I have to decide when that's going to happen."

"Yes, you're right. Give me a hug and come and eat."

The two friends had made their peace and the curry was enticing them downstairs.

The curry was delicious. They chatted over the meal. Brad and Josie had decided to set off home after dinner, meaning they could travel home at night when the roads were quieter and they could both then work on Monday.

The friends said their goodbyes and exchanged bear hugs. Mallory waved them off, feeling a little guilty for their early departure.

On Monday morning, she received a visit from Renee and Cara. Ryan had taken Dylan for a walk. They both looked distracted. Mallory made tea and placed the tray on her beautiful gnarled wood coffee table. Renee and Cara were whispering when she walked in.

"What's going on with you two?" Mallory was intrigued. They both grinned like Cheshire cats.

"Well, we have something for you." Renee clapped her hands together like a teenage girl. It made Mallory giggle.

"Okay, what is it?" Mallory's excitement mounted. She had already received some lovely gifts of perfume, a beautiful scarf and a beautiful white gold bracelet. What more could they have to give her?

"Well, we figured that maybe you wouldn't get around to booking a holiday this year…" Cara began, she looked at Renee. Gesturing for her to continue the story,

"Sooo, we got you this." Renee handed her a long thin envelope.

Mallory opened it and removed the contents. She inhaled sharply and clasped a hand over her mouth. "You got me a ticket to come to Canada?" Her eyes were wide and her heart was pounding. This was too much. "I can't accept this, you've already bought me my birthday gifts…I don't—"

"Oh stop! You *can* and you *will* accept it. We discussed it with Stella and she has happily agreed that a holiday would be good for you. Greg has agreed to take Ruby for a few weeks. So you're all set."

"Wait, what? A few weeks?" Mallory couldn't quite comprehend this.

"Yes, Josie is fine with the shop, Ruby is sorted and the pub will be fine. You'll come home with us on Saturday and stay for three weeks. You will return to *Scotland* in the middle of July. You'll have time to go off and do your own thing but we'll take you sightseeing too."

Cara waved her hands around, her girly giddiness exuding from every pore. "Oh Mallory, it'll be so much fun!" she chirped, "Let me know if you need help to pack."

"Ah, the silly thing is I hardly have any clothes to pack. Nothing is fitting me lately." Mallory admitted feeling rather embarrassed.

"Well, we can take you shopping when we arrive so just get yourself a few essentials." Mallory realised that today was Monday and she was flying on Saturday so she didn't have long to get organised.

On Tuesday morning, Mallory rose early, showered and dressed in the black trousers and paisley top that fit her. She jumped into her car and set off for Oban. She needed to get some clothes to tide her over until the ladies took her shopping in Kingston.

She went in several shops and managed to purchase some new, smaller sized jeans, some leggings, three new tops and some new underwear to better accommodate her smaller assets. She had never really enjoyed shopping, but today was different. She was going on holiday and was quite a bit smaller than last time she had shopped. This made the whole process easier. But that fact in itself angered her. *Why don't more shops cater for curvy girls? Instead of presuming we want to wear gaudy tents!*

She arrived home after six that evening with bags full of new things, feeling quite pleased with herself. Greg was walking down her road toward her. He was wearing his combats, boots and a black fitted tee. She had never really noticed his physique, but she could see through his T-shirt that he was very toned. She broke her eyes away from his abdomen feeling guilty.

"Hi, Matey. You seem to have been busy today." He gestured to the bags she was piling up at the side of the car as she removed them from the boot.

"Yes I have. I think I've bought most of Oban. I only went for essentials," she admitted cringing.

"Are they for your trip?" he asked solemnly.

"Yes they are." She was giddy. "Oh by the way, thanks so much for agreeing to have Rubes. Her and Angus will have fun." She smiled. "You coming in for a coffee?"

"Aye, why not as long as I can make it. You can do me a fashion show if you like."

Mallory felt the heat rise in her cheeks. "Oh I don't think that's necessary. You'd be bored. I only got jeans and tops. Apart from one dress that I couldn't resist." Mallory took her bags into the house.

Greg followed close behind her. "Tell you what, you go put that lot somewhere and try your dress on. Maybe you need a second opinion, eh? I'll make the coffee. Your coffees not as good as mine anyway," he teased.

"Cheeky. Okay, if you're sure." She picked up the bags again.

"Oh I'm positive; it's probably the worst coffee I've tasted."

Mallory smirked but feigned annoyance. "I meant about the dress you cheeky sod." She stuck out her tongue at him and carried on up the stairs. She dropped her bags on her bedroom floor and pulled out the dress that she had simply fallen in love with. Sam would've loved it; except he would've wanted her to be curvier, maybe.

She stripped down to her underwear and slid into the dress. It was red and clingy. It had a slash neck and a very low back. She'd had to buy a special bra to wear with it. It fit like a glove and clung in all the right places. She wasn't sure where she was going to wear it, but she loved how it felt. She slipped on the black strappy sandals she had bought to go with it. She unfastened and fluffed up her hair and made her way down the stairs.

When downstairs she announced her arrival with a loud "Ta daaaaaa!" Greg turned to look at her. He didn't speak. He just stared and swallowed hard.

Mallory's shoulders hunched. "Oh God, I look ridiculous don't I? I knew I shouldn't have shopped alone. I always make stupid decisions." Her hands came around to cover her body as her self-consciousness took over.

Greg cleared his throat. "Ah, no, no… ah…Mallory …you look…I mean…you're…um…wow."

"Is that good wow or *wow I can't believe you were so stupid*?"

Greg blinked quickly. "Erm, I'd say it's a good wow…definitely good." He began walking toward the door. "Anyway, I should go. I've remembered I need to…ah…goodnight." He walked out of the door and slammed it behind him.

"What the—? What just happened?" she asked Ruby, who simply wagged her tail. She went upstairs, removed the offending dress and pulled on her jeans, a clean sweater and her boots. She decided she was going over to Greg's to confront him about what just happened. Had she offended him with her choice of attire? Did she scare him away with her flab? What the hell?

She drove over to Greg's house and knocked on the door. There was no answer. What was wrong with this guy? She would have to wait until tonight when they were both starting work at half seven. It was close to seven now and she would just go straight to the pub. She drove back home, left her car and walked over to work.

Greg was already there, sitting at the bar with a glass of whiskey in his hand. He looked upset.

"What the hell happened to you back there?" she demanded.

"Mallory, not now, okay?" He waved her away with his hand.

"Yes, *now*. What did I do?"

"Oh yes, coz the world revolves around you now doesn't it, eh?" he snapped.

"That's unfair, Greg. All I want to do is understand? You said I should show you the dress, so I did. Then you went all Weirdsville and buggered off." He didn't speak. She held her hands up in defeat, "Okay, have it your way. I will just keep out of your way tonight, okay?"

"No need. I've got the rest of the week off so I'm taking off for a while."

Mallory frowned, "Oh…right…what am I to do about Ruby then for my holiday? Do you know of a boarding kennel? Thanks for dumping me in the shit, Greg, really smooth."

"Don't fuckin' worry, I'll be back by Friday. God forbid I should let you down and disappoint you *again*, eh?"

"Oh whatever, Greg. I can take her somewhere else."

"I said I'd have her and I will. Bring her to mine at five Friday. I'll be there." He stood from his stool, placed the glass with the untouched liquid back on the bar and walked out without another word.

After walking home to clear his head, Greg stuffed some clothes in his duffle bag, thankful that he hadn't drunk any of the whiskey. He decided to leave straight away. He needed to think and to get some distance. Grabbing his small tent from the cupboard under the stairs he called Angus.

They climbed into the car. Greg was trying to make sense of the mixture of emotions he was feeling. He started the engine, turned on his CD player and cranked the volume right up to drown out the sound of the raw growling noise of the *Land Rover* and until *3 Libras* by A Perfect Circle was all that filled his auditory senses. He slammed his foot on the accelerator and pulled away from his house. The lyrics resonated deep within him as he drove.

Chapter Seven

Mallory didn't see or speak to Greg at all for the rest of the week. When Friday came around she was dreading seeing him. She drove to his house with Ruby. Nervously, with more than a little trepidation she knocked on his door at five as he had instructed. The door opened, but it wasn't Greg who answered.

"Hello, can I help you?" A woman, about the same age as Mallory, stood there in front of her. She had long black hair with blue streaks that fell, tied in bunches around her shoulders, big blue eyes lined with thick black kohl and bright red stained lips which stood out against her pale skin. She had nose and lip piercings and a tattoo on her left wrist of a series of Celtic symbols. She was Scottish, like Greg.

"Erm, is Greg here?" Mallory asked, a little bemused at the girl's attire. She was wearing what looked like one of Greg's T-shirts and little else.

Realisation spread across the woman's face. "Oh yes, sorry. You must be Mallory. I've been hearing all about you. And this must be Ruby? Come in, he's just upstairs." Mallory followed her inside. "I'm Trina by the way." She announced. Mallory didn't much care.

Greg came down the stairs. He too was almost naked apart from his black jeans hung low on his hips. God he really *was* defined. She now saw that he had a tattoo stretching half way across his chest that she hadn't seen before. His chest was very toned and muscular, with a small amount of hair scattered between his nipples. He looked good for thirty-seven. He was smiling as he went over and slid his arms around Trina's waist.

"Oh hi, Mally, have you brought Rubes for me?" he enquired, all smiles. A complete contrast to the mood he had been in when they last met. *So mercurial.* Mallory couldn't help but think it all a little contrived.

"Erm, yes but if it's not convenient anymore, Ron said—"

"No, no don't be daft! We're happy to have her aren't we Trina?" Trina nodded enthusiastically; hanging on Greg's every word. Mallory felt physically sick. "We'll take good care of her, don't you worry. She'll have great fun with Angus, won't you girl?" Ruby wagged her tail excitedly at his voice.

Mallory let go of Ruby's lead and the little dog ran to Greg. Tears stung the back of Mallory's eyes and she turned to leave as quickly as she could.

Greg followed, thankfully without Trina in tow. "Hey, Mally, are you okay?" he called after her. "She *will* be fine you know," he said reassuringly as she stopped at her car without turning around.

"I know that. I'm just going to miss her." She wasn't entirely sure that missing Ruby was the reason for her tears.

"Look, I wanted to apologise." Greg walked over to her, his feet bare. He tilted her chin so that she would look at him. "I was an arse, yet again, last week. I don't know what was wrong. But, I had a few days away and met Trina, she's nice, eh?" he enthused.

"Oh yes she seems delightful," she answered rather sardonically.

"Aye, I had a lot of thinking to do, but it's done and I'm over it now." He opened his arms as if to show her the evidence. She looked at the tattoo on his chest; *another homage to Mairi no doubt* she thought; it was a series of foreign looking words. She figured it out to be a Gaelic phrase. She had no idea what it said.

"Good for you." She smiled trying to be genuine.

"Aye, well there's no point wanting what you can't have, eh?" He smiled, glancing back to the house.

"No, no point at all," she agreed, but wasn't sure exactly what he meant by that comment. "I'll be off then, I'm staying at a hotel near the airport with The Buchanan's tonight and then we fly early morning."

"Well have a brilliant time, eh? And don't worry about this place. We'll all still be here when you get back."

"Great…see you in three weeks then." She forced another smile and went to climb into her car.

"Don't you have a hug for your bestie, eh?" He chuckled holding his arms open. Mallory was confused by his mercurial manner, yet again. Reluctantly she stepped into his arms and accepted his embrace. He was surprisingly warm despite his lack of clothing. He did the thing that men do when they hug; he patted her back roughly. Okay, so she was clearly 'One of the guys.' She pulled away and got into her car.

She glanced up at Greg who now looked confused; his frown creating a crease right between his eyebrows. She waved and drove away. Greg simply stood and watched her leave; one hand raised and the frown ever present.

July 2011

It was good to be back in Canada; back in Sam's old room. She felt close to him there.

Renee had put framed photos of the two of them together around the place. There was a vase on the top of Sam's dresser that Renee had been filling with fresh flowers every couple of days. Her first week had been a little emotionally draining. She had cried a lot in the bed where she and Sam had made love. At night she hugged the pillow that Sam slept on and felt sure she could smell him even though the linens were freshly laundered.

She had put Greg and his weird behaviour/midlife crisis out of her mind and had joined in the family outings and meals. It felt good to be surrounded by a real family again. It had been so long and she had missed it.

At the beginning of her second week Cara had taken Mallory shopping in *Kingston*. She had bought nearly a whole new wardrobe of clothes and was wondering if her baggage allowance would take it on her journey home. It was great to be looking around such different shops. Some of which were very quirky. She found some really interesting clothes and reluctantly admitted that shopping at her current size was more fun. She knew herself of old though and wasn't putting pressure on herself to stay unrealistically slim. She was a curvy girl at heart and Sam's acceptance and love for this made her feel free to be however she was and not worry anymore. If she gained weight again, so what. Sam had loved her exactly as she was, curves and all.

The day after shopping was a day of art galleries. Mallory was in seventh heaven. There was a Julian Forster original on display and she stood for what felt like forever just staring at it. She and Sam had been to an exhibition of his in Edinburgh once and they had both agreed on how talented he was. Funny that this piece should be in *Canada* now.

At the end of the visit she purchased a beautiful little print of a painting she had fallen for immediately. It was of a couple standing on a pier, looking out to sea whilst they held each other. It kind of reminded her of standing with Sam on the Atlantic bridge.

That night she went drinking and dancing with Cara, Ryan and a few of their friends. She met a wonderfully colourful character called Reece who she had just adored. He was gay and made her laugh so hard she thought she would suffocate. They danced together all night and swapped email addresses, determined to keep their new found friendship alive when she returned home.

They stayed at Revolutions nightclub for most of the night and she did far too many jell-o shots. Reece wouldn't let her leave the dance floor much at all.

"Oh, honey, I just *love* the way you move!" Reece shouted over the music. "If I wasn't as gay as the day is long I would ravish you right here on the dance floor!"

Mallory had been in pain, her stomach was cramping so much with laughing.

"Now shimmy and shimmy and rrrroll those hips, yeah baby!" His *Austin Powers* impression nearly made her pee in her pants. It felt so good to laugh with free abandon.

The morning after the nightclub Mallory awoke late and was too ill to get up. Her tongue felt like it could be used to carpet the stairs and her head was thumping to a beat of its own making. Renee brought her a tray of breakfast in along with some Advil for her head. She gave Mallory a knowing look and shook her head smiling.

Seeing Renee made Mallory's eyes well, "I'm so sorry, Renee," she sobbed, feeling ashamed of her behaviour. In actual fact she had been a very civilised drunk. She wasn't sick, although in hindsight being sick would probably have taken the edge off the hangover.

Renee stroked her cheek, "Oh darling, we've all let our hair down once in a while. Even me." She winked.

Mallory couldn't imagine Renee doing jell-o shots and dancing on tables. She cringed when she remembered kissing some complete stranger in the nightclub.

~~~~~

"Hi, wanna dance?" The stranger asked right into her ear to make himself heard over the thump, thump of the bass. "I'm Carl." He held out his hand to shake hers.

Reece had ducked out to go to the 'ladies room' as he had called it.

"Hi ya! I'm Mallory." She shook his hand. At this point in the night she was tipsy but not completely gone.

"Where are you from, Mallory?" Carl had asked.

He seemed nice. He was quite handsome, but not her type at all. He was stocky and blonde, not fat, just stocky. He had a kind face, but there was no spark; she didn't want to rip his shirt open to check for tattoos she decided. They had discussed the delights of Yorkshire. He had never been, but he had visited London as a teenager and had always loved the accents of the English.

She discovered that Carl was from a place a little distance away called *Port Credit*, near *Toronto*. He was staying with friends in *Kingston* for a short holiday before going back to start a late post grad course in dentistry. That explained his perfect white teeth.

She got drunker and drunker until the DJ played *Someone Like You*, by Adele. Mallory was initially taken aback by hearing this song in a Canadian club, but she soon pushed the random thought from her mind as Carl swayed her to the music.

She looked up into his sparkling grey eyes and suddenly needed intimate physical contact. Not sex, but something more intimate than a hug. He had lowered his face to hers and kissed her chastely on the lips. She had returned his kiss with passion and need. He had seemed shocked but reciprocated anyway. Sadly, she felt nothing but sadness and guilt at her actions as Ryan and Cara looked on.

All the way home in the cab she had sobbed on Ryan's shirt apologising over and over for her behaviour and for betraying Sam's memory. What she failed to realise is that they understood and wanted her to stop feeling guilty already.

~~~~~

Once she had forced down the bacon and maple syrup that Renee had brought her, drunk her coffee and freshened herself in the en-suite bathroom, she made her way downstairs to face the music. They were all sitting around the breakfast bar in the kitchen chatting and drinking coffee.

"Ah, here's my English little sis." Ryan announced as Mallory appeared in front of them all.

"Morning everyone. Listen I know what I did last night and I wanted to say—"

Ryan held his hands up as he interrupted her, "Mallory. Stop. You have nothing to apologise for. You said sorry around a hundred times last night and you got mascara all over my new shirt." He laughed

Mallory's lip quivered. "I…I feel so ashamed." She put her hands to either side of her face. Tears of embarrassment stung at her eyes.

Ryan walked over and hugged her. "Hey, c'mon, don't you cry again. This is a clean shirt. I'm warning you." He smiled down at her. "You have been through so much, honey. We all get it. We know that you can't be alone forever and we don't want you to be. That guy last night seemed nice. He gave me his number and asked if I would pass it on. Do you want it?"

"Oh, no! I can't believe I kissed him. It was *not* good. I didn't really even think he was attractive. How terrible of me. You must all think I'm such a slut."

Renee shook her head "We think nothing of the sort, dear. You couldn't be more wrong." Renee spoke softly trying to defuse Mallory's anguish.

Ryan chuckled. "Mallory, will you stop? So you kissed a guy and you didn't like it—hey didn't someone write a song about that?" He chuckled at his lame Katy Perry reference. "Next time it may be someone you actually *like* and that'd be cool," he reassured her.

After the family had spent an hour convincing Mallory that they still loved her, in spite of her kissing a stranger, they convinced her to grab a bag with her bathing suit, sun lotion and a towel. They were taking her to *Alwington beach*.

It was a beautiful old beach surrounded by large country estates owned by very wealthy people. Luckily, Renee had friends in high places and so they all went along to sunbathe and splash about in the water.

Mallory enjoyed laying there, sunglasses covering her eyes and the sun beating down on her skin. It had taken some encouraging—getting her to take off her sarong.

Cara tried convincing her that she looked amazing in the navy blue and white spotted one piece bathing suit that she had bought while they were out shopping together.

Ryan picked her up and flung her over his shoulder threatening to throw her into the water unless she relaxed and took off the 'darn sarong'. She had screamed and laughed all at the same time and eventually conceded.

The Sarong was nearby, a bit like a security blanket. Suddenly, something or someone blocked out her light.

"Hey, Mallory." She opened her eyes to see Carl standing over her. She sat bolt upright, shocked by his presence. "What a nice surprise to see you in daylight." He smiled, genuinely pleased to see her.

"Oh…erm…hi, Carl." She took off her sunglasses and nervously squinted up at him.

Obviously he noted her scrunched up facial expression. He sat on the lounger beside her. He was wearing long board shorts and flip flops. His hair was damp and swept back.

"I saw you from all the way over there where my friends are and thought it was you, so I came over to check and here you are."

"Here I am." Mallory laughed sheepishly remembering their kiss.

"I gave your brother…brother? That guy Ryan anyway, I gave him my number to pass onto you. You looked kinda upset after we…danced." He rubbed his bottom lip with his thumb.

"Oh yes, thank you, Carl. But the thing is I'm only here for a short time. I don't think it's a good idea to get into anything…you know…"

He looked disappointed but nodded his acquiescence.

"Hey, we could be friends though right? I could take you for coffee maybe while you're here?" He looked hopeful.

Mallory sighed and briefly looked down at the ground as if the courage she needed was there. "Carl, look, I should maybe come clean. I don't know what came over me last night. I'm grieving for my Canadian fiancé who was killed on his way to our new life in *Scotland* in April. I'm here staying with his family. I really needed something physical last night. That's not like me. I'm so sorry for dragging you into my misery. It was unfair."

Carl exhaled puffing his cheeks out as he did. "Wow, okay. I'm so sorry to hear about your fiancé. That must have been tough. Look, I like you and I totally get that you maybe don't want an emotional or romantic thing at the moment, but that's okay. I would still like to take you for coffee. And maybe we could be…I don't know, pen pals?" He laughed. He was such a nice guy. "I know at twenty-eight I may be a little old for a pen pal but it'd be kinda fun, don't you think?"

Mallory smiled, but her insides churned with guilt and sadness, "I just don't want to lead you on, Carl. I will never be interested you in any other way than as a friend." She felt unsure about the prospect of staying in touch with him.

"Look, I get it. You have been honest with me and I respect that. Here, this is my card. My cell number is on there and my email. You could add me as a friend on *Facebook* too if you have it." She took his card. She had never really understood the *Facebook* thing. Why would she be interested in what someone had for breakfast? Or why would she care about the people that brag about their perfect lives, when under the surface there were cracks? But maybe she should give it a go? She had made friends in Canada. It'd be nice to have an easy way to keep in touch. Snail mail wasn't an option these days.

"Thanks, Carl, that's really sweet of you." She put the card into her beach bag.

He held out his hand to her. "Friends?"

"Friends." She shook his hand.

"Gimme a call if you wanna go for that coffee," he shouted as he walked back to his friends. She waved her acknowledgement.

Ryan came over to check on her. "You okay? That was the guy from the club, huh?"

"Yeah, but he was nice. I apologised and explained. He says he's happy to be friends."

Ryan rolled his eyes. "Poor guy. Believe me, any guy who looks at a girl the way he looked at you is living in desperate hope of a change of heart. He says he's happy to be friends but in 'Man' that translates as 'I will adore you from afar, I will never give up.'"

He smiled and gestured behind him. "C'mon, the water is…ahhh…okay I won't lie, it's freezing, but not too bad once you get in." He ran off to grab Cara and pull her into the water with him. She squealed with delight as he picked her up and spun her around before depositing her into the icy waters of *Lake Ontario*.

Mallory put her shades back on and lay back on her lounger. Greg sprang to her mind. He had given her the 'happy to be friends' speech and then had gone off and picked up some random girl who now seemed to have taken up half-naked residence in his house.

She mentally slapped herself as the thoughts whizzed through her mind. *What right have you got to judge him? He's single. He's attractive. He's a man and men, like women, have needs. So he's screwing an Addam's family reject, what is it to you? You don't want him. You just don't want anyone else to have him.*

She recoiled at the barrage from her subconscious. Was that the problem? She wanted him to want her. She liked feeling wanted; but didn't like it when his attentions were clearly aimed at someone else.

Mallory's heart pounded as she thought through and analysed her reaction to seeing Trina at Greg's house. Immediately another snide comment sprang forth. *He's only known her two minutes. What kind of man moves a woman into his house after that long? A desperate, pathetic, sad and lonely man, that's what.* She shook her head as if doing so would eradicate the mental altercation between the two parts of her psyche. *And anyway, you don't know that she's moved in for goodness sake.* She stood up, threw her glasses down and ran straight for the cold water. That was one way to derail her current destructive train of thought.

~~~~~

The days seemed to fly by and before she knew it she was down to her last three days with the Buchanan family. It had been such a wonderful experience. And in some ways she felt that being there without Sam gave her a sense of closure. She knew now that what she had with Sam was extra special, but that she didn't want to give up on love entirely. She saw the way that Cara and Ryan looked at each other and the way they looked at their baby son. She had listened to stories of Sam's dad from Renee. The fondness with which she spoke about Bill Buchanan made Mallory want to love again.

Sam had always been obsessed with her happiness and had even made her cry once by insisting that if ever anything happened she should move on and re-marry. *Re*-marry. If only she had married in the first place.

Thursday brought rain and lots of it. The family spent a fun day indoors playing on the games consoles and sitting at the table playing cards. Mallory had wowed them with her poker skills and had taken almost all of their matchsticks. Ryan insisted that the next time she came over there would be a re*match*—then he had apologised for the bad pun.

Thursday evening they had decided to go and eat out. They had toyed with the idea of several different restaurants, but couldn't agree on a single one. Mallory had been listening to Renee and Ryan arguing over the Steak House on King Street, which Ryan championed, and the Japanese place on Division Street that was Renee's choice.

"Can we go to Aqua Terra, please?" Mallory's voice was small, but they all turned to look at her. "I…I would really like to go there. It would be hard, but I feel I need to go there before I go home."

Renee immediately picked up the phone and rang the restaurant to speak to the owner.

Their table was booked for eight and she had worn the red dress that she had bought back in *Scotland*. When they arrived her senses were bombarded with the sights, sounds and aromas from the night almost exactly a year ago when Sam had proposed. The music was the same. It drifted through the air and transported her back in time to that happy evening.

Mallory was understandably quiet throughout dinner. Renee kept squeezing her hand to ensure that she was okay. Mallory nodded each time. Eventually, when dinner was done, Ryan asked her to dance. He took her hand and led her to the dance floor. He held one hand at the small of her back and Mallory's right hand in his left as they swayed to the sounds of *'That's Life'* by good old Frank Sinatra. The lyrics seemed somehow apt and Mallory smiled as she leaned her head on Ryan's shoulder. She didn't cry, even though she had thoroughly expected to. At least that was some kind of progress.

~~~~~

Friday came around too soon and Mallory was packing her suitcase. Renee knocked on the bedroom door and entered.

"Hi, Darling. I just wanted to check that you are okay?"

"I'm fine thanks, Renee. I'm just trying to figure out how to get all this stuff in my suitcase." She smiled.

Renee began to her assist her with the mammoth task of folding.

"I hope this time away from home has been helpful to you, honey." Renee touched Mallory's arm.

"I've loved being here, Renee. I've felt closer to Sam. But I feel I've been able to deal with my grief easier being amongst all of you."

Renee nodded. "It's been good to have you here. I think it's helped all of us too. Losing Sam was so difficult, but we made a pact as a family not to dwell on the sadness." She sat down on the bed, "Sam was so full of life. He would hate us all sitting around crying and gnashing our teeth. This leads me onto something else."

Renee paused and fiddled with the hem of a top she was folding. "He always told me that if ever he died suddenly, or after an illness of some kind, that he wanted people to wear bright colours and laugh. I just didn't want to do that at the time. But, I hope you don't mind, I invited some of his friends around tonight for a kind of memorial service." Renee cringed as she awaited Mallory's response.

Mallory sat down too, absorbing Renee's words. "Oh, wow, how amazing. I think it's a wonderful idea."

Renee exhaled a sigh and looked relieved. "Oh that's wonderful, darling. I'm so happy you think so." She held Mallory's hand in hers. "Ryan and Cara are out in the yard hanging coloured lights on all of the trees, whilst Dylan sleeps. I have some food ordered in. We've put up the gazebo and strung that with lights too. I have told everyone to wear bright colours and to write something down to read out and we have some lanterns to release. It will be so beautiful." A tear cascaded down Renee's cheek.

Everything was arranged for eight that evening, in time for when it had begun to get dark. The weather was being kind. Mallory wore her favourite new red top and white linen trousers.

She walked downstairs when she was ready and went out into the back garden. She inhaled sharply as she saw the stunning sight before her. The garden twinkled with thousands of fairy lights in all of the trees. It was so beautiful. Sam would have loved it.

There were coloured lanterns hanging from spikes in the grass and around the edge of the gazebo and a long table displaying an array of rainbow coloured food. There was a large photograph of Sam on the table with a garland of colourful paper flowers strung around it. The photo had been one that Mallory had taken in *Edinburgh* with the backdrop of the colourful buildings of Grassmarket behind him and that wonderful grin on his face. She had sent a copy of it to Renee for Christmas. He looked so very handsome and happy; his green eyes vivid and sparkling.

Gradually people began to arrive and fill up the garden. She had met many of them when she was over in *Canada* last time. Everyone was kind and friendly. She was hugged and kissed more times than she could keep track of. At ten o'clock Renee clinked her glass and a hush fell across the twinkling garden.

"Thank you so much for coming tonight everyone. As you know, we are here to celebrate the life of my son, Ryan's brother and Mallory's fiancé. He was such a special boy, but I know I'm preaching to the converted when I say that." Her words choked in her throat, but after a reassuring squeeze on her arm from Ryan she continued. "I asked all of you to write down a memory on a little tag you were given. We're going to each read our tags aloud and once they are attached to the lanterns we'll release them into this beautiful clear night sky."

Everyone was silent as the first person came up to read their memory. Mallory could feel her emotions rising to the surface and so she took her place by Renee's side and held her hand. They knew they were in for a rough ride.

"I knew Sam from kindergarten. He was one nice guy. My earliest memory is the best one. I had joined kindergarten as the new kid. None of the other kids wanted to play with me, but Sam came over and handed me half his snack and told me his name." The large tough looking man choked back a tear. "That has stuck with me ever since and we stayed friends from that day. And now the world is worse off for losing him." He wiped his eyes as he was handed his lantern and dutifully tied his tag on.

"I worked with Sam at *Woolworths* when we were at college." The pretty red head told the group. "We used to laugh all the time. The most vivid memory I have is when we had to chase a shoplifter down the street. It was a woman who was wearing a wig and as she ran away the wig flew off. Sam and I had to stop running as we could hardly breathe for laughing." She smiled, "I kept in touch via email and he came to my wedding. I miss those emails…I miss hearing his news." She tied her tag to a lantern.

"Sam and I were good friends at High School. When you met Sam you knew that his friendship was for life. He was there for me when my dad got ill. He supported me when I thought I couldn't cope," the mousy haired skinny man fought back tears. "I used to get called 'geek' and all sorts of other names at school by the supposed 'cool' kids. Sam was different. He was popular and compassionate. I love you, man." He ended, looking up to the night sky and stepping down before his emotions got the better of him.

The memories ranged from school to work colleagues. It was so very emotional for Mallory, hearing how well thought of her man had been. There were a few jokes told which lightened the mood.

After a while it was Ryan's turn.

"Losing my bro is one of the hardest things I have ever gone through, losing Dad was bad enough. We weren't like a lot of brothers. There was no real sibling rivalry. Don't get me wrong, he was such an idiot sometimes, like the time he decided to put the Christmas lights on the roof to save Dad a job and we had to get the fire department out 'cause he got scared and couldn't move. We ribbed him about that for years. But he was there for me no matter what. When Cara and I split up briefly in college and I was so sure none of it was my fault. He somehow made me realise that it was actually all me, being an ass. Maybe if he hadn't done that I wouldn't have my beautiful wife and son." He rubbed his eyes and looked up at the sky. "If you're up there lookin' down bro, keep an eye out for Dylan, 'k?" He stepped away and tied his tag on his lantern.

Renee stepped forward to speak. She was shaking and squeezing Mallory's hand the whole time. "My sons have always made me so very happy. They have been loving and kind. They've helped people in need all through their lives. I couldn't be more proud. Cara came along and completed my Ryan's soul. He has never been happier since they got married. She is wonderful and I know Sam adored her too. Sam was always the outdoors type. Even as a child he was always off trekking somewhere or other. Climbing trees or rocks and coming home with grazed knees. He loved to be in the open air and you can hardly get in our loft for all the scenic photos he's taken over the years. We were all shocked when he agreed to go to England and become a white collar worker in his fancy suits. But then one day it all fell into place. It was all meant to be."

She smiled at Mallory. "One day, not so long ago, Sam told us he was finally, utterly, irrevocably, head over heels in love with a beautiful English girl he had met within two months of being there. We were all delighted. When we had the pleasure of meeting the soul who had completed our Sam we all fell in love with her too. And his love of the outdoors was shared by Mallory. They bought their home in *Scotland* and he had his dream come true; Mallory, the outdoors and the amazing backdrop of the Highlands. Sadly now Mallory has to live the dream without him."

A tear escaped and she simply let it fall. "Sam will be missed more than words can say, but I hope Mallory knows," she turned to Mallory, "I hope you know, sweetheart, that some of the best memories I have of Sam are of Sam with you." She hugged Mallory hard as the tears came. Mallory held onto Renee as if she held the very essence of Sam within her.

It was Mallory's turn to speak. She had to muster up every ounce of strength she could find. She had actually planned out what she was going to say to him on their wedding day and it felt fitting to say most of the words now.

Mallory closed her eyes and with a trembling voice, began to speak from the bottom of her heart. "Sam, I literally fell into your life, one cold December lunch time. You made me laugh so much and I knew right then and there that my heart was yours. The way you looked at me, let me know that you saw the real me. Not the girl struggling with low self-esteem, not the chubby girl who hated the way she looked. You saw *me*. You saw the light inside me and you made it glow brighter than ever simply by being with me."

With her lip quivering she inhaled a little courage. "You made everything fun and even when we argued you made me laugh, which I said I hated, but I didn't really and you knew that. I miss you so much that I sometimes forget to eat, which isn't like me." She laughed through her tears, "Being here these past few weeks has helped me to love you more, but also to let you go. You will always be in my heart. I love you, Sam." She could hear little sobs coming from the small gathered crowd of friends and family and her heart ached

The crowd wandered down the garden to the area which left them away from the trees. They stood in silence and in small groups released their lanterns. The sky lit up as they floated away. They looked so beautiful and the silence was a peaceful one. The lanterns swayed and played in the slight breeze as they floated higher and higher. They all stood and watched for a while. Renee, Ryan, Cara and Mallory clung onto each other.

With tears streaming down her face Mallory whispered, "Goodbye, Sam, I love you."

~~~~~

It was raining when she landed back in *Scotland*. She climbed into the limo that had been arranged for her as a treat by the Buchanan's. She relaxed into the seat and thought back to her wonderful holiday. She felt a serene calmness now; one that she hadn't felt since before Sam's accident.

The limo pulled up outside her cottage and the driver opened the door and helped her out. She went to unlock the door and the kind driver, Michael, brought all of her bags inside for her. She thanked him and he wished her well.

She closed the door and looked around her lounge. It felt good to be home. *Home*, she repeated in her mind. She took her bags, one by one up to her room and dropped them on the floor of the guest room. They would have to wait. She wanted to see Ruby-doo.

She started the engine on her little car and it reluctantly spluttered into life. She was a little concerned at the spluttering, but put it down to the fact that it hadn't been driven in three weeks. Pulling away from her cottage she set off for Greg's house. When she arrived, he was outside in the rain messing about under the bonnet of the *Land Rover*. She tapped him on the shoulder and he turned around, startled, banging his head on the hood.

"Ahhh, shit!" He rubbed his head and then realised who the culprit was. "Mallory! You're home!" He went to hug her but stopped, looking down at his oil covered wet clothes.

Mallory sniggered. "Yep, I'm home."

Wiping his hands down his grimy T shirt he gestured to the house. "Come in, I'll make us a coffee."

She followed him in.

Ruby came scurrying toward her making little yappy noises and whining. The little fluff ball had missed her owner so very much, that was clear. Mallory got down to floor level and cuddled her little black dog.

"So, where's Trina?" Mallory eventually enquired, trying to appear nonchalant.

Greg ran an oily hand through his wet hair. "Ah, we…" He looked at the floor.

Mallory held her hands up in apology. "Sorry, it's none of my business, rude of me to ask."

"Na. It's okay. We just weren't compatible, let's say."

Mallory raised her eyebrows. "Oh. Right."

Greg huffed, "Truth be told, she was ready for moving in permanently and getting engaged. I mean, for fuck's sake, I'd only known her a few days." He laughed, his eyes sparkling. "I'll be back in a minute." He ran up the stairs two by two.

Moments later he came back down in dry jeans with a T-shirt flung over his shoulder and a towel in his hand which he was rubbing through his hair. His chest glistened from the rain drops that had seeped through his other top.

"So, good time?" he asked, pulling the dry T-shirt over his fuzzy towel dried hair.

"Brilliant," she replied.

"Make any new friends out there?" He combed through his hair scraping it back off his face.

"Yes quite a few actually. I even got asked out." She smiled, and her cheeks heated as she remembered Carl.

Greg smirked and shook his head. "Why do you sound surprised?"

"Oh, I don't know. It was nice. I'd forgotten what it was like to be asked out."

"So did you go?" Greg was frowning.

"No, he wasn't my type." She followed Greg to the kitchen where he put the kettle on.

"Oh right. Do you have a type then?" he asked inquisitively.

"I didn't think so. But anyway, he wasn't it, that's for sure. Too…oh I don't know. I just didn't fancy him."

Greg chuckled and shook his head. "I've something to ask you, anyways." He handed her a cup of coffee. It was fresh and smelled delicious.

"Oh yeah? What's that then?" She took a sip, but winced as she burned her lip.

"Too eager! I made it with hot water and everything you know," he teased.

She scrunched her face at him. "Ha ha."

"Anyway. It's my birthday next weekend and I thought we could maybe have that beach barbie we'd talked about for your birthday." He looked hopeful. "I know that was just a rouse to get you to cheer up whilst I was planning your actual birthday, but I do quite fancy it."

"Oooh, thirty eight then, eh? BBQ sounds good. Who shall we invite to come along?" Mallory also liked the idea of a beach party.

"Oh, leave that with me, I'll sort it out," he insisted. "You just get ready for around seven and I'll pick you up."

"What's up with the Landy anyway? Looked serious out there."

"Oh, it's nothing. Just a wee oil leak. I think I sorted it. Not bad for a twenty year old car." He took a sip of his coffee, "So what did you get up to whilst you were away?" he asked.

"We shopped, we looked around all the touristy things, went to the beach. It was so lovely and relaxed." She smiled, recalling the things she had done.

"Well, you look...I don't know...refreshed?"

"Thanks, I feel it. We had a kind of memorial service at Sam's mom's place." She clasped her hands around her mug. "It was very touching. All his friends were there. They said some amazing things about him. We all wore bright colours and released lanterns. It was really beautiful."

Greg nodded and looked thoughtful. "Sounds great. Did it help you? You know, to be around his friends and family?"

"Definitely. I felt like I said a proper goodbye. Not like at the cremation where I was so numb I couldn't even cry." She looked at her mug and felt awash with sadness and regret.

"Must have been lovely." He looked wistful.

Mallory had an idea, but wasn't sure whether to broach the subject. "Hey, how would you feel about doing something similar for Mairi?" Mallory asked bravely, hoping it didn't upset him.

Greg's eyes narrowed. "What do you mean?"

"Well, we could get a few friends together and say a few words and maybe release balloons or lanterns for her?"

Greg shook his head. "I don't know…her parents and I weren't close. I only met them once and it didn't go down too well. And her friends already did a climb in her memory. There would be no one to invite." He looked so forlorn. Mallory wanted to hug him, but didn't dare.

"Well, okay, you and I could do it," she said determined to help him, considering Sam's memorial had helped her so much.

"You'd do that…for me?" He seemed surprised.

Mallory smiled, "I would…of course."

"When could we do it? You and me? And where?" He seemed to perk up at the idea.

"Whenever and wherever you feel ready," she said.

"How about on my birthday?" he asked looking a little more positive now, a smile playing on his lips.

"That's fine by me." She could see his mood improving as the plans began to come together.

Greg's smiled turned into a grin, a handsome beaming grin. "Great. I will just write a few words and we'll get some lanterns to release. Leave it with me. You can speak too if you like."

Mallory pursed her lips. "Hang on though. Wouldn't you prefer to have your friends at your birthday? Maybe the memorial should wait until after you've celebrated?"

He placed a hand on her shoulder. "Mallory, you are my friends. The only friend who understands and the only friend I'm that bothered about spending my birthday with anyway. It's fine."

That settled things. Mallory finished her coffee and took Ruby home. She started planning what they could do for the memorial/birthday. It felt so good to be helping Greg. It was what she had hoped for all along, since she realised they had this terrible grief in common.

Chapter Eight

Monday night Mallory's shifts in the pub started again. It was good to see Ron. He said he had missed her smiling face behind the bar and his beer hadn't tasted quite as good with her not pouring it for him. Colin and Christine called in for dinner and she sat chatting with them for a while. Mallory learned that Christine made the most beautiful jewelry. She was wearing a gorgeous amethyst necklace and earrings that she had crafted using real gem stones. It was stunning. They were such a lovely couple.

Tuesday meant Greg would perform at the pub again. As usual he was in top form. He wore a new shirt. This one was white with folded back sleeves and a tiny pale blue paisley pattern on. It made him look tanned. He was so happy when he was performing. Mallory was bobbing up and down and singing along when she knew the words, but she did so quietly so as not to get in trouble with the artiste.

By the time Saturday had come around she was all ready for the beach barbie with Greg. She had made him a gift and wrapped it in home-made wrapping paper—which was actually brown paper with a sun, moon and stars pattern she had drawn in gold pen. It looked quite effective and she gave herself a little pat on the back, proud of her achievement.

She dressed in black linen trousers and a teal long sleeved T-shirt that she had bought in *Canada*. She slipped on a black denim jacket, another treat from her travels. Her black sparkly flip flops finished the look nicely. She went for contacts and left her glasses on the mantle next to the urn.

As promised Greg arrived at seven. He wore khaki cropped combats, flip flops and a cream granddad collar linen shirt. He had sunglasses on the top of his head pushing his hair straight back. He looked nice, Mallory thought. Handsome even.

The weather was warm and dry and the sun was on the verge of beginning its descent. Greg had brought a kettle barbeque, coals, burgers, steaks and sausages. Mallory provided bread, salad and a picnic set. Greg had found some candle lanterns on stalks that stuck into the sand. Mallory had brought the paper lanterns and they had both written and kept their own tags.

They loaded up the Landy and drove a little way along the road to the small beach. There was no one else around. Mallory set out their blanket and stuck the candles in the ground while Greg lit the barbeque straight away. Whilst the coals were heating to the right temperature for cooking, Mallory pulled out the package and handed it to him.

"Oh Mallory, what's this? You didn't have to get me a gift." He protested, but from his smile she knew that secretly he was glad she did.

Greg opened it eagerly and took out the hand-made plaque, reading aloud. "True friends are hard to find, thank goodness I found you." He smiled and she saw water well in his eyes.

He didn't speak but clambered over to her and hugged her tightly. He looked down at her and it looked as though ten different emotions fought for the surface all at once.

"I couldn't have dreamt of anything better, Mallory, it's beautiful…thank you." He paused looking into her eyes. A strange feeling washed over her.

Her stomach lurched and her heart began to pound. She knew that he felt it too. She was terrified that he was about to kiss her and had no clue what she would do if he did.

He didn't do it.

"I...think the temperature should be about right now. Better get the food on, eh?" He pulled away from her and stood to attend to the coals. She felt a mixture of relief, sadness and other things that she chose to ignore. They went back to chatting normally.

"Something has been bugging me, Greg." Mallory's curiosity had been lying in wait for the right opportunity. "How come you didn't want to invite anyone else here today?"

"Mallory, all I can say is that the friends I've had in the past have had a habit of letting me down in big ways. I just feel it's better to keep myself to myself."

"But what about me?" Mallory wondered aloud, immediately regretting that the words had fallen out of her mouth.

He pulled his lips in and then huffing out said, "You're different. Don't ask me why, but I trust you. I don't think you'd ever betray me. I get the feeling I would only ever lose you if *I* was the one who did the wrong thing." He looked directly into her eyes.

"Hmm, better be on your best behaviour then." She laughed trying to lighten the suddenly sombre mood.

Their meal was delicious and they drank a little wine but Greg switched to soda after one glass. Once they were stuffed and had eaten their fill of steak and hotdogs, they carried the lanterns and tags to the water's edge. The temperature had dropped and Mallory was now chilly. Greg had said that she could speak first and so she began.

"Mairi, you were a bright light in Greg's life. You were a brave and adventurous woman, you made my friend very happy and I'm sure, had I met you, we would have been the best of friends too. Now you've left this world you're a bright star in the night sky, you are missed and will always be loved." She let her lantern go and they watched it float away.

Greg turned to her, squeezed her hand and spoke, almost in a whisper, "That was beautiful. Thank you." He turned to face out to sea; tears welling in his eyes. He looked to Mallory again, she nodded in encouragement.

He took a deep breath and let the words go. "Mairi, my heart and my love, you were a vivacious, stunningly beautiful woman, both inside and out, I was so proud of you for all you achieved at such a young age. Your courage knew no bounds. When you walked into a room, all heads turned and you made everyone smile; especially me. Since you left, my world has got a little darker. I've spent the last year feeling a type of pain that no one else could understand. Mallory came along and changed that. She helped me to come to terms with losing you. She helped me to come here today to say goodbye in a way I wasn't able to do before. I miss you so much that sometimes I still feel physical pain, but I know that you can't return and I have to try and let you go." A sob escaped his trembling lips and Mallory put a hand on his shoulder. "Please know that wherever you are I will always, always love you."

He let his lantern go. The two friends stood side by side and watched as their lanterns disappeared into the distance. Greg let out a huge puff of air. He rubbed his face and turned to Mallory.

"Thank you for suggesting this. It's been really cathartic." He smiled and touched her cheek. "You need to know that I would never have let go of all this if it wasn't for…your help." His hand dropped to his side.

Mallory was shivering now and Greg put his arm around her, making her feel a little warmer. They wandered back up the beach to where their blanket and candles still remained. Greg grabbed a fleece from the Landy and threw a blanket to Mallory.

After sitting, looking at the stars for a while, and drinking hot chocolate from a flask that Greg had produced from the car, they decided it was too cold to stay longer so they packed their things away in silence.

Greg drove them back to Mallory's house. He put on the handbrake and they sat for a few moments. There was a palpable tension in the air between them. They had been through a lot this evening and Mallory suspected it was the weight of all the emotions they had shared and experienced.

"Do you want to come in for a coffee?" she asked eventually, immediately wondering if the suggestion was a bad idea.

Evidently Greg felt the same as he shook his head. "Ah, thanks, but I should get back to Angus really. I've had a great birthday. Thanks for making it so special." His eyes sparkled in the moonlight.

"You're more than welcome. I had fun too. And you were right, you cook a mean steak." She punched his arm playfully.

"Why thank you Miss Westerman, how kind you are."

"I speak only that which is true Mr. McBradden." She giggled in a posh voice.

"Enough of this nonsense, now bugger off so I can get home to my dog and my bed." He waved his hands toward the house.

She obeyed and climbed out of the car giggling. She waved from the door as he drove away.

~~~~~

Monday morning was rainy and cold for July. Mallory decided to get her laptop out and have a look at Facebook. She was relieved to have finally had the internet installed prior to her trip to *Canada*. She was an *eBay* addict and had had to go cold turkey for months. She fired up the computer and typed in the address for the infamous social networking site.

After completing her details she started the laborious hunt for 'friends' going through the list of people she had met on her holiday in *Canada*. She immediately found Reece, then Carl. Josie and Brad were on there and had been badgering her for over a year to sign up so they would be happy to find that she had added them too.

She spent a good few hours sorting things out, uploading photos and accepting friend requests from people who had beaten her to it. It was good fun, and she could see that it could become addictive. She had several conversations back and forth with Josie, Reece, Carl and various other new friends she had made.

Since returning from *Canada* she had thought long and hard about Sam's ashes. She was beginning to feel that it was time to set them free. She rang Josie to see if she agreed.

"Mallory, it has to be done when you're ready. But I think maybe you are. The service in *Canada* was a big step for you and it sounds like it really helped. Maybe it's time."

Mallory sighed, "Maybe. I have thought about driving around the places we went in *Scotland* and releasing them bit by bit. Is that weird?"

"Not at all. People do that kind of thing all the time. Remember that scene in the film '*Elizabeth Town*' where Orlando Bloom's character takes his father's ashes on a road trip? I thought that was really sweet. You could do the same kind of thing."

Mallory smiled. "Oh, I love that film. Never fails to make me cry."

Josie chuckled down the line. "That's 'cause you're a sap. Hey, do you want me to come up to go with you?"

"No, don't worry. I know you're busy in the shop right now and you've been up and down a lot. I think maybe Greg will go if I ask him. He knows his way around better than I do and I think he would drive me."

"Good idea. You guys seem to be getting on really well since you came home."

"Yes, he's great. He's fun to be around."

Josie laughed. "I don't believe a word of that," she teased.

"He is! We laugh a lot."

"Well they say laughter is the best medicine. Let me know how you get on."

"I will. And Josie?"

"Yes hun?"

"Thanks ever so much for all the hard work you're doing in the shop."

"Ahem, you don't have to thank me for doing something I love."

Mallory was relieved to hear that Josie was still enjoying running the place. "Well, I appreciate it. Right I'm off. Speak soon. Love you."

"Love you too chick."

The next day Mallory had a busy time in her workshop painting signs and packaging them up to post to Josie for the shop. She loved being covered in paint again and came up with some funky new designs. She had chatted briefly to Colin and Christine about her work and they had asked if she would like to sell some in their shop. She jumped at the chance and had produced some signs ready for display. She had chosen to hang them from a beautiful piece of gnarled and twisted, almost sculptural, driftwood she had found when she and Greg had been to the beach.

Later when she was working her evening shift with Greg at the pub she decided to ask him about her idea for Sam's ashes. She told him what she was hoping to do and then took a deep breath, hoping she didn't sound cheeky.

"I wondered if you would mind driving me?" She cringed and awaited his answer.

He smiled, "Mallory, I would be honoured to go with you. Thank you for asking me to be a part of it." He seemed genuinely touched.

They agreed that they would go on a mini trek the next weekend. Mallory had chosen several places that she felt were appropriate. She hoped she was strong enough to go through with the difficult task.

At home late that night and for the next few days Mallory looked through old photos of her adventures with Sam and planned the places she would love to go. It was a difficult plan to make. The photos made her cry. The two of them smiling, kissing and laughing from the glossy pages as if all was perfect. It had been.

~~~~~

Saturday was bright and fresh. Greg picked her up at seven for their early start. They had a lot of distance to cover. Mallory had her map with little red stickers on the main places. Greg had brought a flask of coffee. He had also done a CD of music for the car with songs that were special to Mallory and Sam. When he told her of this she burst into tears at the thoughtful gesture. He had held her whilst she cried. Today was going to be emotionally fraught. There was no doubt about that.

After an hour and a half of chatting, listening to music and the odd lengthy pensive silence, they arrived at *Kentallen*, the first destination on the list. Mallory and Sam had spent a week in a log cabin here on the shores of *Loch Linnhe*. They had eaten at the beautiful Art Deco hotel on the shore. Then they had gone walking and been bitten by midges. They spent the next day lathering each other in lotions and potions to ease the itching.

Mallory opened the urn, grabbed a handful of the dust in the bottom and let it fly in the breeze. Greg stayed by the car and gave her some space to deal with the raw emotions that bubbled to the surface.

When she was ready to leave they got back in the car to head for the second stop, *Glencoe*. The journey was a shorter one and took them through the most stunning mountain scenery. The Peak of the Buckle, the base of which was where Greg met Mairi, was visible in the distance. Greg stayed silent as if he was making sure that this was about Mallory, not himself. She appreciated the unspoken act of kindness. The colours were so vivid. Hues of brown covered the rocky ground like a lumpy carpet. The azure blue sky stretched like a blanket overhead.

They eventually arrived at *Glencoe* and Greg stayed in the car again as Mallory wandered off for a while in solitude to scatter the next handful of dust. It almost sparkled as it dissipated in the warming air. It was at the gift shop here at *Glencoe Visitors Centre* where they had bought a tree for the garden at Railway cottage and a CD of music by the Peatbog Faeries which became the soundtrack of their holiday. She remembered the way that the Highland cows had all wandered toward them as they had stood looking up at the view. One of the cows had sounded asthmatic and it had made Sam laugh hysterically whilst Mallory had talked to the cow trying to reassure it. Thinking back to that time made her smile.

She returned to find Greg leaning, arms folded, eyes closed and head back, against the Landy.

She suddenly felt ravenous.

"C'mon, breakfast is on me. The café should be open by now," she called to Greg.

He jogged over to where she stood and they tramped up the wooden walkway side by side.

Once their order of coffee and bacon sandwiches was placed they sat at a table which gave them a wonderful view outside.

Greg had been quiet for a few moments. With a frown on his face he announced, "You know, I'm kind of jealous of the relationship you had with Sam. And I don't mean because I have feelings for you or anything. I mean because of how intensely you loved each other."

She bit her lip before answering, "Your love for Mairi was intense."

He exhaled loudly. "The thing with Mairi was…she was adventurous. She was always looking for that next natural high. I supported her, of course I did, but since I lost her I've often wondered how long it would have taken for her to move on anyway."

Mallory felt concern for her friend's unhelpful train of thought. She shook her head. "Greg, you can't think that way. I'm sure she loved you just the same."

"Na. The more I've looked back, since meeting you and witnessing how strong things were for you guys, I got to analysing my relationship. You see, Mairi was a good deal younger than me. If I'm honest I think maybe things were one sided." Greg paused as their food arrived.

He thanked the waitress and looked back to Mallory. "I think that all along I feared that she'd leave. Her being killed like that almost suspends her in time. It makes me look at how wonderful things were. I was always happy in the Highlands. It's where I belong; where I feel safe and at home. Mairi was always looking to the horizon. I reckon it wouldn't have been too long before she found someone else on one of her trips. You know…someone who was a bit more adventurous, like her." A sad expression came over his face and his soliloquy had shocked Mallory into a bewildered silence. "Sorry. This day isn't about me. I'm waffling on."

Mallory looked down feeling sorry for him, but sure that he didn't want her sympathy. "No…no it's fine. I-I'm just shocked at your disclosure. I'm surprised to find that you feel that way." She wasn't really sure what to say.

"I'm just being realistic. What you and Sam had…I want that. It was real and genuine…It was true love." He looked at his food but didn't eat. "All that said, I still loved Mairi with all my heart. Don't get me wrong, I would have married her after the first date. And all the emotions I felt…feel…are still real. Nothing can change that." He smiled.

They finished their breakfast and headed back for the car. They set off on the next leg of their journey and a little while later they arrived at the *Corran Ferry Terminal* and boarded the ferry once it arrived. Their journey across the water on the two car vessel was a smooth one and they were quickly delivered to the other side of the water.

The next part of their journey was a little longer. They headed for *Glen Finnan* via the *Ardnamurchan Peninsula*. The virtually unspoilt scenery was timeless and vast. The rocky landscape made up of dormant volcanoes was the stuff of Sci-Fi movies. They passed through the lush green village of *Acharacle* with its little school and holiday makers. The remains of *Castle Tioram* were just visible from the road.

Two hours later they arrived at *Glen Finnan*. From the car park they could see the statuesque monument, which commemorated the *Jacobite rising*, standing proudly looking over *Loch Shiel*. The majestic loch behind glistened in the early afternoon sunshine. They walked toward the monument and Mallory thought back to when she was here with Sam. It had been virtually deserted. Sam had climbed the internal staircase right to the top of the monument and Mallory had taken a zoomed photo looking up at him from ground level. She smiled at the memory.

Mallory asked if she could have few moments alone at the water's edge. The huge piece of twisted tree trunk, where an old man had taken a photo of Sam and Mallory, was still there. The photo was one of her favourites. They looked so happy and windswept with the sparkling loch and the mountains creating a v shaped valley for their backdrop. Mallory let another handful of dust fly freely toward the heavens.

She allowed herself a few tears at this point. It had been such a special place for them. They had visited here a few times and never got bored of just sitting cuddled up on the twisted tree trunk looking out over the water.

As they strolled back to the car, Greg put his arm around Mallory's shoulder and squeezed her to him.

He kissed her head "How are you holding up, Matey?" he asked quietly.

"I'm good. It's just hard. But it has to be done." After a pause she continued, "Greg, I'm glad you're with me."

"Me too, hen, me too."

They decided to stop for an impromptu lunch at a pretty little pub they saw on the way to Fort Augustus.

"I don't know about you but I'm starving!" Greg announced as they walked through the doors.

Mallory nudged him. "No wonder, you hardly ate any of your breakfast."

Mallory excused herself to go wash up and check her red eyes and puffy face in the mirror. She splashed cold water on her cheeks and applied a little lip balm. She was glad she had decided against wearing her contacts today. Her eyes would have been too sore.

Greg was hungrily perusing the menu when she arrived back at their table. He had ordered her a large glass of wine.

"What are you having then?" she asked.

"I think I may have to go with the steak pie and chips" He rubbed his hands together looking greedy and excited. "Although, I doubt it will be as good as Stella's eh?"

Mallory wasn't that hungry. She still felt full from her bacon sandwich so she chose a salad and Greg went to order.

When he returned he sat and leaned across the table toward her "Where are we off to next then?" he enquired as they waited for their food and Mallory looked at her itinerary.

"*Fort Augustus*," she replied. "Sam and I visited there a couple of times. I remember standing on the little bridge over the locks watching the water pouring in to lift a boat up. It was fascinating. We had ice cream sundaes in a little café just by the *Caledonian Canal*. Sam thought they were the best sundaes he had ever eaten. I say 'they' as he ended up eating most of mine too, greedy sod." She chuckled at the memory.

Their food arrived and Greg wolfed down his meal like a vacuum cleaner. Mallory was aghast at the sheer lightning speed of it. She munched through her salad but didn't finish it all.

They set off again for *Fort August* and arrived around an hour later. They parked in a little car park next to an old fuel station and convenience store. They walked around to the little bridge over the lock, the breeze had dropped slightly and so Mallory was able to release a hand full of dust on to the water where it was free to float out toward the loch.

They didn't stay long at *Fort Augustus*. The ice cream parlour was now a normal café which saddened Mallory a little. She stood gazing into the window for a few moments until she realised a little girl sitting at the window table was pulling faces at her. She giggled and walked back over to the bridge where Greg waited.

The final leg of their journey would take them to *Eilean Donan Castle*. Mallory had taken some stunning photos of Sam on the footbridge. The imposing castle on its little island was another favourite of theirs. Sam loved the history of the island fort and had researched it before they went for the first time. He had impressed Mallory with knowledge of the meaning behind its name and the Celtic saint it was named after. He went on to explain to her that the castle she could see standing there was not the original as that had been almost totally destroyed after Spanish soldiers moved in and the British forces opened fire on them in the seventeen hundreds. How he loved his history.

When they arrived Greg began taking photos of the imposing structure whilst Mallory went up onto the footbridge to release another handful of dust. She looked out over *Loch Duich* and remembered Sam also taking photos. He took what felt like hundreds all from different angles. Her particular favourite was a shot that showed the most glorious cornflower blue sky with the castle standing proud in the forefront. It had been framed by Mallory as a gift to Sam. The sky looked photo-shopped but it was actually that colour.

She had two more places to go, but she would do those alone in her own time. This part of her ordeal was over. She headed back toward Greg.

"Hey, are you alright?" Greg asked with concern. He could probably tell that she had been crying again. She felt her swollen eyes were probably a give-away.

"I'm okay. I found that bit so hard." She stifled a sob.

Greg rushed to her enfolding her in his arms. "Hey, shhhh, it's okay. You've done so well. You've been so brave. I'm proud of you." Greg soothed, speaking softly as he kissed her head and stroked her hair.

The journey home was going to take around three and a half hours and it was nearing five o'clock, so they climbed back into the car and set off. They both sat in contemplative silence for a while looking at the stunning views through the dirty car windows. Mallory leaned her head against the door post as she gazed off into the distance.

Greg broke the silence first. "So, it's been a nice day, weather-wise, eh?" He kept his eyes on the road. Here he was again with his terrible attempts at small talk. Mallory smiled to herself.

"I really appreciate you bringing me, Greg. I think I would have hated to make the journey alone," she said without changing the direction of her stare.

"Aye, well, Josie would've come surely?" He glanced over to Mallory, but she wasn't in a mood for eye contact.

"She offered. I just thought that…well you know how I feel about it all. You've lost someone you were in love with." She wiped away a tear that had sneaked out.

"Well, that's true. I loved her more than anything." He sighed.

She turned to face him. "And, Greg, all that stuff you said before about being unsure of her feelings for you…there's no point torturing yourself over that. You loved her. You maybe will never know the true depth of her feelings. So you just go with how you feel about her. What's the point in dwelling on whether she did or didn't love you the same?" Mallory hoped that her tone was neither condescending nor harsh. But she turned away, not wanting to see his reaction.

They sat in silence and eventually Mallory dozed off and slept for the remainder of the journey. A while later Greg pulled up outside Mallory's. The moon was bright and the sky was crystal clear, dotted with millions of tiny dots of light. Mallory inhaled deeply as she climbed out of the car.

"I won't invite you in, if you don't mind. I hope that's not unfair of me. I have a job to do before I go in. Then I just want to go to bed and cry myself to sleep." She smiled as she spoke, not feeling the expression go any deeper than her face.

"Hey, no bother. You take care and give me a call if you need me okay?" He spoke through the open door of the car.

She nodded. "Thanks again Greg. I can't express how much today has meant to me." She wanted to hug him, but didn't.

"You're very welcome. I'm glad I was able to help." He smiled, "goodnight sweet, Mallory. Sleep well, eh?"

She slammed the door and waited for him to pull away. Once he was out of sight she took the urn and walked slowly over to the mid-point of the Bridge Over the Altantic. There she stood, with tears falling freely once again.

"Oh, Sam. I'm so glad we didn't know the future on that first day we stood here. It breaks my heart to think that this is how things ended up. But you loved it here so very much. And now a part of you will be part of this beautiful landscape." She reached into the urn and took half of the remaining ashes. Holding them aloft she released her hold of them over the bridge and let them fly. One more location to go and that would mean a trip to *Yorkshire*.

~~~~~

She arranged to visit Brad and Josie the following weekend. The urn was packed away in her bag. Ruby sat in the foot well of the passenger side fast asleep as they drove the long journey back to *Yorkshire*. After she had arrived and dropped her bag in her room, she and Josie drove into the centre of *Leeds*. It was nearing ten at night. Josie hung back to give Mallory some space.

Mallory walked up the precinct to the place where she had first fallen into Sam's arms. "Who would have thought that after such a chance meeting we would fall in love?" she said as the memory of Sam wrapped its arms around her as she stood. This place had been the start of such an important time in her life. A time that had moulded her into the much more confident person she was right then. She removed a handful of ashes from the pot and let them drift away in the slight breeze that wafted around in the sheltered precinct.

Finally she walked up to the coffee shop which was closed for the evening. She looked through the window where she could just about make out the table she had shared with Sam. Her palms pressed against the window, as did her forehead, almost searching for some connection to the past. She remembered how he looked at her and listened intently as she waffled on about rubbish. He had made her feel worth listening to. He made her feel sexy and attractive; things she hadn't felt before him.

"I owe you so much Sam. I will never forget you." She released the last of the ashes and said her final goodbye.

August 2011

Back in *Scotland* a few days later, Mallory arrived at the pub for her shift, fully expecting to recount the day's events with Greg as usual, but he was nowhere to be seen. Stella had no clue where he was either. There had been no phone call or text to say he wouldn't be in, which was strange.

By ten that night Mallory was beginning to worry. They had been spending so much time together lately that she felt sure he would have mentioned if he was going to be elsewhere.

Admittedly, he had been rather quiet throughout the day, unlike normal when he would just turn up and take her for lunch or call and ask if she fancied a trip out on the boat.

When there was a lull in customers she decided to give him a call. His answering machine kicked in. She looked at her watch and suddenly noticed the date. August twentieth. Suddenly she was filled with horror. Greg was somewhere, alone, on the anniversary of Mairi's death.

She explained to Stella that she needed to go find him and why. Stella whole heartedly agreed that it was a good idea for her to go.

Mallory ran over to her house and grabbed her car keys, slamming and locking the door behind her. Ruby had looked dazed but didn't get up.

She set off for Greg's but on arrival found the house in darkness. She banged on the windows but there was no answer. She tried the front door. It wasn't locked. Filled with dread she entered and ran around the house looking in every room, closely followed by Angus who didn't understand what was going on. She called Greg's name. No reply.

She slumped on his sofa and noticed a pile of photos on the table, glistening in the moonlight that streamed in through the window.

She switched on a lamp and picked up the photos. Mairi and Greg at the beach; Mairi and Greg at a friend's wedding; Mairi and Greg kissing; Mairi and Greg out walking; every photo showed happy, smiling faces in loving embraces. They looked so in love. How could he have doubted her love for him?

The last photo was one she picked up from the floor. Shivers went down her spine when she remembered Greg's words from a few months before.

Every so often I take off up to The Buckle near Glen Etiv, where I met Mairi…there's a little rock…I just sit there. I take my sleeping bag and sleep under the bridge…I feel her there.

"Oh my God, Greg." She sprang to her feet and went over to the front door where Greg kept his keys on a hook. His house keys were there but the *Land Rover* keys were not. Her worst fears realised, she fussed Angus and told him to stay then she ran out to her car slamming Greg's front door behind her.

She scrambled into the driver's seat of her own car and started the engine, fumbling with the handbrake. "More haste, less speed!" she shouted at herself. She vaguely remembered how to get to *Glen Etiv* and knew it'd take her around two hours to get there. She just hoped he was okay.

It was very late when she set off to find Greg and Mallory was relieved to find the roads were fairly clear. She drove at the maximum speed limit the whole journey.

"What the fuck am I doing?" she asked aloud as she drove through the dark, "I must be fucking mad." She hated herself for swearing, something she didn't do often, but she was nervous and scared as to what she may find if and when she eventually found Greg.

It was well past midnight when she eventually found a small road that was signposted to *Glen Etiv*. She figured it must be the one Greg talked about as the moon highlighted the Buckle looming in the distance. She pulled onto the road and drove. Sure enough she crossed a small bridge.

Her eyes were wide open as her headlights fell on Greg's *Land Rover*. She screeched to a halt nearby, jumped out of her car and ran over to the vehicle. There was no sign of him. But there was a hold-all scrunched up in the back seat.

"GREG!!" she shouted as loud as she could. No reply. She walked toward the bridge, "GREEEEEG!!" She tried again. Her voice echoed in the night air and her heart was thumping in her chest.

It was uncomfortably dark, apart from the crescent moon shining down and casting eerie shadows on her unfamiliar surroundings. There was a haunting stillness to the place. The only clearly, audible sound as she walked was the sound of the water crashing around under the bridge, breaking the otherwise silent night.

She decided to follow a narrow path which veered away from the road to the underside of the bridge. She remembered Greg saying he sometimes slept there. It was pitch black. She grabbed her phone from her pocket and switched on its torch.

"Bloody typical. Can't get a sodding signal anywhere, but I pay twenty five quid a month for an effing torch," she chuntered loudly as she walked.

There was a sleeping bag right where she had anticipated; but no Greg. She clambered back up to the road and aimed back toward Greg's car. Tears of sheer anxiety stung at her eyes. Suddenly, the torch glinted on something, making her jump and stop dead in her tracks. It was a man. She shined the torch directly onto him. The figure raised an arm to shield his eyes from the glare of the light. It was Greg. She marched toward where he sat, on his little rock facing the Buckle.

She exhaled a huge sigh of relief as she reached him. He had hung his head.

"Greg. Are you okay?" No response. She tilted his chin up. His eyes were closed and his face was wet. She tapped his face with her free hand. "Greg, it's me, Mallory." Slowly his eyes opened partially.

"Mallory?" He looked confused for a moment. "Oh aye, Mallory, my bestest friend in the world, Mallory, Mallory." His words slurred. Mallory noticed a large, half empty whiskey bottle clutched in his right hand.

"Oh, Greg, you silly, silly sod. What have you done?" She wrestled the bottle from his hand.

"Ahhhhad a wee drinky. In memory of my wee lassie." He smiled, "She's dead, you know."

She sighed. "Yes Greg, I know. Come one, let's get you home. We'll collect your car tomorrow, eh?"

"Fuck off!" He swiped her hand away as she tried to take his arm. "You just fuck the fuck away, am stayin' here with my Mairi." He was not a pleasant drunk.

Annoyance washing over her, she snapped. "Oy, don't swear at me." She grabbed his arm and wrapped it around her neck and struggled to get him to a standing position. "You can't stay here, not in this state."

"Am shorry, Mallilly. I don't mean to swear at you. You're my best friend you know that?" He swayed.

"Yes, Greg, so you said. Now come on. You are going to feel like shit in the morning and I need to get you home. You've had me worried sick," she scolded him.

"Whoops, you swore." He chuckled, "you said *Shit.*" His accent had become stronger in his drunken state. If this situation wasn't so sad Mallory would've been amused by drunken Greg.

Stifling a giggle she said, "Sorry for swearing, Greg, now come on. You can't stay here. It's a car park not a camp site." They wobbled and swayed toward the car. Suddenly Greg stopped and looked back at the moonlit mountain.

"I met her there on that wee path. I'd been out walking and I was on my way back to the car. She dropped her map and tripped over her lace trying to pick it up...I caught her." Greg was now seemingly lucid and Mallory was struck as to the similarities between his story of meeting Mairi and hers of meeting Sam. They stood in silence.

Greg looked down at Mallory. "She was so beautiful, Mally, so beautiful. Long red hair, green eyes." A single tear rolled down his unshaven cheek. "I miss her so much. I don't want to be alone. I hate it." He brought his hand up to cover his eyes as he was taken over by his emotions.

His lower lip trembled and his body shook much the same as hers had that night on the beach when he had rescued her. It was her turn to rescue him now. She hugged him and let him cry.

Eventually he wiped his face on his T-shirt, took a deep breath and looked down at her again. She felt sad too. She gazed up at this broken man, knowing exactly how he felt. Then suddenly she froze as he lowered his mouth to hers. He kissed her softly but it was not the simple kiss of one friend to another. He tasted of whiskey.

Her mind snapped back into action. "Greg, no! What are you doing?" She stepped back from him glaring.

He wobbled a little. "Shit. I'm sorry, Mallory, I-I don't know why I did that." He touched his lips as he stumbled backward.

"No, neither do I…Let's just forget about it. Come on. You need to get home to bed." She knew he was drunk. She knew he was grieving, but boy was she going to have to work on forgiving him for that latest development.

She helped fold him into her car which wasn't really built for huge hulking men. Fastened his seat belt and slammed the door almost off its hinges.

When she had climbed into the driver's seat he was looking at her.

"You're mad with me; please don't be mad with me." He pleaded, "I couldn't help myself, I really couldn't. I'm sorry. I know you don't see me that way."

She huffed. "You don't see me that way either when you're sober, Greg. You probably won't even remember this in the morning so let's not worry, eh?"

"Mallory?"

"Yes, Greg, what is it?" she snapped.

"It is morning."

Chapter Nine

Over two hours later Mallory helped Greg upstairs into his bedroom. She figured that undressing him was probably inappropriate in light of recent events and settled for pulling off his boots and pulling the duvet over him.

"Mallory?" Greg whispered as Mallory put his boots together under his bed.

Mallory sat beside him on the bed. "Yes?"

"I'm not sorry," Greg mumbled.

"Not sorry about what?" He had a lot to be sorry for this evening, but clearly he disagreed.

"For kissing you."

Mallory shook her head as she stood and walked toward the door. She switched off the light and without speaking, left him to sleep off his alcohol fuelled stupor.

She had set her alarm so that she could get up and go to Greg's house early to check up on him. Once awake, she showered and pulled on her dark blue jeans and a lilac T-shirt with an image of the *Eiffel Tower* on the front. It was slightly off shoulder and rested just on her hips. She gave Ruby a cuddle and set off for Greg's.

Greg lived a ten minute drive away in a detached white painted cottage at the end of a secluded track. There were other houses on there, but Greg's was more isolated than the others.

Most of the rooms were on the ground floor, but there was an en-suite bedroom upstairs where Greg slept. He had simple taste and most of his furniture came from junk shops giving it a very eclectic feel. There was an old fashioned juke box in one corner which he had repaired and converted to play CD's. It was full of his favourite bands. Mallory was quite amazed at the variety of music he owned. From Dougie MacLean to Tool, Queens of The Stoneage and A Perfect Circle.

She opened Greg's front door and called his name. He didn't answer. She went up the stairs to his room. He was laid; spread eagled, face down on the bed, butt naked. He must have got up after she left and removed his clothes. His buttocks were shapely and muscular, she noticed. His back was defined, almost sculpted. To save his dignity, she pulled the covers over his lower half. She stroked his hair to try and wake him. He opened his eyes slowly and when he realised it was Mallory he sat bolt upright exposing a little more of his nakedness. Mallory gasped and averted her gaze.

He grabbed the sheet and pulled it over his manhood.

"Shit-fuck, Mallory!" He was rather shocked to say the least. Wincing and closing his eyes briefly, he held his hand up to rub his head. Feeling uneasy yet sorry for him she asked, "Are you okay? I was so worried when you took off. You were in a state when I found you."

"I'm okay; I think...sorry to worry you. I don't know what happened." He shook his head, "I remember bits of it...did I...did I...kiss you?" He cringed.

"You did," she said plainly.

"Oh God, Mallory, I am so sorry."

She pursed her lips and folded her arms. "That's not what you said last night."

He looked puzzled. "What do you mean?"

"When I put you to bed, you told me you weren't sorry for kissing me."

He blushed, beetroot red. She couldn't help the half smile that played on her lips at his embarrassment.

"Ah. Right." He looked down and then a look of horror crossed his face. He rubbed his eyes. "Did you..." He gestured down at his naked body. "Did you…take my clothes—"

"God no!" she interrupted rather harshly, "I took your boots off and pulled the covers over you. You must have got up and done the rest."

He cringed and shook his head. "Regardless of what I said last night, I *am* sorry. Please forgive me."

"Look, Greg, it's difficult for me to sit here talking to you when you're naked. I'll go and put the kettle on, you get a quick shower and come down when you're ready," she instructed.

Greg waited for her to leave the room until he punched his pillow several times whispering expletives as he did so. Why was he such an arse where she was concerned? He slammed his body back into the mattress and wondered why he couldn't be a better man around her. Huffing at himself he unsteadily climbed out of bed and went to the shower.

Mallory found all the necessary items she needed to make fresh coffee, not instant. Although, she didn't much care that he didn't like her coffee this morning. He'd have to put up with it.

When he was freshened up, Greg sheepishly came downstairs in his jogging bottoms and nothing else. She turned her head toward him. His dark, shaggy hair was damp. He smiled but she turned away. Slowly, he walked over to her and standing behind her, kissed the top of her head as she looked out of the kitchen window at his pretty, well-tended garden. Surprised at the gesture he made, she turned to face him. His torso was still glistening a little from his shower and she felt an unwelcome aching deep inside her. This confused her to no end. She looked up at him. He was too close for comfort.

"I *am* sorry I kissed you." He breathed.

Butterflies set about dancing in her stomach. She felt angry at her reaction. "Y-yes, so you said," she whispered. She felt an almost overwhelming urge to lick the droplets on his chest. She scrunched her eyes to liberate herself from her thoughts.

"But…I'm only sorry because I know you don't feel the way I do." He stroked her cheek. "If I thought for a second you felt the same…" His expression was sad, pained almost.

Mallory stuttered, "I – I don't understand." But really, she did.

He clenched his jaw. "Mallory, do I have to spell it out for you? I've wanted you since the first time I laid eyes on you in the pub. That's why I was so angry and unpleasant. I was still grieving. I shouldn't have felt that way, but I couldn't help it."

She could feel his breath on her face as he looked down at her. He smelled of cologne and mint. "But…but you said you were happy to be friends. You were so sincere. I-I believed you." Her legs had turned to jelly and her heart was pounding. Heat radiated from him and she felt flushed.

"I tolerate being only friends. If I'm completely honest, I want more. Much more. I'm sorry, but it's the truth. Can't you find room for me in your heart?" He tucked a strand of her hair behind her ear.

She was so confused; both by how her body was reacting to him and by his words. She longed to touch his muscular arms, to feel them around her, to trace the tattoo on his chest and kiss it. *Why? Why? I can't feel this way. It's wrong to lust after another man so soon.* Half her subconscious screamed.

"I can't, Greg, it's not right." She breathed. But the other half of her subconscious was screaming *kiss me, just kiss me dammit!* She closed her eyes and waited for the inevitable. It didn't happen.

Greg looked down at her standing there with her eyes closed. Her chest heaved as her breathing became irregular. She looked terrified. He hated that. It made him feel nauseated that she could be scared of him. But then he looked at how they were standing. Mallory was backed up against the work surface, unable to move, her hands clenched in front of her. He was about an inch away from her, looming down over her like some menace. He disgusted himself. She opened her eyes as he gazed down at her with an intense stare. His jaw still clenched. Tension wracked his body.

"I know…You don't have to worry, I won't say anything again." He stepped away from her, shaking. "You'd maybe better go," he spoke through clenched teeth and he turned to avoid eye contact. His voice had lost its warmth and now cut her with its icy edge. What had he expected to happen, really? *Idiot.*

"Greg, please, I'm still grieving. It's too soon. Please don't be upset with me. I couldn't bear to lose you." A sob broke free and she covered her mouth as if to stop it but was too late.

Looking at her from under his lowered eyes he spoke as coldly as he could, "I am clearly not yours to lose, now am I?" It was almost a snarl, "just go."

Mallory rushed for the door; unsure as to what had just happened. A terrifying sense of loss once again washed over her. She was torn between running back into his arms and kissing him or running away and getting on a 'plane to *Canada* or a train to *Yorkshire*. She summoned up some strength from somewhere and turned to him once more.

"Greg, you are my closest friend here. If I don't have you then I may as well go home, back to *Yorkshire*."

He turned his lips up into a menacing grimace. "I don't do ultimatums," he stated coldly.

"Please don't be like this," she pleaded. What else could she do?

He closed his eyes for a moment and when he opened them again his gaze has softened a little. "Mallory. We have reached an impasse. I want what you can't give. Enough said. It's over. I can't pretend to be friends with you anymore," he choked on his words. "Now for fuck's sake just go!"

She ran to her car and started the engine. She looked back at the house hoping for a glimpse of him coming out to chase after her. To apologise and take back what he had said. She waited. He never came.

~~~~~

"You fucking IDIOT!" Greg shouted as he slammed his fist into the wall. Tears sprang to his eyes caused by a combination of physical pain from the impact and emotional pain from the realisation of what he had just allowed to happen. He had just practically jettisoned the only woman he had ever cared about, other than Mairi. The only person he could actually call 'friend.' He stomped over to the window. Her car was still there. Why? What was she doing? Should he go out to her? God, he wanted to go out to her so much. His fists clenched.

He went to the door but stopped when he heard the engine of her silly little car start up. She was so going to need a bigger car come winter. That is if he hadn't just scared her away; which he most probably had. *Well done Greg. You've really done it this time you fucking arsehole.* He mentally persecuted himself.

She had been so wonderful about the memorial for Mairi last month. So selfless in her own grief. All he had wanted to do was hold her, kiss her even. He knew she was hurting too, but she did all that for him.

He understood it was still raw for her. But he knew that they could be great together. Why wouldn't she just look at him through different eyes? Okay, so he was eight years older, but as he had always said, age is just a number. God, the way she had looked that night at the beach. She was stunning in the way she just didn't acknowledge her own beauty. He had said goodbye to Mairi, but only because she had given him the opportunity. She was such a special woman and he had just blown everything. How could he make it up to her now?

He had fallen for her. He didn't want to. It had just happened. The timing was terrible. He knew that. Why didn't she feel the same? Probably because at every given opportunity he did or said the totally wrong thing. He was so angry, but at himself; not at her. *She won't have seen that though.* She clearly thought his anger was directed at her. And why wouldn't she after how he'd behaved.

~~~~~

Mallory arrived home from Greg's feeling heartbroken and shell shocked. She collapsed onto the sofa sobbing into the cushion and then, as usually happened, into Ruby when the little dog jumped onto her lap to see what was wrong.

She was angry with herself for feeling something for Greg. She couldn't allow it to continue. But she did feel *something*. She hated herself for it. It was far too early after losing Sam, wasn't it? Why then, when he got close to her had she yearned for him to kiss her? And why did she feel so lost now he had rejected her hand of friendship? Was it just that she needed physical contact? Is that all it was? Lust? Sex? She had never been that 'type' before so why would she start now?

She washed her face and made coffee. The garden was a little overgrown again, so today she would make a start on tidying it up. If she decided to sell up she would need it to be tidy. Maybe selling up was for the best? Maybe being here wasn't healthy after all? Maybe she should just be in *Yorkshire* where she could work in the shop and forget ever moving here. It was a possibility.

She heard the letter box clatter. She ignored it. She didn't make an excited dash for the post anymore. It was usually stuff still addressed to Sam, even though she'd written what felt like a million letters telling people he was deceased. She decided to sit and drink her coffee at leisure. Then she would start on the garden.

She put her empty mug in the sink and walked through the lounge to go up the stairs. She noticed an envelope on the doormat so she picked it up. There was no stamp. *Odd.* She placed it on the mantle shelf thinking she would look at it later.

Mallory pulled on her scruffy clothes and headed out for the garden. The weeds had taken over with a vengeance. She tugged and pulled and made a huge pile of discarded leaves and stalks. She clipped things back paying little regard to the fact that this time of year may not be the right time to do so. She didn't much care. She just wanted to chop things and dig. She needed to exert some energy and get Greg out of her head. Her attempts were futile, however; the analytical side of her brain would not back down.

She didn't understand her feelings at all. But she had to admit she had felt something for a while. Looking back she had felt a stab of jealousy when she'd met that Trina woman. Once again she questioned her feelings. Was it down to lust? Was it love? Was it simply platonic and she was overthinking it? No, she knew it wasn't platonic…

The rain began to fall in earnest. She worked in it for a while but it got heavier and so she decided to give up for the day. She had been at it for a few hours and the garden was looking much tidier. She had made good progress. It was quite dark now and in the air was a strange thick feeling, like there could be a storm on its way. It was only four o'clock.

She grabbed a towel from the downstairs bathroom and scrunched it around her ponytail to soak up as much rain as she could from her hair. Then she dabbed her face. She noticed the envelope sitting there and curiosity got the better of her.

Inside the envelope was a CD and a note. The CD was not a shop bought pre-recorded one. It was blank apart from the words 'For Mallory—I'm sorry—again.' She opened the note that accompanied it.

Mallory, once again I have proved myself unworthy of your friendship and most definitely of anything else. Since meeting you I appear to have lost the ability to communicate my feelings like an adult. In fact, I am not sure I ever could. I made you cry again which makes me sick to my stomach. Please listen to the tracks on the CD. Hopefully they will explain a lot better than I can. Your friend, <u>always</u>, Greg.

He had underlined always twice. On the reverse of the note was a track list. Some songs she knew and others were new to her.

With her heart pounding, she placed the CD into her stereo and hesitantly hit play. The first track began with the haunting melody of violins and guitar. She didn't recognise the voice of the singer but it had a distinct, ethereal quality. Glancing at the note she read, track one: *'3 Libras'*—A Perfect Circle. A cold chill enveloped her. The vocalist sang about feeling almost invisible and unseen. *This must be how he feels.* The words jumped out of the track at her and she was overcome by a feeling of sadness. The singer continued, conveying what she interpreted as Greg's message. A single tear escaped from her eye. Over and over again the words came.

Track two she knew and loved. It was one of her favourite Foo Fighters tracks '*Walking After You*'. She had never really listened to the words of the song; she had only ever swayed around to it, eyes closed, at gigs and clubs.

Greg's determination and need to be with her, now audible in words he could and would never say directly to her himself. Dave Grohl's usually growling voice was a soft, soothing whisper, floating out from the speakers. As she listened on, line after line jumped out at her. Greg's sentiment pierced her heart and a shiver travelled down her spine as Mallory sat staring into space and letting the things that he was communicating to her sink in. He knew that there was a chance she would run away, but he would follow. Perhaps he knew that she felt something too, but was denying it?

Track three came. There was a melancholy quality to the poetry. She wasn't sure of the original intention of the lyricist when The Fray had been writing the song but Mallory read what she thought Greg had put between the lines of '*How to Save a Life*'. One particular phrase released a sob from deep within her and the tears streamed; it spoke of letting friends down and being unable to do the right thing. He was sorry. *So sorry*, she could see that now.

Next, came a song that she loved by Nickelback. '*Far Away*' had always been a song that brought tears to her eyes and here it was being used by a man who loved her desperately to try and convey a message that he felt unable to express in his own words. He wouldn't give up on her. It was as if the lyrics had been written by Greg himself. A smile curled at the corners of her mouth as she listened despite the tears that fell.

She braced herself for the fifth and final track. It was a song she was not familiar with, but the words resonated through her in a way that sent shivers down her spine once again. It was, in her opinion, one of the most personal and heartfelt songs she had ever heard; *'The Reason'* by Hoobastank. The words drove into her soul as tears continued to cascade down her face. The honesty of the lyrics, sent as a message from Greg, made her heart ache, ready to burst out of her chest. She wanted to open the front door and run back to him; slap his face, kiss him, hold him; this hurt and damaged man who was struggling to come to terms with his feelings, just as she was doing the same thing.

As the song played and Mallory sobbed there was a knock at the door. She didn't bother turning off the stereo. She pulled the door open and there he stood, in the rain. *Greg.* His eyes were bloodshot and damp; his chest heaving as if he had run all the way. She stared unabashed as the tears fell.

"I couldn't wait any longer. It's been hours. I was scared you'd packed up and gone." He stepped over the threshold and scooped her into his arms. They clung to each other. He sobbed into her hair and *'The Reason'* became the soundtrack to their embrace, just like a movie.

He kissed her forehead. "I'm sorry, I'm so sorry, please forgive me." His voice was filled with emotion. He hugged her to him. She grabbed at his back, pulling him nearer.

Looking into his eyes she pleaded. "Don't hurt me like that again, Greg, please. I couldn't bear the way you looked at me, like you hated me." She sobbed.

He grasped her face in his hands. "I could never hate you. It's me that I hate. I'll never, ever be so stupid again, I promise. I'm such an idiot. I care about you so much. I would never really want to hurt you, ever. I just don't know what else to do Mallory…I…I love you so much…I don't care anymore if it's wrong…All I care about is you. If friends are what we are then that's what we are. I'll get used to it, I promise I will." He hugged her again, "I can't be without you in my life. I said some terrible things. Can you forgive me? The songs were meant to make you understand, not make you cry." His words came out in a rush. He took her face in both of his hands again and wiped the tears away with his thumbs. "I want to kiss you so badly right now…" he said breathlessly. "Oh God, I just said that out loud didn't I?" He closed his eyes and clenched his jaw.

Without thinking of the consequences and without further analysing the way she felt, Mallory pulled him to her again so that their foreheads were touching. She took a deep breath and said the words she knew she had wanted to say for a long time,

"So do it." She looked directly into his burning eyes.

Greg inhaled sharply. "What?" He gasped, his brow furrowed in confusion.

"Kiss me, Greg." She breathed.

He let out a muffled sob as if she had just pulled him back from a ledge. He crashed his lips into hers. His hands found her damp hair as he devoured her mouth with all of his pent up passion and longing. She kissed him back with the same ferocity. The kiss felt like it lasted forever. Mallory clung onto Greg as if her life depended on it.

They broke apart gasping. She held his face between her hands and, staring into his chocolate brown eyes she simply whispered.

"Greg…I *do* see you."

Hearing the words, he kissed her again just as deeply.

~~~~~

They sat together on the sofa in their damp clothes; just holding each other. Every so often she gazed up at him to see him smiling down at her. Each time he just kissed her hair and squeezed her closer. He had made no sexual pass at her. It was as if what he felt went beyond such carnal desires at this moment; as if he just wanted to be *with* her; to feel her near him; to know that all was not lost and she wasn't going to run away back to *Yorkshire*. And it was what she needed too. She felt safe in his arms. They would probably need to talk about what would happen next. But right now it felt good to just silently be close to him.

Sometime later Mallory woke to a darkened room; Ruby was curled up in front of the unlit fire and the room felt chilly. She looked up at Greg who was still staring down at her, smiling.

She stretched and yawned. "Sorry, I must have dozed off."

"You've been asleep for about an hour," Greg whispered, his voice soft. "You're so beautiful when you're asleep." He stroked her hair and she inhaled the scent of him.

"So…what happens now?" Mallory asked nervously.

"Well, that's up to you. We take things at your pace. When you feel you want to move forward, we do, until then it's whatever you want it to be." He kissed her hair.

This had all been so sudden. Part of her wanted to drag him, cave-woman like, upstairs to her bedroom and part of her knew that time was needed to get used to this new development.

She bit her lip. "I…I'm scared of making huge mistakes…I'm scared of being judged…I'm scared of judging myself and being disappointed that I didn't give myself time."

"Then time is what you'll have." He shifted so that they were facing one another. "Mallory, earlier today was…I felt so happy just being with you." He stroked her cheek. "Kissing you was…wow…not what I expected. I'm so terrified you'll regret it and that's why I didn't try to…"

"I know and I can't tell you how much I appreciated that." *Gosh, he is gorgeous.* She sat upright as if just realising for the first time how attractive he was.

He looked worried at her change in body language. "What? What's wrong?"

"N-nothing…I was just thinking…never mind." she felt heat rising in her cheeks and so she looked at her hands knotted in her lap.

Greg tilted her chin up so that their eyes met. "If you need to say something, please just say it. Don't leave me wondering, I'm terrified here."

"It's silly really…I was just seeing you through fresh eyes, I guess." She bit her lip almost not daring to continue, "you are an incredibly good looking man, you know?" She smiled nervously.

Greg grinned and breathed a sigh of relief. He slumped back against the sofa. Mallory could have sworn she noticed a slight blush in his cheeks.

He glanced up at the ceiling for a moment and then turned to face her again. "I was scared to death of what you were going to say." He took her hands in his. "People around here won't judge you…they won't judge us," he said after a short silence. "The people here absolutely adore you, Mallory, there is no way they want you to be anything but happy." He stroked his thumbs over the backs of her hands. "I know that this is all a bit of a sudden occurrence. But it's not as if it was premeditated or anything, eh? We didn't ask for this to happen. But I am happy to take things at your pace. We don't do anything or tell anyone anything until you are ready. It's just us for now, okay?"

She liked that. *Just us.*

She removed her hands from his and slid closer to him. She climbed into his lap and rested her forehead on his, running her fingers through his thick, dark hair. She kissed him lightly on the mouth and he kissed her back gently; once, twice, three times; the fourth time the kiss became more urgent and then it exploded between them with passion and urgency.

They slid their tongues together, tasting each other, possessing each other. She moved to wrap her legs around him. His hands were at her waist, then up her back to her shoulders. He pressed her to him tightly. A heat washed over her and through her. She grasped at his shirt with desperate hands. He slid his hands down to her bottom pulling her nearer. She could feel his arousal. Then suddenly he pushed her away, letting go of her, breathing fast and deep.

Feeling a little confused and rejected Mallory's voice came out a little strangled. "What...what's wrong, Greg?"

"I...I have to stop now; before we go too far. You're not ready...We need to be careful not to rush things. I don't want to lose you...I can't lose *you* too." He lifted her onto the sofa and stood. He walked over and placed both hands on the fireplace and dropped his head down. He took several deep breaths as if trying to regain his composure. She understood why he felt he had to pull away, but felt a little disappointed.

Mallory touched her lips which felt swollen from the intensity of their kisses. She wasn't sure how to react now. She had been on the verge of giving herself to him. She craved the intimate contact, but he was right. If they moved forward at such a pace it could all be destroyed. Neither of them wanted that.

She stood and walked over to him. She slid her arms around his waist. It felt good to hold him. He turned around and wrapped her in his arms. They gazed into each-other's eyes for a few moments.

"Just promise me one thing," he whispered to her.

She kissed his chin. "Anything."

He took a deep breath. "If you have second thoughts about us, or if I'm taking things at the wrong speed, even if I'm going too slowly, please talk to me. Don't shut me out. I couldn't cope with that, Mallory. I'm afraid I'm in love with you…deeply in love with you. I'm not sure how you feel about me right now. I'm not asking you to tell me. I just hope that we have a chance at a future."

Mallory looked up at this gorgeous, rugged man and her heart melted. But she felt a tinge of sadness. Could she say she was in love with him? Maybe not right now. She thought maybe she loved him, but she wasn't prepared to say so just yet.

"I…can you give me some time? I have so many feelings whizzing around my head right now that I just can't make sense of them. But please know that I *do* have feelings."

"That will tide me over." He smiled. He bent to kiss her again.

They spent the rest of the evening cuddling, chatting, kissing and listening to music. It was a relaxed and sensual evening.

Greg glanced at the clock on the mantle and cringed. Mallory realised then that it was almost midnight. Greg put his empty wine glass on the floor. "I really should go." He exhaled.

She cupped his cheek with her hand. "You could stay."

"I'd love to, but we agreed to take things slow. And…well…I'm not sure I could keep my hands off you if I stayed." He smiled sheepishly.

"We could just hold each other and stay clothed," she suggested, desperate for him to stay.

He thought for a few moments and then sighed. "I'll stay, but why don't I sleep in the spare room?" It was clear that he was determined to give her the time she needed even if she was pushing things right now.

Feeling a little desperate she grasped his hands "Look, I don't want to be alone. Today…in fact this last month has been a whirlwind. I don't want you to go. Why don't we just sleep in the same bed and stay clothed?" she insisted.

He eventually gave in.

Mallory took his hand as they went up the stairs to her room. She wanted to undress in front him seductively and have him do the same. She wanted to kiss and explore his body. But she was still unsure as to the nature of her feelings and his honesty had meant she ran the risk of hurting him. So, instead, she retreated to the en-suite where she changed into a pair of white cotton pyjamas. She brushed her teeth and returned to the bedroom. Greg stood there, waiting, in just his jeans. His chest looked magnificent as she dragged her eyes over his body and her heart rate increased. She had the urge again to touch him there, right where the tattoo scarred him.

She pulled the duvet back not taking her eyes from Greg. He climbed in bedside her. He held out his arm so that she could snuggle into him. They rolled to face each other. He stroked her cheek with his free hand. His gaze was so loving; so tender.

"I love you," he whispered, closing his eyes. A tear escaped Mallory's eye as she looked at him. She felt quite dwarfed by his size in her bed. He was no taller than Sam, but he was wider and something about him made her feel tiny and vulnerable, but safe at the same time.

She traced the tattoo on his chest with her fingertips and then kissed it. She had been longing to do that ever since she had first seen it. Close up the smell of him was intoxicating to her. Desire rose up in her again. But she fought it. She had to be certain that this wasn't just lust. She found him so very attractive; he had an irresistible magnetism that exuded sex and resisting was hard.

These feelings had only just become clear to her. She hadn't been allowing herself to access them until now. She needed to be sure for his sake and for her own that there was more to it. Once they made love she knew that, for him, there would be no turning back. She knew, therefore, that she must fight her urges to clamber on top of him and make him take her. The last few hours had been so intense. She felt emotionally drained, exhausted in fact.

"Can I kiss you one last time before you go to sleep?" he asked her.

The question made her smile. She didn't answer; she just pulled him toward her and took his mouth with her own. One thing was certain. She could kiss him forever.

There was something very contradictory in his kisses. He wanted to go slow for her sake yet his kisses were raw and sexual. She broke away when she felt herself getting carried away and her breathing was shallow. She nuzzled into him and after a while they fell asleep.

When Mallory awoke the next morning she stretched out to find him, but Greg had gone. Feeling a little panicked at his absence she tiptoed downstairs to find him seated at the kitchen table, clutching a coffee cup. He sat there in his T-shirt and jeans, his feet were bare, but she couldn't help thinking he was ready to leave.

She tentatively took steps toward him as if approaching a horse about to bolt.

"Hey you." She smiled as she entered the room.

He looked up at her with sad eyes. "Hey yourself, sleep well?"

She slid her arms around his neck. "Wonderfully well, you?"

He smiled. "I did too."

Kissing his cheek she asked, "Greg, what's wrong? You seem down this morning."

He huffed out all the air from his lungs and looked to the floor as he spoke, "I've been thinking…I…I'm not sure that this is a good idea…you and me."

His words cut her to the quick. She dropped her arms from his body. She couldn't help thinking he was trying to convince himself of his words.

She pulled out a chair and sat down suddenly feeling light headed. "What? Why? What's happened? Did I say something wrong?"

He looked up at her and smiled that smile filled with sadness again. "You were…you are perfect."

"Then what's the problem? Is it…is it because I didn't sleep with you?" She regretted her words immediately.

Greg understandably took offence at the question and stood, knocking over his chair. "How could you even *think* that? Let alone say it out loud?"

"Okay, okay, it was uncalled for, I'm sorry. You've been the perfect gentleman. I didn't mean it. But please tell me what has made you change your mind?"

"There are things you don't know about me; things about my past."

"Greg, we have time to get to know about each-others pasts." She was feeling panicked again.

He shook his head.

"Greg, why now? Why go through all that shit yesterday and then do this now?" she shouted at him, her voice breaking.

"I had a call this morning. While you were sleeping." Dread washed over her, was it Mairi? Was she alive? She didn't dare ask.

"And this call made you not want me anymore?" She felt nauseated and stood ready to run if he confirmed her fear.

"No, it's not that at all, please don't think that, Mallory." He shook his head. "My feelings for you haven't changed. They will *never* change."

She inhaled deeply and thought her words out carefully before she spoke. "You said to me yesterday that if I had second thoughts I was to tell you. Why does that not apply to you?" She was shaking, how could it all be going so wrong after last night had been so perfect?

"Okay, okay, fair point. But I'm warning you. When I tell you it'll be the end of any future we had. Are you ready to lose that before it even begins?" His eyes were pained. He sat.

"Well you're ending this anyway so just TELL ME!" she shouted.

He ran his hands through his hair and rubbed them over his face.

He gestured for Mallory to sit down again. "The call I received was from someone I would rather forget. But unfortunately, she won't let me."

Mallory opened her mouth, but had no idea what to say. She closed it again and pulled her face into a frown. She stared at him, willing him to explain.

"I suppose I should start at the beginning…I met Alice at college. She was studying fashion and textiles and I was studying music. We hung around together. She was pretty and popular. She made it clear she wanted me." He glanced at Mallory who was still staring at him as he spoke. "We had fun. Well, *she* had fun. I was very jealous back then and she made it her job to fire me up at every given opportunity. She flirted with other men in front of me and I hated it. If I did the same though, she got physical with me. I had several black eyes through her temper. She was bad for me and I knew it, but for some reason I thought I loved her. My parents didn't approve at all. They said she was too possessive of me. It caused no end of trouble with them."

He inhaled deeply again, this was clearly not an easy subject for him. "We'd been together for two years and she told me she was pregnant and the baby was mine. I was shocked and terrified, but I felt I should do the right thing by her. So we got married quickly. I was young. But I was determined that if there was to be a child I would make a go of it.

"Anyway, it turns out she'd lied to me. There was never a pregnancy. She made the whole thing up. I think they call it trapping? She well and truly trapped my arse. I was hurt and angry but she said she only did it because she loved me and wanted to be with me. After about six months of arguments and tears we decided to give things a proper go. No more lies.

"By this point I actually did love her. I have no clue why but…I just did. I was so desperate to make it work and so maybe I forced myself to love her, but even so the feelings turned out to be real. We rented a house over by Oban. We stayed there for two years and everything felt great. Then one day I came home from work and found her in bed with my best mate. I beat him up. And I told her I would never forgive her. I walked out and never looked back."

Mallory threw her hands up. "So what's the problem? You got divorced and met Mairi and the rest is history right?" Mallory desperately wanted to be right.

"Mallory…I never got divorced."

"What?" Mallory rose to her feet.

"We just never got divorced. I didn't want to speak to her let alone spend time discussing the finer points of our relationship in front of lawyers. I left her with the house and all our belongings. I thought that would be the last I would ever see of her. Until…"

"Until she called you this morning asking to see you?" Mallory's voice was shaky as she pieced the jigsaw together.

"Yes." He looked up at her. His eyes filled with sorrow and regret. "I'm so sorry."

"I think you had better go now, Greg." Mallory's fists clenched as she spoke.

Greg slipped his boots on. He didn't fight. He didn't protest. He looked at her longingly. "See, I told you I wasn't good enough for you." His eyes glazed over. "I never told you because I don't think of her as my wife."

"No, but she *is* your wife, regardless. It's a pretty huge thing to keep from someone you are supposedly in love with don't you think? What else haven't you told me? How many more lies will I uncover? I nearly slept with you! How can I trust you now?"

His lip trembled. "I don't love her, Mallory, I love you. I don't feel anything for her. Not even hate anymore. I'm apathetic when it comes to Alice. If I could go back in time and tell you everything I would." A sob broke free from his throat, obviously his heart was breaking too. "The sad thing is that yesterday I had a glimpse of you and me together; the whole nine yards; a proper future. And I loved it." His expression was pained as he sighed. "I hope that maybe someday you will forgive me for keeping the truth from you. Please don't move away. Not because of me." And with that, he left.

Chapter Ten

Mallory spent the few days after Greg's revelations decorating the house. The thoughts whizzing around her mind were so mixed up she found it hard to focus. She began to wonder why she had stayed in the first place. With Sam gone, and the mixed feelings around her relationship with Greg, it felt like she had outstayed her welcome. The house was thoroughly beautiful and it should have been a happy place.

She freshened up the paint work. She put a splash of colour in some rooms. It looked nice, homey and a lot different than when she and Sam had fallen in love with it.

This will make someone a wonderful home, her subconscious taunted her. A sadness washed over her that there was a possibility it wouldn't be hers for much longer. After everything that had happened, she had instructed an estate agent to come and give her a valuation and discuss house selling packages. After briefly explaining her situation to the estate agent he had left her with a pile of documents to peruse. He said he understood and that the decision she made would be the right one.

Mallory had called Josie to fill her in with what had happened with Greg. The audible gasp from down the line told Mallory that Josie was shocked. "Oh, Mally, babe. Are you sure coming back here is what you want though? Does it really matter that he has a piece of paper that connects him to another woman? If you think there's a future with him you shouldn't give up. What if you regret it?"

"Josie, whose side are you bloody on?" Mallory snapped

"Yours obviously, that's why I don't want you to make any rash decisions. He clearly adores you not her."

Josie just didn't get it. He had kept something huge from her. It should have been the first thing he told her. He had opportunities before they were even drawn together. He didn't take them. It was over.

She hadn't seen much of Greg; only at shift changeover at the pub. She had swapped shifts in order to avoid awkward meetings with him. She couldn't bare the hassle of seeing him. Their relationship had been tumultuous to say the least. But she had enough of pain and anguish to last her a lifetime.

Greg had been taking Angus into the pub on his shifts. He always came over to say hello and she always greeted him with a big cuddle—funny how dogs didn't show any loyalties when it came to break ups.

After a great deal of soul searching Mallory had taken the decision to instruct the estate agent to try marketing the house for a while. She had been informed that the market was slow and there were more houses available for sale than there were interested buyers.

Secretly she hoped that it would be on the market a long time. She was not quite ready to let go, but felt like she had to take some form of action in a positive direction.

September 2011

August turned into September. The temperature had become noticeably cooler. Her relationship with Greg had become a series of 'hello's' or nods out in the village. He had kept his distance and she had been glad of the fact.

She had awoken early one Saturday. She had no plans for the day apart from a couple who were coming to view the cottage. Everything was presented superbly. She had even followed the advice of the clichéd TV shows and made fresh coffee so that the tantalising aroma would permeate every room. Fresh seasonal flowers filled every available vase.

When she realised she had no milk left she decided to wander over to see Colin and Christine. They had been heartbroken when the *For Sale* board had been knocked into the ground outside her house. She had promised she would keep in touch.

She grabbed her fleece and walked up her lane. As she got to the main road she took a slight detour and ended up at the midpoint of the bridge.

"Oh, Sam, how wrong it all went." She sighed. "If you had been here things would have been so different." She stood for a few minutes looking at the view they had both loved.

She heard voices coming from behind her and turned out of sheer curiosity. Her heart skipped a beat. Walking toward her was Greg. He was with a stunning blonde woman. *How fickle he must be*, she thought. The couple was chatting. The woman kept touching his arm. When he saw her he stopped in his tracks. The woman looked over in the direction of his gaze and her face dropped. He approached Mallory.

"Hi, Mallory." He smiled. His voice was just above a whisper.

"Greg." She forced a smile in response.

"Mallory…erm…this is Alice, Alice this is Mallory."

Oh good grief it's her! He's introducing me to HER! Her subconscious screamed.

"Hi Mallory, I've heard a lot about you." Alice held out her hand, but didn't crack a smile.

"I'm sure you have," Mallory replied sardonically and shook her hand.

"We were just taking a walk, you know clearing the cobwebs." Greg was still terrible at small talk. At least some things never changed. His gaze shifted between the two women.

Mallory began to step away. "Lovely. Well, enjoy yourselves. I need to get going," she said tersely and walked past them in the direction of the shop.

Unwelcomed tears welled in her eyes. She bit the inside of her lip to fend them off. She didn't look back.

Once she had picked up some milk from the shop she wandered back along the road toward her house. Much to her chagrin, Greg was sitting at one of the tables outside the pub. *Come on Mallory, you can do this, just smile and walk by, don't let him upset you, not again.*

She couldn't avoid passing him. She wanted to run but her legs chose that moment to forget how to work.

"Mallory!" Greg called to her. She looked over to where he sat. "Can you talk?"

Now her subconscious screamed a hundred sarcastic retorts, but she couldn't bring herself to say any of them out loud.

"What are you doing here? I thought you were out walking" she said dryly.

"Aye, I was but I wanted to talk to you…alone…so I asked Alice to head on without me. I'll meet her back at the house." He looked at his shoes.

So she's staying with him too. How cosy.

She sighed. "What did you want to talk about?" she asked coldly.

"Will you sit for a while?" He gestured to the other side of the table.

Reluctantly, she sat down, placing the milk and her purse side by side.

"I haven't seen you for a while, how are you?"

"I'm fine thanks. Is that it because I have people coming."

"To view the house?" He picked at a splinter of wood protruding from the table.

"Yes. Not that it's anything to do with you."

"Why do you have to be so hostile, Mallory? Nothing has changed for me. I wish you would realise that."

"It's of no consequence to me how you feel. How is your *wife* liking it here?" The acerbity of her tone did not taste good.

Greg bit his top lip and shook his head. He was angry and she didn't blame him really. "Okay, we're being like that are we? I really thought we had something a little more mature, Mallory. I thought there were feelings on both sides of this. Clearly I was wrong." He looked directly at her, making her fidget uncomfortably.

She felt the sting of his words.

"Greg, you're married. You kept that fact from me just as I was about to give myself to you. Whilst I was still grieving for the *real* love of my life. Excuse me if I'm little indignant."

"Can we at least be civil? Or maybe even friends? We got along so well, Mallory. Don't you miss that? I know I do."

"It's irrelevant. I can't trust you. How can we possibly be friends?" She pushed her glasses up her nose.

"Okay, well, it was worth a try." He sniffed and looked down at the table. "Will you do me one thing? Will you tell me if you do sell the house? I would at least like a chance to say goodbye."

"Greg, we said goodbye that day in August," she said regretfully and left him sitting there.

She walked away from him for the second time that day and again a little piece of her heart broke. She walked fast in case he had decided to follow. He hadn't. When she got inside, she closed her front door behind her and burst into tears. This was becoming a habit now. Her subconscious was quite right.

Her shift started at seven that night. When she arrived outside she was greeted with a sight she would rather not have encountered. The chalk board she had made for Greg was propped up outside the door and it was evident that her former friend was playing. *Great.* She was tempted to turn and retreat back to the cosy womb of her newly decorated house. But instead, she walked through the door putting a fraudulent smile on her face. She would be busy so it would all be fine. Wouldn't it?

She got herself set behind the bar and noticed Greg was sitting in his usual pre-gig spot with *her.* They were chatting and laughing together. Every so often she would touch his arm or toss her hair. From what Greg had told her of Alice it seemed that old habits, did indeed, die hard.

Dammit! Alice looked over and realised that Mallory was glaring in their direction. She muttered something to Greg who turned toward the bar. Mallory quickly dropped her gaze and wiped the glass she was holding so hard that it slipped from her grasp and shards of glass flew everywhere as the vessel shattered. Greg rushed over.

"Hey are you okay?" he enquired, concerned.

"Greg, it's just broken glass. I'm fine."

"Let me help you." He grabbed the dustpan and brush from its place on top of the dish washer, but she snatched it from his hands.

"Greg, just go. You're supposed to be singing aren't you? So go do it," she snapped viciously.

"Look I've said sorry about everything. What else am I meant to do?" he pleaded.

"Nothing. There is *nothing* you can do. Just go!"

Ten minutes later Greg sat in his usual place ready to perform. The bar had filled up and there was a hum of chatter and anticipation. Greg had become somewhat of a local star and his gigs were very well attended. Mallory did her best to stay focused and busy, serving the many thirsty customers.

"Evening all." Greg's voice boomed out of the PA system. "I'm not going to talk much tonight. I'm sure you's don't want to hear me rambling on about stuff all night, eh?" He cleared his throat. "I know you all are gradually discovering how eclectic ma taste in music is. Well just to prove the point even further I'm going to kick off with a little bit of Chicago. The band not the musical." He chuckled and the audience chuckled with him. "This is a beautiful song called *Hard to Say I'm Sorry*." The audience clapped and cheered before falling silent and listening intently as raw emotion poured from Greg's lips.

Mallory tried her damnedest to swallow the lump that had become lodged in her throat as she listened to the words she knew were indubitably for her benefit. She avoided making eye contact with him at all costs and she had to remind herself why this chasm had opened up between them lest she run over and fling her arms around him.

She stuck it as long as she could but when her emotions got the better of her Mallory had to leave the room. She went to the ladies restroom and splashed water on her face. When she stood up and looked in the mirror at her red, puffy eyes, a presence startled her.

"Hello Mallory." The beautiful blonde woman said to her reflection.

"Alice." She dabbed her face with some paper towels and threw them in the waste bin.

"You've broken his heart you know." Alice folded her arms across her chest and leaned on the sink, addressing Mallory directly.

"I think you got there before me, don't you?"

"What you're doing is much worse." Alice snorted.

"How the hell do you figure that one out?" Mallory couldn't quite believe her ears.

"You could just walk away. You could crawl back to your little hole in Yorkshire and let him move on. But instead you're here taunting him with the presence of what he thinks he wants but can't have. It's cruel." Her eyes flashed angrily.

Bile rose in Mallory's throat.

"How dare you? You told him you were pregnant! There was no baby! That is the epitome of cruelty. Then you slept with his best friend! You bitch. And my 'hole', as you referred to it, is more desirable than spending another second in your presence now get out of my fucking way." Mallory was shaking with anger. She didn't swear lightly and the words falling from her mouth sounded like someone else, not her.

"You should know, before you walk away, that he and I are going to give things another go. He still loves me. It won't take him long to get over you." And with that she walked out. Mallory leaned against the sink feeling as if she had been winded.

She gathered herself and went back out to the bar. Greg was just having a drink before his next song. Mallory looked over to him. Was her presence hurting him more? She didn't intend to make things worse. She resolved to take a few days away in Yorkshire. Maybe the distance would help both of them.

Greg looked directly at her with sad eyes as Alice arrived at his side briefly drawing his attention away. She kissed the top of his head.

Stella, who had appeared from the back, saw the display of affection and looked over at Mallory with a sad smile.

"Anyway, onto my next number…ahem…Now unrequited love is a bitch eh? I know I've been there; anyone else?" The audience murmured in agreement. "Aye well, some of you should relate well to this next one. It's by one of my favourite bands, Fleetwood Mac and it's called '*You Can Go Your Own Way*'. Oh and don't sing along, eh?" He forced a laugh and winked at the audience who laughed along with him.

He began to sing yet another song aimed at Mallory. She felt her cheeks burn and saw Alice glaring at her as if to say *I told you so.*

Greg's eye burned into Mallory whilst he sang. She wanted to leave but for some reason she was equally as compelled to stay. She didn't want to run and give Alice the satisfaction of knowing she had burrowed under her skin.

Greg was doing his usual thing of communicating with other people's words and tonight he was on a mission.

"Sorry folks, it's all a bit melancholy tonight. I'm feeling that way out. Must be my hormones." He laughed. "Anyway, this next one is a sad, sad song by a wonderful song writer called John Waite. It's about a guy who's in love with a girl. She left him and moved away. He really doesn't know why she's gone and he misses her desperately but he's trying to convince himself that he isn't…he's failing miserably. She's all he can think about. She's all he sees. He wants her to realise and come back to him…it's called '*Missing You*.'"

He began to play and Mallory stopped what she was doing this time. *If he has something to say then you should damn well listen!*

She listened for a few moments, knowing the song of old. The lump in her throat returned and she was finding it difficult to see through the glassy film over her eyes. She feigned a headache and Stella told her to go on home. She was certain that Stella knew exactly what the real reason for her swift departure was. Mallory slipped out of the back door and made her way home.

"Hi, babe! How you doing?" Josie answered Mallory's call within two rings.

"I need to come and stay. Please, can me and Rubes come tomorrow?" Mallory sobbed down the line at her best friend.

"Of course you can, hun. What on earth is wrong?" Josie sounded concerned at Mallory's emotional, distressed call.

"I just need to get away from here, from Greg; from memories."

"Come whenever you like, hun. I'll make the spare room up."

Before bed Mallory packed a small case with essentials and set it by the door ready for an early start in the morning. Ruby jumped on to the bed and snuggled up to her. Mallory sobbed once again into the fur of the little black dog.

After breakfast the next day Mallory scooped up Ruby and her case and put them in the car. It was nine o'clock and she was determined to set off soon. She pulled up outside Colin's shop and went in to let him know she was going away for a few days. She had already called Stella who had been very understanding, as always. She turned the car around and began to pull away. Greg appeared out of nowhere in front of the car; hands held up to stop her. She slammed the breaks on. He came around to the driver's side and she rolled down the window.

His expression was pained. "Mallory…are you leaving?" He was out of breath.

"What does it have to do with you?" Her frustration was evident in the terse tone with which she addressed him.

"The case in the back. Ruby…are you going for good?"

"Why don't you ask your wife, Greg." She bristled and hit the accelerator.

Chapter Eleven

It felt good to be emancipated, even if was temporarily, from the stress of the chaos that had become her relationship with Greg. She was looking forward to seeing Josie.

She stuck in her Alanis Morisette CD and felt an angry sing along was just what the doctor ordered. The growling, scathing lyrics of '*You Oughta Know*' seemed so fitting and rang through the car and out into the warm September morning through the open windows of her car. Then it was the turn of Pearl Jam and '*Rearviewmirror*' followed by Avril Lavigne's '*So Much For My Happy Ending*'. Good clear-your-head-get-it-outta-your-system songs. She felt better already.

Eight hours later after taking only one brief stop off; and after singing along to as many angry, loud songs as she could lay her hands on, at the top of her voice—much to the amusement of other motorists—she arrived at Josie's house. It was just after six and she was starving. Josie's was a semi-detached estate house not far from Railway Cottages but much more modern.

Josie had seen her pull up and was waiting. Exiting the car and almost running up the driveway, Mallory flung her arms around her best friend.

"It's so good to see you," Josie said as she hugged her back hard.

"It's good to be here, I've missed you," Mallory replied, fighting back the threatening tears.

Josie helped Mallory into the house with her things and then made a pot of fresh coffee. Ruby ran around in the familiar surroundings wagging her tail. Once Mallory had deposited her case upstairs she came down to tell Josie about Alice and her antagonistic accusations.

Josie gasped in shock, her hands on her face. "So do you think they are going to get back together for real? Or is that just her wishful thinking?"

She shook her head. "I don't know. She kept touching him and kissing him, but he looked uncomfortable. All the songs he sang had hidden messages which were clearly aimed at me. I don't know what to think. But it's irrelevant, Josie. I can't trust him."

Josie took a deep breath and paused as if unsure whether or not say what she was thinking. "Mallory, I get that he was economical with the truth, but you obviously have feelings for him or you wouldn't have rushed down here."

Mallory was annoyed by the direct approach, but that was Josie; she was nothing if not direct. Mallory shifted in her seat and her lips were pressed together.

Josie continued on her mission of truth, "You need to think long and hard like I've said before. If he feels for you like he says he does, then Mrs. Conceited-Pants will have no chance at getting into his life again. There are only so many times you'll let someone break your heart you know."

Mallory relaxed a little and sighed as she remembered what Greg had told her about Alice. She was a nasty piece of work, out for her own gains. Greg was just the opposite.

"I just need some time away. I need to be able to think clearly about everything. Not just Greg but the shop too. I was considering selling up and moving the whole thing to *Easdale*, near the house, but then all this happened and I am now thinking of coming back here."

Josie squeezed her hand. "Mallory, you have enough money now to open a second shop. You could do that when you go back. I'm quite capable of dealing with the *Leeds* branch. I do love it and we have a regular customer base now; plus the tourists love the bespoke local signs you make. No one else is doing things like that in the centre." She hesitated again. "Look, don't get me wrong, if you decide to sell I will go find something else, or I can go back to college. This isn't about me. I just think it's a shame to fix something that isn't broken."

Mallory liked the prospect of a second *Le Petit Cadeau* outlet. And judging by the forecasts and current figures, *Leeds* was excelling. Josie was right. But the fact still remained that she was considering coming home to *Leeds*. She would have to figure things out.

The following day was a trip down memory lane. She hadn't been to *Leeds* for a while. It felt good to be back in the hustle and bustle of the busy shopping precinct with its huge department stores and vast array of designer shops. Josie had suggested Mallory came into the shop to see for herself how things were going. She wanted Mallory to see the fruits of her labours as she had managed to encourage other local crafts people to have commission based stands within the shop and so the variety of goods had increased dramatically. Business was booming. Mallory's heart warmed to think that what started as a hobby had become a viable business venture. Sylvia would be so proud, she thought.

As she sat by watching Josie work her sales magic her cell phone buzzed in her bag. She expected there to be a message via *Facebook* from Reece who had met someone and had gone on a date a couple of days before. Excited to hear his news she fumbled around in her bright red bottomless pit of a bag and located the phone. It was a text. From Greg.

Hey, how r u? Am worried u will not come back. I miss u so much. Please just let me know u r ok.

She thought for a moment and hit reply.

Greg, I'm fine. Please just let me be for a while. I need some space, okay? Concentrate on your own life for a while and let me deal with mine.

She hit send. When she re-read the message she realised that perhaps she had been harsh. *Too late now, lady.* Her subconscious chided.

Josie had arranged for them to go out for a meal with a few friends that night. They had been booked into the Tandoori Palace for eight. Mallory was looking forward to some good Indian food. Mallory slipped on a pair of straight leg jeans, a purple v neck top and black stilettos. She wore the bracelet from her first Christmas with Sam.

The restaurant was lively and warm when they arrived. The air was filled with the most tantalising aromas of exotic spices. Mallory's mouth began to water in readiness for the delights she was about to savour. She sat toward the end of the long table with Josie at her right and Brad opposite. It was a kind of an accidental shield created by the friends for their supposedly fragile guest.

However, to her left was Dan; a six foot four, ridiculously handsome, olive skinned, dark haired dreamboat of a basketball player. He had just been signed up to play for the Stags. He was a friend of Brad who Mallory had met before when she was with Sam.

Mallory and Dan chatted throughout the meal. It turned out that they liked the same music, films and TV shows. Interesting. Not at all contrived by Brad and Josie...she doubted that! Mallory had let her nerves get the better of her and had drunk rather a lot of Pinot Noir. She was feeling very giggly and tipsy.

Dan was delicious. Mallory wanted to bite him; he looked good enough to eat. Her train of thought made her giggle even more. At the end of the night Dan walked with Mallory to the taxi that Brad had ordered.

"So, can I see you again?" he asked standing very close to her. He was so tall.

"Erm…well I'm only here for a short visit," she said, fiddling with her hair like a besotted teenager. She was revelling in the fact that he seemed to fancy her. Her!

"Can I take you out whilst you're here? I understand if you don't want anything serious. I just thought we could have some fun." He licked his bottom lip suggestively.

She wanted to bite that now too.

Her brazen thoughts were totally out of character. "I think we could arrange that," she purred and smiled as sexily as she could after a bottle of Pinot.

"How about tomorrow? I don't start training until next weekend."

Crikey, he's eager. She thought, loving it.

"Okay. What do you want to do?" she asked coyly.

"Why don't you get Brad to drop you at mine and I'll cook? I have a place in the centre of *Leeds*…one of the converted warehouse apartments."

Wow, she thought, *those places are very swanky and not cheap.*

"Be there for eight?"

Trying her best to stay upright was a feat in itself, "Okay, I'll see you then. What should I bring?" She hoped her alcohol fuelled mind would remember.

"Just your very sexy self." He lifted her hand to his lips and smarmily kissed it. Mallory couldn't help but giggle at the gesture.

She finally crawled into the cab and Josie was glaring at her.

Mallory was a little befuddled and enquired as to her expression. "What's up with you and your sour face?" *Subtle, Mallory, very subtle.*

"Mallory, you are going for dinner with him. Do you think that's a good idea in your current state of mind?" Josie demanded, arms folded.

"I'm of perfectly mound sind, Josie-posie." She sniggered at her mix up. "I'm just a bit pissed, but I'll be sober tomorrow so stop worrying." That was the end of the subject. It felt good to have something new to think about.

When she woke the next day, Mallory's head throbbed from over indulgence. She managed to tame her wavy locks and bring her countenance back to something vaguely resembling human. She checked her phone and there was a text. *Oh Greg, for goodness sake.* She thought opening the message. It wasn't Greg. It was Dan.

Hey sexy. How's the head? Can't wait to get you alone, Dan x

Blimey, what was he expecting? She wondered feeling excited, but the text was also a little disconcerting. She decided to go into the shop again with Josie and do a little stocktaking. She was aware that her own items were becoming less of a feature in the shop and that needed to change.

The shop was busy again, much to Mallory's delight. Pride swelled in her as she heard the old fashioned cash register go *kerching*, time after time. The day went fast and before she knew it Mallory was showering ready for her date. When she got back to her room Josie was sitting on the bed.

"Hey Jose, what's up?" Mallory was surprised by the intrusion.

"I'm really worried about you going to Dan's tonight." She stated, her expression filled with concern and her eyebrows pulled together.

"Well, didn't you orchestrate our meeting?" Mallory smiled.

"Not exactly. Dan asked Brad if he could sit by you." Her worry visibly increased. "I wasn't happy about it at all."

"Aw, sweet." Mallory felt heat flush her cheeks.

"No…not sweet, Mally. Look, he has a reputation as a bit of a male tart. Just watch yourself. Don't go falling for him okay?"

"God, Josie, you make me out to be kind of serial inamorata!" Mallory scoffed. Feeling rather offended.

"Not at all. I just know how physically attractive he is and I know how extremely vulnerable you are. Just be careful."

"What, no condoms to hand over today then?" Mallory held out her hand, mockingly.

"Believe me, he has shares in every condom company there is," she retorted and left the room.

Brad dropped Mallory off at the flash, gated apartment complex at eight sharp. He didn't offer any words of wisdom. Just shook his head knowingly as Mallory stepped out of the car. She buzzed the button next to where it said 'Dan Camera.' Italian, figures. Her subconscious turned its nose up.

"Hey sexy, come on up." Somehow, in the cold light of day his *Yorkshire* accent didn't have the same appeal. He just sounded like any other guy she'd met in night clubs in her youth. She took the lift up to his floor. It was all very well presented.

He stood at his front door eagerly awaiting her arrival. She walked toward him. Black fitted dress and strappy sandals. She hadn't applied too much make-up just a little lip gloss, mascara and cheek highlighter. His eyes flashed greedily when he saw her. She smiled as he welcomed her inside.

The apartment was a little like a show home. White walls, black furniture, modern art on the walls. It was stunning. She couldn't figure out how he could afford this when he had only just been signed up by the Stags.

"Nice apartment, Dan." She offered, as her eyes took in every visible detail.

"Thanks. It's not mine just yet."

"Oh? Rented?" she asked nosily.

"Yeah, kind of. My dad bought it as an investment and so I pay him back as a kind of mortgage."

She raised her eyebrows. "Cool. Nice dad."

"Yeah, he's a stereotypical Italian male; outwardly emotional, loud, gregarious, family orientated. I think I'm more like my mum. She's from York. She's a little more reserved." He smiled. He seemed anything but reserved.

"Something smells good." She inhaled to take in more of the enticing aromas.

"Surprise, surprise, it's Italian." He shrugged, a little embarrassed at the obvious choice. "My mum was taught to cook by my nonni, my dad's mum. She passed her knowledge onto me." Impressive.

"So what are we having?" She went over to the black granite kitchen space. The splash backs were brushed stainless steel and there was every conceivable modern gadget installed.

"Well…for starter it's a simple Bruschetta Al Funghi, then for main I've made my speciality…Penne Al Salmone. It's delicious. And for dessert I'm afraid it's all out obvious, Tiramisu. I know most ladies like that." He winked. He wasn't wrong and boy he had gone to such a lot of effort.

Dan opened a bottle of Pinot Noir. "I bought this thinking maybe it was your favourite? You drank it at the restaurant."

Mallory nodded and took a sip. It was delicious but also reminded her of her hangover. She would have to seriously pace herself tonight.

The food was outstanding. Dan had made it all from scratch. Mallory was impressed and touched at the same time. Once they had dessert and coffee, Dan asked her to join him on the black leather couch. He sat very close to her, which made her a little shaky and fidgety. Her palms began to feel clammy too. Nice.

"I've been looking forward to this bit all night," he said leaning in to kiss her shoulder.

Whoa, he doesn't waste any time! His light kiss sent shivers down her spine.

She pulled away slightly feeling the heat rise in her cheeks, "Erm…thank you for a lovely meal." She felt a little uncomfortable at the way she was becoming turned on. She hardly knew him. What was with her lately?

"You're more than welcome. I think it may be time for a second dessert now." He slid nearer and mumbled against her neck. Shivers tingled again. She turned toward him to make a vain attempt at conversation, but instead he grabbed her head with his hand and plundered her mouth with his tongue.

She pulled back breathing heavily. "Dan, what are you doing?" She gasped.

"I told you, second dessert. Look don't worry, there are no strings attached here, I'm aware that you will be going home soon and so I have no expectations of this going further than tonight. Let's just enjoy each other and have some fun, eh?"

She leaned back. "Can't we just…you know…talk for a bit?"

He leaned in again and continued to nibble at her ear and neck. "Talk? Ah…been there…it's over rated…I prefer to fuck." His tone was harsh and unforgiving and he slid his hand up to her breast.

She pushed at his chest. "Dan, can you stop? Please? I don't want this."

He was strong and didn't budge.

"Of course you do. You definitely want me. I saw how you looked at me last night, like you could eat me alive." He chuckled as he fondled her.

She gasped for air in between his invasions of her mouth. "Dan…please…I was…drunk last night."

"Relax…take a chill pill…we both know what we want out of this," he continued groping and mauling at her.

Hang on a minute! She thought to herself. *What we want? This is what you want, you arrogant self-obsessed tool!*

He moved his hand down to the hem of her dress and slid it up her body, forcing himself into her mouth again. His tongue was deep and probing, making her gag. Like a crazed octopus his hands were all over. Not in the slightest bit sexy or romantic. In fact, a little bit scary as she was pinned to the couch by his huge, heavy torso. She felt nauseated. Her heart pounded and her mind raced thinking of a way to free herself from his grip. She couldn't scream or slap him. What the hell am I going to do?

Gathering her wits about her, she slid her hand down to his groin. He groaned in pleasure and then, suddenly, he cried out lurching up with an expression of agony and horror combined on his contorted face.

"You bitch!" he shouted holding his manhood where Mallory had just dug her nails in sharply.

"You've seen nothing yet, mate, now unless you let me out of here right now I will call the police and ruin your career. I said I didn't want this! Do you even understand what NO means?" she shouted at him, she widened her eyes at him as her chest heaved.

He snorted at her. "It was only a bit of fun. I cooked for you. You wanted this!"

"I wanted this? Are you kidding me? Oh I get it. You thought, *formerly overweight girl gets slim and now she'll sleep with anyone who'll give her a good meal?* Is that it? You bastard! Wait until I tell Brad. I think you'd better watch yourself. You may be a bloody giant, but he would absolutely flatten you if he knew what you'd tried to do!"

"Tried to do? What do you mean what I tried to do?"

"You know very well what I mean!" she yelled.

She grabbed her bag and made for the door, terrified he would try to stop her. Luckily, he was attending to his bruised manhood. She ran for the lift and hammered at the button, smoothing her crumpled dress down as she waited impatiently for it to arrive.

"You stupid, stupid idiot!" she shouted at herself in the lift. She rang Brad and asked him to come for her without explaining. Dutifully he arrived ten minutes later.

"Shit, Mallory are you okay? You look like you've been fighting."

She pulled down the vanity mirror and addressed her hair which was dishevelled and her lip gloss which was smeared across her face. She didn't speak.

When she got back to their house she explained what had happened. Josie was disgusted and Brad, steaming with anger, stormed out to his car and drove away, tyres screaming as he reached the end of the road. Neither woman tried to stop him as they knew that their attempts would be futile. It took a lot to get Brad angry, but if he thought someone he loved had been harmed in some way, hell the perpetrator had better watch out.

This was not how she had wanted things to turn out. She was shaking from the delayed shock of it all. Josie handed her a glass of neat Jack. She felt so stupid. What the hell did she think she was doing?

She sat with her elbows on her knees and her head in her hands. "This is so not like me," she told Josie who knew her the best. "Has Greg affected me so much that I go out and seek some kind of pathetic revenge on him by pulling some arrogant groping bastard? Not cool, Mallory, so not cool."

Josie's mouth was pulled into a straight line. "Hmm, love makes you do bloody crazy shit, Mally," she said before leaving the room.

When Brad returned his knuckles were red and grazed. It turned out that Dan was on his way out to go drinking in town after the incident with Mallory and Brad had caught him off guard. He was now sporting a broken nose. Brad had left him bleeding at the doors of A and E under the threat that if he reported Brad, Mallory would go to the police. Dan had believed him and agreed he'd been in the wrong.

Mallory decided that the next day would see her return to *Seil*. She concluded that perhaps she had given Greg a rougher ride than he deserved and maybe she should give him another chance at friendship…but nothing more. She couldn't risk getting her heart broken again so soon after losing Sam. It was silly to contemplate feelings for someone else so soon anyway, surely?

Her early start had meant that the return journey home was fairly straight forward. She took a brief break at the Green Welly stop and took Ruby for a quick walk. Grabbing a coffee and croissant to go she set off to home once again.

Walking through the door of the house felt good. It smelled fresh and she felt good about the jobs she had managed to do prior to her trip. This was the first time she walked in and felt at home fully; totally. She sighed in a mixture of melancholy sadness and hopeful happiness. She had serious thinking to do.

After taking a nap she headed on over to the pub. Greg was standing behind the bar. Alice was nowhere to be seen thankfully. She walked over and his eyes lit up when his gaze lifted to meet hers.

"Mallory, you're back." He sounded joyful, but then his expression changed. "How long are you here for?"

"I'm not sure Greg. Not yet. Can I speak to you in private please?" The pub was fairly quiet apart from Ron in his usual spot and Colin and Christine eating a meal. *Do they ever cook?* She smiled to herself. They all acknowledged Mallory with a wave and a smile.

"Is everything okay, Mallory?" he asked with a look of concern as they stepped outside.

"Greg, I've done a lot of thinking whilst I have been away." She made direct eye contact with him.

His eyes were like an open book today. Filled with mixed emotions.

He gave a sad smile. "I'm not going to like this am I?" He winced.

She smiled at him which seemed to relax him a little.

"I think maybe I was...too hard on you about the whole marriage thing. I don't feel able to be anything more at the moment and I doubt that I ever will now...but I think we can maybe be friends...If you want to?" she asked.

He looked very disappointed. "Mallory, I love you. I probably always will. It will be hard to just be friends, but I would rather have that than the icy chill between us." He stroked her arm, his chocolate brown eyes tinged with sadness.

She flinched. She didn't really want to be touched by anyone at that moment. The last few days were still raw in her mind. There was no way she could ever tell Greg about what had happened. He would totally freak out and go looking for Dan. Not a good idea. No, she would keep that quiet.

"Well, as I said, friendship is all I can offer." she reiterated. "Where's Alice?"

"She went home. She...wants to give things another go with me," he admitted.

Mallory snorted derisively. "I'm fully aware of that. Did she not tell you about our cosy little chat in the ladies that last time you played?" Greg's expression changed to one of anger, but Mallory continued. "She accused me of breaking your heart worse than she had and pretty much warned me off you."

Greg ran his hands through his hair. "Shit! Really? Is that why you went—"

"Ha! Greg, I won't be scared off by her or by anyone. I've become quite tough lately. I just needed a break. That's all," she said sternly.

"Okay. Well, I haven't made her any promises and I won't be doing so either."

Mallory raised her eyebrows at him. "Not that it's any of my business, but she told me you're thinking about getting back together with her."

"I'm thirty-eight, Mallory. I admit that I don't want to be alone forever, and I know now that I can't have the person that I want but…if I'm really honest with myself, I think I'd rather stick with being alone than go through another relationship with her. She's asked me to think about things and I said I would, just to appease her enough to make her leave, but deep down I think she knows It's a no-go—"

"Right, well as I say it's nothing to do with me, but I just think she would hurt you again and as my friend, that prospect doesn't sit right. But anyway, I…I'm glad we talked. Look, I'll be off now. I'm not staying for a drink. I just wanted to see you," she said brusquely backing away and turning to make her way home.

She felt annoyed that this reunion hadn't gone quite according to plan. She'd wanted to hug him, but felt that it would blur the already hazy lines between them.

She was shocked that Greg was even pretending to consider taking back that witch. If, God forbid, he did actually take her back she could no longer stay friends with

252 | L i s a   J .   H o b m a n

him, even though they had just reconnected. That cow was simply more than she could take.

Mallory was happy to be back at the pub that night. Greg would be there too as he was playing again. Stella had to ask him to increase his dates. He was being asked for on a regular basis. Mallory was so happy that it was working out for him.

She dressed in black trousers and a black fitted shirt for her shift. She pinned up her hair and went with glasses instead of contacts for a change. She chose red earrings, shoes and belt. Greg was there when she arrived. He smiled when he saw her. He was clutching a half empty whiskey glass.

She frowned. "I thought that stuff dried your vocal chords out," she teased him as she pulled herself a diet cola.

"Aye but I'm a tad nervous tonight. Some guy put a clip of me on the internet and this bloke from some entertainment agency is coming to see me play." He gulped down a large swig of the amber coloured liquid, clearly trying to quell a tumult of nerves in his gut.

"Wow, Greg. That's brilliant," Mallory gasped. "What will happen if he likes what he sees?"

"Ah…I won't be famous or anything quite so crazy, but it could mean I get gigs further afield. He has a list of places all over Highland that I could be booked for."

Suddenly a man and woman walked in. They were definitely not regulars. They were trying to emanate professionalism, but only succeeded in looking awkward and out of place in the country pub, wearing their suits and carrying files. Hmm, a bit OTT. Rather than entertainment agents they looked more like not-so-secret agents or debt collectors. They were trying too hard, Mallory surmised.

Following Mallory's glance Greg inhaled sharply. "Shit, that must be them." He took another gulp of his single malt. Shaking like a leaf he went over to introduce himself.

Mallory watched as the two smartly dressed agency reps chatted to Greg. She saw his anxiety gradually subside. She was relieved for him. The pub had become very busy and she was rushed off her feet at the bar as Greg started his first song.

"Evening all." His usual greeting fell casually from his lips. "Good to be here again and to see the place packed. I'm sure Stella is grateful and I know I am." The appreciative rumble traversed the room as usual. "I'd like to start tonight off with a dedication to someone. They know who they are. The words have to be said and I can think of no better way to say them…It's a song by a band who you may think obscure for a week night in a village pub, but the sentiment is important. It's by a band called Incubus and it's called *Dig*.

Mallory looked over and sure enough his gaze locked on to hers.

The song was beautiful and talked of friendship, forgiveness and being there for each other. Mallory found her arms covered in goose bumps as the words touched her deeply. Greg's voice never ceased to amaze her, hitting every note with precise perfection. Her heart swelled and she smiled despite the tears that stung the backs of her eyes. He reciprocated her smile and all felt good. She was beginning to love that about Greg. He could always find the perfect song to express his feelings.

At the end of the night Greg chatted with the reps again. He looked happy and relieved. There was a lot of handshaking, smiling and nodding.

Mallory waited until they had gone before excitement got the better of her and she made her way over to where he was putting his beloved guitar away.

"Well?" She waved her hands at him eagerly awaiting his response.

"They've taken me on!" He grabbed her and hugged her before she had a chance to protest. It felt good to be hugged by him again.

She hugged him back without reserve. "I'm so happy for you, Greg. How amazing." She was proud of her friend. It felt good to call him her friend again.

"Look, I've something to ask you. Feel free to say no if it's too soon to socialise with me again but…I'm going to an open mic night at the beginning of October in *Oban* and I wondered if you'd like to come along? I've been before and there are some great performers on. What's even better is that you can get up and do something if the mood takes you." He smiled.

She loved the sound of that and she had missed spending time with him "I think I can safely say I'll be there." She smiled. He hugged her again.

~~~~~

Things had settled down well for Mallory and Greg. They were back to joking and laughing again. Every so often there would be a tricky moment where he looked at her in the way that meant he still loved her, but she managed to rein her emotions in.

The first weekend in October was rainy. There had been two couples to view her house but she hadn't received any offers. She was quite relieved. Friday, the seventh was just as wet a day as the rest of the week. Greg picked her up and they set off for *Oban* at seven for the open mic night. Greg was like a kid on Christmas Eve.

"So Mallory, have you ever been musical at all?" Greg enquired as they chugged along in the Landy.

Hesitantly she admitted, "Well…actually I used to sing in choir back in *Yorkshire* a few years back."

"Really?" After doing a double take a wry grin appeared on his face "What happened? Why'd you stop?"

"I had a couple of solos and really enjoyed it, especially when I was asked to sing '*Martha's Harbour*' by All About Eve…I love that song…but then the conductor changed and it all went downhill."

"Soooo, you're a singer then?" He wiggled his eyebrows at her.

"Not for a long time and don't be getting any ideas." She poked him.

He feigned shock. "Me? I don't know what you mean."

The sky was heavy and dark as they drove the journey to the club. The place was alive with excitement and effervescence when they arrived. They got a drink from the bar and listened to the young man who was on stage performing a cover of '*Yellow*' by Coldplay, accompanied by his guitar. He was really good.

They listened to a few more artistes. One of which was a girl with long red hair and green eyes who must have been in her late-twenties. Greg was transfixed on her as she sang a beautiful rendition of '*Somewhere Over the Rainbow*' Eva Cassidy style. Mallory watched Greg as tears welled in his eyes. She realised from his description and from photos she had seen, that the girl bore a striking resemblance to Mairi.

Mallory squeezed his arm and he looked down at her. He shook his head as if he realised he had been staring. He told her he was going to the men's room and disappeared. He was gone quite a while and Mallory was wondering if he was okay.

When he eventually returned he grabbed Mallory's arm and pulled her with him toward the stage. "You know you sang '*Martha's Harbour*' in your choir that time?" he whispered.

Mallory scrunched her nose as she looked up at him. "Yes, yes of course I remember. We were just talking about it." Her mouth fell open and she shook her head beginning to panic. *What has he done?*

"Aye well, I hope you remember the words, coz you're just about to sing it live on stage. It just so happened it's one of my favourites and I know it like the back of my hand." He grinned.

She gasped and pulled against him. "You must be mad! There's no way I'm—"

"Ladies, gentleman it's time for a duet now. Next up this evening we have Greg McBradden and Mallory Westerman performing '*Martha's Harbour*'."

There was a rumble of applause and whistles. Mallory looked at the crowd and realised with horror that she was already on the stage. Unsure as to how she got there she sat on the stool next to Greg as he began to play the opening chords to the haunting melody. He nodded and winked at her. Her mouth felt dry. She closed her eyes and took a deep breath. *Never expected to be doing this tonight.* Somehow she managed to come in at the right time and the beautiful lyrics came flooding back to her.

She kept her eyes closed as she sang. A strange feeling washed over her. It was a sense of calm at the lilting guitar and how well Greg played the piece, but also at her inhibitions melting away. When the song finished there was a rousing, raucous applause which took Mallory by surprise. She looked over at Greg who was grinning from ear to ear and glowing with pride. His eyes looked glassy and he was applauding her too. She felt amazing.

When they had climbed down from the stage, Greg put his guitar down and scooped Mallory up in a bear hug. He kissed her head and both cheeks. She looked up into his sparkling, intense brown eyes and for a moment she was lost. He leaned down close to her face and kissed her chastely on the lips, never taking his eyes off hers.

Her heart was pounding and they were so close she felt sure he could feel it. She desperately wanted to kiss him back but shook her head and looked away. He seemed to have got the point and released his grip on her.

He cleared his throat. "You were amazing up there, do you know that?" he said running his hands through his hair as if to occupy them somehow. "You're a bloody good singer. You've been holding out on me you sod." He laughed.

"I have to admit it felt pretty amazing too.'" She smiled, her heart rate was still galloping, but the adrenaline that had been coursing through her veins was beginning to calm.

Greg got up and did a few more numbers throughout the night. He was wonderful.

Mallory was beginning to feel confused about her feelings again. The pounding of her heart wasn't just down to the rush of being on stage and she knew it. The fact it skipped a beat or two when he was so close was playing on her mind. He made eye contact with her periodically throughout his songs, making heat rise in her face. He did a rendition of Buzzcock's *'Ever Fallen in Love'* and winked at her whilst he sang. The temperature of her cheeks soared yet again.

During the journey home Greg attempted to make small talk, but as always he was better at communicating through song so the conversation melted into an awkward silence. They parked outside her house. He turned off the engine and swivelled in his seat to face her.

"Thank you for a wonderful night." He smiled warmly

"Thank you for making me confront my fears. I loved singing tonight."

"We'll have to do it again soon, eh?" he suggested hopefully.

"Hmmm, we'll see about that." She wasn't sure if she wanted it to become a habit considering how nervous she had been.

Greg looked at her intently. "Can I ask you something, Mallory?" He reached for her hand.

"I'm not sure that's a good idea." She broke away from his gaze and pulled her hand away.

"Mallory, I'm going to ask anyway. I think I'll be able to tell the real answer by your body language."

She turned to him again trying to plead with her eyes. "Greg, don't, okay? We've had a lovely evening please don't spoil it."

"Mallory, can you look me in the eye and tell me honestly that you don't want to be more than friends?" His gaze was intense and filled with emotion.

She sighed. "Greg, you lied about being married. It doesn't matter how I feel. You broke the trust we had. It will take a long time to get that back. I would always be wondering if there was more to come." Her heart rate increased again and she felt the familiar sting of tears behind her eyes. Why couldn't she keep her emotions in check around him?

His eyes became glassy again and his voice strained, "Mallory, I don't love her. I still love you. It's always been you; since we first met." He took her hand in his again. "I know you feel something for me. I know you do. Why deny it?"

She tried hard to be annoyed, but it was so hard when he looked at her that way. "Greg, stop. I'm not going there again. It doesn't matter how I feel."

"Just let me kiss you. It'll all melt away; all your doubt." He leaned toward her and slipped his hand into her hair.

A betraying tear escaped her eye. "I can't," she whispered. She removed her hand from his grasp, pulled herself away and climbed out of the car, closing the door behind her.

The following day she had a second viewing on the cottage from one of the couples who had seen it. Having them in the house made her feel uneasy. Her mind raced with a million different conflicting thoughts. Could she let go? Was it right to leave? The young couple walked around making very positive noises. They were first time buyers. Mallory knew that if they offered, there would be another massive, continental shift in her life. Was she ready? She wasn't sure.

~~~~~

Greg was friendly at the pub and as time went on, but he seemed to become more resigned to how things were between them. Mallory's heart broke a little each time she saw him, but felt that at least things would be more straightforward. Greg's song choices became more generic and Mallory simply stopped looking for the hidden meanings and messages that he used to send in the hope that her heart would change. He even stopped making eye contact with her when he sang. A line had been drawn in the sand. It was over…for good.

Greg had started to play at a variety of other venues following being signed up to the entertainment agency 'Class Act Talent'. His bar work at the pub became less and less.

Mallory missed him. When she did see him he regaled her with tales of the other venues. It sounded like he was having fun. Mallory chatted with enthusiasm and suggested songs for his set list. He was attracting a lot of attention from the opposite sex too. Women were slipping him their numbers on a regular basis. But why wouldn't they? He was, after all gorgeous.

"Aye, they loved me over by *Fort William*. I got handed three phone numbers! Can you believe these women? It's like I'm some celebrity. I still can't believe it." He laughed, shaking his head as they washed glasses at the end of one shift.

"Well, you must be doing something right." Mallory tried to sound happy despite the ache in her chest.

"I just feel like a piece of meat." He joked dramatically. "They only want me for my body. Never mind my talent." He played the camp act well, making Mallory giggle.

"You should be so lucky." She flicked him with a towel.

"You'll have to come along with me to one of the other places sometime."

She forced a laugh. "What? To watch women fawn all over you? No thanks."

Greg shrugged. "Your loss," he simply stated and walked out the back.

~~~~~

One night late in October came the inevitable and dreaded news that he had met a woman he liked very much. Mallory's heart broke a little more. The woman was called Kate and she was a curvy brunette—which made it worse. She was the daughter of one of the venue owners and was training to be a nurse. He hadn't taken her out yet, but was considering asking. Mallory listened to his excitement as he told her all about Kate and her heart sank. She kept reminding herself that she and Greg could have no future. The fact remained that he was married. If Kate was okay with that then more fool her. Or perhaps he was stringing her along too?

"She's really nice. I really like her. I just don't know whether I should take the plunge, you know?" he spoke, but not really to Mallory.

"Well, maybe you should just go for it," she offered without enthusiasm or emotion.

Scratching his beard he thought for a moment. "Aye, maybe I will…"

~~~~~

From that night, Mallory visited *Yorkshire* at every given opportunity. Josie and Brad were starting to see more of her than Greg did. She tried her best to be convivial, but Brad and Josie knew she was just going through the motions.

She covered in the shop a few times and enjoyed being back on the frontline again. She caught the train in just because she could. It was like old times and it felt comfortable.

On one of her journeys back to Josie and Brad's she got chatting to an elderly lady, quite out of the blue. The lady had enquired as to her marital status, as old folks tend to and when the train had broken down due to an engine fault, she had found herself telling this complete stranger all about Sam and Greg. It felt good to talk to someone who just listened without preconceived ideas and without prejudice. The lady, who introduced herself as Edith, spoke candidly, reminding her of her Aunt Sylvia.

"You know, my dear, in the war things were tough. I was very young, but I loved my husband to be so dearly. He was called Geoffrey. He was such a handsome fellow. He was a bit older than me. I couldn't wait to be his wife. But then he was called up to serve his country and my heart broke. He was killed in action the first week out. I couldn't believe it. I never thought I would ever love anyone again. But it just goes to show that love doesn't follow strict timings."

"What goes to show, Edith? What happened?" Mallory asked enthusiastically.

"Well, there were all these 'yanks' as we called them. Stanley was one of the 'over- paid and over here' lot." Edith chuckled at her memory. "He was handsome, sure enough. But I was grieving for my Geoffrey. The trouble was, Stanley fell head over heels for me and was determined to make me do the same."

"What did he do?" Mallory was intrigued by the romance of the story.

"Oh…he gave me extra rations for my family…he brought me silk stockings and chocolate when they were virtually impossible to get hold of…he picked flowers for me." She smiled fondly. "He was a true gentleman and slowly but surely I realised that life is too short to look backward. I was never going to get Geoffrey back, but I had a chance at happiness again." She looked directly at Mallory "If you love someone enough, it doesn't matter what anyone else thinks, dear. It doesn't matter what is in his past. If he truly loves you and no one else and you know that deep in your heart…well, I wouldn't be sitting on a broken down train chatting to some daft old biddy." She squeezed Mallory's hand and Mallory immediately realised that the story had come back to her and Greg.

Mallory's eyes stung. "But…his wife…he lied."

The old lady took a deep breath. "Now dear, I think seeing as I don't know you, I can be brutally honest. The wife he has is what you youngsters these days call 'emotional baggage'. He doesn't love her. It sounds to me like he doesn't even think about her long enough for her to become a concern for him and that's why she never came up in conversation. What you need to decide is whether you are prepared to accept that?"

The train jolted into life again and Mallory sat back, open mouthed at the clarity that Edith had brought to her situation. The train pulled into the next station and Edith rose to alight the carriage.

"Edith!" Mallory was shaken from her thoughts. "What happened…to you and Stanley I mean? Did you get your happy ever after?" Mallory was desperate to know.

Edith smiled warmly. "Dear, we were married for fifty four years, blissfully happy until I lost him to the dreaded cancer." She shook her head. "I never regretted a single moment of 'rushing into it' with him, dear. He was wonderful. Now see that you don't miss that chance at happiness. Take care." And with that, Edith was gone like a fairy godmother.

~~~~~

"I'm going to get a tattoo." Mallory announced the next morning over bacon sandwiches.

Josie nearly choked and Brad burst out laughing, spraying soggy bread and tea everywhere.

"You're what?" Josie spluttered trying not to join Brad in fits of hysterical laughter.

"Yes…I'm going to have it done on the small of my back."

"What are you going to have done? Donald Duck?" Josie mocked, making Mallory even more determined.

Brad slapped his thigh. "Or…or a big arrow pointing downwards that says 'kick here'" He howled with laughter and rolled backward on the sofa.

Mallory bristled at his reaction. "I have a design that I've picked and I have an appointment at noon. My mind is made up."

Brad's brow furrowed. "Why?" He asked. And he followed the question up quickly with "You do know they hurt like hell don't you?"

Josie's laughter stopped. "You're serious aren't you? What on earth has possessed you to make such a decision, Mally? It's permanent you know…once it's done it's there for life."

Mallory didn't speak. She simply carried on chewing her sandwich.

"I'm not sure this is the best idea you've had, Mally." Josie sighed. "Do you want me to come with you?"

A grin spread across Mallory's face.

Mallory arrived at the tattoo parlour and was greeted by a large inked up man with lip and eyebrow piercings and a shaved head. He looked like someone she would normally shy away from, but it turned out that looks were most definitely deceiving as he was a really nice and quite well spoken man. He put her at ease immediately and introduced himself simply as 'Stubbs'. She showed him the design and he said it would take about an hour and a half to complete.

"Are you having it done for a special occasion?" Stubbs asked as Mallory lay on her stomach with her trousers low around her bottom.

"I need to remind myself of a few things and I think this will do the trick." She informed him.

"Well it certainly will for the next few days." He chuckled. The buzzing began and Mallory gritted her teeth.

~~~~~

She arrived back in *Scotland* just in time for the Halloween bash at the pub. Stella had texted and asked her to come in and help decorate the place with accessories for the party and she had cordially agreed to do so. She was so excited. She had done a lot of thinking about things whilst she was away, thanks to Edith and of course there was her tattoo. She was looking forward to seeing Greg.

Before going to the pub she had something important to do. She had phoned and made an appointment the day before to see a little shop in *Easdale* just up the road from home. *Easdale*, with its whitewashed one story buildings, had a nice community feel with restaurants and little shops where *Le Petit Cadeau* would fit in very well.

She had visited it with Sam when they were on holiday and they had chatted about how nice it would be to, one day, rent one of the little shops there. The place she viewed had been perfect. The amount of space had been just right and the owner had welcomed her interest. He had given her some figures to look through and she was going to peruse them to see if it could work out running the two shops concurrently. It was an exciting prospect. She couldn't wait to tell Greg. After the viewing and a look around the other shops in the small retail area she had set off for the pub with butterflies doing the Highland fling in her stomach.

When she arrived at the pub he was there. She grinned like a Cheshire cat when she saw him and had to restrain herself from running into his arms. She was about to shout a greeting to him where he stood behind the bar pinning up streamers. But before she had a chance to speak and much to her dismay, a pretty dark haired woman, presumably Kate, walked in from the back and slid her arms around him. Mallory's heart sank. *Oh. Ship = sailed.* Her subconscious mocked her. Her tattoo rubbed against her jeans.

Later on Greg made introductions and Kate seemed very nice, but a little cagey around her. Mallory had no clue why. She tried hard to be cordial, but found it tricky considering that Kate kept on making romantic gestures toward Greg in Mallory's direct eye line. She was like a cat marking her territory. *Cringe-worthy*, Mallory thought. Greg looked uncomfortable.

Between them they blew up enough balloons to almost make the pub take flight. The streamers were strings of orange pumpkins and black bats cut out of shiny plastic. They placed carved pumpkins complete with tea lights all around the place. It looked fantastic. Mallory was looking forward to the party. The staff was dressing up in costume for the occasion and Greg, aka Dracula, was performing a secret list of songs for the occasion.

Chapter Twelve

On the Sunday night of October thirtieth, Mallory pulled on black tight jeans over a fitted black all in one T-shirt body. She tied her wavy brown locks in a high pony tail and donned contact lenses and an eye mask. She drew on fake whiskers with eye pencil and attached a tail to her jeans that she had made out of a fluffy black scarf. She looked in the mirror. *It'll do*, she thought.

She'd had to buy new jeans whilst she was in *Yorkshire* as it appeared her curves were returning. She could've felt down about that, but she reminded herself of Josie's words 'Men LOVE curves!' So she felt comfortable in her changing shape and happy in the knowledge that when the next Mr. Right came along, he would love her for *her* just as Sam had.

She wrapped a warm coat around her and headed for the spooky pub. Greg was there in his Dracula costume. She hated to admit it, but he made rather a sexy vampire. Kate came through from the back carrying a tray of sandwiches to pass around. She was dressed as Morticia from the Addams family. Mallory smiled and said hello. Greg swung around when he heard her voice and Mallory saw him do a double take. His eyes widened as he scanned her body. Mallory couldn't help smiling to herself.

Greg took to the stage at eight and the atmosphere was electric. Many of the customers had dressed up in costume. Colin had a fake axe attached to his head so that it looked like it was embedded in his skull. Mallory thought it was hilarious. Ron had even joined in, dressing in a suit and a very tall hat. When asked what he was dressed as, he indignantly informed people that he was an undertaker and couldn't seem to understand why this wasn't blatantly obvious.

Stella had painted her face white, back combed her hair and made herself up as a zombie; Christine was a mad scientist in a white lab coat covered in fake blood. Frankenstein was there, along with a giant pumpkin, a werewolf and several vampires, amongst many other ghoulish guests. Everyone was having a brilliant time.

Greg kicked off with *'The Monster Mash'* and managed to somehow to follow that with an acoustic rendition of *'Thriller'*. The tone changed slightly, however, when he announced his next song.

"Now I know this isn't a high school disco, but I have to say that all these decorations are taking me back. I think, in true high school disco fashion, maybes we'll have a smoochy number. So if you're here with a loved one, grab them and give 'em a cuddle. This one is dedicated to all those who are lucky enough to be in love." He smiled and briefly looked at Mallory for the first time in a long time whilst he was performing. As he looked away he announced, "This one is by The Calling and it's a lovely song called *'Wherever You Will Go'*."

People in the pub paired off and smooched in the small space. Greg's rich voice sounded gravelly and filled with emotion as he sang the beautiful lyrics. He hadn't done this in quite a while. She wondered if she was being conceited. Maybe the song was for Kate. She looked over to where Kate was sitting only to find her gone. She looked over to Greg who was now singing with his eyes closed, oblivious to the absence of his girlfriend. Mallory felt unable to move as the tears pooled in her eyes and she listened to Greg, hoping that the message in the song *was* meant for her.

As the song was finishing, Mallory's thoughts transferred to Kate. She had been there at the end of the previous song so where was she? Wiping her eyes, Mallory decided to go outside and check. She clambered through the freakish, smooching couples and made it out into the chilled October evening. Kate was sitting, shivering on one of the seats outside. She was crying. Her make-up was now streaked down her face. Mallory immediately felt sorry for her.

Making her approach Mallory asked the sobbing woman, "Kate? Is everything okay?"

"No. Everything is most certainly *not* okay. I'm an idiot!" she blurted out.

Mallory twisted her hands together. "Mind if I ask what's wrong?"

"*You* really need to ask that?" Kate scoffed.

Feeling affronted by the unspoken accusation she asked, "Have *I* done something, Kate?"

"He won't let go of you will he? He *still* thinks there's a chance. I was willing to get passed the marriage thing until it's dealt with but, oh no, *Mallory* can't be replaced."

"Kate…I'm sorry but Greg and I are not…together. We're friends but that's all. He is with you now and I won't stand in your way." She swallowed the lump that had appeared in her throat as she spoke the painful words.

"Well don't waste your time helping *me*. He lives in hope that someday you will forgive him. He told me tonight that he can't see me anymore. That it's unfair whilst he still loves you."

Mallory's heart skipped a beat. "Oh, Kate, I'm so sorry. Really I am. I did have feelings for him. But…Look you should come inside and I will call a taxi for you…if you like." She offered.

"Thanks. I'd appreciate that…but I'll wait here." Her resolve appeared to be set firm.

Mallory went inside and called a taxi for the broken hearted woman. She waited near the door to make sure that Kate was alright. The taxi turned up ten minutes later.

Before making her getaway Kate looked over to Mallory. "You know, I don't know you so I can't pass comment on you as a person, but I think I know Greg well enough now. He's such a wonderful, caring man and he clearly adores you. You'd be silly to let him go over a piece of paper that means absolutely nothing to him. If I were you I'd be getting back in there and telling him how I felt. And if you say you feel nothing then you're kidding yourself girl." She climbed in the taxi and it pulled away.

At the end of the night Greg was surrounded by his groupies. Mallory watched in amusement as the cell phones came out one by one and they all took photos of their friends with the minor celebrity. She resolved that she would give him a little space after what had happened with Kate and that she would speak to him over the next couple of days and see how things went.

She waved goodnight as Greg was packing his gear away and she headed for home. She felt a tingle of anticipation about what could potentially be the start of something official if Greg still wanted her. She would have to wait and see.

Monday morning was very cold. She had decided to spend a day in the workshop getting some stock made up for the shop in *Leeds* and the potential new place she had seen up the road at *Easdale*. She received a phone call from the estate agent. The young couple who had viewed her property twice had made an offer. Mallory was shocked and didn't quite know what to say. She had almost forgotten about the house being for sale as nothing had really happened in a while. She asked if she could take some time to think about it which had annoyed the agent. She would need to think; and a lot was riding on speaking to Greg.

She had a very productive day in the workshop and produced some lovely new designs that she knew Josie would be happy with. It felt good to be creating again. She had listened again to the beautiful CD that Greg had made her with heartfelt songs on and mentally made a list of songs she could put on a CD for him. She thought back to her conversation with Edith on the train and wondered if there was a song called 'I've been a silly cow can you forgive me now?' *Maybe I should write one!* She laughed to herself.

She knew she had a shift with Greg on Tuesday night. It was November already. She mused, shocked at how quickly the last seven months had passed. She decided she would dress up nicely and invite him round for a nightcap after work. She had planned some of the things she wanted to say, but was concerned it was all sounding a little contrived and so she had decided to say whatever came to her when he was here. She hoped he still felt the same. Kate seemed to think so.

November 2011

On Tuesday night the weather was atrocious. The worst she had experienced since moving here. *Bang goes dressing up nice!* She thought to herself, feeling rather disappointed. She had showered and heard the rumbling thunder as the water cascaded over her body. She hated storms. When it was time to go to work she wrapped up warm and pulled on her big waterproof jacket. She checked her watch after messing around trying to ensure that her hair would stay dry and realised it was seven already which meant she was late.

She opened the front door just as the lightening lit up the sky as if it was daylight; making her jump almost out of her skin. She pulled the door closed and locked it behind her. There seemed to be an awful lot of people hanging around which was really odd in this weather she thought. She trudged over to the pub, head down against the rain. The pub was heaving when she got inside. But no one seemed to be drinking and there was an eerie hush around the place. It was then that she noticed the two police officers.

Stella pushed through the crowd of people toward her. "Oh Mallory thank goodness! We weren't sure if you'd gone with him!" She hugged Mallory hard. "Colin banged on your door, but you didn't answer."

Mallory was puzzled. "Gone with whom? What's going on, Stella?" She could feel the panic rising inside her.

"Greg…Didn't you know?" Mallory felt a strange ringing in her ears and everything began to spin. Stella's words sounded muffled, but she made out odd words. "Boys in a dinghy…out sailing…got into trouble…Greg went out…little blue…Mallory!" Everything went black.

When Mallory came to and opened her eyes, Stella and Ron were hovering over her. Someone was pressing something to her head. It hurt. Everything echoed. She blinked her eyes open.

"She's waking up, Ron." a familiar female voice said.

"Stay still Mallory. Just let's make sure you've no neck injury." That was not a familiar voice. She glanced in its direction and a man in a bright fluorescent yellow and green coat was looking down at her. He was the one pressing something to her head.

"What happened? What's…what's going on?" Mallory tried to sit but she was held down. The room was spinning.

"Don't move, love, you'll be fine we just need to stop the bleeding and check you over in case of concussion." The man said.

Mallory began to panic again, "What? Why? What's going on?"

"Oh, sweetheart, you blacked out. You hit your head so it's bleeding a little."

"Aye but the table's fine so don't worry." Ron chuckled trying to lighten the mood.

"Ron! Not the time or place!" Stella snapped. "Sweetheart, Greg hasn't been found yet." Stella informed her.

"Found? What do you mean? Will someone please tell me what's going on?" She shouted, getting angry.

The Paramedic helped her to a sitting position and checked her eyes with a little torch.

He examined the back of her head. "You won't need stitches, I've dressed the wound you'll be fine, but you must take it easy, okay?" He demanded as he ensured the gauze was firmly in place, making Mallory wince.

"Yes fine. Thank you…Stella?" She pleaded.

"Mallory, please don't black out again…There was a terrible incident. The Carrick boys, you know, Tom and James? They were out fishing in their dinghy when the weather turned for the worse. They managed to ring their dad from Tom's mobile and Greg was with him, fixing their kitchen sink, when they got through. They contacted the coastguard but Greg took Little Blue out to try and reach them. That was two hours ago and the wind has really picked up and now with the storm…The Coastguard is out there now."

"Oh my God no!" Mallory pushed the paramedic away, clambered to her feet and bolted for the door. She was dizzy but she ran and ran to the marina where Little Blue was usually moored. *This can't be happening, not again. Please no.*

Colin came out after her. "Mallory, love, the Coastguard is doing all they can, please come inside. You'll freeze out here especially with you being in shock." He put his arm around her shoulder. "You won't help anybody by getting yourself ill, hen."

She knew he was right. Her legs were like lead as she walked; propped up by Colin, back to the pub.

An hour later they were told that the boys had been found. A mumble of relief shuddered around the room. There were tears of joy at the news that, although they were in severe shock, they had only suffered minor injuries. There was, however, no report on Greg. They sat in the pub for hours, waiting.

Mallory was horrified when the news came in that parts of Little Blue had been found, but there was still no sign of Greg. Her heart was breaking all over again. She couldn't bear the thought of Greg being hurt or worse still being found dead. She cried out in physical agony at the terrible thought of losing him; tears relentlessly pouring from her clenched eyes. Ron, Colin, Christine and Stella fussed around her as her body shook uncontrollably and her anguish poured out.

The pub telephone rang at eleven o'clock. Stella ran to answer it. Her colour drained and her hand came up to her mouth as she sobbed. *That's it, he's gone too.* Mallory's subconscious concluded.

Stella spoke to Colin in low murmurs. They both came over to where Mallory sat. Colin sat beside her and took her hand.

"Mallory, you need to come with me. I need to take you to the hospital in *Oban*."

Mallory began to shake her head frantically and recoil in her seat as if gripped by absolute terror. "No! Please no! Please don't make me be the one to identify his body! Please! I can't do that again! I can't do it! Please?" She was almost hysterical, remembering what she had gone through after Sam's accident. Colin took a firm grip of her shoulders.

"Mallory, stop! Please calm yourself and listen to what I have to say!" His voice was firm, forceful and quite loud. She had never heard him raise his voice before, it grabbed her attention. When he could see that she had calmed down, he spoke again, softer this time. "Greg was pulled out of the water an hour ago. He is in a critical condition, but he is asking for you. I would like to take you to him."

Mallory let out a strange, convulsive grunt of relief as what Colin had said sunk in. She threw her arms around him. "Thank you, Colin, Thank you, let's go. I want to see him."

Ron and Colin helped Mallory to her feet and toward the door. Colin went ahead to bring the car over to the pub. The rain had slowed and the storm had calmed.

"I have your spare key. I'll go over and check up on Ruby for you," Ron reassured her.

"Oh no! Angus!" Mallory was terrified that he had gone out with Greg.

"Don't worry, hen, he's at Greg's. Stella has a key and she's going over there to bring him to the pub now that the weather is calmer." Mallory breathed a sigh of relief and turned her concentration to thoughts of Greg as she mentally prepared herself for what she may see.

Colin pulled up in the car and Ron helped Mallory into the passenger seat. Her head was throbbing, but she didn't care. She just wanted to get to the hospital. Eventually Colin parked the car and they made their way into the hospital to the reception desk. They were pointed to intensive care. Mallory almost ran to get there and Colin followed close behind.

They buzzed on the door and were let in by a nurse. They explained who they were and after initially being told it was family only, Colin had convinced the nurse that Mallory had been asked for by the patient. Reluctantly, and after protest, she let Mallory in alone. She was shown to a side room.

Mallory's eyes were assaulted by a vision of a bruised and swollen man she hardly recognised. She let out a sob when she saw that he was laid out on the bed surrounded by machines; tubes going in and coming out of him; an oxygen mask over his battered face. It was a truly horrific sight.

She walked slowly over to his bedside. His eyes were barely visible under all the swelling, his head was bandaged and his ribs were strapped up. She sat on the chair at the side of the bed and held his hand.

A nurse walked in to check on the machines that bleeped and flashed myriad numbers and letters.

She smiled at Mallory kindly. "Are you Mallory?" She asked in a soft Scottish accent.

"Yes," Mallory whispered.

The nurse smiled. "Good, he's been asking for you repeatedly. He keeps drifting in and out of consciousness so you'll have to bear with him. He is heavily sedated due to his injuries and the tests we've had to do, but talk to him. He can hear you. It'll help him very much to know that you came." She patted Mallory's shoulder and left the room.

"Greg, it's me, Mallory." She let out another sob, "I want you to open your eyes for me and talk to me. I need to know you're okay." She stroked his hand. He didn't respond.

"Greg, I want you to know that I'm sorry for how I reacted when you told me about Alice. You said you don't love her and I should've accepted that. It doesn't matter that you are still married if you don't love her. It's just a piece of paper that can be dealt with…You said you love me. I should have just been happy and now I'm scared I'm going to lose you, too. You need to get better, Greg. You need to come home." Still nothing.

She stroked his hair where it poked out of the top of the bandaging. "It's strange how it's taken something like this to kick me up the arse and make me realise exactly how I feel. I was intent on talking things through with you tonight to see if we could get past what happened between us. But when I found out that you had gone missing I thought through everything we've been through. The arguments, the kisses, the laughs. And it dawned on me. Nothing else matters.

"The thing that matters most is that I love you, Greg." Her face was wet with tears. "Greg, can you hear me?" She squeezed his hand. "Greg, I'm in love with you. Please don't leave me. I'm stupid and I'm stubborn and self-righteous. I judged you and made assumptions about you and I was so, so wrong. You told me exactly how you felt and I threw it back in your face. And now I realise that I love you and don't want to be without you. It doesn't matter how soon this has happened. It's no one's fault. It doesn't make it wrong. Please just wake up and tell me you still love me." She sobbed. She sat just holding his hand for a while staring at his unresponsive face. Then she stared at the rain drizzling down the window mirroring her tears.

After what felt like hours she felt Greg squeeze her hand. She looked up at him. His eyes had opened a little and he squinted at her.

He lifted his free hand and removed the mask from his face. "Hey, Mally." He smiled, his words slurring as he spoke. "You came."

She squeezed his hand in return. "Of course I came, Greg." She laughed through her tears.

"It's good to see you…Oh, no, please don't cry. I'm always making you cry," he croaked.

She kissed his hand. "Oh Greg, no, I'm fine…It's so good to see you."

Greg's eyes widened, filled with dread and fear. "The Carrick boys…Tom and James…are they okay?"

"They're fine, please don't worry. Just shocked and a little bruised, that's all."

"Oh thank God." He closed his eyes and puffed out a long breath, relieved at the good news. After a pause in which confusion washed over his face he squeezed her hand. "I had a dream earlier." He smiled as he watched her. "It was such a good dream…but…I think you woke me from it." His brow furrowed again as he seemed to be trying to make sense of things.

"Oh, I'm so sorry Greg. I just wanted to hear your voice and see your eyes open again."

"The dream was strange. You were in it, crying and stroking my hair…and you told me you were in love with me and it made me so happy." A tear escaped and trailed down his cheek soaking into the bandages on his head as he closed his eyes. "But then I woke up." His lip quivered and her heart felt like it would rupture. The hand that had pulled his mask off now covered his eyes as his raw emotions broke free. He shuddered and sobbed with a deep, deep sadness.

"Greg, look at me, open your eyes, please," she begged him fighting back her own tears.

He lifted his hand to halt her. "I'm sorry, I know all that's gone now, I ruined it after Alice and Kate…I'm so sorry. I blew it. I always mess everything up," he struggled to form the words as he fought against his sedation.

"Greg, look at me please." He opened his eyes again as best he could and looked at her. "Greg it wasn't a dream. I said and did those things. I stroked your hair and squeezed your hand. And…and I told you I'm in love with you and that I never want to be without you again." Her tears cascaded down her already damp face.

His brow furrowed and his eyes closed briefly. When he opened them again his gaze was intense. "You did? You love me?" His voice wavered as he searched her expression.

"I love you. Greg, I want to be with you, always." She leaned down and kissed his cut lips gently. "Do you still…want me though Greg?"

His lips curled upward. "Do you really need to ask me that?"

She blew out a long relieved breath. "That's so good to hear." She stroked his hair. "Now please get well so we can get you out of here and decide where the heck I'm going to live…seeing as I think I may have sold my house." She kissed him again.

His hand came up to touch her hair. "Mallory?"

"Yes Greg?"

"I love you. More than anything in this world."

Somehow, Mallory had managed to convince the nurses to 'forget' she was there, she had told Colin to go home. She slept in Greg's room in a rather hard and unforgiving chair with a single blanket for warmth. She was as uncomfortable as hell, but she didn't care. In the night she was woken by Greg shouting out.

"NO! No, please! No! Mallory?" Mallory stood and went to his side immediately.

She took his hand, "Shhhh, Greg, shhhhh, it's okay, I'm here."

His eyes snapped open. His breathing was shallow and ragged. "Mallory? You'd gone. You left me. Was it all a dream that you loved me?" He grabbed onto her hand as tightly as he could.

She kissed his furrowed brow. "No, Greg, I'm not going anywhere, I'm here to stay." He calmed and drifted back off to sleep. He kept his grip on her hand and she had to drag the chair over to his bedside and rest her head on the bed near his hip.

When she awoke it was daylight. Greg was already awake and stroking her hair. When she lifted her head to look at him, the oxygen mask had been removed from his face and he looked a lot brighter. He was still attached to the machines but his whole demeanour was much more alert.

"Hey. How are you feeling?" She asked him softly.

"Much better for seeing you beside me," he croaked. "I'm still terrified you'll tell me it was the drugs or that I was dreaming." He looked at her with pleading eyes.

She reached up and stroked his face. "Well, that's not going to happen. I'm not going anywhere this time."

"Do you promise? Because I'm in this for the long-haul, Mallory."

"I promise. After what we've been through since we met I think we can deal with whatever gets thrown at us, don't you?"

"I hope so…but I'm scared." Greg squeezed her hand.

"You have nothing to be scared of Greg. When I thought I'd lost you last night I realised that some things are totally insignificant. You and I can work things through together. No more secrets, eh?"

"Well…there's one more I need to tell you…"

Mallory's heart sank and she braced herself for what was to come. She closed her eyes and took a deep breath. His grave expression was not instilling her with confidence for what he was about to impart.

She opened her eyes and looked directly into his. "I…I…quite like the Bee Gees…" He smiled and Mallory burst out laughing.

She kissed her funny, bruised and sore man gently on his poor swollen lips.

~~~~~

Mallory went home to freshen up and pick up some things for Greg. She bought him a couple of music mags and picked up his MP3 player from his house. Sure enough as she flicked through the discs on his old Jukebox there it was, plain for all to see, *The Bee Gees Greatest Hits*. She chuckled, it was a far cry from heavy metal but very sweet. She carried on collecting a few more things.

She noticed a pile of official looking documents on the coffee table. She knew they were private, but couldn't help herself. *Curiosity killed the bloody cat!* But she ignored the voice in her head and picked them up to quickly examine them. *Divorce papers.* She breathed a sigh of relief when she realised that both Alice and Greg had put their signatures to the documents. She placed them back on the table as they were and left the house.

Stella was out and about as she drove back from Greg's. She was walking Angus…well, if the truth be told Angus was actually walking Stella. Mallory was laughing as she pulled to a stop beside them.

"Hi, Mallory. How are you doing, hen? And how's Greg?"

"He's doing much better now thank you and I'm just relieved that he's okay. They're talking about letting him go home this weekend. He's bruised and sore, but not in any danger now. Thanks for taking Angus. I'm sure he's getting spoiled rotten just like Ruby is with Ron." She giggled.

"Oh, it's nay bother. He's eating me out of house and home, mind. Look Mallory…I wanted to say that…I hope you and Greg work things out…you'd make such a lovely couple." Stella waved and took off to finish her drag; as opposed to walk.

When Mallory arrived back at the hospital, armed with goodies for her new love, his bed was empty. She panicked. There was no one at the nurses' station so she had to hang around tapping her foot and waiting. The thing she hated most in the world was waiting.

Eventually, a nurse came along and informed her that Greg had been moved onto a general ward. She breathed a huge sigh of relief and made her way to his new location.

He was sitting up when she got there. His chest still gloriously bare, apart from a few remaining disconnected electrode pads and bandages. The drips had been removed and the heart monitor had gone too. He looked a little like he'd had the proverbial altercation with Mike Tyson, but his eyes sparkled all the same.

She nearly ran to the bedside. "Oh, Greg, look at you. So much better." She leaned in to kiss him gently, but his hand came up to the back of her head pulling her in for a deeper kiss. When she broke free she looked around to see if anyone had just witnessed the veraciously passionate exchange between them. Thankfully no one was taking the slightest bit of notice. She looked back to Greg who was smiling and shaking his head.

"If being out there in that icy water, fearing for my life, has taught me anything, it's that from now on I'm not going to hide my emotions any more. I love you and I want you and I don't care who sees or who knows it." His low growl sent shivers down her spine. Her cheeks heated and she returned his gaze with just as much passion.

"Have they said when you can come out?" She asked, hopeful that it would be soon.

"Well, it turns out I have no internal bleeding, just bruised ribs and a bust up face so they are happy for me to go home at the end of the week. I've been so lucky, Mally." He looked pensive.

"What happened to Little Blue?" She asked cautiously, knowing how much he loved his boat.

"Capsized. I got thrown overboard. There was quite a bit of damage, but they managed to tow her in. Hopefully I can repair her. But she'll be out of action for a while. That'll teach me for trying to be the hero, eh?" He looked puzzled for a while until he spoke. "Mally...did you tell me you'd sold your house? Or was I dreaming?" His brow was scrunched in confusion.

She bit her lip, feeling anxious at telling him now that he was fully conscious. "I had an offer on Monday from a young couple who came to look around twice." She fiddled with the sheet on the bed, nervously. She knew what was coming.

"So you were serious? About leaving here?" He looked shocked.

"Yes, Greg, I *thought* I was serious. I still feel that maybe I should sell up. I just don't feel that things have worked out since we...I moved in there."

Greg took her hand and tilted her chin up. "That's all about to change. Please don't sell up. I think it would be a shame. It's got your fantastic workshop. I saw some of your stuff in Colin's shop and was so impressed. Don't give that up."

Maybe he was right. She would have to think long and hard about it. The young couple, however, had nothing to sell and were keen to get their offer accepted.

"I don't know, Greg. The people who have offered seem to love it."

"Well so do you if you're honest. And...so do I."

"But you don't live there. I do and it's lonely. And it was mine and Sam's house. Maybe I need to move on."

"Look, It's your decision but don't let them pressure you into accepting the offer. There are things we can do to make it feel like home. Just think about it."

She nodded her acquiescence.

The next few days were filled with hospital visits for Mallory. By the end of the week, Greg said he was itching to get home and begin his relationship with Mallory in more private, comfortable and intimate surroundings.

Mallory picked him up in the Landy as she figured it would be easier for Greg to get in and out of in his current bruised and battered state.

She helped him down to the car and he grinned, clearly surprised when he saw his hunk of a vehicle there waiting for him. "Bloody hell, Mallory, you brought my car?" He laughed, impressed at her bravery in driving the old bone shaker.

"Yes, and boy that was a fun experience. It put a smile on my face that's for sure."

"See, I knew I could convert you. We'll need to get you one instead of that pocket sized, pretend car you drive around in now," he teased. "Winters around here are a sight to behold but my, oh my, will you know about it if you try to go out in your toy car." He chuckled and she shook her head at his audacity.

He was really happy to be going home. And Mallory was happy to be taking him. She had been around earlier in the week to clean his house and stock his food cupboards for him. She even placed fresh flowers around the place to make the basic and mismatched surroundings of his bachelor pad more conducive to a homecoming welcome.

When they arrived at Greg's house, she manoeuvred the rather stiff and achy six foot tall, broad, muscular man inside and onto the sofa, with great difficulty. He grabbed her and pulled her to him, wincing in pain as he did so. His hand found her hair and he pulled her mouth to his. The kiss was deep and passionate and made Mallory's insides turn to jelly and her core clench.

"God I've wanted to do that properly for so long," he gasped. "And I'm willing my ribs to get better quickly. I'm not sure where we are on the *taking it slow* thing, but I'd appreciate a heads up 'cause I'm just about going to go crazy here." His eyes flashed and her breath caught in her throat.

"Please, just get well, Greg; quickly." She kissed him again. She couldn't get enough. When she released his mouth she stared into his hot, melted chocolate gaze, smiling. "You have the most amazing eyes, Greg. I could fall right in and drown."

"Feel free," he growled.

How had she managed to hold back from this? How had she nearly let him go?

Suddenly a worrying thought crossed her mind. "I…maybe I should call Renee?"

"To tell her about us?" Greg asked.

"Yes. Or is it too soon? I mean we don't know what will happen do we? Maybe I should wait?"

Greg's brow knitted as he bit his lip, "It worries me that you think something will break us up again. You can't think like that or you'll always be waiting. I have no intention of this ending." He tucked her hair behind her ear. "But if you still have doubts maybe we *should* go back to taking things slow until you can trust me again?" He looked a little disappointed at the thought.

"No…no, Greg it's not that. This feels right." She gestured between the two of them. "We *do* feel right. I think I'm just scared because I was so in love with Renee's son. What if the Buchanan's decide they don't want to know me anymore? That'd break my heart." Her eyes dropped to where her hand was entwined with Greg's.

"That won't happen. You know that they want you to be happy. I'm sure they'll be fine. Just explain everything exactly as it happened."

"I may leave it a few days so I can figure out what to say. Is that okay with you?"

"Mallory, you don't need my permission. It's entirely up to you." He squeezed her hand in reassurance.

"Okay, well I will maybe ring after the weekend. Right, coffee?" She jumped up off the sofa.

"Oh no…are you making it?" He chuckled.

She pursed her lips at him and placed her hands on her hips. "Oooh Greg if you weren't injured already…"

~~~~~

Later that evening when she realised that Greg looked exhausted, Mallory decided to help him up to bed. He protested quite a lot, but eventually gave in to her. She helped him up the stairs.

He gingerly lowered himself onto the bed and looked up at her longingly.

She smirked and shook her head. "Don't go getting any ideas Mister. You're still in a state. I'll go home and sleep there. I daren't stay in case I kick you in the night or something."

"Don't go, please. It's been a while since I shared your bed and that didn't end too good. Stay?" He gave her the puppy dog eyes and she giggled.

"Greeeg. I don't want to hurt you if I roll into you. Your ribs are still black and blue under those bandages. I'm worried…"

"Ah, but what if I need to go pee in the night? And I can't get up? You wouldn't leave a poor wounded man to fend for himself would you?" He stuck out his bottom lip in a pout and fluttered his eyelids.

Mallory laughed. "Good grief, you're worse than a kid!" She teased. "Oh, for goodness sake…alright then." She acquiesced as he kept pouting and fluttering. "Now let's figure out how to get you undressed." She stood hands on hips and assessed him like a project.

"Ooh I love it when you talk dirty." He chuckled.

She wiggled her eyebrows at him. "Don't push your luck, I'm in a position of immense power here."

Together they struggled to free him from his T-shirt. And then he lay back whilst she unzipped his jeans and pulled them down over his long lean legs. A shiver went through her as he lay there in just his fitted black boxers. Just looking at his body caused her thoughts to be diverted along the wrong route.

"Ahem…Mallory…can you help me so I can go brush my teeth please?" He chuckled and Mallory blushed as he interrupted her fantasy.

"I wasn't staring!" She insisted and then, "Oh, who am I kidding, I was staring." She giggled feeling rather embarrassed. She helped him to stand.

"All in good time, my gorgeous girl." He smiled, taking her hand and reading her thoughts.

She breathed deeply trying to calm the fire of lust burning low in her belly. "What does your tattoo mean?" She asked. "This one on your chest." She traced the lettering with her fingers as he stood in front of her. His skin trembled under her touch which didn't help her state of mind.

"It's Gaelic. I studied it at school and it's always been special to me. The tattoo translates, roughly, as 'Love conquers all'."

Her heart melted.

"I got it to remind myself that no matter what life throws at me, whether it's my wife and best friend betraying me, Mairi being killed on a mountain, or me balls-ing anything up in a big way…for example with the woman I'm in love with now, whatever it is, love will still find a way and I've not to give up on it. And you see…" he kissed her forehead. "I was right."

Mallory's heart swelled when she heard his reasons behind the beautiful scarring on his chest.

When Greg had finished up in the little en-suite Mallory helped him into bed then went to change into one of Greg's oversized T-shirts and a pair of his shorts, hiding in the en-suite to do so. She then gingerly climbed in beside him. She snuggled up to him and he made a cute little murmuring noise.

"Hmmm, feels good to be next to you again."

"It really does," Mallory agreed. She gave him a tender kiss goodnight. They both drifted into a deep, comfortable, contented sleep.

Chapter Thirteen

The next couple of weeks were mainly focused on rehabilitation. Greg was healing quickly and Mallory was relieved to discover that the bruising was subsiding rapidly.

The people in the village had figured out that they were an item on account of the number of times they had been caught having a sneaky kiss when they thought no one was looking. The villagers smiled and chatted about it together.

"Isn't it lovely that they finally sorted themselves out?" and, "Don't they make a handsome couple?"

Mallory had rejected the offer on her house and decided to remove it from the market. She had decided she loved it here after all. She stopped seeing the negative about the place and began to really make it her own home.

Greg stayed over a lot whilst he was in the throes of the healing process. It was beginning to feel like *their* house.

Mallory phoned Renee at the end of November to inform her of what had happened. Renee had cried and Mallory thought at first that this was due to anger or upset at the betrayal of her son's memory.

But eventually she had sighed and said, "Oh Mallory, Ryan, Cara and I said as soon as we met Greg that he was the one for you. We just knew how much he thought of you. It was so obvious to us, sweetheart. I am so very happy for you. We all are. But promise me the two of you will come out and visit? And please don't lose touch because you're worried about how awkward things will be. They won't be at all awkward, darling. You are and always will be a part of this family. We all love you dearly."

Mallory had cried and cried at hearing such kind and heartfelt words from Renee. She was relieved to have got it out in the open with Sam's family and she felt that she and Greg had everyone's blessing.

December 2011

Early December was an exciting time. Greg and Mallory's relationship had remained, all be it reluctantly on both sides, in the realms of celibacy since their first kiss in the hospital after the accident. Greg's wounds had been healing and neither had been prepared to rush things and ruin what they potentially had. She had remained covered up in front of him and he had yet to see her tattoo.

Mallory had always loved December. The joy of Christmas lay around the corner. How wonderful to be spending Christmas with Greg, in her lovely home, near the beautiful Bridge Over the Atlantic; her favourite place in the whole world.

Saturday December third and Greg was almost back to his former self apart from a scar on his head, one on his lip and slight shadows under his eyes.

He had been with Mallory to buy a Christmas tree. It was standing in the corner of the lounge and they were just about to decorate it with a combination of their respective ornaments.

Greg had brought over a bottle of Sherry and Mallory had put on the Christmas CD that she would happily listen to in June as she loved Christmas songs so much.

Greg poured them a wee dram and they began to go through their boxes of tree ornaments. They squabbled jokily over whose were better, but Greg knew that Mallory's were much more tasteful, although he wouldn't openly concede. His were bright, garish and mostly, if they were both honest, ugly.

The battle did not end there. Greg was placing his ornaments on the tree in prominent positions with a wry, playful grin and Mallory, using her womanly powers of subterfuge, was removing them and placing them at the back of the tree, hidden out of sight. Greg caught on to this fact quickly and decided to make a tactical move himself, which involved grabbing Mallory around the waist and wrestling her to the ground to tickle her until she relented and allowed him to place the gaudy ornaments where he chose. Once finished they sat back on the sofa to admire their handy work.

"This Christmas is going to be so special, gorgeous." Greg announced to Mallory as they snuggled together on the sofa. "Are Josie and Brad coming up?"

"I think they may come up for Hogmanay. I can't wait for Hogmanay." Mallory was filled with excitement just thinking about it.

Greg turned to Mallory, his melted chocolate eyes burning into her. "Do you know what I'm looking forward to?" He stroked a finger down her cheek and brought his face close to hers until they were almost touching.

Her breath caught as she was willingly trapped by his gaze. "What?" She felt her temperature begin to rise and her heart rate increased.

His breath was warm on her lips and she noticed his breathing had changed. "I'm looking forward to unwrapping you on Christmas morning and kissing you all over." His voice was a deep, low whisper as he leaned closer still and rested his forehead on hers.

Desire clenched deep within her and she placed her hand on his chest where she could feel his pounding heart. She kissed him deeply, her tongue dipping into his mouth. "Why wait until Christmas morning?" Their eyes remained locked. She wanted him…now. His wonderful full mouth turned up at one side and he took her hand.

He stood and pulled her up to meet him. "Come with me," he whispered.

This time her temperature soared as the need for him coursed through her body. He led her to the stairs and still holding her hand made his way up to the bedroom.

Once inside the room he pulled her into him. He looked down at her, his eyes hooded with avidity. He cupped her face in his hands and lowered his mouth to almost touch hers again. "I've waited for this moment since the day I met you." His throaty voice still no more than a whisper, his sweet breath danced over her lips.

His hands slid down her back to her bottom making her insides turn to liquid. "I want to savour this. I want to savour you, Mallory. I love you with all my heart, but I want you with every inch of my being." One hand travelled up her body and into her hair, but his lips still didn't touch hers. There was only an electric current running from his words down her body and into her soul. She brought her hands up to touch him, his chest was firm underneath his T-shirt. She smoothed her hands over his torso. He closed his eyes just for a second and breathed deeply as if struggling with self-control.

When he opened them again his eyes bore into hers. She wanted desperately to kiss him but she, too, was enjoying the spark between them; the anticipation. Slowly he let his lips connect with hers and he inhaled sharply and deeply. This first kiss was the promise of what was to come. Her hands slowly slid up over his shoulders, around his neck and into his hair. His kiss became more urgent and his tongue sought entry into her mouth. She opened for him and welcomed his tongue with her own, caressing and tasting him.

He groaned as he ran his hands down her back to squeeze her bottom, pulling her closer. She felt his arousal through her jeans and her hands fell to the hem of his T-shirt where she began to lift it up over his taught body, sliding her hands over him as she did so. He raised his arms and stooped for her to remove it and cast it aside. She lowered her face to his chest where she kissed his tattoo. He breathed out a rush of air and stroked her back as his head rolled backward in sheer pleasure.

He lowered his gaze back to hers and pulled her sweater over her head kissing her lips, both before and after the item was removed. Their eyes remained locked on each other. He traced the line of her collar bone with his finger tips and bent to place kisses where he had touched her. His kisses moved to her neck. She gasped and grabbed onto him as her core clenched. She slid her fingers around the waistband of his jeans and unbuttoned them, slipping her hands inside to help push them down. He stepped out of the jeans and then it was his turn to do the same.

He gently unfastened and slipped her jeans down her trembling legs, smoothing his hand delicately over her bottom as he did so. She shivered in anticipation. They stood in just their underwear devouring each other with their eyes. Greg was broad and muscular, taught and olive skinned. His jaw angular and covered in stubble which drew her eyes towards his goatee and up to his lips. His ink made him even more masculine if that was possible and that made her feel ravenous for him. Greg smiled and shook his head as he stroked her face.

"Why are you smiling?" She asked nervously, her eyelids fluttering.

"I'm just looking at you and thinking that I must be the luckiest man on the planet right now." Mallory felt her cheeks heat under his appraising gaze.

He ran both thumbs over her lips as he fixed his gaze on her mouth, "You truly are beautiful Mallory. So very sexy. And you just don't seem to realise that. Your curves, your skin…I mean you're just…so beautiful. I can't put into words how much I want you."

She smiled up at him, her heart nervously fluttering in her chest. "You did a pretty good job with words right there. But…maybe if you can't…can't find words…just show me?"

He bent to kiss her, once again his hands slipping around her back and unfastening the clasp of her bra. He slipped the pretty blue lace down her arms and it was thrown to join the rest of their relinquished clothing. He cupped her breasts tenderly, stroking the little pink buds with his thumbs. Mallory's head now rolled back in ecstasy. He kissed each one ardently with long wet kisses until Mallory's legs nearly gave way beneath her.

Whilst she stood trembling before him, he kissed all the way down her stomach, and crouched to a kneeling position. He slid the matching blue lace panties down her legs, kissing her hips and sliding his hands slowly down her thighs. Her hands found his thick dark hair and she massaged his scalp.

He nuzzled her mound making her moan loudly before he let his tongue slide lower. When he rose to his feet, his tongue was replaced with fingers teasing and caressing her most intimate place. It all felt so strange, so different, but so amazingly good.

The tension was building inside of her and her breathing became shallower. He stopped, causing her to whimper. But he removed his fitted boxers to release the full potential of his desire. Mallory wanted to touch him, but he slowly turned her around so that his arousal pressed deliciously into her lower back and he continued the tantalising torture with his fingers whilst his other hand moulded her breast and he kissed her neck sending shivers right through her body.

He stepped back slightly and smoothed his large hand over the curve of her waist and hip, savouring her every curve just as he had said he would. Suddenly, he stopped and stepped further away from her. She heard a sharp intake of breath.

He had finally noticed her ink.

He dropped to his knees again to examine the design on her lower back more closely.

"Mallory." His voice was choked with emotion.

She felt him trace the design with his fingertips; it tickled. The Serch Bythol, with the letters G and M at either side.

"That's…that's the Celtic symbol for everlasting love," he stated. "And…you've got my initial…wait…our initials on your body?" He grabbed both of her hips and pressed his lips to the image. "Mallory it's beautiful; it's perfect."

He stood and gently turned her to him holding her by her shoulders, a frown etched his face. "When…?" His eyes had turned glassy as tears hovered ready to fall, he looked totally overwhelmed at this display of her love for him.

She caressed his face and looked into his damp eyes. "Greg, I realised how I felt about you when I was in *Yorkshire*, the last time. I was so angry with myself for how I handled things. I figured I'd probably ruined everything, but I wanted a permanent reminder of you. I wanted something to keep forever in case I had blown it by being so wracked by guilt at loving you. Something that was out of sight to everyone else, but that I knew was there."

He shook his head. Disbelief washed over his gorgeous features and he touched her face. "How could you think that you'd ruined everything after the way I'd lied to you? After I had blown it all, myself?"

"I love you, Greg, so much. I was so scared to even acknowledge my feelings until I went away. I was terrified that you'd fallen for Kate. I'm so glad you hadn't stopped loving me. Now you know how I feel and whenever you look at my tattoo you'll know how much I truly love you. There is no going back for me now."

He pulled her into him and stroked her hair muttering his love for her. Their kisses became deeper and needier. Breathing became ragged as their hands explored each-others bodies. His fingers found that special place again and her hands found him. She stroked and he groaned, his pleasure making her move faster. She was on the brink as his fingers teased and teased.

Suddenly he tumbled onto the bed taking her with him. He reached down to where his jeans lay, under the bed and found a small foil packet. He ripped it open and stretched the sheath down.

Moving over her he caressed again her until she exploded into a million tiny pieces of her former self, floating somewhere above the stratosphere; he slid into her and she pulsed around him as he moved inside her. He kissed and caressed her adoringly as their bodies became one.

The tension was building in her once again and she looked up into his face but his expression troubled her. He stared down at her with fear in his eyes as if he was expecting to wake from some cruel, tormenting dream.

She placed her hands on either side of his face as he moved. "Greg," she gasped staring intently into his eyes, "I love you and I want you…and I mean forever." A tear escaped her eye as the verbalisation of her true feelings for this soft hearted, rugged man struck her once again. Her words were the only catalyst he needed as he cried out her name in sheer ecstasy taking her with him once again.

~~~~~

They held onto each other as their bodies shuddered in the immense afterglow of the pleasure and love they had shared. Their gazes were still locked and tears streamed down Mallory's face.

"Mallory, I love you so much, please don't cry." Greg gasped as his heartbeat began to calm. He wiped away her tears as he clung onto her.

"I'm not crying because I'm sad. They're happy tears." She smiled and kissed him as he stared at her worriedly.

"I didn't hurt you?" He asked, his breathing slowing.

"No, not at all, you were wonderful. Making love with you was just…amazing. I'm just so very happy that we got here after everything we've been through." She stroked his cheek as relief became evident and his features relaxed.

"No regrets?" He was clearly still waiting for her to get up and leave or say she had changed her mind.

She had thought of a way to drive the point home. She pulled herself up so that she was looking down at him.

She took a deep breath and spoke, "I want you to move in with me, Greg." She exhaled quickly feeling relieved to finally speak the words she had been thinking since the accident had nearly torn them apart for good.

He sat bolt upright and stared down at her taking her face in his hands "Are you serious?" His eyes were wide and a face splitting grin appeared nonetheless.

She looked him straight in the eyes again. "Is that a yes then?" She asked raising her eyebrows at him. "I'm perfectly serious."

"Hell, yes I'll move in!" He grabbed her into a strong embrace and they tumbled backward into another lingering, passionate kiss.

~~~~~

Christmas 2011

Two days later, Greg pulled up outside Mallory's place in the Landy. It was packed to the gunnels with his belongings.

His house was going to rent out easily according to the estate agent.

Mallory came out to help him unload. Angus sat in the passenger seat wagging his long tail frantically, almost taking Greg's eye out in the process.

Greg climbed down from the car and ran around to scoop Mallory into his arms. "I'm so bloody excited about this!" He spun her around.

She clung on, laughing with her head back. "Me too. I just hope it all fits in."

"Well if not, we'll have a mega car-boot sale, eh?"

They carried box after box into the cottage. Stopping to kiss or embrace at every possible opportunity. When they had finished, they collapsed onto the sofa and snuggled together out of breath.

"Guess what?" Mallory suddenly remembered her news. "Brad and Josie are definitely coming for New Years!"

It hadn't taken much persuading to get her friends to agree. Josie had pretty much squealed in delight down the phone when she had heard all of Mallory's news.

"Fantastic. I know how much it means to you to have them here. It'll be great to have them share Hogmanay celebrations with us…in *our* home." He squeezed her gently. "I can't wait. They'll be able to come over and see me play and then we can have a wee celebration back here." He kissed her for the millionth time, "Fancy a wee bit of Christmas shopping this afternoon?"

"Sounds like a plan." She jumped to her feet. "I think I'll go shower and get ready. You coming?" She bit her lip and held out her hand. He didn't take much convincing and grabbed it.

As they walked past the lounge window which looked out to the water Mallory gasped. "Greg! It's snowing." The snow was beginning to blanket the ground in front of the house and turn their view into something usually seen on Christmas cards. "It's perfect." She smiled as Greg slid his arms around her waist whilst they stood, watching the feather-like flakes float to the ground.

~~~~~

Christmas Eve was quiet and romantic. Greg cooked whilst Mallory put the finishing touches to a gift she was making for him. He'd been quite cagey about his gift for her, but she had a feeling he had spent too much money. His savings were from his inheritance and she hated the thought of him frittering it away on her. She had opted for making him a gift, as he said that was what he wanted more than anything. He still raved to everyone about the chalkboard she made him.

Greg called Mallory down to the house for dinner. She had finished and was ready for washing up.

He had opted for Moroccan lamb with couscous and the delicious aroma teased Mallory's nostrils, making her salivate. The wine was chilling and Mallory went to change and rid her hands of the paint.

She returned to the dining table where Greg had lit candles and placed out all the best dinnerware. It looked wonderful. He stood when she entered the room. He looked amazing in his black jeans and grey shirt, open just enough so his pendant was visible. He gazed lovingly at her as she walked toward the table.

"You look beautiful, Mallory." He smiled. She had slipped on black trousers and a lilac cashmere sweater she had bought when they were out shopping for gifts. *Well it was a bargain,* she had convinced herself. Her hair was loose around her shoulders just how Greg liked it. She smiled across at him and his eyes twinkled in the candle light.

"Can I make a toast?" She asked, her head tilted to one side as she gazed at her love.

Greg nodded, his eyes locked on hers.

"To us. May this be the first of many Christmases we share, until we are old and grey." She thought back to Edith on the train and smiled. They clinked glasses and tucked into the delicious meal.

Christmas morning finally arrived and Greg was like a kid, bouncing on the bed beside Mallory to wake her up.

"Can we get up now? Can we get up now? Can we get up now?" He resorted to tickling and prodding at her at which point she attacked him with a pillow.

"Good grief, McBradden, remember how old you are." She laughed as she pushed him back and straddled him trying to pin him down.

"I've reverted back to childhood, but it's your fault. I never got the whole Christmas thing until you." He wrestled her off him and flung her over his shoulder. "C'mon lazy bones it's prezzie time!"

Mallory squealed and hit his bottom as he carried her down the stairs. He only placed her on her feet once they were in front of the tree. She stood there in his oversized T-shirt and nothing else except for a smile.

"Now you, sit." he demanded. He proceeded to switch the twinkly lights on and go to the fridge for the bottle of Bucks Fizz that was chilling. He had already lit the fire and there was a smell of bacon diffusing through the air from the kitchen. Two minutes later Greg returned with a tray, one of Mallory's creations, upon which were the Bucks Fizz, two champagne flutes and two plates of bacon sandwiches.

"Ah, well if I'd known you'd got up early to make bacon butties I may not have taken so much cajoling." Mallory laughed. They huddled together in front of the fire. She had no idea what time he had got up, but he seemed determined to get Christmas day officially underway.

Once they had eaten, Mallory took out the parcel she had wrapped for Greg, late the night before. He stared at the package for a while and kept glancing up to smile at her

"Open it then." She prodded him.

"Now who's being impatient?" He chuckled. He opened it slowly, taking care not to rip the pretty brown paper that Mallory had decorated with golden love hearts and snowflakes. He took out the rectangular sign and read aloud

"Welcome to Greg and Mallory's Home." His eyes misted over. "Mallory, this is the best Christmas gift I think I have ever been given." He smiled over at her and then leaned in to kiss her sweetly.

"What? Did you never get a bike or a Scalextric?" she teased.

"Aye…yes, course I did. But this means so much more because you made it for me and it makes our moving in together official. Best gift ever, just like I said."

Mallory's heart swelled.

Mallory picked up the small package with her name on which she knew to be from Greg. It was flat and rectangular. She was puzzled.

"Now before you open it and go all ape-shit on me, I just want to defend myself and say that it's something for us both. But I think you'll be happy and that's what matters."

She took a deep breath and opened the package. Inside was an envelope with 'British Airways' emblazoned across it. She took out the contents.

"Bloody hell, Greg! Two first class return flights to *Canada*?" She pounced and flung her arms around him without protest.

"Whoa! That's not the reaction I was prepared for!" He hugged her grinning widely like the Cheshire cat.

"I know and I should be angry with you. But how can I be when it's just so perfect?" She kissed him over and over.

"Well, I spoke to Renee and she says we can either stay with her or if we don't feel comfortable doing that she will book us into the hotel in *Kingston*, her treat."

"How wonderful! I love you Greg McBradden." She squealed and kissed him again.

The days following Christmas were filled with snowy walks in boots and scarves, mulled wine over at the pub and lazy evenings of making love in front of the fire at home.

Josie and Brad arrived on December twenty-eighth for the preparations leading up to Hogmanay.

Greg had surreptitiously arranged to go shopping with Brad whilst Mallory and Josie headed off in search of suitable Hogmanay attire.

The girls' first stop was a little designer boutique which had become Mallory's favourite shop in *Oban*. Mallory made a beeline for a silver grey dress peeping out from one of the rails. It was fitted and had a sweetheart neckline.

The fabric had a slight shimmer when the light caught it and Mallory hoped it would suit her now curvier frame. She gingerly stepped out of the changing room. Josie gaped at the stunning vision she encountered.

"Fu-...cra...Blimey!" She eventually fought and succeeded in her battle with the expletives. Well it was a rather posh place, afterall.

"Is that good?" Mallory scrunched her nose up at her stuttering friend.

"Well, put it this way, if I was a lesbian I'd be total in lust with you right now and trying to get you out of it."

Mallory burst into hysterical laughter at her friend's rather bizarre comment.

"Buy it, buy it, buy it! Ooh, ooh and you've got to get these silver shoes to go with it!" Josie grabbed the shoes from the display, much to the chagrin of the boutiques manager who looked disgruntled at the way her display was being manhandled and dismantled.

Josie was right though. The shoes finished off the whole ensemble perfectly.

Josie chose a fitted red dress which only served to reiterate how tiny she was. And as always, she was stunning until she opened her mouth.

The girls were all sorted and decided to get back home to the men. When they arrived home Brad and Greg were nowhere to be seen, so the girls opened a bottle of wine and chatted until the wanderers returned.

As soon as he walked through the door, Greg took bags quickly upstairs and Brad shrugged his shoulders in a "Don't ask coz I can't say nothing," kind of gesture. He grabbed a bottle of beer from the fridge and joined the girls as they chatted.

Hogmanay ~ New Year's Eve

Greg and Mallory were so pleased to have Josie and Brad to share their first Hogmanay celebration as a couple. They weren't doing anything too flashy. They had made arrangements to spend the celebrations at the pub as Greg was playing up to just before the countdown to midnight.

Josie and Mallory were getting ready in the master bedroom whilst their men drank beer together in the lounge. They were getting on well. The sound of laughter permeated the floorboards up to where the preening and preparing was taking place.

Mallory slipped on her beautiful silver grey dress. She was glad Josie had convinced her to buy it, even if her methodology had been unorthodox. Josie squeezed her petite frame into the very sexy fitted red number. They both applied lip gloss and helped each other with their hair.

Once ready they teetered down to the lounge where the guys were waiting. Mallory's jaw dropped open at the sight of her rugged man looking even sexier in his kilt. Mallory had always liked to see men in kilts, but nothing had prepared her for this man in one. She caught Greg's expression and he too was agog at the vision of her and her fitted dress which showed off her curvy figure in the best possible way. They both realised they were staring; both blushed and then burst out laughing.

"Get a bloody room you two." Brad chuckled in his broad *Yorkshire* twang as he watched the outward display of lust on his friend's faces. They all laughed together and after grabbing their coats, headed out for the pub.

Greg shivered. "Geez, it's night's like these when I wish I was from Eskimo heritage instead." He laughed as he pulled his coat tighter around his exposed legs.

Thankfully the pub was a warm haven against the bitter icy chill. The snow had all but gone, but the clear sky meant the bite in the air was a vicious one. They set up by the fireplace with their drinks as the pub began to fill up. Greg took his place ready to perform.

"Evening all!" Greg shouted his usual greeting over the PA system. The chatter subsided in readiness.

"Hey Greg! What's worn under your kilt?" Ron heckled from somewhere near the back.

"Hey, Ron, there's nothing *worn* under my kilt, matey! It's all in perfect working order, thanks for asking!" A ruckus of laughter rumbled around the room. Mallory, Josie and Brad were in hysterics and Josie was trying her best not to pee, as she'd so boldly added.

"I thank you." Greg laughed and did a little bow. "Right, now guys, as you know, this rollercoaster year is drawing to a close and I'm happy to be sharing this special evening with you's all tonight. I won't be doing much blathering. So enjoy the music, and dance if you have the room around you but remember…"

"DON'T SING ALONG!" the audience shouted back in unison at the smiling and nodding man holding the guitar.

Greg sang an eclectic mix of songs and the audience revelled in the wonderful music, defying his orders to stay quiet at every opportunity; never more so that when he sang '*500 miles*' Mallory's favourite Proclaimers song. The pub was in uproar and the atmosphere was electric.

Five Minutes To Midnight

When his set was over, Greg announced that it was five minutes to midnight and there was a huge cheer. He grappled through the crowd, his sights set on Mallory, but it was like swimming against the tide. People wanted to hug him, pat him on the back and congratulate him on a brilliant show. He locked eyes on Mallory determined he would get to her in time.

When he finally reached her he grabbed her hand and pulled her toward the door, a grin fixed on his face. Someone announced over the PA that there were four minutes remaining. They made it outside and he was virtually dragging her along.

She was giggling uncontrollably.

"Greg! Where are we going? We're going to miss the countdown."

He said nothing but continued on, pulling her behind him, teetering on her silver high heeled shoes. He was on a mission.

They arrived at the midpoint of the Atlantic Bridge. They could still hear the ruckus in the pub; the announcement came that three minutes remained.

"I think we should celebrate here, Mallory." He said as he pulled her in for a lingering passionate kiss. Her legs weakened.

"Two minutes to midnight!" Came the voice over the PA.

Greg looked deep into Mallory's eyes with such love and adoration. "Mallory...I love you more than anything in this world, do you know that?"

A wide smile spread across Mallory's face as she stroked his cheek. Greg took a deep breath, "I love your laugh, I love your body, I love how you make me feel...I want to feel that way for the rest of my life..." His words came out in an emotional rush and Mallory's giggles subsided as she melted into the sincere gaze of the man she loved.

"One minute to midnight!" Came the announcement in the background.

Greg looked terrified, his chest heaved and his eyes stared into hers as he stood before her "Please would you make me the happiest man alive? Mallory, am pos thu mi?"

Mallory was confused by his Gaelic words; not quite sure what he was asking; she could tell it was a question by his inflection. But then he held out a small, black velvet box. She froze, her brow furrowed.

"Ten, nine, eight, seven," could be heard from the pub.

Greg dropped to one knee holding the box aloft. "Mallory, will you marry me?" His eyes sparkled with unshed tears as he gazed lovingly up at her, filled with hope.

"four, three, two."

Her mouth fell open and her hands reached her face. "Oh Greg...YES!"

"Happy New Year!" Loud cheers and whoops came from the pub as people began to celebrate.

Greg rose to his feet and kissed her holding on to her tightly. People spilled out of the pub cheering and singing *Auld Lang Syne*.

Greg and Mallory just stared at each other, both out of breath if they had been running and both with tears tracing warm tracks down their faces. The enormity of the wonderful situation was dawning on them both.

Greg realised he was still clutching the box. "You haven't even seen the ring." He laughed as he opened the lid.

Mallory gazed in awe at a single princess cut diamond, set on a white gold band engraved with Celtic love knots. It was simply stunning. More tears escaped and streamed down her face. He took the ring out of the box and she held out her left hand for him to glide it onto her finger. Suddenly someone at the pub saw what was happening on the bridge.

"Greg has proposed to Mallory!" the onlooker shouted "He has! He's proposed!" A cheer rang around the cold midnight air and everyone ran to join them on the bridge.

Colin was the one who had shouted and he was the first on the scene. He hugged Mallory and said, "You've become like a daughter to me and Christine these past months, Mallory, and we're so very happy for you, love."

Mallory's tears were relentless. Josie squealed in delight and Brad lifted her and spun her around. People were hugging Greg and congratulating him. Through all the excitement and furor Greg and Mallory still gazed at each other lovingly, smiling; beaming. Greg mouthed the words "I love you" and she reciprocated.

"Back inside for champagne," Stella announced.

Mallory was impressed. She found Greg and slipped her arms around his waist as everyone headed back to the pub.

Greg held her back for a moment. "I hope you didn't mind me proposing here on the bridge." He tucked a strand of hair behind her ear and tilted her chin up to kiss her. "I want this to be our place too." He stroked her cheek.

"It is our place. I have more memories of you and me here now. This is our Atlantic Bridge." Another tear escaped as she looked up into the eyes of the man she adored.

He curled his arms around her. "Come on, you're freezing and I've an icy breeze blowing around places I would rather I didn't have, let's go have champagne before it's all gone." He chuckled

Mallory smiled. "Champagne…who would have thought it? Didn't realise Stella stocked it."

Greg grinned sheepishly. "Erm, she doesn't usually. I went out with Brad and bought a boot load just in case you said yes. Stella knew all along." He squeezed her to him.

"Oh yeah? What if I'd said no?" She poked him playfully.

"Don't joke. I've been terrified and wondering if they did sale or return." They laughed together.

Someone had put an old Cliff Richard classic *'Congratulations'* on the CD player when they arrived back in the pub. When they walked through the door everyone sang at the tops of their voices as Mallory and Greg blushed. The majority of them sang the whole song and those who didn't know the words sang along, badly to the tune. It was hilarious and quite sweet. At the end of the song people were baying for a speech.

Greg took the microphone from his stand. "Alright, alright! I'm guessing you have all figured out that it's over between me and Mallory." Boos and laughter roared around the place. "Okay, okay so I asked her to marry me and I am totally and utterly in shock because this beautiful," he pulled her next to him, "sexy, amazingly talented woman whom I am utterly, irrevocably in love with has said yes!" The whole place cheered. "Now of course you'll all be invited along to the wedding, but you have to promise one thing as a collective." Everyone clapped and whistled. When the noise had calmed he shouted "NO MORE BLOODY SINGING!"

The place exploded in laughter and applause again. Greg kissed Mallory passionately much to the delight of the crowd.

Everyone went back to their celebrations. Josie and Brad came over to the couple. They all hugged and Brad and Josie congratulated them again.

"Listen honey, me and Brad have arranged to stay here just for tonight so you too love birds can celebrate in private if you know what I mean." She gave them a salacious wink.

Greg hugged Josie. "That's brilliant, thanks you guys. We appreciate that." He shook hands with Brad, the handshake turned into a masculine, back slapping hug.

They said their goodnights and the crowds began to dissipate so Mallory and Greg made their way home. Ruby and Angus were waiting to greet them with frantically wagging tails and yips of delight. It was as if they knew their mum and dad were getting married.

The dogs were let out and subsequently put to bed in the kitchen. Greg lit the logs in the fire and switched on the tree lights. He then produced a bottle of champagne from outside the back door and brought it into the lounge with two flutes.

"Where has that come from?" Mallory asked quizzically.

"Ah, the joys of hidden, natural, outdoor refrigeration." He smiled as he popped the cork. "I kept a bottle back in the hope that things would all go according to plan." He poured a glass of the sparkling liquid and handed it to Mallory. Then he poured one for himself. They sat together on the rug in front of the fire which was roaring nicely.

"A toast." He held is glass aloft "To my beautiful fiancée, you have made me happy beyond words. I will love you forever." He clinked their glasses together and kissed Mallory lightly on the lips.

"May I make a toast too?" She asked politely, feeling rather coy. He nodded. "To my wonderful husband to be. We've had some pretty steep ups and downs but at least that proves we can handle anything. I hope I can continue to make you as happy as you make me. I love you, Greg." They clinked glasses again.

Greg took both glasses and placed them on the hearth. He pulled Mallory into his lap and kissed her deeply, his hands in her hair. Mallory gazed down at him. His hands moved to her face where he stroked her cheeks with his thumbs. He bent forward to kiss her gently. His hands slid to the zipper at the back of her dress and he slipped it down, pulling the sleeves from her arms. She pulled him in to her breasts in a strong, loving embrace, stroking his hair.

She leaned back and watched him as he unbuttoned his shirt still gazing lovingly into her eyes, "I have a surprise for you," he announced.

"Really? Another one? What is it?" She asked.

"You know how I disappeared with Brad earlier today?"

"To buy the champagne?" Mallory asked

"No, I already had that. No I went with Brad into *Oban*. And I had a little ink done, especially for you." He removed his shirt and there was a large white dressing covering the space above his other tattoo. He gently peeled the dressing back to reveal an exact copy of the tattoo she had on the small of her back.

Mallory gasped as the salt water she had become very much accustomed to lately, welled up and overflowed from her eyes. After replacing the dressing, being careful not to hurt the raw skin, she cradled him in her arms.

She slid out of the remainder of her silver dress and removed her pretty silver lace bra. They held each other skin on skin for a while, relishing the closeness and warmth. The glow of the fire sparkled in their eyes. They removed the rest of each other clothes and lay back down on the rug.

Greg eased Mallory onto her back as he placed kisses down her neck, to her shoulder, to her collar bone. He caressed each breast with hands and mouth and onward down her abdomen. He kissed his way all the way down to the mound of her pubic bone. He kissed her there and she arched and moaned.

He didn't play there for long before he climbed back up her body and caressed as he went. Rolling over he pulled her onto him. Her hands slid down his body to his very manhood. She worshipped him with her hands loving his little growls of pleasure. Then, whilst he was on his back he slid herself onto him. His hands were at her hips as they moved together.

There was urgency to their love making this time. Neither could quite get close enough nor take enough of one another. The heat of the fire glowed over their beautiful nakedness. They both climbed higher and higher until they were sky bound with the dizziness of orgasm; two people desperately in love giving themselves to each other whole heartedly; forever.

They lay there for a while, revelling in the closeness and basking in their post orgasmic bliss, holding each other, smiling and kissing.

"So when do you want to get married? Or am I asking that too early?" Mallory stroked his 'Love Conquers All' tattoo as she spoke, musing that just maybe it did.

"You kidding me? Can we do it yesterday please?" He smiled. "Seriously, gorgeous, as soon as possible for me." He brought her engagement ring finger up to his mouth and kissed it gently.

"We'd better get planning then, eh?" She snuggled down into him making sure to avoid his newly scarred skin.

"We certainly better had do that, gorgeous, yes."

"Hey, I've just had an idea." Mallory propped herself up on her elbow and looked down at her handsome fiancé. "We have a honeymoon all sorted! We can use the *Canada* tickets"

She smiled as a strange look crept over Greg's face. "Oh my goodness! That's what you had planned all along." She gasped as it all dawned on her.

"I'm afraid so my sweet, gorgeous, Mallory. I would have proposed at Christmas too but I thought maybe it was too soon after moving in together."

She kissed the tip of his nose. "Just for the record…I would have said yes."

~~~~~

March 2012

Greg's divorce papers had dropped through the door at the end of January which meant all systems were good to go. Much to Greg and Mallory's relief, things had been resolved quickly on account of how long they had been apart.

Alice had made one last ditch attempt to get Greg back and was astounded when she discovered that he had become engaged to Mallory. She told him he was making the biggest mistake of his life. Mallory was sitting beside him when she rang.

"Alice, the biggest mistake I ever made was giving you a second chance. Do you honestly believe you deserve a third? I'm head over heels in love with Mally and nothing you say will change that." He had given Mallory's thigh a reassuring squeeze as he spoke. It seemed she had relented and hung up.

"Was she okay?" Mallory asked when he threw his phone onto the cushion at the side of him.

"Oh yeah, she was fine. Faked a few sobs, but she'll get over it. She has no choice. I am utterly yours, gorgeous."

"And are you okay about it all?" She asked tentatively.

"Me? Of course I am." He began to sprinkle her with kisses in between his words, "I have never…ever

…been…happier…than…I am …now that…I'm… with you." He kissed her more deeply with hunger. To reiterate just how fine he was about the whole situation, he made love to her there and then on the squishy old sofa, slowly and lovingly, cherishing her returning curves as if they were long lost friends.

In order to avoid the cliché of getting married on Valentine's Day they had set the date of Saturday March third. The beautiful nineteenth century Kilbrandon church had been booked since the engagement. Mallory and Greg were so excited to be committing themselves to each other.

Wedding dress shopping had been great fun. Mallory had visited *Leeds* where she looked in every wedding dress shop that she and Josie could find. Eventually, they ended up back at the very first one. Mallory knew she had found the right dress when her best friend was utterly speechless on seeing her in it.

"Oh, Mally, oh…you look…oh." Josie had wiped tears from her eyes and hugged the bride to be so hard, Mallory almost passed out. But that was all the confirmation she needed. The dress was a done deal.

Mallory had messaged her friends in *Canada* to tell them of her impending nuptials. Reece had left her a virtual scream of delight on her timeline. She had laughed when he posted a photo from his cell phone of him actually screaming. *Crazy man*, Mallory had giggled.

Carl had been very sweet about the engagement. He had said he wished it was him she was marrying, but that he wished her every happiness all the same. He had a girlfriend, but apparently he didn't think she was 'the one.'

Renee, Ryan, Cara and Dylan were flying in for the wedding and the honeymoon was going to start two days after the wedding when Greg and Mallory were flying back with the Buchanan's. Everyone was very excited.

On the night before the wedding, Greg had stayed at the pub where Stella had cooked him a lovely meal. The Buchanan family was staying at the little cottage they had hired last time they stayed. Josie and Brad were staying with Mallory. Colin had agreed to give Mallory away and Brad had been signed up for Best Man duties.

The day of the wedding arrived at lightning speed. Josie, Brad and Mallory drank Champagne for breakfast along with their toasted bagels and cream cheese. Although, Mallory struggled to eat anything she was so very nervous. She disappeared upstairs to get ready. After around an hour of hearing nothing from her, Josie was beginning to worry.

"How are you getting on Mally?" Josie called through the door.

Mallory was standing in the bathroom staring at her reflection. She was trying so hard to fight back her mixed emotions. The stunning ivory dress was off shoulder and had a fitted, beaded bodice with crystals adorning the front. The skirt was just the right level of fullness; not meringue-like but not straight. Her hair had been partially pinned up, but the tendrils that hung down framed her face beautifully.

She adored Greg and couldn't wait to marry him, but she also remembered Sam and how this day, her wedding day, was originally supposed to be about her marrying him. The fact that Sam's family were here made matters more difficult than she could ever have imagined.

"Mally, you're worrying me." Josie knocked on the door. She tried the handle, but the door was locked. "Mallory, what's going on?" Josie knocked harder.

Mallory unlocked the door and sat on the side of the bath as Josie walked in. "Sorry...I...I just needed some time on my own." She sighed as Josie looked on.

"Why? Are you getting cold feet?" Josie asked bluntly, folding her arms across her chest like a chastising parent.

"Not exactly…just thinking about Sam." She nipped the bridge of her nose as if it would halt the tears that were threatening to make an imminent appearance.

"Thinking what about Sam, honey?" Josie sat beside her on the roll top bath in her pretty, knee length, purple bridesmaid dress and held her hand.

"Just that this should've been me and him. Maybe it's too soon? Maybe I shouldn't go through with this?"

Josie sighed. "Mallory, you know how we always tell each other when we are being ridiculous?" Mallory nodded. "Well…and I know maybe you don't want to hear this right now…but it's one of those times." She took a deep breath, "If Sam was still alive, maybe we wouldn't need to be having this conversation. Or, maybe you were meant to be with Greg all along and it was Sam that brought you to him. Have you ever thought that? Maybe Sam was your guardian angel. After everything that has happened between you and Greg I am beginning to believe in fate. Mallory, you stuck it out here when it would have been so easy to just run back to *Yorkshire*. You came here because of Sam…but you stayed because of Greg." Mallory had certainly never contemplated such a thing, but hearing the words now made her heart swell and tears pool in her eyes.

"Do you love Greg?" Josie continued.

Mallory didn't hesitate in her answer, "Of course I do, with all my heart."

"Well then, let's go and get you married to him, eh?" Josie stood and pulled her friend to a standing position. "You and Greg are meant to be together. He adores you…always has. You tattooed his initial on your arse for goodness sake!"

Mallory laughed at the bluntness of her friend's words, "Erm, my back actually." She pointed out.

"Back-shmack…same bloody difference." Josie waved Mallory's comment aside with her hand. "You wouldn't have done that if you just thought he was just 'a bit of alright' and nothing else now would you?"

"Absolutely not." Mallory confirmed with a smile.

"Then what are we going to do? Colin is downstairs."

"Well…I don't know about you, but I have a wedding to go to." Mallory made for the door winking at her best friend.

They arrived at the church and a red carpet had been laid from the place where the car parked, right up the path to the front of the church. Greg had thought of everything. Colin clung onto her hand and looked proudly at Mallory, just as he would his own daughter. Josie stood in front with her small hand tied bunch of white roses which was a smaller version of Mallory's large bouquet. The music from inside the church could be heard just under the sound of friendly chatter.

Suddenly the background music was replaced with the opening bars of Hoobastank's *'The Reason'* tears welled in Mallory's eyes once again and she took a deep breath. She hadn't expected yet another romantic touch. Greg was full of surprises.

"This is it, my flower." Colin squeezed Mallory's hand as they stepped toward the doors. They opened and Mallory got her first glimpse of the beautifully flower adorned church interior. It looked amazing and smelled even better. Fragrant white roses filled every available window ledge and pew end. Greg had chosen the flowers.

"*Yorkshire* roses for my *Yorkshire* rose," he had explained to her about his choice when they were planning the wedding.

She looked toward the front where Greg stood facing the altar in his wedding suit, complete with kilt. Slowly, almost as if he feared that she may disappear if his eyes touched upon her, he turned to meet her gaze. His face lit up with love as he laid eyes on her. Brad leaned in to hand him a hanky when it was clear his emotions were getting the better of him.

Mallory, Colin and Josie walked slowly down the aisle toward the altar until Mallory and Greg were face to face. Colin handed his 'adopted' daughter over to the handsome groom and stepped back. Mallory's own tears were the issue now and Josie handed her a lace hanky. What a pair they were.

Greg leaned toward her and with trembling lips, whispered, "Thank you for marrying me. I know this must be a hard day for you. But I've never loved or admired you more than I do right now." It was the perfect thing to say and she loved him all the more for it.

The Vicar began the service. The couple dutifully repeated the words uttered by the man. They held hands and stared lovingly at each other through the whole service.

"Mallory and Greg have written some words to each other that they would like to say." The Vicar announced and stepped back.

Mallory was first to speak. "Greg, since the moment I met you I've been on a rollercoaster ride. We've supported each other through grief and our own individual issues and it's been difficult at times. But I cannot imagine my life without you in it. And I don't want to. Whatever life throws at us, we'll get through it. We've proved that we can…I think my guardian angel was watching over me when he brought me to you." Her words caught in her throat as she fought to keep her emotions in check, she smiled and breathed deeply. "There's a saying that someone close to me says…'Love Conquers All' and I never believed that to be true until I met you and now I believe it irrevocably. I love you with all my heart."

Little sobs could be heard from within the congregation.

Greg wiped his eyes and kissed her tenderly resting his forehead on hers for a moment. He then stepped forward. Brad handed him his guitar. Mallory gasped when she realised what was happening. She held her hands over her mouth and waited with baited breath to see which song he had chosen.

Greg cleared his throat. "Erm, I usually use other people's words to express how I feel; which is daft when you think about it 'cause I've been writing my own songs for years. Mallory, I wrote this for you. I think the words say it all." His voice cracked as he spoke, raw emotion trying to escape the cage of his body. "And everyone else this is called '*Mallory's Song*'." Mallory watched in adoration as he began to strum chords on his beloved guitar. She was past the point of caring about her perfect makeup getting smudged as the tears cascaded down her face. He began to sing his heartfelt words to her,

> "From the moment I met you
> It was love at first sight
> I wanted to hold you
> Each day and each night
> Maybe we weren't meant to be
> But that's not what my heart kept on telling me
>
> I want to hold you forever
> And that's what I'll do
> Whatever life throws our way
> It'll be me and you
> And we'll both stand tall
> Because love conquers all
>
> Our future together
> Means more than I can say
> Together forever
> With a family one day
> Who can say we're not meant to be?
> I know that my heart keeps on telling me

I want to hold you forever
And that's what I'll do
Whatever life throws our way
It'll be me and you
And we'll both stand tall
Because love conquers all
Yeah we'll both stand tall
Because love conquers all"

Greg just about managed to get through the song without breaking down. That couldn't be said for the wedding congregation. As soon as the song finished the church erupted in applause and Mallory flung her arms around Greg, sobbing.

"Greg, I love you so much, thank you for such a beautiful gift," she whispered into his ear and he clung onto her.

"There was no other way for me to tell you how I feel." he kissed her hair. "I can't be without you ever again Mallory. This is it. This is forever."

"Well, I'm going nowhere unless you come too." She breathed.

The Vicar brought the proceedings back to order. When the bride and groom were back in their places he began to speak, "Ladies and gentleman, it gives me the greatest of pleasure to declare before God that Mallory and Greg are now...Husband and Wife. Greg, you may kiss your bride...one more time with feeling." He chuckled and the congregation joined him

Greg swept Mallory up once again into a long, lingering embrace as the congregation cheered and applauded the newlyweds.

They had been though such a lot to get there, but they both knew that despite all the ups and downs, despite the things that had placed obstacles in their path before now, this was it. This was real love. This was always and forever. For Mallory and Greg, at least, love had conquered all.

Epilogue

December 2012

Mallory gazed at the little bundle in her arms. Nothing could have prepared her for the way she felt looking at the tiny fingers and toes. It had been a traumatic journey, but they got here in the end. The beautiful baby girl sleeping peacefully, wrapped in a white crocheted blanket. All that the little bundle needed now was a name.

They had expected a boy and had prepared for a boy right up to the last minute. The surprise arrival of baby *girl* McBradden had left them with a little dilemma. But it was a sweet, lovely dilemma. Mallory had never felt such a glow as she did holding her new baby. The most precious thing she and Greg had ever created. And Greg was such a proud daddy.

He had gone off to buy pink things that morning; vowing to return with lots of gifts as speedily as he could. He was so excited about having a baby daughter; even more so than when they had been told at the scan that they were eighty percent sure the baby was a boy, but not to buy specific colours just in case. So they had bought neutral coloured clothing. But they had picked out a boy's name, feeling pretty certain that's what they should do.

Mallory had looked adoringly into Greg's face as he had wept when he had first held her. "Oh my precious, beautiful, little baby girl. You're going to wrap me around your little finger you know." He had wiped away his tears on the back of his hand and stroked her tiny little scrunched up face. "I reckon you're going to cause me more trouble than I will know how to deal with, but I will love every minute of it.

And I will protect you and your mummy forever, don't you ever worry about a thing."

They had discussed a number of beautiful names; Gaelic names; names of places they had visited together. Greg liked 'Skye'; Mallory liked 'Iona' and they had almost settled on that combination, but then they had discussed naming her after their mothers. The discussion had not ended. There had merely been a short reprieve whilst Daddy Greg had gone shopping.

Whilst he was temporarily absent Mallory had done a lot of soul searching and had thought long and hard about names. She would talk to Greg when he returned from his expedition. On the nurses advice Baby McBradden had gone back into the crib so that Mallory could get some rest; it had been an exhausting forty eight hours. She slipped into a calm and restful sleep.

~~~~~

Her water had broken at four in the morning and Greg had calmly brought her into the hospital whilst she had been pretty much hysterical.

"I'm not ready, Greg! I can't be a mum! I am rubbish at everything!" She had sobbed as the reality of their situation soaked in.

Greg had smiled at his panic stricken wife. "Mallory, you will be a wonderful mum. Stop worrying. We will get through the next eighteen years as a team."

The labour had been prolonged and very painful. There were some issues with the placenta and there was talk of an emergency C-section which terrified both Greg and Mallory. Some hours later and a check had revealed that the situation had righted itself. The labour continued on—and on—and on. Mallory was exhausted.

The time to push came and Mallory had found some hidden resolve from the depths of her soul and had pushed with every ounce of strength she could muster. Twenty-four hours after arriving at the hospital Baby McBradden had been born healthy and crying loudly; which was a very good sign, they were told.

~~~~~

An hour after she had dozed off, she was awoken by someone sneaking, not-so-quietly, around her room. When she opened her eyes she realised she was surrounded by fragrant flowers and pink balloons.

Greg appeared from behind a huge bouquet of pink and white roses and a huge helium balloon reading 'It's a girl!' his grin was as wide as *Loch Ness*. His hands were red with the weight of the carrier bags full of purchases from every baby shop conceivable.

He placed the bags down near the door to the private room and came over to Mallory. He kissed her gently on her forehead and whispered, "I'm so very proud of you. You've made me the happiest man alive yet again, Mrs. McBradden. And I will never let either of you down, ever, I promise."

Malory grinned, "I love you too Mr. McBradden." She kissed him tenderly. "Listen, I've been thinking about the name of our new little addition." She stroked his face as she gazed lovingly into his smiling eyes.

"Aye, me too. You go first though eh?"

"Okay, I was thinking that Mairi is such a pretty name and it's Gaelic just like we wanted if we're honest. And Mairi was such an important part of your life and mine too in a lot of ways."

Greg's eyes filled with tears as he picked up their little sleeping bundle. "Funny, I was thinking along the same lines." He smiled at his wife as he sat beside her and kissed her forehead. "Mallory…my love…meet our new baby daughter…Mairi Samantha."

Meet the Author

Lisa is a happily married Mum of one with two crazy dogs. She especially enjoys being creative; has worked as a singer and now runs her own little craft business where she makes hanging signs and decorations for the home. Lisa and her family recently relocated from *Yorkshire, England* to their beloved *Scotland*; a place of happy holidays and memories for them.

Writing has always been something Lisa has enjoyed, although in the past it has centered on poetry and song lyrics. The story in her debut novel has been building in her mind for a long while, but until the relocation, she never had the time to put it down in black and white; working full time as a High School Science Learning Mentor and studying swallowed up any spare time she had. Making the move north of the border has given Lisa the opportunity to spread her wings and fulfill her dream. Writing is now a deep passion and she has enjoyed every minute of working towards being published. Novels two and three are works in progress so watch this space!

3878065R00186

Printed in Great Britain
by Amazon.co.uk, Ltd.,
Marston Gate.